D0971071

Trouble
Loves
Company

Also by Angie Daniels

In the Company of My Sistahs

When I First Saw You

Love Uncovered

When It Rains

Trouble
Loves
Company

ANGIE DANIELS

Dafina
BOOKS

KENSINGTON PUBLISHING CORP.
http://www.kensingtonbooks. com

DAFINA BOOKS are published by

Kensington Publishing Corp.
850 Third Avenue
New York, NY 10022

Copyright © 2007 by Angie Daniels

All rights reserved. No part of this book may be reproduced in any form or by any means without the prior written consent of the Publisher, excepting brief quotes used in reviews.

All Kensington titles, imprints and distributed lines are available at special quantity discounts for bulk purchases for sales promotion, premiums, fund-raising, educational or institutional use.

Special book excerpts or customized printings can also be created to fit specific needs. For details, write or phone the office of the Kensington Special Sales Manager: Kensington Publishing Corp., 850 Third Avenue, New York, NY 10022. Attn. Special Sales Department. Phone: 1-800-221-2647.

Dafina Books and the Dafina logo Reg. U.S. Pat. & TM Off.

ISBN-13: 978-0-7582-1745-5
ISBN-10: 0-7582-1745-5

First Kensington Trade Paperback Printing: September 2007
10 9 8 7 6 5 4 3 2 1

Printed in the United States of America

Acknowledgments

I'd like to thank everyone who read my first book, *In the Company of My Sistahs,* and shared your opinions. I hope this sequel is everything you have been waiting for.

To my girls Maureen Smith and Kimberly Kaye Terry, for bouncing off so many ideas and sharing information. The two of you have made this adventure so much fun. Also, to my girl Tanya Henderson—even though the times are few and far between, I've enjoyed all the laughs we shared. Has anybody bought those stilettos yet? I wish I was in San Antonio with the three of you.

To my kids, Ashlie Kelly and Evan Smith, for being such big supporters. To my son, Mark Kelly, for reading everything his mother has written. My daughter refuses to read what her mother is thinking. Like I've told her before, I was doing it long before she was born.

To Sergeant William Green of the Columbia Police Department for answering all the questions that helped breathe life into this book. Dinner is on me.

To my cousin Verl Powell Williams, the first lady at Sugar Grove Baptist Church, for helping me with every spiritual and biblical question I had. Girl, I know, I need to bring my butt to church more often.

I want to give a shout out to my family because they have all been such strong supporters of my career. To my mother, Kathleen Anderson, who tries to read my books even though she can't see worth a damn. To my daddy, Dennis Daniels—regardless of what I say or do, you are the only father that I know, and I love you.

To my siblings, Arlynda and Dennis Daniels, and Terrence, Taneisha, and Nichole Moore. Y'all make your big sister proud.

I want to give a shout out to all my aunties, who continue to show their love and support: Cynthia Hayot, Sylvia Stringfellow, Dorlinda Miller, Eunice Edwards, Elizabeth Moore, Geraldine

Moore. I guarantee I forgot someone. If I did, please don't strangle me.

To my wonderful husband, Kenneth, for all your years of love and support and stepping in when I needed it most.

To my home girls Tonya Hill and Kim Ashcraft, for just being you and making it easy to create these believable characters.

I love to hear from my readers, so please don't hesitate to drop me a line at angie@angiedaniels.com.

Chapter 1

Renee

If I had known my girl Danielle was going to call and spend the last half hour whining about her sorry-ass boyfriend, I wouldn't have answered the phone.

"Whaddaya think I should do?" she asked in a low whisper, as if someone else might be listening.

I clicked my tongue and answered, "You already know what I would do."

"Yeah, but I ain't like you."

See, that's one thing I've never understood. Why ask for advice when you really don't want it? I have never been able to figure that out, especially when the answer is obvious. Kick his ass to the curb! As my grandmother always said, "Can't nobody tell a woman to leave her man. She has to decide on her own when she's had enough." I understand what Big Mama was trying to say, really I do. But it's a shame how much shit a woman is willing to take before she finally decides enough is enough.

Take my girl Danielle, for instance. Her ex-boyfriend Deon fucked around on her for years. Not only did he fuck around, but he brought home the kind of shit you have to take a trip to the free clinic to get rid of. Yet and still, she forgave his trifling ass. It wasn't until one of his baby mamas clocked her upside her peanut head, while he stood by and watched, that she finally decided enough was enough.

Now Ron, the latest thug in her life, is never home, can't keep a job, and has bitches calling her house at all hours of the night bold enough to ask for him, yet she's determined to stick by him.

I love my girl, really I do. We talk on the phone at least five times a week and I know if I ever needed her, she'd have my back. Her brain is short a couple of screws, though. There ain't no way, at thirty-six, I would be putting up with that kind of shit. But unlike me, Danielle loves a thug, and will go crazy without daily drama in her life. And that's why her ass is always getting dogged.

"That muthafucker got off work three hours ago, and I ain't seen his ass yet. He ain't got no respect for me," she complained.

I couldn't help but laugh in her ear. "What do you expect? He's only twenty-four. I doubt he respects his own mama."

"Yeah, right!" she laughed. "But that's ai'ight 'cause he's got the shit twisted. I'm gonna get all in that ass when he gets home."

Ooh! Like that's gonna make a world of difference. "It's been a year. He's not gonna change. What you need to do is put his lazy ass out."

While Danielle tried to justify why she wasn't ready to end the relationship, I rose from the couch, turned the light off, then moved up to my bedroom and changed into a nightgown. It was late and a school night, so my kids, Quinton and Tamara, were in their rooms, probably pretending to be asleep. That's okay with me just as long as they're in bed by ten.

As Danielle rattled on I half-listened, because she really didn't want to hear what I had to say. If it was me, Ron would never have moved into my house. So, instead of giving advice, I pretended to be paying attention and said, "Uh-huh" on cue. I really think she just likes for someone to listen. Shit, I ain't mad, because I do the same thing. Nevertheless, it's late and I am tired. I yawned rudely in the mouthpiece, hoping she'd get the hint.

She didn't.

Okay, she's got ten more minutes, then I'll come up with some kind of excuse and hang up.

I had just stepped into the adjoining bathroom and dropped my clothes in the hamper when I heard the garage door rising. "Oh shit!" I exclaimed as I dashed back into the bedroom.

Danielle gasped. "What?"

Leaning over, I turned out the Tiffany lamp on the nightstand. "John's home."

"Already? I thought he didn't get off work until midnight."

"He doesn't, but I guess he decided to get off early." I glared at the clock—it was barely eleven.

"It must be nice being the boss." I heard the envy in her voice.

"Look, I'll holla at you tomorrow." I hung up the phone, then slipped beneath the covers as quickly and quietly as possible, and waited. As soon as I heard heavy footsteps coming up the stairs, my stomach felt all tied up in knots. Damn! I can't deal with him tonight. I was irritated, because if John got off early from work, it was for one reason and one reason only—he wanted some booty. *Girl, quit trippin'! Everything ain't always got to be about you. Maybe he's tired,* I thought to myself. Okay, maybe I'm being silly. Maybe I'm wrong.

When John entered the room and turned the lock behind him, I knew my luck had run out.

Shit!

While he undressed, I lay perfectly still on my back and breathed deeply, praying he'd think I was asleep and would leave me the hell alone. From the corner of my eyes, I watched him move about the room in the dark. Then he stepped into the bathroom, took a leak, passed gas, and flushed the toilet. I turned up my nose, totally disgusted, but relieved when I heard the water running. At least he washed his hands. A few minutes later, the mattress beside me sagged from the impact of his weight, and within seconds he was underneath the covers with his large arm pressed against mine. My nose began to itch, but there was no way in hell I was going to scratch it, because the slightest movement and John would spring into action.

The clock on the dresser ticked and seconds became minutes and finally I began to relax. Yes! He's not going to touch me tonight. Then, just as I started to really fall asleep, I felt his hand creeping up my thigh. I tensed because I knew that in the next five seconds he was going to ask me that same stupid-ass question.

"Can I have some?"

I wanted to yell, "Hell nah, you can't have none!" No, what I really wanted to say was, "If I wanted to give yo' fat ass some, I would've been lying in the bed butt-naked instead of in a long gown and a pair of grandma draws." Instead, I remained stone-faced and tried to pretend I hadn't heard him, but at this point it was obvious he wasn't falling for it.

"Hey, Renee, you hear me?"

I gave a long, exasperated sigh because for once I wished my husband would just get the hint and leave me the fuck alone. "Not tonight," I said as nicely as I could manage, then rolled onto my side. I even threw a little sleep in my voice since I hadn't quite given up on that trick yet.

"Aw, come on," he begged. "I'll be quick. I promise."

I know his *quick*. Thirty minutes of him playing with my left titty, then he'll want me to play with his dick before he'd finally climb on top of me for another half hour of torture. I blew out another angry breath, then rolled over onto my back and looked up at him. "Why can't you wait until I want you sometimes? I mean . . . I can't understand why you always want some when I'm not in the mood."

There was a long moment of silence and one would have thought I had hurt his feelings, but not John. He gave me this sad, pleading look. "So you gonna give your husband a little bit or what?"

I couldn't help it. I tossed my arms in the air and gave a frustrated laugh. He was obviously not going to let up until I gave him some coochie. And as usual, I felt guilty as shit for depriving him of what he felt he was entitled to have on an "ass-needed basis." "I'm not in the mood," I snapped with attitude. "I don't want no dick! But if you want it, if you really, *really* want it, then go ahead and do the damn thang!"

Now any other brotha would have said, "Fuck you, bitch," and rolled over. Not John. He rose long enough to shrug out of his t-shirt and tighty-whities, then eagerly climbed back in the bed. The moment I felt his limp dick on my thigh, I sighed because I knew I was in for a long night.

Lord, why me?

Now, I could have refused, but Big Mama taught me never to bite the hand that feeds you, so as usual I gave in, and let him have his way. Within seconds, I felt his hand slide underneath my gown. I cringed as his fingers grabbed my nipple, tweaking it like he was trying to tune a transistor radio. I have discovered in the five years of our marriage that playing with my breasts for five to ten minutes is one of the only ways John can get an erection. The other is me going down on him, but that shit's not about to happen. John lifted the gown over my head while I lay there like a stiff board. He suckled one nipple between his dry, cracked lips while he twisted and pulled at the other with his fingertips.

The entire time, I stared at the ceiling fan twirling above while tears ran from the corners of my eyes and onto the pillow. I'm so sick of this shit, I don't know what to do. Every time he touches me I feel like I'm being violated. I've never been raped, but it can't be too far from what I'm feeling. As he slid my panties down to my ankles, I allowed my mind to disappear to another time in my life. A time when I was free to do what I wanted with whomever I wanted. I then traveled back even further to happier times when I was in grade school before all the madness in my life had begun. My sister Lisa and I used to lie in our bunk beds, laughing and creating make-believe worlds. I bit my lip and forced myself not to cry. Even after a year, thinking about my sister still brought tears to my eyes. At thirty-eight, Lisa had lost her battle with ovarian cancer. I didn't even know she had it until it was too late. One of her last wishes was for me to give my marriage an honest try, and because of her I was still trying to hang in there with John. As much as I loved my sister and tried to be a woman who stood by her word, I wasn't sure how much more I could endure.

"Play with it," John instructed as he reached for my hand and moved it over to his limp dick.

I was so pissed off, I lashed out at him. "I don't understand this shit! If your dick ain't hard, why're you bothering me? Why can't you wait until it wants to work?"

My voice cracked but he didn't seem to notice because he gave an impatient sigh and said, "Just play with it a minute."

I practically yanked at his shit because I just don't get it anymore. For the last year his dick has only half worked. Not that it has mattered to me. Even when it was still fully functional, the sex between us had been bad. I just didn't think it was important. Seriously! It may sound crazy but I really thought that what I was getting out of the marriage far outweighed what I had to give in return. That shit sounds crazy as hell now. When he met me I was a broke bitch trying to rub two nickels together and when he asked me to marry him I jumped at the chance, thinking that life could only get better. Now I wasn't so sure.

By the time my hand was about to fall asleep, John's dick finally rose to the occasion. Quickly, before it grew soft, he climbed between my legs and searched for the hole. "Help me find it."

I don't understand why John can't find my coochie! Damn! We've been fucking for over five years but he still aims for the wrong hole. What the hell is up with that shit? Reaching over into the top drawer of my nightstand, I pulled out a tube of KY Jelly because my coochie was as dry as the desert. I squeezed a little in my hand and lubed the head of his dick. Damn! He was starting to get soft already.

"Mmm, baby, that feels good. Rub some more on me," he crooned.

I closed my eyes and prayed for strength, then squeezed another dab in the palm of my hand and jacked him off some more. By the time he was hard again, I quickly guided him to my hole and he entered me.

I sighed while he pumped his little dick in and out like he was hurting some damn body. He was moaning so loud, you would have thought it was me. As he thrust, his fingers tweaked my nipples. And tweaked and tweaked and tweaked some more.

"Dammit, would you stop before they fall the fuck off!" I yelled, then slapped his hand away. I've told him I don't know how many times to stop playing with them so much, but that shit goes in one ear and out the other. I don't even think plastering a note across my chest that read, "leave them the hell alone," would have made a difference.

John sighed, then slid me down to the middle of the bed and entered me, again pumping and pumping like he was doing some damage. I could have lain there and gone to sleep if he wasn't dropping balls of sweat all over me. I put a pillow over my face to stop the next droplet that was sure to fall in my damn eye. Thank goodness he paused long enough to wipe his face off on the sheets. He then tossed my pillow aside.

"Is that better?"

"Yeah, just hurry up," I managed through gritted teeth.

Draping my legs over his shoulders, John began to plunge all three hundred pounds into me. I couldn't feel shit, but I knew if I wanted this ordeal to end I had to pretend that I did, so I started to moan. As usual, the sound of my voice excited him.

"That's it, baby. Come with me," he said as he reached for my nipple. Instinctively, I slapped his hand away, then rocked my hips and met him stroke for stroke. "Yeah, that's it. I'm about to come."

I was so happy to hear that, I started moving my hips faster, moaning even louder, and urged him on. "Come on, big daddy, you can do it. Come all inside this pussy!"

"Okay," he said like a good little boy. "Okay." He pumped faster.

I reached up and stroked his nipples, since he seems to get

off on that shit. "Come on, Daddy. I want to feel you nut inside of me. Wet that pussy!"

"Yeaaah! I'm getting ready to come!"

"Me, too!" I lied.

While he was howling like a hound dog during a full moon, I felt that wet, warm feeling as he squirted inside of me. The bed rocked. John was slamming the headboard against the wall so hard, I know the kids heard it, until finally, he collapsed on top of me. Thank you, Jesus! I lay there waiting for him to get off of me. He finally rolled over and within seconds he was snoring. Overcome with relief, I eased out of bed and went into the adjoining bathroom and cleaned myself up. Catching a glimpse of myself in the mirror, the tears began to fall again. What has my life become?

I'm miserable, but nobody seems to believe me. Especially not the big muthafucka who happens to share my bed. I feel trapped. Being trapped in a bad marriage is bad enough, but being trapped in a marriage with a good man who you don't love makes you want to stand in the corner and bang your head against a cement wall. Don't get it twisted. If it wasn't that John was an excellent provider and that my kids adored him, I would have left a long time ago.

John and I have been married five years and I've been miserable for three. A one-night stand I met at a club. I was horny and after a night of no other prospects, I went home with him. I was too drunk to remember the specifics of his performance. The only reason why I know we fucked was because I woke up naked and spotted the used condom wrapper on the nightstand beside me. We dated a couple of times after that. None—to his disappointment—ended with sex. I found John to be a kind, generous man, but too damn nice and touchy-feely for my taste. He was also dull, very lonely, and needy. Not to mention he wasn't much to look at—dark, five-eleven, over three hundred pounds, with a waist I couldn't even wrap my arms around, and a face that resembled Shrek. What's even worse, the brotha can't dress! And even when I try, it's no use. Phat

Farm on John just looks like the fat farm. But despite his appearance, he had a six-figure salary, which meant he took me to the finest restaurants in town, his company had box seats to all the sporting events, and he drove a Lexus. I know my reasons for dating him were purely selfish, but hey, it isn't every day a girl from the streets gets the opportunity to sample the finer things in life. After a while, though, even those weren't enough to make me want to keep seeing him.

The second time I gave him some was because I couldn't bring myself to say no after he had spent over two hundred dollars on a lobster dinner. As soon as we were in the bed, he was all over me, touching, feeling, sucking, and, of course, tweaking. When I reached down and felt what he was working with, I almost laughed in his face. Good Lord, my thirteen-year-old son had more than he did! Nevertheless, I endured the hourlong session, and when I finally left his place, I had every intention of ending the relationship. Unfortunately, the next day at work I got fired, and who did I call? John. He let me cry on his shoulder. Back then, I didn't know what I was going to do. I was already behind on my house payment. After a month of hitting the pavement hard, I panicked—then John offered a solution.

"Let's get married."

"What?" I looked at him like he had lost his damn mind.

He simply shrugged. "Why not? You need help and I want to help you."

I tried to think of every reason I could why that wasn't even a possibility and ended up stating the obvious. "We've barely known each other three months."

He shrugged and smiled. "It wouldn't matter to me if it had been two years. In the short time we've been together, I have fallen in love with you and your children."

I was at a loss for words because although he was starting to grow on me, love wasn't even a factor, not to mention that the sex had gotten worse instead of better, and I was ready to move on to the next guy.

John noticed my hesitation, because he added, "Listen, I

know you don't love me and that's okay. You can learn to love me later. Let's try it out for a year and if it doesn't work out, then we can go our separate ways."

If I hadn't known it before, I definitely knew it then—his ass was desperate. Why else would someone ask a woman he barely knew to marry him? With two kids, and a foreclosure notice from the bank, I did the only thing any desperate single mother would do. I accepted.

His face lit up like a Christmas tree. "You just made me a happy man."

John then gave me one of those kisses that lacked passion, as well as tongue, then moved into the kitchen. I was about to yell, "Wait! I changed my mind," When I saw him grab the stack of bills I'd left lying on the kitchen table. When he removed his checkbook from his back pocket and took a seat, I didn't say a damn thing. That night I lay in his arms, trying to imagine a life with him, and all I saw was boredom and lousy sex. Still, I kept my mouth shut. Three days later, John got down on one knee in front of my kids, holding a one-carat solitaire. I didn't even feel my lips move but I definitely heard myself accept. Within the next two weeks, we were standing in front of the justice of the peace with my sister Lisa and her husband as our witnesses.

After that I tried to make the best of it, even though I knew I didn't love him. John was so good to me, I thought nothing else mattered, and that in time I could surely learn to love him. Making him happy was easy. I fucked him when he wanted to be fucked and told him what he wanted to hear.

A year passed with me trying to convince myself that I had made the right choice. With his six-figure salary, I made myself believe that I loved him and everything that he was able to do for me. I was financially secure. I didn't have to work. I was home when the school bus arrived. I attended PTA meetings and made brownies, things that so many mothers wished they could do. I started getting into that Suzie Homemaker shit and began planning meals. I even learned how to crochet.

John loved me to death and showered me with so much affection that I tried to tell myself this was the best thing that could have ever happened to me. I even tried to enjoy sex with him. I would fondle and play with him and for hours we would lie in the bed, kissing and hugging between rounds one and two. I convinced myself that I had a lot to be thankful for. Sex was a small price to pay for the lifestyle I was living.

John built a four-bedroom home for me and my kids and I got the joy of decorating it myself. Then, when I had nothing left to do, I started looking for a job. I applied for every management position I could find, and after a year, I still hadn't found a job. Every rejection was proof that marrying John had been the right decision. However, at the end of the first year, I thought I was going to lose my damn mind. I had too much time on my hands and all I did was sit around and think.

"Why don't you write?" John suggested after I started complaining about being bored. "You said you always wanted to write a book."

It had always been a dream of mine to become a famous author someday. So, I decided to give it a try. John bought me a computer. Before long, the words began to flow and I got so wrapped up in my writing that I discovered a way to fill the void in my life for the next year. After that, every time I thought about leaving him, a voice in my head would say, *Bitch, look at all you have accomplished with this man. You'd be a fool to let him go.* Then I would glance over at his kind face sitting in a chair like a damn puppy just waiting for me to scratch his head, and I would feel guilty for even thinking about leaving him. But still, even after I had published three erotic romance novels, I realized with a sinking feeling in the pit of my stomach that no matter how much I tried to hide behind the stories I was writing, my marriage wasn't going to change. I realized that after three years, I still wasn't in love with him. I liked him and loved how good he had been to me and my kids, but I didn't love him.

I mean, come on. To this day, I'm embarrassed to be seen in public together. With our fifteen-year age difference and his old-school spirits, it's like having my daddy on my arm. I dread going out alone, just the two of us, because we have nothing to talk about. Vacations are a bust because we never have any fun unless I create it. I didn't realize until we were married that John had no friends, no hobbies. Anything I do, he wants to do. He has become so needy that his entire life revolves around me and my kids, and it is driving me crazy. I'm not kidding you. I do almost anything to get away from him. Book-signing tours, vacations with my girlfriends, any excuse to put some distance between him and the boring life he wants me to continue to share with him. The only reason we have lasted this long is because of financial stability, and after my divorce I wanted to offer my children a stable home. Something I never had.

I never knew my real daddy. He died in a car accident when I was barely four. Growing up with my stepfather was pure hell. Paul Perry made it no secret he didn't like me. No matter how hard I tried, it was never good enough. To hide my pain, I rebelled and generally gave him a hard time. My mother, Bernice, was and still is a crackhead. Talking to her was a waste of time. A week after my sixteenth birthday, she left and didn't bother to come back. During that time, I had already met my first husband. High-school romances seldom work, and my marriage to Mario was just that. By the time I received my diploma, I was already pregnant with Quinton. Tamara came three years later. After Mario put his hands on me one time too many, I took a bat to his head, and filed for divorce.

Now you're probably wondering, after all that drama, how I could even think about leaving a man like John. Believe me, I hear it a lot, and I've been asking myself the same question for years. Only I can't come up with one good excuse except to say, I am unhappy. I just wished I felt the same way he does. I've tried so hard, but I've got needs and wants that he just can't meet.

The thought of him touching me turns my stomach. His kisses make me want to run to the bathroom and throw up. I can't help the way I feel. I love John for who he is, but I am not in love with him. There is a difference. I didn't believe that at first, but I know it now. I just can't take it anymore. I know now he isn't my soul mate. That I can't spend the next fifty years with him because, in the process, I'll be losing a piece of myself. I need a man who challenges my mind, body, and soul, who I look forward to sharing my evening with, talking about our day. I want a man who holds me in his arms through the night after making me come.

With John, if you give him a hug he wants sex. If you kiss him, he gropes your breasts. Any form of affection results in sex, so eventually I've stopped touching him altogether. Also, with John I can't initiate sex, because if I do, I kid you not, his dick won't work. He has to be the aggressor and even then he asks for permission. What brotha do you know asks for the coochie? I want a man to flip my ass over and bury all ten inches in before I can take a breath. John is so kind and obedient that if I ordered him to bark like a dog, he would respond like that princess in *Coming to America*.

After the first two years, I couldn't take it any longer. I started hanging out on the weekend and messing around with one man after another, trying to find what I was missing at home. John never once complained about me being in the streets as long as I gave him some whenever he asked. I didn't mind at first, but now that his dick only works half the time and I have to spend the majority of it whacking him off, I'm fed up and can't take too much more. I am dying inside. I just wish I could get him to understand.

During our marriage, I have suggested splitting up at least four times. And every time he has talked me out of it. I just don't understand it. I remember what he said the last time I tried to tell him I was unhappy.

"What do I need to do to make Renee happy?"

I shrugged. "I don't know anymore."

"I'll do anything you want, but you've got to give me a hint."

After a moment of hesitation, I said, "Time away from each other."

I saw the flash of panic in his eyes before he pulled me in his arms. "I don't want you to leave. We can work this out if you tell me what I've got to do." His chest began to heave and his tears stained the side of my neck. "I love you so much."

I was overcome with guilt. This man had given me everything and here I was, trying to bail out on him. I held him in my arms and promised to try harder. But I continued to mess around and the months passed with me stepping out on my husband every chance I got. Then, two years ago, he accepted a position hundreds of miles away. I stayed behind with no intention of joining him until my sister made me promise only minutes before she had gone into surgery to pray to God for answers, and to give my marriage one last chance. Then, only days after agreeing to try harder, my sister died from a blood clot to the heart. Overwhelmed with grief, I stayed true to my word, and gave John another year of my life. I've prayed regularly and have given up all the other relationships. I can honestly say that I haven't messed around on my husband, not once, in a year. Okay . . . make that nine months. Damn . . . all right, in the last six months. And that is a record for me. But my ass is so horny that I don't know how much longer I'm gonna be able to hold out. Why do you think I write all those erotic novels? Because I need some real dick, and not that cracker-box shit I'm getting at home. That's why it's time for me to start building another life. It's time for me to get a job teaching. I already have a bachelor's degree in Journalism and a master's in English. Teaching would allow me to get back into the workforce again so I can support myself. Writing pays well but not as good as everyone thinks. I have a fat savings account but how long will that last without John's help? I love to shop and have gotten used to living an upper-class lifestyle. Change is not going to be easy. Okay, so all I need is a job—then I can save up enough to move and buy my own house. One more year, that's all I have to survive, then I can pack my bags and get the hell up out of here. It sounds easy enough, but somehow I know that leaving him won't be that easy. Freedom will come at a price. I just hope I can afford it.

* * *

I awoke the next morning to John's snoring. I don't know how I ever managed to get any sleep with the ruckus he makes. Making him lie on his back's a big waste of time.

I reached for my robe and walked into the bathroom, splashed water on my face, and headed down to the kitchen to fix breakfast. I like to make sure my kids get a balanced meal before they go off to school each morning. I moved to the counter to prepare coffee. By the time the pot was brewing, I could hear John coming down the stairs. My stomach churned. Why does he always have to get up in the morning with me? As long as I lie in bed, he'll lie in bed, but the minute he realizes I have left, he has to come and find me.

"Good morning," he said merrily as he moved into the kitchen, smiling. I've never known anybody to be that damn happy this early in the morning. I personally don't come alive until after my second cup of coffee.

"Morning," I mumbled as I moved to the cabinet and removed the waffle mix.

John took a seat at the table, waiting for the coffee to finish brewing. I glanced over at him. He hadn't put in his contacts yet so he was wearing his birth-control glasses. Those bifocals were better than condoms. That's for damn sure. Because as long as he was wearing them, he didn't have to worry about a woman giving him some.

I put the batter in the bowl, the whole while aware that he was sitting there, watching me like a damn retard. "Why are you staring at me?"

"Can't I look at my beautiful wife if I want to?"

"Whatever," I mumbled. He was obviously happy because he got some last night. I wish he'd just go back upstairs and wait instead of staring at me. I could see if we had shit to talk about, but we don't. We never have anything to discuss. It has always been that way. I used to try to keep a conversation going, but after a while I quit doing that shit, hoping that he would see how dysfunctional our relationship really was. So far it hasn't worked.

If I was a man, and my wife and I rarely talked, hardly did anything together, and she hated having sex with me, what the hell would I want to hold on to her ass for? But not John. The first thing out of his mouth is, "What do I have to do to make Renee happy?" He'll then go out and start buying me all kinds of shit. The worst part about it is my kids are so attached to him that it would break their hearts if I left. So as you can see, I am stuck with his ass . . . for now.

"I want to go back to work." I stared down at the waffle iron and waited several seconds before he finally spoke.

"What kind of work?"

I shrugged. "Teaching, maybe," I said, still avoiding eye contact. "I want to start using my degrees."

I could tell he was trying to put his words together carefully before he spoke. "I thought writing was your career."

Here we go again. "It is my career but I also need something else to fall back on."

He gave me a ridiculous laugh. "Fall back on for what? I make plenty of money."

I looked him in the eye. "Yeah, but I want my own money."

"Don't you get paid from your books?"

"Yeah, but not enough yet to feel comfortable about my future."

He gave me a smile that said, *be patient.* "It will come in time. With every contract you make more money. Eventually you'll be making enough that I'll be able to retire."

I rolled my eyes. Sometimes I think John looks at me as an investment. As long as he supports me while I get my writing career off the ground, eventually he'll be able to reap the benefit of my success and hopefully retire early. What I can't seem to get him to understand is that I no longer want him to support me. I'm dying inside and need to be able to stand on my own two feet. I also know if I am going to leave him, it has to be before I make it big, because if not, he will be entitled to half.

"This is something I need to do for me."

"If that's what you want to do, then I'll stand by you one hundred percent. I just think you need to stick to the one thing you want to do the most and you said it was writing."

I rolled my eyes again because he was starting to sound like my father, as usual. "I want to do both."

"How are you going to find time to prepare lesson plans and grade papers? Teaching isn't easy."

I hate it when he reminds me of how hard it had been for him when he was a graduate teaching assistant. "You act like I can't do it," I replied with straight attitude.

He shook his head and gave me the same scolding look he gives my daughter, Tamara. "That's not what I'm saying. I'm just saying it's going to be a lot of hard work. I just hope you can juggle that around your writing deadlines."

"I don't see it being a problem."

He chuckled. "If you think you can handle it, then I stand by your decision. Have you thought about how many days a week you're planning to teach?"

"I was thinking two or three days a week would be enough."

He nodded, looking pleased. "And when are you going to write?"

"Afternoons and weekends."

"Good, then it sounds like it's settled." Marking the end of the conversation, he reached for yesterday's paper on the table and turned to the sports section. "Why don't you fix your husband a cup of coffee? And make me two waffles. I'm starving."

As I removed a coffee mug from the cabinet over the sink, I told myself, *Hang in there girl, it's just a matter of time.*

Chapter 2

Danielle

One Year Later

The sorry muthafucker.

Danielle tossed a fake Prada purse onto the passenger's seat of her Dodge Durango, then climbed in with straight attitude. She'd had it. Another deadbeat. At thirty-seven, she was getting too old for this shit.

Peeling up the street, she hurriedly moved into the flow of traffic, then glanced down at the clock on the dashboard. Danielle blew out a frustrated breath as she realized she was going to be late for work again.

All because of a man.

Yesterday marked exactly two years since the day she and Ron had first started dating, and she had planned to make the evening quite special. Shortly after work, she had dropped her sixteen-year-old daughter Portia at her parents' house for the night. She then made a quick trip to the Olde Un Theatre, where she picked up some naughty thangs to kick the evening off just right—flavored oils, edible panties, and a porno tape for an un-inhibited night of getting their freak on. By eight she had bathed and dressed in a white teddy, including garter, thigh-highs, and a pair of five-inch white heels. After changing the satin sheets on her bed, she slipped in an old Gerald Levert CD, lit a bunch of candles, and lay strawberries and whipped cream on the nightstand. Satisfied, she had poured herself a glass of white wine, then took a seat in the living room and waited for Ron to finish his eleven-to-seven shift at Quaker Oats.

Only the bastard never showed up.

By eleven o'clock, Danielle was pitching a bitch and tossing all his shit in a box. By one, the box was on the porch. Somewhere between three and four, a fire truck pulled up in her front yard to put out the fire.

Danielle whipped around a slow-ass car and veered left at the light. "Wait 'til he gets home," she mumbled; then, voice rising, she said louder, "I'm gonna kick that muthafucker's ass!" She pounded her fist on the steering wheel. She had expected Ron to show up some time before she left for work, but to her disappointment he had not, and that pissed her off even more.

"Who the fuck does he think he is, anyway?" She sucked her teeth as she swerved the SUV around the next corner. When one wheel hit the curb, she took a deep breath and told herself to slow down. However, even as she let up on the gas, she couldn't stop thinking about how used he made her feel. Growing angry, her white leather mule slammed back down on the pedal harder and she sped down the street just in time to make a yellow light.

As she neared the hospital, she glanced down at the clock again and noticed it was ten minutes before shift change. If she could find a metered parking space close to the building, she just might make it in time to hear a report from the night-duty nurse. Then at lunch she could come back down and move her Durango to the employee parking lot before she got a ticket.

Her cell phone vibrated on her hip. Danielle reached down, expecting to see Ron's number display. Instead, she frowned when she recognized another frequent caller. *Fuck!*

"Hello," she said.

"Ms. Brooks?"

"Yeah?"

"This is Marcy Carter, the nurse at Hickman High School. Can you come down to the school right away?"

Danielle grumbled under her breath. Dammit! Her daughter was a hypochondriac. The school nurse called her at least twice a month. What could possibly be Portia's problem today? she wondered before racking her brain and remembering that her daughter was scheduled to serve detention for skipping gym last week. She figured that whatever Portia was up to, it was nothing more than a scheme to get out of being confined in a small, hot classroom on the last week of school.

Tightening her hands on the steering wheel, Danielle finally asked, "Why? What's wrong now?"

Nurse Carter hesitated. "I prefer not to say over the phone."

Danielle blew out a long breath. "Well, I'm sorry, but you're gonna have to say. I'm already runnin' late for work. Is it somethin' life or death?"

The nurse hesitated again, then Danielle heard something that sounded like a door closing before Nurse Carter finally responded in a low voice, "Your daughter was sexually assaulted on campus yesterday."

"What!" Startled, Danielle swerved to the left and almost ran into the side of another car before she managed to swing out of the way. She pulled away from the flow of traffic onto a side street, a block from the employees' parking lot, and put her SUV in Park.

"Are you okay?" Nurse Carter asked after a moment of prolonged silence.

Danielle felt as if her heart had momentarily ceased to beat. She took several deep breaths. "Yeah, I'm fine," she choked out.

"I'm sorry I had to be the bearer of bad news this morning," she said with what sounded like a sincere apology. "I don't want to get into the details over the phone but I need to know if you can take Portia to the ER this morning so she can be examined?"

Closing her eyes, Danielle shook her head. Not today. She couldn't deal with her daughter today. She had enough problems of her own. Yet what type of mother would she be if she refused? "Yeah, I'll be right there."

Nurse Carter sounded relieved by her response as if for a moment she had feared Danielle might have said no. "Good. I'll give you all the information you'll need when you get here."

Danielle thanked her and ended the call.

She paused for a few seconds to catch her breath and to think about what the nurse had told her. Portia had been sexually assaulted. Why was she having such a hard time believing her daughter? she wondered. *Because your daughter's a drama queen. She'll do or say anything for attention.*

Just last year when she had scheduled her daughter to see a gynecologist for the first time, afraid that her mother would discover that she was sexually active, Portia had concocted a story about being raped by a man who had followed her down an alley. It wasn't until Danielle told her she was taking her down to the police station to file a complaint that Portia confessed that she had lied because she didn't want her mother to find out she was having sex with the nappy-headed boy around the corner.

Noting the time on the dash, Danielle cussed. She was now officially five minutes late to work. Quickly, she dialed the hospital where she worked as a licensed practical nurse (LPN) and gave her boss a lame-ass excuse that she had been throwing up all night, and thought she might have a twenty-four-hour virus. Five minutes later, she pulled away from the curb and headed toward the high school. Halfway there, she reached for her phone again and dialed her mother. Victoria answered on the second ring.

"Good morning, Sunshine. How was your evening?"

"About as bad as my morning," Danielle replied dryly. Then, before her mother had a chance to control the conversation— as she typically did—she continued, "Mom, where'd Portia go yesterday after I dropped her off at your house?"

"Well, let's see. I took her back to school. She went to some track meet, then said she was going to have pizza afterwards. One of her friends brought her home around ten."

Danielle groaned. How many times did she have to tell her

mother Portia wasn't allowed to do anything on a school night? With all of the classes she was failing, her daughter was lucky her ass was even permitted to watch television after her homework was done. Feeling the start of a migraine, Danielle rubbed her temple. Trying to get her mother to respect the way she raised her daughter was a big waste of time and would just cause another argument.

"Mom, I just got a call from Portia's school. She claims someone raped her last night."

When Danielle heard her mother's quick intake of breath, she almost felt sorry for telling her the way she had. But her mother needed to understand that she had put rules to govern her daughter in place for a reason.

"Dear Lord! Why didn't she tell me?"

She paused to ask herself the same question. As close as the two were, she would have expected her daughter to run and cry on her grandmother's shoulder the way she normally did whenever she didn't get her way. Unless, as she had considered before, her daughter was up to something.

"I don't know, Mama, but I'm on my way to the school right now to find out."

"You want me and your father to meet you there?"

Shit, no! The last thing she needed was her mother blowing the whole thing out of proportion. Before answering, Danielle honked her horn at a Pathfinder that had cut in front of her without signaling. "No, let me talk to her first. I'll call ya back."

She turned at the next corner, cussing under her breath when she found the street closed for construction. *If it ain't one thing it's another,* she thought as she made a left turn at the corner. Between Ron and Portia, she felt like she was about to lose her damn mind.

Ever since her daughter had turned sixteen, she had been wearing on her nerves. All she cared about was those nappy-headed boys. The phone rang so doggone much one would have thought her house was a call center. Danielle finally had to take her phone privileges away just so she could get Portia to do her homework and chores. Even then she still tried to sneak on the phone when she didn't think Danielle was looking.

But like she had told her daughter not once but several times before, "I'm smarter than the average bear." Everything her daughter tried to do she had already done. "You can't out-slick a slickster," as her mother used to say. She, too, had been a girl once and knew firsthand every trick in the book. As a result, Portia rarely got away with shit.

Danielle thought she had the problem pretty much under control, until two months ago when she had discovered Portia chatting online. Walking past her computer, she had caught the words, "sucking dick" before Portia could toggle onto another screen. Danielle tried to knock her daughter's head off before she unplugged the computer and put it in the trunk of her car. Gary Graves, a good friend and computer analyst, had a look at the hard drive, and informed her that Portia had been chatting and meeting men online for quite some time.

She just didn't understand it. She had discussed with her daughter the dangers of meeting men over the Internet. Every time there was an article about a girl who had been killed by some pervert she met online, pretending to be a teenage boy, she shared it with her. So why in the hell her daughter would want to meet a total stranger was beyond her. Nevertheless, she wasn't taking any chances and definitely hadn't listened to Portia's promises never to do it again. She had cancelled the Internet subscription immediately.

As she moved onto Providence Road, she tried to look at the big picture. Danielle knew part of the problem was the way Portia felt about herself. Her daughter reminded her so much of her older sister Constance. Both were overweight with very low self-esteem. She tried working with her daughter and had even taken her to see a therapist once a month for almost a year, but nothing seemed to help shake her daughter's low opinion of herself. It puzzled Danielle, because it wasn't as if Portia wasn't pretty. She had thick, shoulder-length hair, high cheekbones, and a small, upturned nose. Her best assets were her slanted, dark-brown eyes and her compassion for others. Despite her daughter's constant need for attention, she really wasn't a bad child.

As she pulled into the high-school parking lot, she thought about the boy she saw dropping her daughter off after school the previous week. Danielle happened to be out in the yard planting flowers when she spotted a brown car pulling up at the corner. Something told her to watch and sure enough, shortly after, the passenger's door opened and Portia stepped out. Danielle waited for the car to drive past her house, then made eye contact with the driver—a young African who had to be at least eighteen. When Portia made it to the house, she looked surprised to see her mother already home from work. Little did she know that Danielle had taken a day off for herself.

"Why weren't you on the bus?" she asked as her daughter moved up the driveway.

"Carmen's mama gave us a ride home." Carmen was the cute biracial girl who lived around the corner.

Danielle rose from a sitting position on the grass. "Then who the hell just dropped you off at the corner?"

Portia knew she had been caught in a lie because she didn't respond.

Danielle cupped her ear. "I'm sorry, you're gonna have to speak up because I can't hear you."

"Nobody," she finally said.

"He was definitely somebody. That's why you had him drop you off at the corner. What I tell you about lyin'? Let me catch you lettin' some muthafucker drop you off again and see what happens!" Without a word, Portia stormed into the house.

Returning her mind to the problem at hand, Danielle took a second and lowered her head to the steering wheel and closed her eyes. Her life had to get better. She didn't know how much more she could take before she reached the breaking point. Maybe it was time for her to take a vacation. She then remembered that she was planning to spend the weekend with her two closest friends. At least she had something to look forward to.

Her best friend Renee Moore was flying in from the East Coast. Any time they were together, her life was anything but boring.

She finally climbed out of the SUV feeling like she had the weight of the world on her shoulders. As she moved across the parking lot, she thought about her ex-husband.

At this point, calling Portia's father would be a mistake. Alvin Patterson would blow the situation all out of proportion, then blame it all on her. No, she would wait and call him when she had more information, if she bothered to call him at all.

Danielle tightened her grip on her purse strap and stepped into the building. Staring straight ahead, she moved down the hall to the nurse's office. Stepping into the carpeted waiting room, she found Portia's best friend Celina sitting on the couch with her daughter's head across her lap.

Danielle planted a hand to her waist. "What's going on now?" she barked, completely aware her voice lacked empathy.

Celina waved weakly with an apologetic look. "Ms. Danielle, I'm sorry. I'm the one who told the nurse, but I felt it was something Portia needed to report," she said in a low, nervous tone.

"Don't worry. You did the right thing." Her eyes shifted to her daughter's golden-brown face, stained with tears, and didn't feel an ounce of sympathy because as far as she was concerned, her hot ass didn't have any business being on a college campus. Before she had a chance to question what happened, the nurse stuck her head out the door.

Her light-blue eyes crinkled in the friendliest way. "Ms. Brooks, hi. Come on into my office."

Forcing a smile and nodding at the redhead, she stepped into a small room. Nurse Carter closed the door and gestured for her to take the chair across from her. Once seated, Danielle met the woman's sympathetic gaze.

"I am really sorry about this, but as you probably already know, I'm required by law to report this incident," she said as she adjusted a pair of round, black wire-rimmed glasses on the bridge of her nose.

Danielle gave her a grim look. If she didn't know, she definitely knew now. She just wished her daughter had given her a heads-up about what was going on before she had broadcast it to Celina. They both knew good and well that girl didn't know how to keep her mouth shut. Thank goodness the school year was almost over.

"Did she say anything to you last night?"

Danielle sat back on the hard chair and shook her head. "No, she stayed the night with her grandmother. Did she tell you what happened?"

Nurse Carter nodded. "Apparently her boyfriend Andre picked her up after school yesterday, and while he was out of the dorm room taking a final exam, his roommate took advantage of her."

Her head was spinning. Andre was her daughter's so-called college boyfriend that she had yet to meet. Her gut told her he was the same guy she'd seen dropping her daughter off at home. Danielle took a deep breath, trying to keep her anger in check. She knew that boy was no good. "Was there a track meet yesterday after school?"

The nurse looked surprised by her question, then turned and looked at a small calendar on her desk. She shook her head.

Ain't that a bitch. She released a frustrated sigh. Her daughter was up to her sneaky tricks again. Danielle sighed. "She told my mother she was going to a track meet."

"I'm sorry." Before the nurse could say anything further, a knock was heard at the door and an older woman stuck her head in. Nurse Carter rose. "Excuse me, I'll be right back."

Danielle rested her purse in her lap and waited.

More and more she regretted not sending her daughter to the small, private high school on the city's south side. Instead, she had allowed Portia to attend the large inner-city school. Hickman High School was within walking distance of housing projects. Every week it was one thing after another with Portia: skipping class, not getting on the school bus, and hanging out in Douglas Park.

She shook her head. If the weather was nice, black folks swarmed Douglas Park like roaches. It had always been that way. Danielle knew because when she was a teenager she broke her neck to get down to the projects to hang with her girls. They would walk to the park in their skimpiest gear, then sit in the bleachers and watch a bunch of fine, no-good brothas play basketball. Only times had changed. Now the park was full of drug dealers and fights that now involved knives and guns. Just last week when she had picked her daughter up after drill team practice, two cops were spotted on foot, chasing a suspect across the park. Only this time things were much worse. It was too unreal for words. *Maybe I should have called her father.* After all, she was tired of dealing with a defiant teenager alone.

"Sorry about that," the nurse said as she stepped back into the office and shut the door behind her. When she returned to her seat, Danielle sat quietly and listened as the nurse explained the process.

"I've already contacted the hospital. All you have to do is take her to the emergency room. They are expecting her."

Danielle nodded.

"As I said before, I am required to report these incidents. As soon as Celina brought her in here to talk to me, I contacted the rape crisis hotline. A rape crisis advocate will meet you at the hospital. Just ask for Nurse Tolliver when you get to the ER."

Danielle gave a reluctant nod. The entire process was going to take up the rest of the morning and part of the afternoon. If the circumstances were different, time would be the last thing on her mind, but with her daughter she knew that things were never as they seemed. Sitting up straighter on the chair, she asked, "Which hospital?"

"University Hospital."

Danielle shook her head. "Nope. I work there. You're gonna have to call over to Boone."

The nurse looked at her like she had lost her mind. "Ms. Brooks, I think your daughter's welfare is more—"

She held up a palm, halting the rest of her sentence. "Look, this is embarrassin' enough as it is. I'm not takin' her to my job so that everybody and their mama will know my daughter was raped."

The nurse seemed stunned by her admission before she finally nodded and reached for the phone. Danielle almost felt sorry for giving her more work to do, but as far as she was concerned, Nurse Carter should have asked her first.

As she made the arrangements, Danielle sat back in the chair and waited. She took in the short, round woman's simple attire, white slacks and a red button-down blouse. She had been certain that working as a school nurse was easier than her job as an LPN, working in the labor and delivery unit at the University of Missouri Hospital and Clinics. Now, seeing Nurse Carter with a bunch of loud, horny-ass teenagers on a daily basis, she wasn't so sure.

Danielle allowed her eyes to travel around the room. A thousand emotions were running through her mind, but compassion for her daughter was not one of them. Columbia was a small town and the black community even smaller. The last thing she needed was for everybody to know her daughter was ho'ing on campus. She would never hear the end of it.

As soon as the nurse completed the call, Danielle rose from the chair and swung her purse strap over her shoulder. "Thanks for understanding."

She nodded. "Good luck. I've already signed her out for the rest of the day."

"I 'preciate it." She stepped out in the waiting room to find Portia still lying across the couch looking pitiful as shit. "Let's go."

Her daughter rose slowly and kept her head down. The nurse stepped over and gave her a big hug. "Everything is going to be okay, don't you worry."

Portia simply nodded.

Lips pursed, Danielle waited impatiently for Portia to grab her things, then turned and headed out to the car. Portia followed several feet behind. As soon as they were both seated,

Danielle stared pointedly at her daughter and said, "What the hell was you thinkin' sneaking on campus?"

Portia dried her face with a tissue and answered while still casting her eyes downward, "I don't know."

"What you mean, you don't know? I thought you were at a track meet."

She started crying. "I lied because I-I knew if I asked you if could I go see Andre y-you were gonna say no," she answered between sobs.

"And why do ya think I would say that?" When she didn't respond, Danielle felt like screaming. Instead she took a long breath, then continued. "Because shit like this happens. A sixteen-year-old girl has no doggone business in some college dorm room. Them horny muthafuckers ain't tryin' to do nothing but get in yo' draws."

"Andre wouldn't do that," Portia looked straight at her and countered defensively.

"Uh-huh," Danielle said, eyes narrowed and not at all convinced. "What did he say when you told him what his roommate did?"

Portia lowered her gaze to her lap again and seemed to shrink on the seat. "He didn't believe me." She started crying, but Danielle refused to be swayed by tears.

Danielle exhaled her annoyance. "He and his roommate probably planned the whole damn thang." Seconds away from screaming, she reached down and put the key in the ignition. She had yet to meet this Andre because her daughter refused to invite him over. All she knew was that they met at the mall, and when her daughter wasn't on the school bus—if she bothered to compare notes with Carmen's mother—she would know how often this college student named Andre was dropping her off on the corner. Demanding that she stop seeing him was a big waste of time. Fighting her was a losing battle, because the more privileges she took away, the more rebellious she became.

She shook her head. "I don't know why you put me through this shit every week. I'm not gon' tell you this again. Leave them muthafuckers alone!" She started the Durango, then peeled out of the parking spot. Realizing she was on school grounds, she quickly put her foot on the brake and slowed down. *Relax, girl.* The last thing she needed was a speeding ticket on top of everything else. Taking a deep breath, she tried to calm her nerves but after last night, what had already started out as a bad day had suddenly gotten much worse.

They rode in the SUV, not saying a word to each other. Portia stared out the window the entire ride and that was fine with Danielle. She was so fed up with her daughter that she didn't know what to do.

"Ya better not be lying."

"I'm not," Portia said between sobs.

Danielle wanted so badly to feel sorry for her but she couldn't bring herself to do it. Part of her felt that she had brought this shit on herself. If she had kept her hot ass at her grandmother's, none of this would have happened.

They arrived at the emergency room, and as soon as Danielle told the receptionist their reason for coming, they were ushered off to a private room. She took a seat in a hard chair in the corner. Portia was told to climb onto the examination table. A nurse came in and asked several embarrassing questions, then left to call the campus police. She informed them a few minutes later that they would be sending an officer over shortly. As soon as the nurse left, the rape crisis advocate arrived.

"Hello, I'm Allegra," said the young, willowy blonde. She looked like a recent college graduate.

Danielle introduced herself and Portia.

Allegra gave Portia a sympathetic smile as she squeezed her hand. "Don't worry, sweetie, none of this is your fault. He took advantage of you. You are doing the right thing reporting this because if you let him get away with it, then he will do it to someone else."

Danielle listened and as she watched the tears fall from her daughter's eyes again, all that she felt was pity. All her lecturing had been a waste of time. It took a man snatching some booty for Portia to realize the road she was heading down was the wrong path. Maybe something good would come out of this embarrassing experience.

She started to feel her heart soften and began to think that maybe for once her daughter was telling the truth. Last year there had been a story in the paper about a girl who had been sexually assaulted by her stepfather. When she finally found the guts to tell her mother, her mother called her a slut and kicked her daughter out of the house. Three days later, the girl had hung herself. As much as her daughter drove her crazy, if anything happened to Portia because she refused to believe her, Danielle would never forgive herself. Regardless of her daughter's history of "crying wolf," it was her job as her mother to stand by her side.

Taking a deep breath, she rose and moved over and stood by her daughter. When Portia glanced up at her with swollen eyes, she reached out and smoothed back a wisp of hair that had escaped her shoulder-length ponytail.

"Princess, the counselor is right," she said softly, using her nickname. "Just tell the police everything that happened and we'll make sure he gets everything that he deserves." Portia appeared stunned by her mother's sudden change of heart. She nodded as Danielle handed her a box of tissues, then returned to her seat.

There was a knock at the door and after being granted permission to enter, two campus police officers stepped into the small examination room.

Oh, hell nah! Danielle groaned inwardly when she spotted Calvin Cambridge. Her temple immediately began to pound in concert with her racing heart. Could this day possibly get any worse? He glanced in her direction and appeared not to recognize her. She released a sigh of relief. Maybe he wouldn't remember her after all.

"Are you Ms. Patterson?"

Danielle shifted her eyes to the short brunette standing beside him and nodded, not bothering to tell her she hadn't been Patterson in years.

"If you don't mind, we are going to ask your daughter a few questions."

She nodded and listened as Calvin questioned Portia about the previous evening. As she listened, she found herself watching and remembering.

Calvin was tall enough to be a professional basketball player and he definitely worked out. After twelve years he still looked good as hell. He had a handsome, mocha-brown face with deep, dark eyes. He wore his head shaved and she couldn't imagine anything being sexier. Calvin was the type of brother she had always dreamed of having but never seemed to find.

She snapped out of her trance when she heard him ask, "What is your relationship to Andre?"

After a moment, Portia answered, "We just friends."

Danielle frowned and stared at her daughter.

Calvin noticed her hesitation. "You sure the two of you are just friends?" he asked.

Dropping her eyes to the floor, she nodded. "Yeah, we just friends."

The look Calvin gave said he was having a hard time believing her, which Danielle couldn't fault since she knew otherwise. Only minutes ago she had decided to give her daughter her support—now she was starting to have doubts again. However, instead of stepping in, she decided to remain quiet and see how the situation played out.

"Okay, so let me make sure I got this right," Calvin began as he glanced down at the notes he had scribbled on his notepad. "Andre picked you up after school and took you to his room. While he left to take a final exam, his roommate Travis returned and took advantage of you."

Portia nodded. "I was lying across the bed watching TV in Andre's room when he showed up."

Danielle wanted so badly to yell, "What the fuck you doin' in some nigga's bedroom!" but forced herself to remain quiet.

"Did Travis hit you?" Calvin inquired.

"Nope."

"Did you try to scream or get away?"

She shook her head.

"Did he threaten to hurt you if you refused?"

Portia tugged in several short breaths and held her tears in check. "No. He stepped in the room, locked the door and sat next to me on the bed. He then moved on top of me and pulled my jeans down."

"How did he manage to get yo' jeans down?"

When the two officers turned their heads and looked at her, Danielle realized she had asked the question out loud.

Portia glanced at her mother through lowered lashes and answered as if the question was obvious. "He pulled them down my hips."

Calvin narrowed his gaze skeptically. Danielle gave an even more confused look. Her daughter didn't wear jeans, she wore coochie cutters. As tight as they were, she couldn't see how anyone could pull them off without a little help. Besides, the minute he started pulling them down she could have kicked him in the face. Danielle inhaled deeply. *It was easier to say what you coulda woulda done when it isn't you.* No matter how hard a time she had with this situation, she needed to support her daughter, regardless of what she might be thinking.

Calvin continued his questions. "At what point did he stop?"

Portia cleared her throat. "When the condom broke."

His brow rose. "He used a condom?"

She nodded.

Danielle noticed the two officers look at each other but didn't bother to comment. Calvin reached for his pen and started writing again.

"Where did he get the condom?" he asked.

"From Andre's top drawer."

Danielle shifted on her seat. When he had stopped to get a condom, that's when she would have kicked him in his nuts. She was becoming more baffled by the minute.

"Is there anything else you might have forgotten to tell me?" Calvin asked.

Portia glanced up, then back down at the floor and shook her head.

"How many times did ya tell him no?" Danielle asked since neither of the bubble-headed officers had. Regardless of what happened, she knew no meant no.

Portia sighed with relief. "Mama, I kept telling him the whole time."

Danielle crossed her arms and looked at Calvin with a look of challenge in her eyes. "That's all I need to know. It sounds to me like the two of y'all need to get on yo' job."

Calvin took a deep breath, then closed the notepad and nodded at Danielle. "We're going to go back to campus, pull the boys in, and start an investigation. As soon as the nurse finishes the examination, we'll be back for the kit and her clothes."

Portia's eyes grew large as she looked to her mother for help.

Danielle cleared her throat. "Those aren't the clothes she had on last night."

"They're not?"

Danielle exhaled deeply. "No, she has showered and changed since then," she said, realizing that Portia may have already destroyed all of the evidence.

Calvin looked like he was starting to get frustrated and Danielle couldn't blame him. She was getting equally irritated.

He shook his head. "We really need to get those clothes. There might be evidence directly on them, linking Travis to your daughter."

Danielle massaged her temple. "They're at my mom's. I can bring them to ya later."

"How about when you're done here, you give me a call and I'll come out to the house and collect them myself?" Calvin suggested.

She gave a weary nod. It was going to be a long day.

The officers excused themselves and Danielle was left alone with her daughter and the advocate. She glanced over at Portia, who was wearing that same blank expression. Danielle wished she could make herself get up and hug her child, but part of her would not do it because now that the officers were done questioning her, she was even more doubtful than before.

The nurse arrived and explained the procedure. She was going to take samples of hair from both her head and pubic area, then do a Pap smear along with collecting other DNA samples, such as saliva and tissue. The entire process was going to take two hours. Danielle groaned inwardly, then told herself she was being selfish.

The nurse glanced over in her direction. "Mom, you can be present during the entire process."

Portia gave her mother a humiliated look. Danielle shook her head. "No, I'll save her the embarrassment. I'll wait down here."

"I'll go in with you if you like," Allegra offered.

Portia smiled, pleased at her offer.

The nurse also smiled. "Good—then let's get started." She escorted Portia out of the room. Danielle decided to go outside and get some air while she waited.

Her phone vibrated. It was Ron calling from her house. He had obviously waited until she had gone to work before he had bothered to bring his tired ass home.

"What?"

"Nucca, what da fuck you do to my clothes?" he barked into the phone.

"What does it look like? I burned them."

He sighed with disgust. "Yo' ass is crazy."

"No, yo' muthafuckin' ass is crazy, thinkin' you could stay out all night. You got life twisted," she said loudly with a sharp edge to her voice.

"I worked a double."

She wasn't buying his lame excuse. "Double my ass. You should have called."

"Yo, straight up, I forgot."

She snorted a laugh. "You must be on some dumb shit. I ain't that crackhead you used to fuck with."

"Man, I'm not fin to argue wit' you. I just wanna know why you burn my shit?"

"'Cause I'm tired of playing games!" she screamed. "Look, I got other problems and I ain't got time to listen to no more excuses. Pack your shit and move back home with ya mammy."

"Damn, boo, why you gotta be like that?" he asked innocently.

"'Cause I'm tired of your triflin' ass." Danielle ended the call, then turned the ringer off just in case he decided to call back, and went inside the hospital again. She didn't have time to play games with him. She had already been doing that for the last two years. Although she knew he wouldn't take her seriously and his shit would still be scattered all over her room when she got home. And because she loved his fine ass, she knew she wasn't even going to push the issue.

Danielle walked back into the emergency room and fumbled through her purse for a bottle of ibuprofen and a dollar so she could get a soda from the vending machine.

She and Ron had met one evening at the grocery store, of all places. Shop & Save had been running a sale on ground chuck and there wasn't any left in the bin. She rang the bell for the meat department and Ron came out. He was fine as all get-out. Tall, dark, sexy, and dripping with charisma, she was instantly attracted. After he brought out a family-pack of meat, he asked for her number with a sexy, white-tooth smile. That night he called, and by Friday, they had gone out on their first date. It didn't bother Danielle that she was twelve years his senior. She had dated men younger than that before. Cornrows braided straight back, jeans hanging off their butts, long, white t-shirts, and Timberland boots—there wasn't anything sexier. She didn't know why. Maybe she watched too many music videos, but a man her age couldn't do shit for her. She couldn't stand a nice, clean-cut brotha. Whoever had said nice guys finished last wasn't lying. She needed a challenge and an educated, refined brotha wasn't it.

It wasn't that she liked young dudes, she just had a thing for thugs and preferably one with a job. As an LPN, she could have dated and probably married a doctor by now. But she knew that would've led to a life of boredom, like her best friend Renee had, and she loved living on the edge.

People thought it strange, her choice in men, especially since she grew up middle-class with both her parents, two sisters, and a brother. Renee grew up in the ghetto, and she spent most of her time in the summer hanging with her. She didn't know why, but hanging in the 'hood excited her, made her heart pump wildly. Her own life has always been so sheltered and boring. She loved the excitement you could always find in the projects. There was never a dull moment. She wanted drama. Her mother used to do everything in her power to try to keep her from hanging in the projects, but she always found a way to sneak out.

Although she might be a little naïve at times, Danielle was far from stupid. Men took advantage of her and took her kindness as weakness, but she eventually figured the shit out and kicked their asses to the curb. Now it was time for Ron to go.

What she liked about Ron was that he was easy to talk to. She had discovered he was the kind of guy who loved to tell jokes. He would do anything to make her smile. One minute he was acting all tough and shit, and the next he was so kind and gentle. However, with Ron came plenty of drama—unfortunately, more than she bargained for: losing jobs, baby mama drama, and his ghetto-ass, mooching family. But even with all of the problems with their relationship, it wasn't often that she came across a brotha with a ten-and-a-half-inch dick and a tongue to match, which was why she'd kept him as long as she had. But lately, with him staying out so much, and the hang-up calls in the middle of the night, she was beginning to believe that good sex wasn't everything. At one point, the thought of some other woman riding her man's dick had scared her, but now she didn't care as much.

Temporarily dismissing all thoughts of Ron, Danielle fed the dollar into the machine and pushed the button and waited for the diet cola to drop. She didn't know why she drank diet, especially since she'd been wearing a size six for as long as she could remember, but since it was all her slightly overweight mother drank, she had acquired the taste. Now if she tried to drink regular soda, she found it to be a bit too sweet. She washed down two ibuprofens, then took a seat in the waiting room and closed her eyes while she waited.

She dozed off because the next thing she knew, the advocate was tapping her arm.

"All done," Allegra said with a cheerful smile. "Portia is definitely a trooper. She handled the entire process quite well." She then gave her some contact information and told her she would call the next day to check on her. By the time Danielle made it back to the room, Portia was dressed and ready to go home. She looked tired and alone. She could only imagine what she had gone through.

"Ready to go?"

Portia nodded eagerly.

When they made it out to the car, Danielle asked her daughter if she was hungry and when she said yes, she stopped at Burger King. While at the drive-thru she groaned as she remembered she was supposed to meet Calvin at her mother's house. As soon as she ordered their food, she gave Calvin a call.

"Lieutenant Cambridge."

His deep voice gave her goose bumps. "This is Portia's mother. We're all done. I'm on my way to my mom's so you can get those clothes."

He took a deep breath, and something in his voice told her the investigation wasn't going as smoothly as he had anticipated. "I want you to come down here instead. I need your daughter to positively identify Travis's picture. I also had a chance to interview the roommates and I have some more questions for your daughter."

She could hear the reservation in his voice. "All right. We'll be there shortly."

After she paid for their food, she headed toward the University of Missouri-Columbia campus. She didn't speak because she didn't know what to say. Something told her that what Calvin was about to tell her was something she wasn't going to like.

When they were a block away from campus, she took a swig of her soda to wash the lump from her throat, then said, "The officer wants you to ID Travis and answer a few mo' questions."

Portia shifted on the seat. "But I already told them everything."

"I know, but they've met with Travis and Andre, and have a few more questions."

Shock filled her eyes before she turned and stared out the window.

"Is there anything I need to know 'fore we get there?"

"Nope," she answered without hesitation.

"Well, if there is, you better tell me now."

"I said there wasn't anything else," Portia said, sounding testy. "I wish you would believe me sometimes."

"It ain't that I don't believe you. I just know how yo' ass likes to lie." Portia huffed and pouted the rest of the way.

Danielle pulled into the parking lot, then walked alongside her daughter into the university police station and asked for Cambridge. He immediately stepped out of his office and greeted them. "Do you mind if my partner shows Portia some pictures while I talk to you in private for a few minutes?"

She shook her head and he ushered Portia into a room across the hall from his, then signaled for Danielle to follow. They sat. He leaned back in the chair, his eyes sparkling with recognition. He did remember her!

"Cambridge, I—"

"Let's quit pretending we don't go way back."

His dark eyes were locked on her. They were compelling and challenging, which bothered her because he always looked like he was determined to have her. Her nipples hardened beneath her blouse and she cussed under her breath. He had always made her react this way, which was one reason why he was all wrong. The other was that he used to screw her best friend Renee. With friendship, there was an unsaid rule never to fuck the same man.

Sitting up straighter in the chair, she cleared her throat. "I ain't pretendin'—considering the circumstances, I'm tryin' to keep things professional."

He grinned. "All right. I'll accept that . . . for now."

She purposely ignored the comment and rolled her eyes.

He obviously realized that now was neither the time nor the place, because his expression sobered. "I had a chance to meet with both boys and I must say I am getting contradicting stories. According to Andre, he and your daughter have been sexually involved for almost six months."

Danielle frowned with embarrassment. The thought of her daughter spreading her legs made her sick to her stomach. "I suspected as much."

Folding his hands on top of his desk, he continued. "He also said he has caught her flirting with Travis on several occasions."

"That's his roommate. Of course he's gon' take up for him." Just like it was her job as the mother to defend her daughter.

Calvin shook his head. "I don't think so. These two can't stand each other."

"So you saying you think my daughter's lyin'?" He didn't have to say it, but she could tell that he did.

"It's not that I don't want to believe your daughter—there's just more to this story."

"More like what?" she snapped.

Before he could answer there was a knock on the door and the female officer entered with Portia. "Please, have a seat."

Wearing a weary look, Portia came around and took a seat beside her mother.

Calvin steepled his hands on the desk. "Portia, we take rape cases very seriously around here and it is vitally important that you tell the truth." He looked at Portia hard to be sure the underlying message came across.

"Now, I've spent the last two hours interviewing Travis and

Andre. I'm going to ask you some of the same questions I asked them. Okay?"

She shrugged. "I guess I don't have a choice."

Danielle swung around on the seat and made sure her daughter knew she was only seconds away from knocking her head off for her smart-ass mouth. The only thing stopping her was that she had an audience.

"How did you meet Andre?"

Portia gave her mother a sidelong glance. Calvin had to repeat the question before she finally mumbled, "Over the Internet."

"No. Isn't it true you met Travis on the Internet and then he introduced you to Andre?"

She nodded.

Mouth gaping, Danielle stared across at her daughter.

Calvin rubbed his forehead. "You liked Travis first, didn't you?"

Portia nodded again.

"The same day you met them at the mall, where did y'all go?"

She played with the ring on her finger, then answered. "Celina and I went to their dorm."

"And do you want to tell your mother what you did with Andre that night?"

Danielle's eyes grew large. She turned to her daughter just as Portia mumbled, "No." It was obvious from her behavior that she had done something her hot tail had no business doing.

"Andre said you and Travis flirted with each other all the time."

Her head flew up in defense. "No, we didn't. He's lying." Portia started crying again.

Danielle sighed. "Can we just stick to last night?"

Calvin didn't look too pleased but he moved on. "Where did Travis get that condom?"

"I already told you, in Andre's drawer," Portia replied, growing testy.

Danielle focused her attention on her daughter, who looked determined to look at anything but her.

"Okay, let me rephrase the question. How did he know where the condoms were?"

"I told him," she said nonchalantly.

Danielle gasped. "You did what?"

Portia shrugged. "He was gonna do it anyway, so I figured he could at least wear a condom." She cut her eyes and slouched in the chair.

"I can't believe this shit." Danielle shook her head. "How you expect me to press charges against the boy if you're tellin' him where to find the condom? Then, on top of that, he stopped the second the condom broke!" She was too through.

"I knew you wouldn't believe me," she said sarcastically, as sharp as a sudden slap.

Her mother's voice softened. "I want to believe you, but you've got to give me something to work with."

Portia's eyes suddenly swelled with tears again.

Calvin tried another approach. "Andre said afterward when he returned to the room, Travis was gone. When he didn't believe your story about being raped, you stormed out the room. Now, you told me earlier Andre brought you home but he said he didn't."

Portia dropped her head to her hand.

"Who brought you home?"

She didn't answer.

Danielle was ten seconds away from choking the shit out of her. "Excuse me, you hear that man askin' you a question. How did you get home last night?"

She sighed theatrically. "My friend brought me home."

"What friend?" her mother asked.

"I'd rather not say."

Danielle sprang from her seat. "I've heard enough." Turning to the two officers, she said, "I'm so sorry for wasting both y'all's time." Heading toward the door, she signaled for her daughter to follow. Calvin called after her, but she ignored him and stormed out of the building and across the parking lot. "Get yo' ass in the car."

Portia was crying and walking with her head down low, but Danielle wasn't falling for that. Not after wasting an entire day from work. She was not about to let her daughter think for a moment she could get away with the stunt she had pulled today.

She studied the sober look in Portia's puffy eyes. "I don't understand you. You had every chance to come clean, yet you lied. I just don't understand why ya do half the shit ya do."

"I'm not lying," she wailed.

"Well, it sho' in hell sounded like it!" she shot back.

Portia didn't respond.

"I'm not puttin' up with any more of yo' bullshit. For the next month, no phone, and no weekends hangin' with yo' friends. You understand me?"

"Yes," she hissed with attitude.

"Little lady, I advise you to get yo' attitude in check—otherwise you can pack yo' shit and move in with yo' dad."

Portia let out a sigh and nodded.

As Danielle drove home, her anger increased. There was no way in hell she was pressing charges against Travis, because as sad as it may be, she didn't believe her daughter had been raped.

She pulled into the driveway and pushed her electronic garage opener, and after three tries realized it wasn't working. "Damn, what else can go wrong?" she asked. Once on the porch, she opened the screen door and found a disconnection notice from the electric company hanging on the doorknob. "Ain't this some shit!"

"Mama, what's wrong wit' the lights?"

"They're off—now, go to yo' room while I figure out what's goin' on." Danielle angrily clicked her jaw. She was seconds away from crying. The day had gone from bad to worse. As soon as Portia had gone upstairs, she reached for the kitchen phone and called Ron's job.

"Quaker Oats, may I help you?"

"Yes, I need to leave a message for Ronald Gross to call home as soon as possible."

"One moment, please." There was a momentary pause before the receptionist came back on the line. "I'm sorry, but he no longer works here."

"What? Since when?"

"Ma'am, I'm afraid I can't give out any more information."

Danielle ended the call without even saying good-bye, and tried his cell phone.

"Hey, boo," Ron purred.

"I thought you paid the light bill."

"My bad. I forgot."

"You forgot? I told ya twice and you told me you took care of it."

"Yeah, I know. Pookie owed me some money, and when I got over to his crib, don't you know that bitch-ass nucca came up short. Yo, don't trip. I got chu payday."

"Uh-huh. How you gon' pay anything when you ain't even got a job?"

He hesitated. "Yo, them white muthafuckas were trippin'. They let me go ova some bullshit. But I pick up my check Friday. I'll pay it."

"What the fuck good is that gon' do me! My shit's already turned off. You were 'posed to pay it last payday." He was so stupid he made her head hurt.

"I ain't have it."

"But ya had the money to buy those new Jordans."

He sucked his teeth. "What you want me to do, wear the same sneakers two months in a row?"

"And what am I 'posed to do, come home and my shit's cut off?"

"Look, holla back later 'cause I ain't fin to argue wit' you."

Danielle gave an angry laugh. "You sho' right, and tonight you gon' get the hell outta my house."

"For what?"

"'Cause I'm tired of yo' shit."

"Man, whatever." He hung up.

No, he didn't hang up on me. I got something for his ass. She dialed another number.

"Hello."

"Kee, wake yo' monkey ass up!"

"Danny, I'm trying to sleep," her brother grumbled in the phone.

"It's the middle of the damn day. Ya probably got one of them hoochies up in there with you."

"Danny, whassup?"

"I need a favor."

"What?"

"I want you to make Ron understand he needs to move his shit up out of my house."

"Man, I ain't gettin' in the middle of yo' shit. I told you not to mess with that punk in the first place."

"Yeah, well, I did. Now I want him out."

"Yeah, ai'ight. I'll run up on him in a lil' while."

She smiled, pleased. Her big brother Kendall Brooks was going to fix everything—as usual. "Good, and get my key back, too." She hung up the phone with a silly smirk on her face. *Ron just don't know who he's messing with.* Swinging her purse back over her shoulder, she yelled up the stairs. "Portia, I'll be back. Ima go pay the electric bill. Make sure you stay yo' butt off the phone!" Without waiting for her response, she walked back out the door and climbed in her car. "Damn!" she cussed under her breath as she pulled down the driveway. "I guess I better go pay the phone bill, too."

Chapter 3

Kayla

Kayla Sparks was sitting in front of her computer, trying to transcribe the minutes from this morning's meeting, but so far she hadn't been able to do anything but watch the clock all day. Nervous energy had a stranglehold on her. She was anxious to see her man again.

Removing the headset from her ears, she decided any further attempt would be a big waste of time. She closed the document. Glancing up at the clock, a smile curled her lips. *Finally!* Fifteen more minutes until closing. She breathed a sigh of relief. In less than three hours she would be lying in the arms of the Reverend Leroy Brown. Giggling, she logged off her computer.

"I love when you laugh."

She went completely still at the sound of his velvety voice. After taking a second to regroup, she glanced over her shoulder to see Jermaine Whitlow, an academic advisor, poking his head inside the door of her small office.

"What's so funny?" he asked.

Straightening her white blouse, Kayla swung around in her chair and met his amused expression. "I'm just looking forward to the weekend, that's all." What she said wasn't a complete lie, although her giggles had nothing to do with the weekend ahead.

Jermaine nodded, then, without waiting for an invitation, strolled into her office. As he moved, Kayla admired the way his broad shoulders strained against the crisp fabric of his navy blue jacket. He reminded her of a Marine in uniform. When he took a seat in the chair directly across from her desk, the intoxicating scent of his cologne floated around her.

"Does that mean you've got big plans?" He gave her a mischievous grin, waiting for her response.

Kayla leaned forward, resting her elbows on the desk. She usually avoided questions about her personal life, but for some reason, Jermaine made her feel like they were friends. He always found the time to drop by her office and make her feel that even though she was only an administrative assistant, her job was just as valuable as his.

She shrugged. "If hanging out with my girl is big plans, then I guess so." She briefly told him about her best friend, who was flying home for the weekend. He was relaxed as she spoke, keeping his gaze on her. She liked the way he always seemed interested in what she had to say.

Jermaine gave her a curious glance. "Are you talking about Renee Moore, the author?"

The smile disappeared from her face. Why was she not surprised to hear that he knew Renee? Everyone in town did. Especially the men. *Humph!* She wouldn't be surprised to discover the two used to screw.

"Yep, the one and only," she replied dryly.

Nodding, Jermaine leaned back in his chair. "She writes under the pseudonym Caeramel, right?" When she nodded, he continued. "The only reason why I know that is because my baby sister is a big fan of her work. She called me yesterday to reschedule our weekly Saturday afternoon lunch because her favorite author will be at the mall this weekend signing copies of her latest erotic romance."

Kayla was relieved and almost felt guilty for jumping to a conclusion about the two. Renee may be quick to spread her legs, but as average as Jermaine was, he probably wasn't even Renee's type. However, as far as her best friend was concerned, as long as he had a big dick, he was Renee's type.

Her gray eyes brightened. "She's signing at Barnes & Noble."

"Maybe I'll drop by and meet the infamous woman myself. Although . . ." he chuckled softly. ". . . romance isn't my idea of educational reading."

She wasn't surprised. Most men wouldn't be caught dead reading women's fiction. "Well, there are thousands of women who would disagree. She really is popular." When his eyes sparked with renewed interest, Kayla shrugged. "I'll be there helping her pass out bookmarks and keeping the line moving."

"In that case, I'll make sure to drop by," he said with a wink.

His voice had dropped several octaves and Kayla felt her nipples tingle. Thank goodness she was wearing a jacket. For several moments they stared at each other in awkward silence. She had never been very good with one-on-one conversations with the opposite sex, and she didn't know what else to say.

Finally Jermaine cleared his throat and rose from the chair. "Well, I guess I better go get ready to head home. Don't forget, I'll be out the rest of the week."

She tapped her desk. "I've got it right here on my calendar." He was scheduled to attend a leadership conference over at the main campus. She knew because she had made the arrangements.

"Great. Enjoy the rest of your week."

"You, too," she whispered as he strolled out of her office, leaving the intoxicating scent of his cologne behind. She stared out into the lobby for what felt like an eternity, as if she expected him to return.

Dang, he's fine. Jermaine stood well over six feet tall. A deep, dark chocolate teddy bear, just the way she liked them. *Too bad I'm already spoken for.* With Leroy on her mind, she decided to call it a day. She reached for her purse in the bottom drawer of her desk, then rose from her chair and headed down the hall.

On the way out, she waved to several other employees who were also getting ready to leave.

She had been working in the Dean's office at the medical school for almost a year, and she loved the atmosphere and the students. At the end of the hall outside of Jermaine's office, she spotted him chatting with one of their fourth-year medical students. When he saw her coming down the hall, to her amazement, he moved and opened the glass door for her.

"I'll see you Saturday," he said with so much passion one would have thought they were going out on a date.

Kayla shook her head. No, she was being ridiculous. There was no way anyone would think that. However, one quick glance over at the curious look on the student's face, and she knew it hadn't been her imagination at all. Without uttering a word, she waved and briskly left the building.

As she moved toward the employee parking lot, she allowed her mind to wander and couldn't help wondering what it would be like to date someone like Jermaine. He had a beautiful personality and all of the medical students loved him, especially the females. Since Kayla was responsible for his calendar, she knew Jermaine's daily activities. Most of the female medical students insisted that they meet with their academic advisor on a weekly basis, while the male students saw him twice a quarter. The women showed up dressed to impress with hair and makeup, hoping to capture the eye of the sexy advisor. Although this annoyed her, Kayla couldn't blame them. Jermaine was in his early forties, recently divorced with no children. Any woman would be lucky to have him. However, after the last advisor was caught with his pants down at his ankles and a third-year medical student bent over his desk, chances were the students were all wasting their time. The Jermaine she had grown to respect and admire wouldn't dream of stepping over the line.

Reaching her car, Kayla allowed her mind to return to the evening ahead. The last time she had seen Leroy was ten days ago, the night before he left to spend a week in Atlanta at a T.D.

Jakes retreat. Climbing into the car, she recalled that their last night together, there was something different between them. To her embarrassment, Leroy's penis wouldn't stay hard. No matter how much she played with it and slobbered all over the head, he couldn't keep an erection. He told her it was nothing to worry about, but she couldn't help spending the last couple of days wondering if there was possibly more to it than that.

As she thought about a possibility or two, she slipped out of her jacket. The June heat mixed with anxiety was getting the best of her. Thoughts of Leroy losing interest rose to the surface. Could that be the case?

Pushing her uneasiness aside, she told herself to think positive and to quit letting her insecurities get the better of her. Tonight, things were going to be different. He was supposed to return this afternoon, and the e-mail he had sent yesterday said that he was looking forward to seeing her.

Kayla started the car and by the time she had kicked on the air conditioning, she was giggling like a teenager again. She didn't even know why she wasted so much time and energy worrying. Leroy loved her and despite everything, nothing or no one could change that.

As she neared home, an idea came to mind. She pulled into a large grocery chain store a couple of blocks from her house and climbed out. T-bone steaks were his favorite. Food was the key to a man's heart, and right now she was willing to do whatever it took to please her man. Tonight she was making him dinner, then serving him a little Kayla afterwards.

Kayla stepped through the sliding double doors, thankful for the rush of air that cooled her body. Reaching for a cart, she moved down the aisle and was disappointed to discover the steaks weren't on sale. Yesterday she had received a child-support check from her oldest daughter Kenya's deadbeat daddy. She had planned to buy her a new pair of gym shoes, but they were going to have to wait. Taking care of her man's needs was a priority. Besides, Kenya had barely had the ones she was wearing for three months. She grabbed a pack of three, then moved to the check-

out lane. Tonight she would grill the steaks, along with baked
potatoes and steamed broccoli. Kayla was thinking about the
night ahead when she heard laughter. She glanced over her
shoulder at the two women in the next lane and her heart skipped
a beat. It was Carlita James and Darlene Brown—Leroy's wife.

She blinked rapidly and turned her head, but not before
Carlita noticed her.

"Well, Sister Sparks, how have you been?" she asked as she
moved over toward her and gave her a hug.

Slipping away from her embrace, Kayla forced a smile. "I've
been fine, and yourself?"

"Good. I thought you had left town. I haven't seen you in
church in over a year."

Kayla glanced over the petite woman's shoulder at Darlene,
who had a hand propped on her slim hip. The sparkle in her
eyes communicated volumes.

"Yeah, tell us—why haven't we seen you in church?" Darlene
said with a sickening smile.

She and Darlene both knew the reason why she'd stopped attending Mt. Carmel Baptist Church. She had a sneaky suspi-
cion Carlita also knew, but instead of letting them get the best
of her, she played the game.

She returned her gaze to Carlita and shrugged. "My work
was needed elsewhere."

"That's too bad. We sure miss you," she said, sounding obliv-
ious to the whole situation. "Well, take care of yourself."

Kayla breathed a sigh of relief when she finally returned to
her lane. Things had gone better than she could have imag-
ined.

It had been two years since Darlene had discovered that
Kayla was sleeping with her husband, and for weeks she had
watched her back, expecting to find the woman lurking in the
shadows, waiting to beat a sistah down. However, as the weeks
turned into months, she started to believe what Darlene had
told her when she had confronted her on the phone. She would
never forget her haunting laughter as she said, "I could care

less who's riding Leroy's little dick, because ain't nobody spending his money but me." Darlene was right about one thing— Leroy had never given her a dime.

Anxious to get out of the store, Kayla quickly put the steaks on the belt. Some old lady in front of her was questioning the price of a head of lettuce. The cashier called for a price check. All the while, she could hear Darlene and Carlita snickering. She didn't dare look their way. It was her turn in line when she overheard Darlene talking loud enough for everyone in the entire store to hear.

"Carlita, did I tell you Leroy's taking me to the Bahamas next month?"

"Darlene, you're so lucky to have a good man like that."

She sucked her teeth. "Don't I know it. We are going to renew our vows. It's been fifteen glorious years. Leroy still makes me feel as if we'd just met."

Kayla tried to pretend she wasn't listening, but how could she ignore them talking about the man she loved? It was hard but she forced herself not to look in their direction.

"Are y'all taking the kids?"

"Nope. Just me and Leroy."

Carlita snorted, then said jokingly, "Chile, you're gonna be walking sideways when you get back." Both women dissolved in hushed laughter behind their hands, straining to keep their voices in check.

Kayla was relieved when she finally paid for her groceries and hurried out to her car, where she loaded the backseat quickly for fear of finding herself face-to-face with Darlene in the parking lot. She climbed into her car, feeling like she had just been slapped across the face. She couldn't believe Leroy was taking his wife to the Bahamas. He was supposed to have taken her to Las Vegas last month but backed out at the last minute. He'd been doing that a lot lately and it was starting to be a regular thing with him. Now his wife had the nerve to boast about their upcoming anniversary. Kayla had asked him over and over about his marriage and he promised her that he was ending it within the next couple of weeks, but after what she had over-heard she wasn't so sure.

As she drove home she tried not to allow self-doubt to cloud her mind, but it wasn't easy. Leroy had lied to her countless times before. She tried to have faith. She had stood by her man for four years, so there was no sense in doubting him now. If he said he wasn't planning to take his wife on vacation, then the best thing she could do was believe him. Besides, Darlene was just jealous.

Kayla hadn't planned on falling in love with the minister at Mt. Carmel Baptist Church, but after several abusive relation-ships, the Reverend Leroy Brown made her feel important and beautiful for the first time in her life. Once Leroy confessed that his marriage was falling apart, and that the attraction was mutual, she tried to fight it with everything she had, but Kayla eventually gave in to the feeling. She truly believed that God had brought them together for a reason. They started meeting and attending conferences together that his wife was too busy to attend. The next thing she knew, they were having an affair, and if anyone found out about it, that would have destroyed everything he had worked so hard to build. Leroy served as the president of the local chapter of the NAACP. He was also an in-surance agent with his face on billboards all over the city.

Kayla released a heavy sigh as she made a left at the next cor-ner. Even back then, she knew what they were doing was wrong. As the granddaughter of a minister, she had grown up in church, knew by heart all ten of the commandments, and was well aware of the consequences for breaking any of the laws. But she was human and the temptation was too great. She felt so good, knowing that she had caught the attention of a handsome and intelligent man who was a prominent member of the commu-nity.

His face danced before her eyes. Leroy was tall, dark, hand-some, and extremely charming. He had a presence that was al-most impossible to resist. She knew that she should have put a stop to their sexual rendezvous years ago, but it was also a spiritual connection that she couldn't begin to explain. Besides, deep down inside she knew that it was just a matter of time before Leroy would leave his wife and finally be with her. As she pulled into her driveway, Kayla took a deep breath, thankful she had made it home without any ugly consequences. She just hoped that Darlene would go ahead and let Leroy have a divorce so they could finally marry.

Kayla stepped into the house to find her oldest daughter, Kenya, lounging on the couch talking on the phone. As usual, shoes and book bags were lying in the middle of the living room floor. Strolling into the kitchen, she found the breakfast dishes still in the same place they had been this morning. Obsessed with things being organized, Kayla's temper began to rise. She stormed into the living room again. "Kenya, get your narrow behind off the phone this instant!"

Rolling her eyes, Kenya answered, "Mom, I've already did my homework."

"But you didn't clean the kitchen or start dinner. Now get off."

"I've gotta go," Kenya said and hung up. She sat there sulking, her arms folded across her small breasts, her Tommy Girl-clad legs crossed.

"Where's Asia?" Kayla asked.

"She's up in her room taking a nap."

"Then wake her up and get that kitchen clean. I don't know why I have to keep telling the two of you the same thing day after day. Do I need to start docking your allowance every time I have to remind you?"

"No," Kenya mumbled after a moment.

"Well, obviously I do. This doesn't make any sense. You go in the kitchen to make a sandwich, yet you don't notice the dishes waiting in the sink." She stood there glaring at Kenya. While she played with the phone cord, she scanned her daughter from head to toe.

She was almost an exact replica of her father. Almond complexion, with a splash of freckles across her nose. Light brown eyes, high cheekbones. Her shoulder-length hair was parted to the side and hung loosely around her shoulders. Rings adorned every finger, while her long acrylic nails gleamed with candy-cane-pink polish. She was a beautiful and bright young lady, just lazy as all get-out.

"And when you get done, go ahead and prepare that Hamburger Helper. The meat is in the refrigerator." Kayla motioned with her chin toward the stairs, her meaning clear.

Shoulders slumped, Kenya went up the stairs to wake her younger sister.

Kayla followed and went to take a shower, deciding not to let her daughter ruin the evening she had ahead. Hopefully things would be better tonight, she prayed as she stood under the spray of the water. Leroy wasn't impotent. He had five children, the youngest one being eighteen months. She figured the problem he'd had the other night must be because of her or maybe she just wasn't trying hard enough to please her man.

She stepped out of the shower, then stood on a towel on the floor and glanced into the full-length mirror behind the door and looked at herself. During their relationship, her weight had increased by a couple dozen pounds. Not that she'd ever looked like a cheerleader. She had always been fat, only now she was at her heaviest. With the scale hitting well over two hundred and eighty pounds, she was certain her appearance had a lot to do with his recent behavior, although Leroy had assured her on several occasions that it did not.

Kayla moved into the adjoining bedroom and prepared for her evening. She slipped into a pair of black slacks and a button-down white blouse, then reached inside her drawer for a sexy new gown she had bought at Lane Bryant the week before. She giggled to herself as she thought about him seeing her in it. He was sure to be pleased. Even though she found it hard to believe, Leroy swore he loved her voluptuous curves.

That was something she'd never understood, considering his wife was skinny. Despite the kids she had a trim waist, wide hips and shapely thighs. Even Leroy, who'd turned fifty-one on his last birthday, looked good for his age. He had a broad football build that attracted women of all ages. He had dark curls that were generously sprinkled with gray and large walnut eyes hooded by heavy, dark eyebrows and the prettiest smile. Kayla giggled and a smile curled her lips because soon he would be all hers.

She quickly brushed her thick, sienna-colored hair back into a twist and secured it with a black clip, then painted her eyes with cinnamon-colored eye shadow and brushed on matching lipstick. She was satisfied that she looked just the way Leroy liked her to. He didn't tolerate a woman looking painted. Although she was big, she knew her face was her best feature. When she looked in the mirror, what she saw wasn't a woman who turned heads, but she knew she was tolerable. She was pretty in a calm, unexcited way with big gray eyes, alabaster skin, a small, upturned nose, and a rosebud of a mouth. Nothing about her hinted at sexiness, but tonight that was exactly what she planned to be.

Grabbing her purse, she moved into the kitchen and was pleased to see that Kenya had started dinner. The dishes had already been washed and dried. Asia was sitting at the table doing homework.

"Hey, Mommy."

"Hey, sweetie." She planted a kiss to her cheek. "Mind your sister. I'm going out for a while."

"But I need help with my homework," Asia whined, her gray eyes misty.

Kayla put a hand to her hip. She didn't have time for this. There was no way she could be late. She yelled into the living room where her daughter was back on the couch talking on the phone. "Kenya! Come help your sister with her homework."

"I want *you* to help," Asia pouted as Kenya stepped into the room.

She shook her head impatiently. "I've got somewhere to go. I'll be back later tonight." Ignoring the look her teenager gave her, she headed out the door.

To her dismay, Kenya had stumbled upon her relationship

after eavesdropping on a phone conversation. When she confronted Kayla about it, she simply told her to stay out of grown folks' business. The look her daughter gave her was the same one she got every time she left to meet Leroy. She never told her daughter where she was going, but she had a feeling she didn't have to.

She lowered the back of the seat and reached for her keys. Kayla didn't have time to deal with her daughter's disapproval. She was grown and could do whatever she wanted to do. She knew what was best for her and her heart told her it was Leroy. However, she was growing tired of her daughter judging her, and it was time for her and Kenya to have a long talk. She cleared the problem from her mind. There was time for that tomorrow. She had more important things to worry about right now. She wanted to have dinner ready and change into her gown before Leroy arrived at the house.

As she pulled out of the driveway, she saw Asia standing in the window with a long face. Ignoring a feeling of guilt, she waved, then drove down the street. Kayla sighed as she tried to convince herself she was doing the right thing, although there were times she felt like a teenager sneaking away to spend time with a boy her parents had forbidden her to see.

Leroy aroused her in so many ways, she couldn't begin to explain it. He satisfied her sexual appetite, challenged her intellect, and as the pastor of the largest Baptist church in the city, he fulfilled her spiritual needs as well. Yep, her girls needed to be patient just a little while longer. After she and Leroy were married and living in a big, new house, she could quit her job and spend all the time together that her daughters wanted. Until then, they had to understand that she was on a mission.

Kayla slid in India.Arie's latest CD and bobbed her head as she moved onto the highway. She was in a great mood as she headed to a small ranch fixer-upper Leroy used as a rental property. Two years ago, Kayla had discovered Darlene was pregnant with their fifth child and threatened to end the relationship. Leroy swore that even though she was expecting, having another baby had not changed a thing between them. He promised he would make it up to her by spending more time together. Instead of finding new tenants to rent the house, they used it as their special place. Leroy had even given her a key that she was allowed to use when he told her she could.

On the drive, she thought about his wife. A stuck-up woman like that didn't know how to please a man like Leroy the way she did. As far as she was concerned, the sooner Darlene realized it, the better off she'd be. She was destined to be the next Mrs. Leroy Brown, and as soon as they were married and moved to another town, Kayla was going to have another baby before it got to be too late. She almost pinched herself to interrupt her thoughts. She had an entire life planned for them. Often she found herself spending hours at a time thinking about the glorious years to come.

As she turned onto the wooded cul-de-sac, Kayla found Leroy's car was already in the driveway. Pulling in behind him, she felt a mixture of disappointment and excitement. She couldn't wait to be in his arms again, but she had looked forward to making him dinner before his arrival.

She climbed out of the car and grabbed the bag with the steaks inside, then moved up the driveway and entered through the side door, stepping directly into the small, blue-and-white kitchen. She lowered the bag and her purse onto the counter. They would have dinner later. Right now, she wanted a little Leroy to tide her over until then.

Hearing music coming from the bedroom, she strolled through the living room and down the hall. Wrapped up in her excitement, she walked through the bedroom door and right into the shock of her life.

Her brain was in denial for several seconds before her blurred vision cleared. There on the queen-size bed were Leroy and Tracy Branch. Leroy was breathing hard as he pumped between her legs like he was seconds away from the finish line. Her eyes were closed with her arm flung over her forehead as she cried out. The headboard was slamming against the wall. Kayla shook her head from side to side, not wanting to believe what she was seeing. With her hand over her mouth, she backed up slowly and accidentally stumbled over one of Tracy's shoes. Hearing the sound, Leroy glanced over his shoulder and his face changed from pleasure to shock.

He jumped from the bed. "Kayla, what are you doing here?"

Her reply was a mere grunt. She turned and walked quickly down the hall. Unfortunately, her feet couldn't get her away from him fast enough. Before she could grab her purse, Leroy caught her about the waist and pulled her close.

"Let me go!" She whirled on him.

"Sssh! Let me explain."

"I don't want to hear it!" she snapped as she moved into the kitchen to retrieve her things.

He had the nerve to chuckle and say, "I don't know why you're so angry. It's your fault. You shouldn't even be here."

Swinging around, Kayla tried to hide her shock and disbelief behind a bland expression. "How is it my fault? You told me to come."

Leroy leaned against the wall inside the small kitchen with a cool expression, arms folded across his chest, dick dripping with cum. "No, you were supposed to come over tomorrow."

She stepped forward with a confused look. "Thursdays are our night."

"Today is Wednesday."

She lowered her head a moment and realized he was right. In her excitement, she had mixed up the days of the week. As soon as she fixed her lips to apologize, his words penetrated her brain. Wait a minute—what the heck difference does it make?

She sucked her teeth and offered him a scowl. He couldn't possibly think she was that stupid. "It doesn't matter what day of the week it is. The fact of the matter is, you're messing with Ray Branch's daughter. I can deal with your wife but I will not tolerate you sleeping with anyone else."

As if she knew they were discussing her, Tracy sashayed her

naked behind into the kitchen, moved over to the refrigerator, and removed a soda. "Whassup, Leroy? You coming back to bed or what?" she asked with a taunting smirk.

New fury shot through Kayla with every step. She bored her eyes on the trifling girl. The twenty-something woman had a reputation of being a ho. Showed up at church every Sunday in tight dresses and stiletto heels, smelling like liquor after a night of partying at the club. Female members of the church didn't trust her within twenty feet of their husbands. She already had three kids with different daddies. Last year she had won a large sexual harassment case against her former employer, whom she claimed had fired her because she refused to sleep with him. People who knew Tracy had sense enough not to believe that claim. Nevertheless the court awarded her over half a million dollars. Now a woman with money, she managed to look like a girl half her age with her perky new breasts and a flat stomach. Studying her naked body with growing envy, Kayla could see why men flocked to her.

"Tracy, go back in the room," Leroy's loud voice boomed.

She sucked her teeth, rolled her eyes at Kayla, and said as she turned on her heels, "Don't keep Ms. Kitty waiting too long."

As soon as she was gone, he turned to face Kayla, who had already swung her purse over her shoulder. "Baby, we'll talk about this tomorrow," he said. His voice was almost pleading for her to understand.

Understand what? She leaned against the kitchen counter for strength that she just didn't seem to have. She wanted to scream. It was a good thing she was a Christian—otherwise she would have cussed him from here to Chicago. Instead she said in a huff, "It looks like there isn't anything else for us to talk about."

He shifted his weight and his voice softened. "Kayla, honey, yes, there is."

Swinging around, she glared over at him and said, "Answer one question. Why? I tolerate your wife, but why do you need anyone else? I thought I was enough for you. I thought you wanted to marry me." She paused, then asked, "Is it because I'm fat?"

He moved up to her and grabbed her forearms. "Baby, you got it all wrong. Tracy came to me for spiritual counseling and guidance. She didn't want anyone to know, so I told her to meet me here and one thing led to another. After that lawsuit, I should have known better than to be caught alone with her. She manipulated me, baby."

His wet dick brushed against her hand and she jumped back in disgust. "Do I look that stupid to you?" She held up an open palm. "Don't even answer that because you see me just as I have allowed you to see me. All these years I have broken my neck trying to prove to you how much I loved you. I believed one false promise after another. You told me you were leaving your wife, then the next thing I know she's pregnant. You promised to leave her after the baby was born and we would move to Tennessee but then you changed your mind." He had some nerve, trying to play her like she was stupid. She hadn't just gotten off the short yellow bus. She folded her arms and gave him a pointed look. "Were you planning to tell me that you were taking your wife to the Bahamas or did that piece of information slip your mind?"

"Man!" He gave a small laugh like one did when caught in a lie. "I was going to tell you tomorrow."

Tears started running down her face freely and she did nothing to wipe them away. She had loved this man with everything she'd had and he had tossed it all away. She reached for the grocery bag, turned, and walked away.

"We'll talk tomorrow," he called after her, his voice a blend of annoyance and plea.

Sadly, she shook her head. "We have nothing else to talk about."

Before she could reach the door, Leroy grabbed her by the neck and slammed her back against the wall. Kayla screamed and dropped the bag. His hand was pressed firmly against her windpipe and she struggled to get free, but Leroy refused to let her go. He leaned forward and whispered close to her ear, "It's not over until I say it's over." He then softened his grip and kissed her, forcing his tongue between her lips. Kayla tried to resist but could not. Leroy had power over her body. He always had. He ground his hips against hers and her traitorous body responded to his aggressive behavior. By the time he finally ended the kiss, she was whimpering.

Leroy smiled. "Like I said before, we'll talk tomorrow. Now go home." He then released her and headed back into the bedroom where Tracy was waiting.

Breathing heavily, Kayla watched him go and didn't even bother to reply. As soon as he shut the door, she obediently reached down for the groceries, then headed back out to her car.

Chapter 4

Danielle

On Friday, Danielle went home after a long day at work, ready for dinner and a hot bath. Renee was due in tomorrow and she needed all the rest she could get. Her home girl suffered from adult Attention Deficit Disorder with symptoms so obvious it was enough to drive another person crazy. *But not me*, she thought with a smile. Renee, although loud and callous at times, always managed to bring a smile to her face even if it was at someone else's expense. The weekend ahead was going to be loads of fun.

As she pulled into the driveway behind her Chevy Impala, a frown wrinkled her forehead. The car that she paid for, but Ron helped her pick out, had twenty-inch rims, tinted windows, and a sound system that could be heard a mile away. Now that he was gone, the vehicle would be a constant reminder of what could have been between them. As soon as she could get her garage cleaned out, she would put the car inside. Portia would be taking driver's education in the fall, and if her daughter ever learned how to drive, maybe she would consider giving the vehicle to her. Although the way she'd been acting lately, she would be better off making her get a job and buy her own car. Danielle turned off her Durango and frowned. Knowing her parents, they would go behind her back and buy Portia a car anyway.

While climbing out of the SUV, she thought about how much her parents spoiled Portia and it pissed her off. Since the day of the alleged rape, her mother had been dropping by every evening bearing gifts that Danielle refused to let her daughter have. Her daughter would then stomp off to her room, muttering under her breath. Portia didn't act like a rape victim; instead, she had been acting like a spoiled brat.

With a deep sigh, she stuck the key in the lock and went into the house. Her temper rose as she noticed that the vacuum cleaner was still in the living room in the exact spot she'd left it this morning, which meant when Portia got home from school she had not bothered to do her chores. Moving into the kitchen, she found dishes piled in the sink and the trash waiting to be emptied. School was officially out for the summer and Portia obviously thought she was going to spend her vacation doing nothing. Angrily, Danielle lowered her purse to the counter and went to remove the trash from the can when she noticed a discarded Tony's Pizza box and two crushed beer cans in the trash.

What the hell? "Portia!" she yelled.

The phone rang and she hastily went over to answer it, hoping it was one of Portia's hot-ass friends so she could have the pleasure of telling them not to call again because Portia was being punished for an indefinite period of time.

"Hello."

"Portia Patterson, please."

Hearing the grown man's voice on the other line, Danielle quickly became suspicious. "This is her mother. Who's calling?"

"This is Dr. Henric from Boone Hospital."

"Is this regarding her lab results?"

He hesitated. "Ma'am, I'm not at liberty to share that information. Your daughter's results are confidential."

"Then I guess you better go check her file because I know the law. My daughter is only sixteen. I'm the one who brought her to the ER."

He paused. "Just a moment."

While he went to check her file, Danielle cupped the mouthpiece and yelled upstairs again. "Portia!" After more silence, she was growing angrier by the second. Portia was either asleep or had her headphones on her ears. She paced impatiently across the kitchen floor. First thing tomorrow, she was getting a cordless phone for the kitchen. Being confined to one space when she'd rather be upstairs choking the shit out of her daughter was driving her crazy.

"Ms. Brooks?"

"Yes," she said impatiently.

"Sorry about that. I just had to make sure you had accompanied your daughter. I hope you understand that legally the hospital would be in a world of trouble."

She rolled her eyes heavenward. He must be a medical student.

"Your daughter's tested negative for sexually transmitted diseases."

Her shoulders sagged with relief. "Thank God."

"Ummm . . . however, her pregnancy test came back positive."

Danielle felt herself sway and tried to support her body with a wooden chair. "Did you say my daughter is pregnant?"

"Yes, ma'am. As soon as possible, she needs to see an obstetrician."

"But the nurse dipped her urine while we were there."

"These things happen sometimes."

She barely heard another word as the phone hung loosely on her ear. As soon as Dr. Henric ended the call, she put the phone down on the cradle, then stood there for the longest time, stunned.

Oh, no! This can't be happening to me.

A baby? Portia was still a baby herself. The last thing in the world she needed was to be raising another child. Her heart raced. Lowering her eyes, Danielle took a moment to try and pull it together. What in the world were they going to do? Portia was too young and immature to be a mother. The burden would fall on her own shoulders.

Hearing movement upstairs, her head jerked up towards the ceiling before she stormed through the living room and up the stairs. She passed her bedroom and the guest room before reaching Portia's door. Not bothering to knock, she barged into the room and found Portia lying on her bed naked from the waist down with a vibrator between her legs.

Danielle froze, completely stunned by what she saw. Portia had her headphones on. Her eyes were closed. She was moaning as her hips bucked against the fat, twelve-inch device. The way she sounded, she was obviously only seconds away from finishing. Good Lord, Danielle thought, the one she kept in her bottom drawer wasn't anywhere near as big as that thing.

Portia was in the middle of an orgasm when her head lolled to the side and her eyes opened. As soon as she spotted her mother, she jumped up and the vibrator went flying across the floor. "Mama!" she screamed.

"Sorry to interrupt," Danielle said sarcastically. "Put some clothes on yo' naked ass and meet me in my room." Furiously, she turned and walked into her room and took a seat on the end of her bed. Shaking her head, she couldn't believe she had actually found her daughter fucking a vibrator. She actually felt like laughing. If the vibrator was the only issue, she probably would have. Unfortunately, it wasn't.

Danielle slipped her Reeboks from her feet. She carried them to her closet just as she heard her daughter come down the hall. Turning around, she spotted her standing just inside the door with her head hung low.

"Why is it that I get home and nothing has been done?"

"I was going to get to it."

"When? After you got done getting some? What? Don't get shy on me now. You want to be grown, then start acting grown. You've been here since noon and I come home to find you haven't done a damn thang."

"I was fin to do it."

"I just bet you were." Danielle pursed her lips and propped a hand to her hip. "The hospital called. Is there somethin' you need to be telling me?"

Portia gave her a puzzled look, then shook her head. "Not that I can think of."

"You're pregnant."

She looked stunned and then started crying. Watching her, Danielle felt herself softening. This was one moment she hoped never to have experienced with her daughter. She sat on the bed and patted the mattress beside her. "Come over here and have a seat."

Dragging her feet, Portia moved to the bed. Instinctively, Danielle draped an arm around her and Portia rested her head on her shoulder. "Did you get yo' Depo shot last month?"

Her body was shaking and she was crying so hard it took her a while to answer. "I forgot."

"You for . . ." Danielle allowed her voice to trail off and took a deep breath. *Too late now to point the blame.* As a parent, it was her job to make sure her daughter got her birth control shot every three months instead of relying on an irresponsible teenager to get it done on her own. Portia continued to cry and she stroked a soothing hand down her hair and across her back. Despite all the drama Portia put her through, she was still her little girl. "We'll get through this. I'll support whatever decision you decide to make about the baby." She dropped her lips to her hair. "Do you know who the father is?"

Portia hesitated, then shook her head.

Danielle closed her eyes and took a deep breath and remembered what her mother had always said when things got rough. *The Lord doesn't give you any more than he thinks you can handle.* Well, she definitely had been delivered a truckload. Her parents had raised four children together and she couldn't even manage to raise one. Where had she gone wrong?

Chapter 5

Renee

After I landed in St. Louis, I rented a Chrysler 300C and started the ninety-minute drive to Columbia. It wasn't that my girls hadn't offered to pick me up—I just prefer having my own wheels so I can go where I want when I want without waiting on someone to get me there. You know what I'm saying? Besides, I like driving. It gives me a chance to clear my head and think. And I definitely have a lot to think about.

"Mom, can we stop and get some Church's chicken?" Tamara called from the backseat.

I rolled my eyes because I hated trying to get food in St. Louis. That place is so damn ghetto it's ridiculous, but if my kids are hungry, then who am I to deny them? Besides, the sooner I got them fed, the sooner I could get to Columbia. I pulled into the drive–thru, gave my order, then drove around to the window where the cashier was waiting. I handed her the money, she gave me my change. While waiting for my food, I tuned the radio to 100.3 the Beat.

"Mama, can you please turn that down?" Quinton complained. The two of them were in the backseat watching a DVD.

Now, don't get it twisted. Since he said *please*, I granted his request, then breathed a sigh of relief. They were going to their dad's for the summer. *Thank you, Lord!* In two hours I can officially start *my* vacation.

The cashier stuck her head out the window. "We ain't got no wings. It's gon' be anotha twenty minutes."

What? That's like Taco Bell running out of soft tacos. Okay, I know that's not the same thing but you know what I mean. "Why didn't you tell me that before I ordered?"

She sucked her gold teeth like she had an attitude. "You wanna order somethin' else?"

"Nah, I want my money back."

She had the nerve to roll her eyes, then went to get her manager. Shortly after, some big amazon came to the window. "Is there a problem?" she huffed in what she probably considered good customer service.

"Yeah, the problem is I don't feel like waiting twenty minutes for wings."

"How about we throw in a couple of free pies?"

Did I stutter? "How about you just give me my money back?" What part of *give me my money back* did she not understand?

She looked like she wanted to say something else but decided against it. I stared her dead in the eyes until she reached for the key and punched in a bunch of numbers. As soon as she handed me back my money, I peeled away from the drive-thru window.

Tamara groaned. "Mama, you are so embarrassing."

I glanced over my shoulder at my daughter and gave her the look. "Girl, be quiet! I could see if she'd offered to give us one of our meals free, but nah, she wants to give me some dry-ass pies." I drove up the street to White Castle and ordered a dozen cheeseburgers and drinks. My kids seemed to be happy to get those little-ass burgers. They make my stomach hurt so I got a shake instead, then whipped onto the highway.

While they ate and laughed in the backseat at some crazy comedy they had me buy, I thought about my life. With the kids gone for the summer, it was time for me to start thinking about what I was going to do next. Last night, I gave John some and it was horrible. He played with my breasts for so long, my nipples were now sore and cracking.

I took a deep breath and weaved into the far left lane. It had been a year since I made that vow to start teaching and begin building a new life. You would think after all this time I would have a plan and a wad of money stashed away somewhere. I have neither. I'm no closer to getting away from John than I was a year ago. It's crazy, but I like the life John offers me and after six years I don't know if I'm ready to give all that up. Now hold up—before you pass judgment, give me a moment to explain.

Growing up, I was one of those children who worried about where my next meal was coming from, and if we were going to have lights. I went to school wearing the same clothes twice in one week with generic labels, and was ashamed because I qualified for the free lunch program. Even as an adult, I worried. I had two kids and worked two jobs. They disconnected my phone several times and repossessed my car. I played beat the check and dug between the cushions on the couch for loose change. I even collected cans so I could get back my deposit.

I moved into the passing lane and shook my head. Not knowing what tomorrow may bring is a terrible way to live, and as much as I want to leave John, there is no way I can return to that life.

Yeah, yeah, I know it isn't fair for me to be with him while I crave the touch of another man. But you have to understand—I am a woman who needs some good dick. Plain and simple. Long, hard, and in a hurry, because I am about to lose my damn mind! It's a shame, but if John was working with more, I could put up with all of his other faults. It just don't make any sense, but it's already been another year and I honestly don't have any idea what I'm going to do except take it one day at a time. As for now, I'm anxious to get to Columbia and forget about John and all of my problems for the next week.

I got within ten miles of the city limits and felt a warm feeling inside. I don't know why. When I was a kid, all I could think about was getting far away from this place and never looking back. But, I've learned you can't run from your past. Columbia will always be the place where I lost my virginity to some football player on a dare. It is the same town where my crackhead mother walked out on me with no food in the fridge and a disconnection notice hanging on the front doorknob. Hell, that was reason enough to want to leave this place, but no, I stayed and later became the laughingstock of the black community when I was supposedly caught in the bathroom sucking Wayne Williams's dick. The lies, in addition to being abandoned, were enough to take any teenage girl off the deep end. Instead, I finished high school, married my boyfriend, and gave birth to Quinton and Tamara. It was a hard, rough ride, but here I am, at thirty-eight, a published author, living an upper-class lifestyle with two kids, a spoiled schnauzer named Nikki, and my husband John. Only my life was far from a fairy tale. I've done shit I wouldn't even dream of telling my friends about, and my marriage is nothing to brag about. John's failure in the bedroom is starting to wear on my sanity. And the last thing I need is to snap and end up like my crazy-ass mama. Well, that's enough of my life for now.

I pulled off the highway and turned into the mall parking lot. After retrieving my briefcase, I climbed out. Quinton put the portable DVD player in his bag and the two of them grabbed their duffel bags and followed me to the food court.

"Mama," Tamara whined, "do I have to spend the whole summer with my daddy?"

"Yep." She started pouting and I just gave her a long look. "Poor baby." I draped an arm loosely across her slender shoulders and gazed down. Tamara is short and petite, and at fifteen, she has enough curves to put any woman twice her age to shame. Thank goodness she has her head in the books, because I would hate to have to stick my foot so far up some negro's ass for trying to holla at her. When I'm not around, her brother does a pretty good job of keeping his eye on her.

It was Quinton's turn to plead his case. "Mama, I'm too old for this. I should be at home working this summer like all my other friends."

"We've already had this discussion. Summers belong to your father. " What my kids don't understand is I need a break, too. I clothe them, feed them, and put up with their spoiled asses nine months out of the year. The least I deserve is the summer off. "Talk to your dad. I'm sure he doesn't have a problem with you gettin' a summer job. Since you'll be starting your senior year, maybe you won't have to come next summer, but that's between y'all."

Quinton nodded, then hurried across the parking lot. I watched with pride. My son is handsome. He's well over six feet and takes his height and dark features from my family. The good hair and thick, bushy eyebrows and long lashes he and Tamara both inherited from their father. We stepped into the air-conditioned building and spotted Mario sitting in the corner, sipping a soda.

"Daddy!" Tamara raced over to him, her thick ponytail swinging. It's funny how seconds ago she was upset about having to spend the summer with him.

As I moved closer, he rose from the chair and greeted me with a wide grin. Smiling, I shook my head. I don't know why I used to have a thing for short men, because that is exactly what Mario is.

"Hey, girl." We hugged and I got this warm feeling inside like I had gone back in time. Back then, Mario was the only man who ignored the rumors, and loved me for me, and I'll be forever grateful for that. But after several years of him acting jealous and possessive, and putting his hands on me, I had to kick his midget ass to the curb. We've now been divorced almost fourteen years.

I chitchatted for a few minutes, then said good-bye to my kids and pulled my rolling briefcase through the mall. As I walked toward Barnes and Noble, I thought about how much I hated book signings, even though I know they're part of the game. It's the luck of the draw. Some signings have readers wrapped around the corner waiting for me to autograph their books. Others, I might be lucky if a handful of people come out. I hate just sitting behind that table at the front of the store waiting for someone to show up, which is why I always invite someone to hang out with me. Luckily, my girls will be there.

I moved into the store and found a table set up right inside the door stacked high with a variety of my books. I sat my briefcase in a chair and within minutes the manager was standing by my side.

"Ms. Moore, thank you so much for joining us again," she greeted with a high-pitched, perky voice.

I shook her hand, then gave her a simple nod. It's funny how they quickly forget. I remember the first time I had called her to schedule a book signing. The first thing out of her mouth was, "Are the books returnable?"

I was floored. "Returnable?"

"Well yes," she said as if my surprise was ridiculous. "We'd hate to be stuck with a bunch of books we can't sell."

I was completely insulted and hung up on her ass. What kind of marketing rep was she? Hadn't she heard of customer service? I had immediately called a smaller, independent bookstore I'd worked with over the years. Unfortunately, they went out of business two years ago, like most bookstores that have to compete with the major chains. I ended up contacting B&N again and with five books under my belt, she jumped through hoops to have me sign at her store. Now I actually receive a yearly e-mail from her before the release of my next book. Like I said before, how quickly they forget. If there had been any other decent bookstores, I would have told her to kiss my juicy caramel ass.

While she ran off to find a diet soda, I reached into my briefcase and set up the table. Within minutes, my girl Danielle came strolling my way.

Now, of all my girls, Danny's my best friend. We've always had each other's back. When I started making money and everybody started hating, she was in my corner. Now that Lisa's gone, Danielle is the closest thing I have to a sister. Hell, I feel closer to her and her family than I do my own. We've been girls since high school and I've always envied the fact that she was raised with both parents in a loving environment.

Danielle and I did some shit in our day, but when you're cute you can do thangs and get away with it. She has a clear honey complexion while I'm caramel. She's tall and thin with dancer legs and I'm thick and sexy. We're also both members of the itty-bitty-titty committee. What can I say—we attract brothas like flies to shit. The only problem she has is her attraction to broke-ass niggas. "Whassup, girl?"

"Not a thang."

I quickly gave her a hug, then lowered into the seat while checking out her outfit. She always looks her best. She was sporting a Tommy Hilfiger jean outfit with high-heeled, red-and-white gym shoes. Her shoulder-length brown hair was pulled back from her face, exposing large hoop earrings. My girl has taste, a good-ass job, and her own home, so why in the hell does she like messing around with them fake-ass bustas? I don't understand it.

"Girl, I've had one helluva week."

Oh, hell. Here we go again. I ain't in the mood to hear about Ron's no-good ass today.

"Portia's pregnant."

"What?" My head snapped around in time to see her give me a weary nod. "Hell, nah." I don't think I've ever seen Danielle look that hurt before. "Oh, my God! What're you gonna do?"

She gave me a weary shrug. "We're not sure yet. She's spending the weekend with her father, who's pissed and blamin' the shit on me. Hopefully, he can help her decide what to do 'bout the baby. In the meantime, I made her a doctor's appointment."

Damn, I feel for her. If it was Tamara, I don't know what I would do but I definitely wouldn't be that calm. I'd be screaming and hollering, and looking for the little muthafucka responsible for knocking my daughter up. "Who's the suspect?" I said *suspect* because as hot as these girls are nowadays, there's no telling how many horny little boys might be guilty.

Danielle shrugged. "Who knows?"

I just shook my head.

"I don't know what I'm gonna do."

I squeezed her arm. "Girl, don't worry. It'll all work out."

"Sure hope so," Danielle said, though she didn't look too sure.

I was so glad the manager returned with my soda because teenage pregnancy is a depressing subject and I didn't know what else to say. Shortly after, the crowd started to line up. I signed books while Danielle handed out magnets and personalized pens. She seemed pleased at the distraction.

"Sorry I'm late."

I looked up at my girl Kayla, who came bouncing over to my table, then glanced down at my watch. I had been signing books for over an hour. Rising from the chair, I gave her a big hug. "Missed you, girl."

"Me, too."

I lowered back into my seat while Kayla moved to the other end of the table and got readers to sign my guest book.

Kayla and I are also close. She just makes me so mad at times. She wears a size twenty-two and has low self-esteem. Because of it, she's been fucking around with this no-good Baptist minister for years. No matter what we tell her, she won't let him go. For some crazy reason, she believes he's gonna leave his wife for her. I don't understand it. Really I don't. That's probably why she's late. She had to go suck his dick. Ooh, let me shut up.

Seriously, though, it pisses me off because Kayla is a beautiful woman. What? You didn't expect me to say anything positive about Kayla? Well, yeah, it's true. She is a gorgeous woman. High yellow with light gray eyes, long, thick hair, and fat. But shit, Monique is a big sistah, too, yet she is beautiful inside and out. I just wish my girl felt that way about herself.

"Hello, ladies."

I glanced up at the man standing over my table. Dayum! My eyes traveled from Kayla to Danielle. "Who is that?"

"That's Jermaine."

I looked over at Kayla. By the way she was cheesing, it was obvious she'd been holding out on her sistahs.

"Danielle, Renee, I'd like you to meet Jermaine. He's one of our advisors at the medical school."

He granted us a generous smile. "Hello, ladies. It's so nice to finally meet you both. I've heard a lot about you."

Oooh! His voice and smile are sexy. If Kayla doesn't want him, I definitely do. I offered him my hand. "Nice to meet you. Unfortunately, this is the first time I've heard about you."

Danielle added her two cents. "Yes, and it's a doggone shame. With yo' fine ass." She mumbled that last line under her breath just loud enough for me and Kayla to hear. Just as I thought, Kayla nudged her in the arm before moving to the side and signaling for Jermaine to follow. Danielle and I watched, then looked at each other and shook our heads. The man was *fiine!*

"You think she's doing him?" I asked.

"Shit, no!" Danielle replied. "She's too busy sniffing behind that minister to be interested in anyone else. But check that out. Look at how he's looking at her."

She was right. Jermaine was really feeling my girl. Too bad he didn't have a chance in hell of getting her attention.

Danielle moved all up in my face. "Renee, don't look now but here comes your Uncle Larry."

Oh, hell nah. Sure enough, here he comes with his seventies Afro and beer belly, wearing blue jeans and a t-shirt two sizes too small.

"What's happening, niecy!" He moved around the table and kissed my cheek. Good Lord! He's reeking of malt liquor.

I glanced around to see if anyone noticed. Sure enough, anyone that didn't have shit else to do was paying attention. I looked up at his raggedy-tooth smile and gave him one of my own. I love my family, really I do. They're just embarrassing as hell. Big Mama was the one who had held us all together and when she died, all hell broke loose. Family went crazy. Fighting over money. Grabbing everything they could. I hung around long enough to make sure Big Mama was buried properly, then I got the hell out of town while they tried to kill each other. The only sibling who wasn't present was Bernice, my crackhead mother, who I haven't seen in almost ten years.

I looked up at my uncle and remembered all the times he had taken me out for pizza when I was a kid and smiled. Fuck what everyone thinks. This is my family. "How have you been?"

I should have known he'd get straight to the point. "Tough. I got laid off at the plant and been trying to find another j-o-b."

I pursed my lips and nodded because I knew what was about to come next.

"You think you can spot your uncle forty-five dollars? My electric bill is past due and they won't give me another extension," he began as he scratched his stomach. "The payday loan folks won't give me another loan until I pay off the first one."

"No problem," I mumbled, then turned to my right where Danielle was trying to keep a straight face. I signaled for her to hand me my purse from under the table. I don't mind helping my family from time to time because I plan on just writing it off on my taxes as charity, anyway. Besides, it's too hot for Uncle Larry to be without electricity. See, I really do have a soft spot after all.

"Thanks, niecy," he said as I handed him a fifty-dollar bill.

"Don't mention it." And I meant that—otherwise all the rest of them freeloading muthafuckas will be trying to track me down. Uncle Larry thanked me, then excused himself so he could get down to the electric company before they closed. Knowing him, he was going to spend the change on beer and lottery tickets. "Play the Powerball for me!" I yelled.

I signed my book for another dedicated reader, shared a little small talk, then breathed a sigh of relief when she finally left. I love the people who support my career, really I do. I appreciate them buying my books and standing in long lines to see me because without them there would be no me. It's just that sometimes they never know when to say good-bye.

Danielle patted me lightly on the shoulder. "Girl, I think

you're gonna sell out this time." I could hear the pride in her voice.

I looked down at the table and was quite pleased at how few books were left.

"Whassup, Caeramel!"

I looked over at the door and spotted Nadine and her partner coming through the door. It's been two years since she came out of the closet about her craving for pussy. I ain't mad at her, because I say to each his own. However, I still can't compare licking clits to sucking dicks.

"Hey, girl." I looked at her short ass. Nadine has the biggest titties. Easily double D's, and, as always, was dressed country as hell. But I love her just the same.

"You remember Jordan."

I shifted my eyes over to the woman next to her and nodded my head. The last time I had seen her was at my sister's funeral. Her girl ain't a butch—you know, those manly looking women who walk around with a strap-on dick swinging between their legs and their breasts taped down? Nah, she was a beautiful woman.

"Hey, Renee—oops! I mean, Caeramel. I really enjoyed your last book," Jordan said.

I smiled, sucking that shit up. "Thank you." I autographed a copy for the two of them, then stretched my arms over my head. "So what's been going on, Nadine? Still sticking it to the man?"

Nadine is an attorney. She handles divorces and custody battles. "Oh yeah, you'd be surprised how far people go to try and hide their assets."

I snorted. "Nothing surprises me these days." An elderly woman came up to the table. "Hello." It's amazing how many old folks still try to get their freak on. I signed two copies, one for her and one for her daughter, then reclined in the chair again.

Nadine leaned over the table and said, "We need to get together before you leave."

The look in her eyes told me she wanted to talk about Lisa. I

dropped my eyes to the table to keep the tears away. Nadine
had been Lisa's best friend. We were all close, although at times
I pretend I can't stand her ass. She is goofy as hell and gets on
my nerves but she really is a good person and I love her like a
sister. Nevertheless, the last thing I wanted to do was sit and talk
about Lisa. It was just too hard.

"I'll call you," I said.

She rolled her eyes as if she didn't believe me. I guess that's
because I've been ignoring her phone calls for months. "Don't
worry. I'll be calling *you*," she warned, then, hand in hand, she
and Jordan walked back out into the mall.

By five, I was completely sold out. I sat around for a while
and handed out covers for my next erotic tale while I started
packing up my things to leave.

Danielle lowered into the seat beside me. "Are we going out
tonight or what?"

"Count me in." I heard Kayla say.

What? Danielle and I locked eyes, then looked over at Kayla.
I can't remember the last time she'd gone out with us. The
good pastor would have a fit. "What's Reverend Brown gonna
say?" I teased.

Kayla dropped her eyes to the table. "We're not together anymore."

"Hell nah!"

"About damn time!" Danielle and I responded at the same
time. "What the hell happened?" I asked, because inquiring
minds wanted to know.

She looked up at the ceiling as if she was trying not to cry.
"Let's just say I know he's never going to leave his wife."

Ya think! I've been telling her that shit for over four years.
Damn! I just can't see being second-best to no one. Reverend
Leroy Brown's in the pulpit every Sunday, and fornicating with
vulnerable members of the congregation the rest of the week. I
ain't sharing nothing. By now, you're probably thinking "this
ho thinks she's all that," and true that I do. I'd rather be stuck
on myself than stuck on stupid.

Chapter 6

Renee

I checked in at the Holiday Inn Executive Center. My girls think I'm bourgeois but I don't see shit wrong with staying in a nice hotel when I'm away from home. Who the hell wants to sleep on cheap sheets and worry if they are going to live through the night when staying at some sleazy-ass motel? Not me. I'm a firm believer that you get what you pay for.

I took a shower and fell asleep. I woke up shortly after eight, ready to get my swerve on. We were planning to hit Sparkle's, a new twenty-five-and-over spot that had been open less than a month. It was either that or the little hole-in-the-wall juke joint that's been around since long before I was old enough to drink, but I wasn't in the mood for smoke or young thugs with bling-bling trying to holla all night. The dress I was planning to wear, I needed an audience worthy of my time. By ten, I was dressed and rolling over to Kayla's. As usual, she stepped out the door in black slacks and a white blouse.

"Damn, girl. Now that you're no longer with Reverend Brown, we need to work on that wardrobe."

"Renee, shut up. There is nothing wrong with what I got on." She looked offended. I don't know why, because she knows how I am. Renee don't hold the punches for anyone.

I clicked my tongue and pulled away from in front of her house. "If you say so." The local radio station was jamming, which meant I didn't have to hold a conversation. Good, because Kayla was staring out the window like she had lost her best friend, and knowing her, she was missing Leroy's tired ass. I turned up the music and bit my tongue because I know if I say something she doesn't like, Kayla's going to make me take her back home, and I didn't want that. Tonight I plan to hang with my girls and hopefully help Kayla find some new dick.

Five minutes later, I pulled into the packed lot and giggled with excitement. Tonight was on and I was looking fine as hell. I turned off the car, then glanced in my visor to make sure my hair was in place. Check! Lipstick looked good. Double check! I stepped out of the 300C and slammed the door just to draw attention. Before Kayla had even gotten off her seat, brothas were hollering. I sucked that shit up and left Kayla in the dust while I strutted to the door.

The crowd was fierce. Sparkle's appeared to be the happening place to be, and I was glad to be part of the excitement. The music was loud and bodies were heating up the dance floor. I moved through the crowd, leaving Kayla behind, swaying my hips to the music. Brothas were whistling, trying to get a sistah's attention, but I just smiled and kept going. I know I looked good and it was gonna take a lot to attract me tonight. I spotted Danielle dancing in her seat at a small table in the corner. Not the most ideal location, considering I wanted to be seen, but I guess it would have to do, especially since there wasn't anywhere else to sit. She was wearing a slamming outfit—white mini, a gold halter top and matching sandals. Maybe I can get her to talk to Kayla about her tired wardrobe. I strolled past a table filled with old heads and took a seat facing the crowd. "Whassup, girl?"

"I was wondering when y'all were gonna make it."

Kayla moved into the chair across from me. "You know how she is. Late all the time."

I gave them both the look. "Girl, you know how I do. Who shows up at a club before ten-thirty?"

"You do, when the club closes at one," Kayla preached over

the beat of the music. "I've never understood why black folks wait until two hours before the club closes to go out. That's barely enough time to order a drink."

I rolled my eyes. "I don't know why your holy ass is tripping. It ain't like you drink no way." Kayla didn't drink anything stronger than a ginger ale.

Danielle reached for her drink. "Can we all just get along tonight?"

She didn't have to ask me twice. I was out to have a good time. "Shit, what are you drinking?"

Danielle took a sip. "A caramel apple martini."

That sounded good as shit. I signaled for the waitress at the next table where an old head in a lime green suit was staring at Kayla. I nudged her in the leg. "Yo, Kayla, that pop-pop over there is staring at you."

She glanced over her shoulder, then back again. "Then he needs to quit looking because I'm not interested."

I laughed, then ordered a martini for me and a soda for Kayla. After the waitress left, I glanced back over at the table again. Lime green was still watching.

"Kayla, he ain't half bad. Girl, you better go get yours."

"Renee, you need glasses. Quit flirting before he comes over here."

"What's wrong with that? All he probably wants is a dance."

"Then you dance with him," Kayla snorted rudely.

"Naw, I don't do butterfly collars but he seems to be exactly what you need. I don't see a ring on his finger." I gave him an inviting smile and then signaled for him to come join us. Danielle choked with laughter.

Kayla's eyes grew large when she noticed the man walking toward us. "What are you doing?"

"Trying to hook you up," I said sincerely.

"Why does it have to be someone who looks like Chewbacca?"

I tried to keep a straight face and smiled up at the man standing at our table. "My girl here really wanted to meet you." I moved my legs out of the way just as Kayla tried to kick me.

He grinned down at her, then offered his hand. "Wilbur Wallace."

Wilbur? I hid a laugh behind a cough.

"Wilbur, this is my girl—"

"Carmen," Kayla hurried to say and this time she kicked me right in the shin.

"Nice to meet you, Carmen."

I joined in on the fun. "And I'm Rhonda and this is my girl Danita."

He took the seat beside Kayla and tried to engage in a casual conversation. Being the Christian woman that she was, she felt she had no choice but to follow along.

I was ear hustling and adding my two cents. "So Wilbur, what do you do?"

"I own a car lot," he replied over the loud music.

My interest was piqued. "Really? New or used?"

He fingered the diamond-encrusted ring on his right hand as he spoke. "Both."

I gave Kayla a long, hard stare. She better jump on him 'cause he was far better than Reverend Brown's ass.

I glanced over at Danny, who was trying to make eye contact with another one of those old heads at the table and then had the nerve to point at me. When she realized she had gotten caught, Danielle tried to keep a straight face. I had something for her ass.

Underneath the table, I tapped him lightly on the leg. "Hey, Wilbur, my girl here wants to meet your partner."

While he moved over to the other table to ask his friend to join us, Danny punched me in the arm. I exploded with laughter.

Danielle sucked her teeth. "Why'd you do that?"

Grinning, I stared over at her. "'Cause I saw you pointing at me."

"I was just tryin' to be funny," she admitted with a laugh as she sipped her drink.

"And so was I."

Kayla leaned forward and said for our ears only, "I did not come here to spend the entire evening doing charity work."

"And I don't have time to be fighting some old man with liver spots all over his head. Nae-Nae, he looks like an ostrich on crack." Danielle sucked her teeth. "What he needs to do is go put his head in the ground."

I laughed, then glanced over at their table—they were both looking over at us. I raised my hand and pointed at Danielle. She slapped the back of my head.

"You're always playing."

I was ready to fall out of my chair. "Shhh! Be nice. Here they come."

Liver spots moved around to Danielle's side and offered her his right hand. "I'm Horace, nice to meet you."

She forced a fake smile. "I'm Dan—I mean, Danita."

I knew Danny was ready to kill me. Thank goodness the waitress returned with our drinks.

Chapter 7

Kayla

A half hour later, Kayla excused herself and hurried off to the bathroom. Another moment with Pa Kettle and she was bound to get sick. Maybe Leroy wasn't the best choice in a man, but he was a far cry better than what the club had to offer.

She stepped into the last stall and frowned. No toilet paper. The one next to it was stopped up with a bloody tampon floating on top. Kayla shook her head with disgust. She could never understand how women could be so nasty. She could only imagine what their bathrooms at home were like. Moving to a middle stall, she lowered her slacks and stooped. There was no way in the world she was going to sit—who knew what germs were lurking around? Reaching into the side zipper of her purse, she retrieved a napkin and used it to wipe off, then flushed and moved to the sink. While washing her hands, she glanced up at her reflection in the mirror and noticed the dark circles beneath her eyes. The last several days had been hard. Leroy had been calling and leaving messages both at work and at home but she had not returned any of his calls. Instead, she had prayed to the good Lord to give her the strength to resist.

For the first time in years, she was afraid of him. Yes, Leroy had always been dominant and demanding and had always wanted his way. He'd even pushed her around at times, but this was the first time he had physically handled her in a way that made her fear for her life. She knew his behavior had changed but she hadn't expected it to shift so drastically. Sleeping around with other women besides her and his wife was bad enough, but abusing her was another thing altogether, and something she just couldn't accept. She had already endured years of mental abuse as a child that had scarred her for life.

Taking a deep breath, she thought about all the times Nadine and Renee had tried to tell her she wasn't the only woman he was messing with. Only she never wanted to believe it. It was normal for women to gossip about people they knew nothing about, and neither of them knew anything more about Leroy than what they heard floating around the community. Most of it she had thought was just a bunch of jealousy gossip, but now she knew that wasn't the case. He *had* been screwing around. A thought came to mind. Maybe Jennifer Tolliver's baby really was his. And maybe he was on the down-low, as Renee tried so many times to tell her. Dear God, she hoped not. She had heard so many horror stories about that. Everybody was starting to come out of the closet. Women across the country were killing their husbands for infecting them with the AIDS virus. Nope. She couldn't take that risk anymore. Leroy was one man she could no longer trust.

Reaching inside her purse, Kayla removed her small compact and blotted the circles beneath her eyes. She had come a long way since Wednesday. While driving away from his house, distraught and crying her eyes out, all she could think about was what it was going to take to get her man back. She didn't care about the pain radiating from the back of her head or that Leroy was in bed with another woman. All she had cared about was finding a way to make things right between them again. It wasn't until she remembered the abuse she watched her mother endure while she was a child that she finally came to her senses.

It still felt so unreal. She had discovered something about Leroy that scared her. How could a man she knew so well turn out to be a totally different person? It was a hard pill to swallow. Leroy had been good to her, in his own way, and had never once laid a hand on her. The love she had for him surpassed feelings she'd had for anyone other than her children. She would have taken a bullet for him. After hours of pondering the situation, Kayla still could not understand how he could do something like that to her. She wanted so badly to brush it aside as stress or that he just wasn't himself that day, but the fear he had inflicted on her made that impossible. As the days passed, she started thinking about all the occasions when rage smouldered in his eyes, and all the times he got mad when she refused to perform oral sex or allow him to penetrate her from behind. On those occasions he had looked mad enough to hit her, but since she quickly agreed to comply, his eyes had immediately softened and a smile curled his lips. What would have happened if she had continued to refuse? Would he have used his fists to get what he wanted? She squeezed her eyelids tightly together, refusing to think about it any further. What happened was in the past and she was thankful God helped her to see the light before something far worse happened.

Tears pushed to the surface. Lowering her head, she splashed water on her face. How in the world could she have been so stupid? *Four years.* She had given that man four years of her life. No matter how many doubts lurked around the back of her mind, she had waited. In her mind, she was the better woman, and in time Leroy would finally leave his wife and the two of them would live happily ever after. Thinking about it now, it sounded so ridiculous. She'd never had a man of her own before, so what made her think that things with Leroy would have been any different?

Because he's a minister. Yes, and she believed any man who could stand before God and the church would be different, that she had met the one man she could finally trust. She wiped her eyes as she realized how badly she'd needed to believe in him. Since childhood, her life had been one disappointment after another, and at this stage of her life, she needed something she could hold onto. Something she could believe in, and that thing, that person, had been Leroy.

A sharp pain shot across her chest as she remembered walking in on Leroy with Tracy. Regardless of how much he pleaded that it was all a mistake, she would never trust him again. Her life, her dreams of being with Reverend Leroy Brown, were over.

Only he refused to take no for an answer. Kayla lifted her chin defiantly. Well, he was just going to have to accept it. No means no. Leroy had used and misled her for too long, and enough was enough. She was done committing adultery. She knew it was wrong to violate any of the Ten Commandments. Now she prayed that the Lord would forgive her.

Finding all the paper towels wet and on the floor, Kayla flung her hands through the air trying to air-dry them, then exited as two loud women with enough weave in their heads to aid Rupunzel pushed into the room. She walked across the red floor and was turning the corner when she felt a hand at her waist. Abruptly, she swung around and gasped.

"Jermaine."

He gave her an irresistible smile. "Sorry. I didn't mean to scare you."

"It's quite all right. When did you get here?"

"I've been here for a while. Watching you." He pointed to a table to the far left. "I started to come over to say hello, but I noticed you were with your man."

Kayla pursed her lips. "That's not my man."

He looked pleased by her response. "Good. Then you won't mind keeping me company at my table."

"I would love to."

He placed a hand at the center of her back as they moved past the table where Renee and Danielle were still entertaining. She waved good-bye to her girls' stunned faces and followed Jermaine's lead to his table.

"Would you like something to drink or eat?"

"A soda and some wings would be nice."

He signaled for their waitress and ordered her standard soda, Jack and Coke, and a plate of wings and fries. She settled back in the chair and stared over at the dance floor as the music changed to Keushia Cole's "Love."

"You want to dance?"

She quickly shook her head. "I'm not much of a dancer."

"Then just follow my lead." He rose and held his hand out toward her.

"I-I can't." There was no way she was going out there and embarrassing herself. Renee would never let her live it down.

"Yes, you can. You trust me, don't you?"

Kayla gazed up at his kind eyes and smiled. "Yes."

"Good." He grabbed her hand. "Now get your sexy behind out that seat and come join me on the floor."

She rose out of the seat, grinning like a fool. It had been a long time since anyone had called her sexy or anything close to it. And it felt good. Yes, indeed. "Well, in that case, lead on."

Chapter 8

Renee

After getting them old cats to buy us another round of drinks, Danielle and I convinced them that we were a pair of gold diggers and sent them rushing back to their seats.

"You need to quit playing with brothas' minds like that," Danielle warned. "That's why that muthafucker tried to whup yo' ass."

See, now why'd she even have to go there? I mean, it wasn't like I told that psycho that I wanted to marry him. He just assumed since I had given him some coochie that I planned to spend the rest of my life with him. That was his mistake, not mine. I'm the type of chick that's going to do what the hell I want to do and deal with the consequences later. Although that was one time I did get my ass kicked. Damn, why'd she even bring that shit up?

"Fuck you," I hissed, then sipped from my martini glass.

"That's what you get for inviting Fred Sanford and Grady to our table."

We shared in a laugh, then sat back in our chairs and enjoyed the music. I glanced over onto the floor and watched Kayla in Jermaine's arms. I have to admit that they looked good together. A tall, big woman needs a brotha with a little meat on his bones, and Jermaine had just the right amount. Hopefully, she would give him a chance.

"She caught Leroy in bed with Tracy."

I looked at Danielle. "Tracy who?

"Tracy Branch."

I gave her a puzzled look. "The one who has all them kids by—"

"Luke Jackson," she interrupted with a nod.

"Damn! How you know?"

"Nadine called me while I was getting ready and told me that Kayla told her," she replied between sips.

"That ho! Does that no-dick bastard have any respect for himself or his wife?"

"Obviously not."

I shook my head. Let me catch John in bed with another woman, I will cut his dick off. Now that probably sounds crazy from someone who ain't even wanting the dick, but it's the principle of the whole thing. If he needs to fuck around, that's fine, as long as I don't find out about it, 'cause when I do, I'm gonna do a Lorena Bobbitt on his ass.

My eyes traveled around the room, looking for anything that had potential, and I turned up my nose. Nothing but a bunch of mud-ducks. Anything halfway decent was already taken. Couples were dry humping on the dance floor. Bodies rubbing. Hands groping. Titties jiggling. To the far right I spotted Ron. He was on the dance floor, bumping and grinding with some short ho dressed like a video hoochie.

I nudged Danielle in the arm. "Danny, look." She followed the direction of my eyes. Her back straightened with anger written across her face.

"I bought the negro that Rocawear outfit."

"Looks good on him, too," I said. Although she rolled her eyes at me, Danny knew what I had said was true. Ron is fine. Maybe it's the cornrows he was rocking or his tall, chiseled body, or that sexy smile that made you want to drop your thong. I don't know what it is but the brotha looks good enough to lick from head to toe. Muthafuckas like him didn't need a job because there was always some bitch stupid enough to take care of their asses. Like Danielle. Oops, did I say that?

"I'ma go over there."

Oh, hell nah. I pushed her back into her chair. "For what?"

"He owes me money."

"Money you ain't gonna get, so you might as well quit trippin'. You knew what type of man he was when you started fucking with his ass."

Danielle glared across the room as Ron and his hoochie moved like they were trying to make a baby together. I held onto her arm so she couldn't jump out of her chair, then happened to glance over at the door and my heart stopped. Calvin Cambridge. I hadn't seen him in ages, but the years had definitely been good to him. He strolled across the room like he owned the place, in a two-piece slacks and shirt that sang Sean John. I got so wet watching him that I had to cross my legs.

Calvin and I go way back. Let's just say, Calvin was the one that got away. We were dating at a time in my life when I needed a man, not a boy. I had two kids, working full-time and taking college classes in the evening. Danny and I were out one night when he approached me. We danced all evening, then fucked all night. He was a lot of fun and the kids adored him. Unfortunately, he was going to school at the time and had a part-time job. After a while I got tired of him eating up my food and dirtying up my sheets. All I was getting was dick, plenty of that, but I wanted something more. So I dumped him for an army brotha who I ended up marrying, only to find out that the muthafucka already had a wife. Years later, I realized that I had made the biggest mistake of my life. Calvin's now a university police officer with a large house, a fat Lexus, and did I mention he had a big dick? Okay, maybe I did, but it was definitely worth repeating.

While Danielle continued to glare at Ron, I watched Calvin, trying not to be obvious. After ten minutes I got tired of waiting for him to notice me and got up from my chair and swayed over to holla at some chick I knew back in high school. I could care less about Ginger's Jeri curl-wearing ass. I just wanted to make sure Calvin saw me in my new spandex dress. Sure enough, by the time I returned to my seat, he was heading toward our table. I tapped Danielle on the arm and got her attention.

"Look who's coming."

She finally tore her eyes from Ron and followed the direction of my eyes. "Oh, damn!"

"What?"

"He's the one that investigated Portia's so-called rape."

I chuckled under my breath. She had called and given me the details but she had left out that vital piece of information.

"Whassup, ladies?"

I studied his beautiful brown eyes and faked surprise. "Calvin, is that you? I ain't seen you in, what, ten years?"

He grinned and licked his lips LL Cool J style. "Give or take a few." His gaze shifted to Danielle. "Hey, Danny."

"Whassup?" She stared down at her drink, avoiding eye contact.

"What are you doing in town?" he asked.

I crossed my legs. And just as I had hoped, he started salivating. "Dropped my kids off with their daddy for the summer." I motioned for him to take the seat beside me. As soon as he flopped down in the chair, I caught a whiff of Armani. Mmmm, it smelled good on him.

"Danny, how's Portia?" he asked.

She glanced up with a look of embarrassment. "On punishment for the next century."

Calvin gave her a sympathetic look. "Teenagers."

The music changed to something slow. Suddenly I wanted to feel Calvin in my arms but before I could ask him, I heard him ask Danielle instead.

She shook her head. "Nah, I'll pass."

He wasn't giving up that easy. "Why?"

Danielle rolled her eyes. "Because I said so."

While they went back and forth, I sat back in my chair feeling

some type of way. *Helllooo*. Was the brother blind or what?
Finally, I rose and grabbed Calvin's arm. "Come on before the
song's over." I was relieved that he followed me to the dance
floor, 'cause for a second he didn't act like he wanted to go. I
draped my arms around his neck, feeling his hard body against
mine. He wrapped his arms around my waist. I smiled seduc-
tively, my eyes locked on his.

"What?" he finally said.

"You," I purred.

"What about me?"

"It's good seeing you again."

"You, too."

He pulled me into the circle of his arms and I closed my eyes
and inhaled while we moved our bodies together. I knew at that
exact moment that I was taking him back to my hotel room. No
was not even an option.

"You married?" I asked.

"Nope."

"Seeing anyone?"

"Nope."

"Good."

He pulled back slightly so he could stare down at me. "Why is
that?"

"Because I plan on taking you back to my hotel room tonight." Do you know he had the nerve to start laughing? "What
the hell is so funny?" I asked with straight attitude.

"You. You still want things your way." He was still chuckling.

I grinned because he knew me too well. "And what's wrong
with that?"

"The problem is, I don't go backwards. You and I had what
we had and when you got tired, you tossed me aside like a pair
of worn-out Air Force Ones. It is what it is, and what it is, is
over."

The song ended. I turned on my heels and tried to hold my
head high. I couldn't believe he had the nerve to turn me

down. It wasn't until I had settled in my chair that I noticed he had followed.

"Danny, let's dance." Calvin moved around and carefully yanked her out of her chair, refusing to take no for an answer, and led her out to the dance floor.

I sat there fuming, hot as hell.

Chapter 9

Danielle

Danielle really wasn't in the mood for dancing. What she wanted to do was run over there and pop Ron upside his head for disrespecting her in public.

"Hey, you look like you're ready to kick someone's ass."

She glanced up at Calvin and couldn't resist a grin. "Somethin' like that. My no-good ex is over there grinding with that video reject."

He followed the direction of her eyes and chuckled. "He looks a little on the young side."

She simply shrugged.

"How about we piss him off?" he whispered close to her ear.

"You'd do that for me?"

He answered by pulling her close to his body. "He's staring you down."

"Good." Danielle reached down and squeezed his behind, grinding into him. "Is he still looking?"

Calvin pulled back slightly and smiled. "Oh, yeah. He's watching."

Good. She couldn't resist looking past his arm at Ron, whose eyes were practically popping out his head. *Hehe!* He was jealous and she was enjoying every moment of it, especially after all the mess he had put her through. Calvin pulled her even closer and nuzzled her neck. She'd be lying if she said that shit didn't feel good, because it felt damn good leaning against his rock-hard body. As they swayed to the music, she snuck another peek at Ron. He was mad and it made her heart flip-flop. He had to care about her. Otherwise, he wouldn't be staring at her like he wanted to choke the mess out of her. While giggling softly, Danielle turned her head at the exact moment Calvin moved his and their lips met. She didn't even realize they were kissing until she felt his tongue invade her mouth. *Ohmygoodness!* He was an excellent kisser. No one had ever kissed her that way before. Ron didn't tongue-kiss. He was a nibbler, but now she realized she had been missing so much. Calvin's hand came up to cup the back of her head and he deepened the kiss passionately. For a split second she didn't want the moment to end. Danielle opened her eyes long enough to make sure what was happening was real, and sure enough, Calvin Cambridge was attached to those thick, succulent lips. She was so wrapped up in the kiss that it took a moment to realize the music had stopped and everyone was clearing the stage for the electric slide.

One minute she was moaning, the next she gasped as she was suddenly pushed away and Ron was standing all up in Calvin's face.

"Nucca, what the fuck you doin', disrespectin' me like that?"

Before she or Calvin could react, Ron reeled back and sucker punched Calvin in the face.

"What the hell are ya doin'?" she screamed as she tried to get Ron off of Calvin. Ron pushed her away and she slid across the floor. By the time Danielle managed to get up, Calvin had recovered and was throwing punches of his own. Everyone quickly cleared the dance floor. Security had been alerted and was on their way over. Ron noticed and took off running across the club and out the door.

Calvin reached out a hand and helped her up from the floor. "You ai'ight?"

Danielle simply shrugged. She was so embarrassed she couldn't even look him in the eye. "I should be askin' you that question. You okay?"

He pressed a hand gingerly to the side of his mouth. "About as good as can be expected. That janky-ass nigga caught me off guard." Danielle followed him off the dance floor.

Kayla came rushing over. "Are you okay?"

Danielle nodded. "Yeah, I'm all right."

"Danny, girl, Ron ran out of here like he stole something."

"He probably realized that Calvin's a cop." Danielle glanced over at her table and found Renee dying with laughter. The last thing she needed was to hear her mouth. "I'm outta here. Calvin, walk me to my car."

Kayla gently squeezed her shoulder. "I'll call you tomorrow." She watched them leave, then headed back over to the table with Jermaine.

Chapter 10

Renee

Okay, I was probably wrong for laughing, but that was some funny shit. Calvin had gotten knocked the fuck out before he even had a chance to see it coming. Ha-ha! Calvin's my boy and all, but he ain't from the streets like Ron.

I leaned back in my chair while sipping on my third drink. I could still see the look on Danny's face when she went sliding across the floor, skirt up, thong showing. Yo, that was crazy. Now, any other time I would have jumped out of my seat and ran to my girl's aid, but you know, truth be told, Danielle brought that one on herself. What the hell was she doing on the dance floor lip-locking with my ex? We had vowed never to mess with each other's men, past or present. So what do you call what she was doing? They were grinding and rubbing all on each other. I don't blame Ron for clocking Calvin, although the person he should have been checking was Danny's ass. Yes, I'm not even going to front—I am jealous because Calvin would rather spend his evening with my girl than me.

"Renee, let's dance."

I startled because I didn't even hear him walk up to me. David Lovell. Nice dude. Short as hell but cute. I finished my drink, draped my slender purse over my shoulder, and followed him out onto the floor. It was a fast number so I didn't have to worry about him trying to cop a feel. I swayed the way I always do when I know I look good, and grinned over at him.

"Whatchu know good?" he asked.

"Not a damn thing. Whassup wit' you?"

"Same ole, same ole. Dee-Dee and I split up so I'm tryin' to adjust to bein' back in the game."

I almost laughed in his face because this was his way of letting me know he was available.

"I hear you're writing books?"

I nodded. "And what are you doing with yourself these days?"

"I'm a Columbia police officer."

"Really?" David nodded. "Well, I'm impressed." I was, really, because most of the dudes I knew from back in the day weren't doing a damn thing with their lives. They were all in jail, still living with their mamas, or gay.

Reaching down, he removed his cell phone from his hip. "I want yo' number now before you run off and I don't see you for another fifteen years."

I rattled off my cell and watched as he danced and programmed in the number at the same time. My purse started vibrating.

"That's me calling, so you now have my number. Make sure you hit a brotha up from time to time."

I nodded. The music changed to Young Joc and I started rocking like all the other young folks. I watched David move and I'll have to admit he had some skill. I checked him out from head to toe. He'd gained a little weight over the years but it seemed to be in just the right places. His chest was buffed, and his arms had some muscle definition going on.

It's funny how you never think about a person until you see them again and then you're flooded with all kinds of memories. David was a year older than me in high school. I remembered having the biggest crush on him while he was dating Genice Prince. When I had found out they had split up, I had jumped at the chance to be with him, but by the time I found the guts to ask him out he had moved on to someone else. By then I had met Mario.

The music slowed down and I met David halfway. He draped his arm around my waist and gave me a long, dimpled smile. "I see you're still lookin' good."

I nodded. "So do you." He pulled me close and I could feel the evidence of his attraction. I rubbed, trying to get an idea of how much the brotha was working with. I'd heard the rumor. Now I wanted the facts.

"I used to have a crush on you."

I'd be lying if I said that didn't make my day, because it did. For the next few minutes we stared at each other, thinking about what could have been, until the end of the song.

"How about we go get some breakfast and see where the rest of the night leads?" His voice was thick with need. David was moving his hips the right way, grinding against me. I was loving every minute of it. On the sly, he took my hand and I thought he was guiding it to his crotch; instead, he pressed the palm against the side of his thigh. Good Lord! His thang hung halfway between his ball and kneecap. If I had known David had it like that, I would have rode his ass years ago. As hard as it was, it was obvious he wanted some of this real bad. Shit, why not? I hadn't had any real dick in a while.

"I'm not in the mood for any breakfast."

"What do you want, then?"

I reached down between his legs and squeezed. "This," I purred.

"Shit!" David groaned. "That's what I'm talkin' about. One mo' dance and we're outta here."

He ain't said nothing but the word. I was more than ready.

Chapter 11

Danielle

Danielle pulled her Durango into her driveway. As soon as she opened the door, a car came to a complete stop behind her. While climbing out, she couldn't resist a grin. Calvin had followed her home to make sure Ron wasn't hiding in the bushes, waiting on her. She shut the door and walked over to his silver Lexus as he rose from the seat.

"Thanks for following me."

After shutting the car door, Calvin got out and stood beside her. "I'm not leaving until I've made sure you're safe inside your house."

"You don't have to."

"Yes, I do." He took her hand and followed her up the driveway and onto her porch. When she unlocked the door, he stepped inside first. The kind gesture caused a warm feeling to stir inside her.

"He doesn't have a key. My brother got it back from him." And without altercation, which she found surprising.

Calvin glanced over his shoulder and said firmly, "That doesn't mean he didn't make a copy."

"Oh, really?" Danielle dropped a hand to her waist. "Is that somethin' you would do?"

Calvin took a deep breath before answering hesitantly, "If I had a fine woman like you . . . yeah, I would."

Laughing, he went back to searching her house while she stood by and watched. Calvin was such a nice guy. *They all are in the beginning,* she thought with a scowl. Then they turn psycho. Kicking off her high heels, she took a seat on the couch and watched the police officer in action as he moved through her small, three-bedroom home, checking every door and window.

"So, am I safe?" she asked when he finally came down the stairs.

Calvin moved towards her with long, confident strides as he spoke. "Safe from Ron. Now me, that's another story altogether."

Danielle paused for a second, then asked point-blank, "What's that 'posed to mean?"

"What do you think it means?" He pulled her to her feet, then snaked an arm around her waist and hugged her against his long body.

Oh, hell! Renee was gonna kill her if she found out, but right now, Danielle could care less. Her coochie was screaming, "Get 'em, girl!" and that was exactly what she wanted to do.

Calvin pressed his lips to hers and Danielle relaxed and got into the softness of his lips. He had skills. That was for damn sure. He took his time and moved with her. When he pushed his tongue between her lips, she allowed him access into her mouth and met his strokes. Her body was responding and she knew he was doing his job when a moan escaped her lips.

The doorbell rang, startling her. Danielle dropped her arms and moved across the plush, oatmeal-colored carpet toward the door.

"Danny, I know that nucca's in there wit' you!"

She froze, then looked at Calvin, and back at the door.

"You want me to answer it?" he asked.

"No!" she practically shouted. With the palm of her hand she stopped Calvin from taking a step further. The last thing she needed was the two of them battling in her house. "Just ignore him and he'll eventually go away."

Reluctantly, Calvin nodded, then sat on the couch while Danielle walked over to her stereo system. Within seconds, the sounds of Janet Jackson filled the room. Danielle moved back over to the couch and lowered herself onto Calvin's lap. She pressed her lips to his and they kissed while trying to ignore the knocking at the door, but it was impossible to do.

"Open this got-damn door now 'fore I knock it down!"

Danielle shook her head just as Calvin started to rise. "He isn't worth it."

He leaned back against the couch and shook his head. "How can you even deal with that type of drama in your life?"

Danielle shrugged in response.

"Listen, I'm not trying to come between you. If you want, I'll leave so the two of you can work things out." There was a hint of frustration in his voice.

"I wouldn't have let you in if I didn't want you here."

He nodded, then his voice softened when he turned to her and asked, "How long you been together?"

"Too long," she replied. Ron had started kicking on the door with his Timberland boots. She shot up from the couch. "Let me handle this." She walked over and yelled through the door. "Ron, if you're not gone in two minutes, I'm calling the police!"

"Fuck you!" he yelled, but the pounding stopped and it wasn't long before she heard footsteps.

With a sigh of relief, she returned to her seat. "Sorry about that. Now, where were we?" She wrapped her arms around Calvin's neck and kissed him.

Chapter 12

Renee

It was shortly after one when David and I finally made it out of the club and into the parking lot. My cootie-cat was wet. Nipples were hard. My desire for him had me light-headed. I hadn't been long-dicked in quite some time and was looking forward to a night to remember. I felt a little guilty, but not enough to put an end to my plans. Not when my body was humming with need—and I desperately needed David tonight.

I followed him to the nearest motel, then waited in my car while he got the room. This may sound crazy, but what was about to go down was going to strictly be a booty call, which is why there's no way in hell I was taking him to my four-star hotel to stank up my sheets. No way. No-how. All I wanted was to get mine, then get up and get the fuck out of there and hurry back to my room. You feel me?

It wasn't long before David came out of the building. I watched him go into room 2B. After about two minutes, I climbed out and followed. As soon as the door was closed we were all over each other. I was so horny my body was on fire and I couldn't get my clothes off fast enough. David stripped down and I breathed a sigh of relief. He was everything I could have hoped for. Thick and long. I planned to appreciate every inch.

"Lay down."

I moved over to the bed and lay back against the pillows with my thighs spread wide. My nipples were hard and erect and begging him to come and taste. David stood there for the longest time, stroking his meat while staring at my cootie-cat. A wicked smile glimmered in his eyes.

"What? You waiting on a formal invitation or something?" Hell, I had waited long enough.

He chuckled. "Hell, no. I just like looking at you. You're sexy as hell!"

True that. I smiled, then, using my pointer finger, signaled for him to come and join me. David lowered onto the bed between my parted legs. His mouth traveled along the side of my neck where he nibbled and sucked, at times a little too hard for my liking.

"Hey!" I flinched. "Watch the neck. I bruise easily." Last thing I needed was a hickey.

"Oops, my bad," he murmured, then dropped even lower and made up for it by running his tongue deliciously across my chest, then stopped. After what felt like forever, he finally captured a nipple between his teeth, kissing one and then the other. Now that's what I'm talking about. They needed attending to. His hand smoothed down along my side and slipped between us. I rocked against his hand. With the tip of his finger he traced my coochie. It throbbed and tingled. I could feel the hard length of his erection pressed against my stomach and was loving the way it felt. I was lying there, moaning and groaning, and thinking, damn, hurry the fuck up.

"You want me to put something there, don't you?"

"Yes!" I was practically begging. "Please."

His thumb caressed my clit and caused slickness to dampen my coochie. Oh, shittt, was that good! Reaching down, I grabbed and stroked his balls, then slid my hand up ever so slowly to the tip where I teased until it released a drop of precum. I played with it, swirling the head with my thumb at the same exact moment he plunged two or three fingers inside. In. Out. And in again. I released him and rocked, meeting the thrust of his fingers instead.

"Do you want me?" he had the nerve to ask.

"Can't you tell?" I moaned.

"I want you to tell me."

Dammit—at this point I would have said or done anything just to get some of him. "I want you. Now come and get it."

He chuckled softly, then rose. "Girl, you gonna have to spread your legs a little wider if you're gonna accommodate all this."

Yeah, yeah, whatever. Just hurry the fuck up. "How's this?" I pulled my knees all the way back against my chest.

"Hell, yeah!" He was stroking his dick again. "Hold up a second." He moved to grab a condom from his wallet, then returned. Thank goodness someone was thinking about practicing safe sex. All I cared about was getting me some.

"Here, give that to me," I demanded impatiently as I snatched the foil from his hand. He was moving way too slow. I quickly ripped open the packet. My hands were trembling so hard. I couldn't wait to feel all that up inside of me. By the time I got it on, I was on the verge of losing my mind. I wrapped my legs around him while he got in position.

Bang! Bang! Bang!

"What the hell?" I practically jumped off the bed. Someone was pounding on the door to our room.

"David! David! I know yo' ass is in there wit' some bitch!" a woman screamed.

I glanced over at his panic-stricken face and frowned. "Who's that?"

"My wife," he mumbled as he rolled off the bed.

"Wife! I thought y'all were divorced."

He reached for his boxers. "Well, not exactly."

"What the hell you mean, not exactly?"

"Listen, I don't have time to explain." He grabbed his boxers and slipped them on.

"I can't believe this shit." That nigga had gotten me all wet and shit for nothing. At least if I had gotten some before his wife had come to the door I might not have been so mad. Because of her, I didn't even get a chance to sample his merchandise.

"David, by the time I count to ten you better get out that room!"

I was so mad, I moved over to the door, wrapped in a sheet, and opened it. Standing there was some fat, cross-eyed woman, holding a black leather belt. "He told me he wasn't married."

"Well, he lied." She stepped into the room and David looked like he was about to shit his pants. "Get yo' ass outta here."

"Dee-Dee, it's not what you think."

"You must think I just came over on the *Mayflower*." She swung the belt in the air and he jumped across the bed. I moved out of the way and watched her chase him around the room and out the door, then across the parking lot. I shut the door and shook my head. Lying ass. I gathered all his things and tossed them in the corner. I'm certain he or his wife were bound to show up again later.

I took a quick shower, getting the smell of him off my body. It's a damn shame the games people play to get some. I don't get it. All David had to do was tell the truth, then let me decide if I still wanted to give him some or not. Shit, there are a lot of sistahs who don't give a damn if a brotha is married. All they want is the dick. Unfortunately, I'm not one of those sistahs. I don't believe in messing with someone else's husband. Now, I might only attend church once a year (no, I'm not talking about Easter), but I do believe there is a God up in heaven and if He says don't sleep with someone else's husband, then I'm listening. That probably sounds crazy coming from a married woman who messes around on her husband, but it's pretty simple. Just because my marriage is fucked up doesn't mean I have to fuck up someone else's. I just don't need that type of guilt on my conscience, especially when I'm already losing my mind as it is.

I finished lathering my body, then rinsed off and reached for the fluffy white towel hanging on the glass shower doors. After wrapping it around my body I moved back to the bed and dried off. It was late and in Columbia the only thing open at this hour was a bitch's legs. And since Dee-Dee fucked that up for me, this cootie-cat was closed for the night. I wasn't ready to go to bed just yet. I decided to ride over to Danielle's and make sure she was okay. Part of me was curious if Calvin had gone home with her, while the other half was truly concerned for her well-being.

I got dressed, reached for David's clothes, and went out to my car. His blue Toyota Camry was still in the same place he left it. I checked his doors to see if by chance one of them was unlocked so I could toss the clothes inside. As soon as I pulled on the handle, two heads popped up in the backseat. They startled and I shrieked.

"What the . . ." I looked through the fogged-up window at David and Dee-Dee locked in each other's arms. Both were topless. I smirked. Them freaks was getting busy in the backseat! "Here. Get a room." I sat his clothes and the key to the room on the hood. Shaking my head, I moved over to my car. I wasn't mad. I was glad I could be of service. That fool definitely owed me one.

Pulling off, I started shaking my head again. Like I said, I wasn't mad at David but I was definitely upset that I wasted the evening with him when I could have been hollering at someone else. I was still thinking about that when I pulled onto Danielle's block, so imagine how I felt when I spotted Calvin's Lexus in her driveway.

Pissed the fuck off!

I had barely parked the car in front of the mailbox when I climbed out and stormed up the driveway. Stepping around a rosebush that was growing wild, I almost twisted my ankle. Instead, I stumbled and caught myself just before landing face-first on the porch. Oh, was I hot! I pushed the doorbell with a vengeance. The door opened, and would you believe Calvin had the nerve to be standing in Danny's doorway in nothing but a pair of boxers?

"Damn." He looked just as surprised to see me as I was him. "I thought you were someone else. Whassup, Renee?"

I pushed passed him, screaming Danny's name. Shortly after,

she came down the stairs into the living room while tying the belt to her robe around her waist. As soon as Danielle noticed me, she slowed. "What are you doing here?"

Oh, no, she didn't. With a hand planted at my waist, I answered with straight attitude. "I came to check and see if everything was all right with you, but apparently so."

"Yeah, Calvin came over to make sure Ron wasn't here," she replied nervously.

"And he just happened to fall into your bed."

Calvin cleared his throat. "Listen I'ma go get dressed and let you two ladies talk."

I watched his fine ass move up the stairs before I glared at her again. "I can't believe this! How could you? You know we used to fuck around."

Danielle gave me a dismissive wave as she lowered onto the couch. "Nae-Nae, that was a long time ago."

"It doesn't matter if it was in kindergarten, the fact of the matter is, you're wrong."

"Yeah, I'll admit, I shouldn't be fucking around with yo' ex." She shrugged. "But shit happens."

I got all in her face, neck rolling, finger pointing. "Now, how would you like it if I went out tonight and fucked Ron?" I said loudly. "Huh? How would that make you feel?"

"Knowing your track record, you probably already have." She was looking at me, daring me to say something.

"Nah, I don't do my friends that way." I sucked my teeth in mock indignation.

Danielle started laughing. "Ho, puhleeze! Just because I wasn't there doesn't mean I didn't hear about yo' behavior in Jamaica."

I simply rolled my eyes because I stuck my foot in that one. Technically, he wasn't Kayla's man at the time, and besides, it wasn't like they'd had a sexual relationship. Truth be told, she didn't want him, so I had willingly filled that slot.

"What's wrong, Nae-Nae? Cat got your tongue?"

I simply stared and ignored her ass.

"See, you can talk all that smack with Kayla and Nadine but

you know good and well I'm not puttin' up with yo' shit. The world doesn't revolve around you and the sooner you realize it, the better." She crossed her legs and gave me a sly look. "You had Calvin. You didn't want him. Now I do." Danielle paused long enough to moan. "Mmm, and I like *everything* he's working with." She started laughing and I pulled her ass off the couch and onto the floor. She was getting a kick out of teasing me. I was two seconds away from twisting her arm behind her back when I heard glass breaking and then a car starting. Danielle's eyes grew large before she got up off the floor, dashed out the door, and across the front lawn. I ran behind her in time to see Ron pulling out of the driveway in her Chevy Impala.

"Ron, get out of my got-damn car!"

He rolled down the window, stuck up his middle finger, and peeled out of the lot with Ludacris blaring from the rear speakers.

Calvin came out on the porch, fully dressed. "What the hell!"

I followed the direction of his eyes. Damn! Ron had broken out the front windshield of Danielle's Durango and had carved the word BITCH on the passenger's side door, in big letters.

"Hell, nah," I mumbled under my breath.

Danielle started screaming and going off. "That no-good nigga done stole my car, and fucked up my truck! Call the got-damn police!"

Calvin tried to calm her down while I went inside and contacted the police. I was tempted to laugh and say, "That's what yo' ass get," but I changed my mind. Danny's my girl, and although she was wrong for fucking Calvin, she can have his ass. With all the dogs she'd had, maybe she just might get it right for a change.

The police arrived and took their report. Danielle was pissed off and had every reason to be. She was talking to the police and trying to report her car stolen when I heard her say the Impala was in both their names.

There was no way I could shut up. "Why the hell you put his name on your car?"

Danielle looked over at me with a long, stupid look. "'Cause I thought we were going to be together."

"Did he help pay for it?"

She hesitated. "No."

I shook my head. "You do some stupid stuff."

Angrily, she brushed tears away from her eyes. "Nae-Nae, I ain't in the mood for yo' shit."

"Whatever." I finally rose. "I'm out."

Chapter 13

Kayla

"You're quiet tonight."

Kayla glanced over at Jermaine and smiled. It felt so good having a man hold her hand that all she could do was sit back and enjoy that wonderful feeling.

Ever since Wednesday when she had caught Leroy with that slut, she had been feeling the lowest of the low. All she could do was sit at her desk and think about what she had done wrong. But tonight, after spending the evening with Jermaine, he made her realize that she deserved so much better.

For over four years she had been meeting Leroy at seedy hotels on the outskirts of town for a quick romp in the hay and him leaving only seconds after ejaculating inside her mouth, vagina, or behind. He never took her anywhere, yet he swore that as soon as the time was right, he was asking his wife for a divorce and they were running off together. She laughed inside. She had been stupid enough to believe all of his lies and promises. Well, no more. She and Leroy were over. It was time for her to be loved and appreciated for once.

"You sure you're okay?"

She nodded, touched by his concern. "I'm the best I've been in days."

"I hope I have something to do with that smile on your face."

"You do."

"Good." He pulled up to the house, then climbed out and walked her to the door. "I really enjoyed spending time with you this evening. How about I take you out to dinner after church tomorrow?"

Kayla nodded. "That would be nice."

Jermaine then leaned in and kissed her on the lips. She sucked it up, enjoying every moment. When he finally pulled away, she stood back and stared as he walked back to his car. Jermaine started the engine and told her he wasn't leaving until she was safely in the house. With a nervous wave, she turned and stepped inside. The girls were asleep and she was glad because it gave her a chance to think about her evening. She turned the lamp on in the living room and jumped when she discovered she wasn't alone.

"Leroy, you scared the mess out of me. What are you doing in my house?"

"You gave me a key. Remember?"

He stepped from out of the corner near the window toward her and for some reason her pulse raced with fear. When they had first started dating four years ago, he had insisted on a key so that he could slip in sometimes while she was asleep, and make love to her. He never did. So why now? Nervously, she took a step back. "Why are you here?"

Leroy gave her a sickly smile that made her stomach churn. "Do I need permission to come see you?"

"N-no. It's just a surprise. That's all."

"Who was that man?"

"Uh . . . someone I work with."

"You've been messing around on me all this time." It was a statement, not a question.

"No, I've never—"

Whop! Before she could finish, Leroy had knocked her to the floor with one hard punch. For a few seconds, Kayla was dazed and totally in shock. She felt wetness on her upper lip, so she gently touched her nose, then looked down at her fingers. She was bleeding.

"I can't believe you did that," she said, holding her nose.

"Baby, I'm so sorry," he said and leaned down to help her off the floor.

"Get away from me!" she screamed, then backed out of his reach until she reached the sofa. While hugging her knees to her chest, tears filled her eyes.

"Come on, Kayla. I didn't mean to hit you. Just seeing you with that man, I lost it. You have to believe me," he pleaded.

Using the back of her arm, she wiped her nose again. "I can't go on like this. I'm tired of waiting around for you to leave your wife—meeting you for quickies and being second-best. I want to be loved."

"I do love you."

"No, you don't. The only person you love is yourself." She paused and brushed the tears away from her eyes. "It's over. I'm ready to move on and you need to get home to your wife and five kids."

"What, you replaced me with someone else?"

His eyes bored down at her and immense fear snaked down her spine. "No."

"You're lying!" he barked.

Leroy was standing over her with his fist balled and his legs parted in a fighting stance, casting an angry shadow over her. Kayla tried to crawl away but he fisted her hair and flung her onto her back. She screamed before his fist landed at her mouth. Terrified, Kayla tried to roll away but he kicked her hard, knocking the air from her lungs. She was holding her chest and gasping for air when Leroy grabbed her by the neck and dragged her across the floor. Kicking and screaming, Kayla tried to pry his fingers from around her neck, but he held on firmly.

"Quit screaming before you wake the girls. I'd hate for them to come down and see what I'm about to do to you."

Panic filled her eyes. The last thing she wanted was for her girls to witness this madness. She stopped screaming and lay still and eventually he removed his hand.

"Good girl."

"What do you want?" Kayla asked as she gasped for air. Tears were falling down her face.

"What do you think I want, Jezebel? You should be ashamed of yourself, fornicating with a man you barely know."

She couldn't believe how crazy he sounded. "You are such a hypocrite. It's no different than when I'm committing adultery with you."

"That's where you're wrong. I told you once. I told you twice. You belong to me and only me." He lowered his head and left a trail of kisses down her neck. For the first time she felt disgusted by his touch.

"Leroy, please don't."

When he raised his head, anger burned in the depths of his eyes. "I bet you let him touch you. Didn't you?" She shook her head and his fist came down and landed a blow to the side of her head. "Liar!" He hit her again. "Tell me the truth."

"I'm not lying, I swear!" she shouted.

"I saw his lips on you. Tasting and seeking with his tongue."

Leroy had a crazed look in his eyes and she was suddenly very, very frightened.

"Did he consummate the relationship?"

She shook her head.

"Liar!" He reached down and ripped the blouse from her body, then slid her pants and underwear down over her hips. She pleaded for him to stop but he refused. "Never! You're mine. This is mine."

Kayla tried to fight him, but she couldn't match his strength. He tossed her onto the couch and despite her protest, he started kissing her across the belly and thighs. He then flipped her onto her stomach and parted her butt cheeks.

"No, please!" she cried.

"Shut up and take this punishment," he said and he plunged inside. She muffled her screams in the cushions of the couch. "Please, no!" Kayla wept.

"You want to act like a whore, I'm going to treat you like one," he said as he brutalized her from behind. She cupped her mouth and screamed. "Whore!" he managed between breaths. "Take your punishment!" She closed her eyes and tried to forget what was happening as he huffed and puffed and moaned in her ear and he moved in and out of her butt. After what felt like forever, Leroy finally pulled out and grunted like a pig as he shot hot cum all down her back, hair, and the side of her face. Crying softly, she watched out of the corner of her eyes while he pulled up his pants.

"Now I want you to get down on your knees and ask the Lord for forgiveness," he commanded between breaths.

She slowly slid off the couch and down onto the carpet, but she was crying and shaking too hard to pray.

Leroy quickly grew impatient. "I don't have all night. Pray and ask the Lord to forgive you for being a whore!"

"Dear Lord, father in heaven, p-p-please have mercy on my soul and forgive me for straying from your teachings." Unable to say anything further, she collapsed in tears.

"Good, now come over here and give your man a kiss."

Shaken and terrified, Kayla slowly rose. Before she reached him, Leroy grabbed her by her hair and yanked her over against him. He pressed his lips firmly to hers, then licked her lips with his tongue before releasing her. He looked pleased. "Good girl. Hopefully we won't ever have this problem again." He then turned and walked out the door, whistling "Amazing Grace."

Kayla collapsed onto the floor and rolled into a ball.

Chapter 14

Renee

I swung by Kayla's the next morning to scoop her up for breakfast. I drove down the road, still pissed off from the night before. I couldn't believe Danielle had put that muthafucka's name on her car. Dang, was the dick that good? I'm gonna have to ask her if Ron's name was on the title of her house as well, because if it was, his dick was *fire* and I definitely need to get me one just like that. Ha-ha! I sound like a fool. I think I'm just jealous and pissed off today. Danny got her some, Kayla's got her somebody new, and I still haven't found any. Six months was a long time to go without the real deal. Something had to give fast.

Speaking of dick, my phone vibrated and I glanced down at the number. Hell nah! It's David's punk ass.

"Yeah?"

"My bad about last night."

"I thought y'all weren't together no more."

"We weren't, but when one of her friends spotted us together at the club and called her, she realized that she still loved her big daddy and wanted him to come home."

"Uh-huh. I'm glad I could be of service."

"Thanks. Um . . . you think maybe I can still get some of that before you leave?"

Click.

See what I'm talking about? I don't do married men. There

are a lot of women who could care less. I'm just not one of them. Men are dogs. That's a given. But all I can give a married dog is a bone.

I pulled into Kayla's driveway and blew my horn. As soon as I climbed out of the car I heard her yell from her bedroom window, "You and Danny go without me. I'm not hungry."

Not hungry? Since when had Kayla skipped a meal? Never. More than likely, her ass was broke. "Bitch, I didn't drive all the way over here for nothing. Let's go. My treat."

"Really, I don't feel like eating."

Something was up. I could sense it. I tilted my head back and used my hand to block the June sun from my eyes. "If you don't come down and let me in so I can pee, I'm gonna climb up there and snatch them braids out yo' head." I really did have to pee.

She huffed and acted like she was surprised by my response. I don't know why. I've been this way for as long as she's known me. Finally, she stepped away from the window. I counted backwards from ten because if she wasn't down by the time I reached one, I was going to start banging on the door and act ghetto and shit. Kayla knows how I do. Luckily, by the time I had reached two, the lock turned. She stood there in her usual black pants and white blouse, wearing dark shades in the house. What's up with that? Before she could react, I snatched them away from her face.

"Hey, quit playing!" she cried as she tried to retrieve the glasses out of my hand, but I held them out of her reach as I took in every bruise on her.

I don't know how she thought she could hide them. Kayla is vanilla. If it wasn't for her nappy head, she could have passed for white. The longer I looked at her, the more pissed off I got and could have kicked someone's ass. And that person was Reverend Brown. He had beaten the shit out of her.

"What the hell happened to you?" I asked, like I didn't already know.

Kayla refused to make eye contact and kept staring down at the floor. "I fell," she mumbled.

"Yeah, it looks like you fell into someone's fist." I pushed past her and entered her house and glanced around. "Where's Kenya and Asia?"

"I took them to my mom's this morning," she replied as she took a seat on the brown leather couch.

She looked so pitiful and shit. I moved over to the couch beside her and cupped her chin with my hand so I could get a better look. She looked fucked up. Lip busted, eye blackened. "Did Jermaine do this to you?"

Her eyes grew wide with alarm. "Of course not."

I didn't think so, but I just had to ask. "Then I guess it's safe to assume that Reverend Brown paid you a visit last night."

She pulled away from me and lowered her head. The answer was obvious. Damn! You know, I've tried being nice to his ass. I even asked Reverend Brown nicely to leave my girl the hell alone because I was sick of watching him fuck with her head. Now it's on!

Kayla held her face in her hands and started crying. I'm not the most compassionate person, but I've been trying to get better. I began rubbing Kayla on her back with a comforting hand. "Hey, girl. It's gonna be okay." I tried to smile and reassure her but inside I was so mad I was crying as well.

"This is so unreal. Gosh, why do things always happen to me? Why can't I be so lucky to have a man in my life like John?"

Be careful what you wish for, I thought but didn't bother to comment because no one would ever believe that what I got ain't nothing to envy. Shit, she could have him, for all I care. Now, you know my ass is lying. Although John's draws are empty, his pockets are too fat to give up just yet.

"Girl, looking like you've just gone nine rounds with Mike Tyson, the last thing in the world you need to be thinking about is another man." I rose and retrieved a box of Kleenex from the coffee table and handed it to her. She blew her nose. I couldn't begin to explain the anger raging inside of me as I watched her sit there on the couch looking so helpless. No matter how much I talk about Kayla, calling her stupid and fat, she is still one of my best friends and has always been there for me even when I haven't been there for her. "Has Reverend Brown ever touched you before?"

She lowered the tissue and slowly gazed up at me. I shook my head. She didn't have to say a word. The answer was obvious.

"What happened?"

"He saw me with Jermaine and got mad," she replied, then blew her nose.

"Now, how the hell is he gonna trip about you being with someone else when his ass is married?" Can you believe that shit? I wrapped my arms around her and let her slobber all over my shoulder. I can buy another shirt but I'll never find another friend like Kayla.

Her shoulders deflated. "He raped me."

"What!" I was shaking now because this was like a television show. I hugged her tighter and the next thing I knew tears were running down my face. It took a while but she somehow managed to tell me everything that happened the previous night. I could almost feel her pain. But what bothered me the most was that Kenya had found her mother lying on the floor bruised, abused, and naked. I was so mad, I wanted to hop in my car and drive over to Reverend Brown's house and beat his ass in front of his knock-kneed wife and ugly kids. But I knew doing that would nowhere near equal the pain and humiliation Kayla had endured. It would have to be something far worse than an ass-whooping. Suddenly, I remembered one question I hadn't even thought to ask.

"Have you called the police?"

Kayla shook her head. "I don't want to call the police. I would be too embarrassed."

"But you can't press charges against him if you don't."

She closed her eyes, probably pretending she was invisible. "I don't need to press charges. I prayed about it."

"Prayed! Girl you should have knocked him upside his head, then called the cops."

"The Bible says, 'Vengeance will be mine.'"

"And the Lord also helps those who help themselves."

She gave me a long, sad look. "I can't press charges."

I knew exactly what she was afraid of. Pressing charges against one of Columbia's most prominent members of the community would be a scandal that would affect the lives of her and her children. Leroy had so many people backing him that she would be fighting a tough and difficult battle. As committed as his wife was, she would probably provide him with an alibi. Nope. We would have to handle Reverend Brown ghetto-style. I reached into my purse for my cell phone.

"Danny, put some clothes on your naked ass and get over here. Leroy busted Kayla in her eyes, lips, and put a couple of lumps upside her head."

I hung up and sat with her while we waited for Danielle. Kayla started crying again and I hoped and prayed that Danny would get here quickly. I can't stand to see another woman cry. The more she cried, the madder I got. How dare that pencil-dick muthafucka put his hand on my girl?

While she continued to cry, I couldn't help wondering if it was finally over. Kayla had been messing with Leroy for over four years, regardless of how many times we've told her to leave his no-good ass alone. But he has her brainwashed. It's like some Jim Jones shit. Leroy's this pastor with all this power and so many people have put him up on this pedestal, flooding his church on Sunday, and given him all their hard-earned money. Whatever he says, whatever he wants, they give him. Now he rides around in this phat-ass Benz, living in this bad-ass house on the hill like he's God, looking down on everyone from heaven.

Leroy has a reputation of being a ladies' man, which I can't understand because I've seen the pictures and he ain't got no dick, yet the women want him anyway. He preys on vulnerable women like Kayla with low self-esteem. He makes her meet him at sleazy hotels on the outskirts of town. He has never helped her financially. She even passed up an opportunity with a pro-fessional football player to be with him. (I still ain't figured that shit out.) She's not his wife, yet he doesn't want her fucking anyone but him. Leroy's a manipulator and he doesn't deserve a woman like Kayla. By the time Danny came through the door, tears were running down my face again.

"What all happened?" she asked, looking from me to her.

Before Kayla could answer, I jumped in. "That bastard raped and beat the crap out of her. Look at that shit!"

Danny looked from me to her, then placed a comforting hand against Kayla's arm. "Have you called the police yet?"

I intervened. "The police? What's the po-po gon' do but get all in her business. Don't worry, we don't need no police, I'm gonna handle this shit."

Danny rolled her eyes. "Ho, whateva. You always tryin' to get some shit started. I guess you haven't learned anything after that psycho tried to slice and dice yo' ass."

See, now why did she even go there? They're always trying to bring up old shit. A couple of years ago, I played with this cat's emotions and he tried to kill a sistah, but what's that got to do with anything? "I'm not going to sit around and let some fat fucker hit my girl and get away with it. I'm going to call my boy and get this handled."

Kayla panicked. "No, please, let's just leave it alone."

I jumped back and stared down at her. "Have you lost your mind? Why you always trying to defend that no-good mutha-fucka?"

"I know that's right," Danny chimed in. "Although I don't believe in an eye for an eye, I think we should at least get the police involved."

"Please, no police." A sob blocked her windpipe, causing her to cough. "I don't want to get Leroy in trouble." I could tell by the look on her face she didn't mean to blurt that out. I was too through.

"Leroy beat yo' ass like you're a runaway slave and you're worried about getting him in trouble? He don't care about you. You were just some more pussy to him, and the sooner you re-alize that, the better off you'll be." I told you her ass was stuck on stupid, and stupid is Leroy Brown. What gets me is that the man ain't even cute. Now mind you, he's tall and has large bedroom eyes, but he has that Grizzly Adams beard thing going on that he needs to either cut or take an Afro pick to. And the worst thing is, he has a little-ass dick. See, why you even have to go there? No, I never fucked his ass. However, I have a friend that took a picture of him naked while he slept. So like I said, he ain't got shit. So you tell me what the hell does Kayla and all the other women he's fucking see in him? It ain't like he's giving up any money. Everyone knows he's a ho—even his wife, and she doesn't care what the hell he does as long as he keeps her round, apple-shaped head in Gucci and diamonds.

Danny was sitting on the couch, patting Kayla's back and speaking in a low, soothing tone. I rolled my eyes. I was through babying Kayla. It was time for her to stand up for herself for once. I'm a strong believer that the Lord helps those who help themselves. And that is something my girl has yet to figure out. "Okay, so since you don't want to call the police, what are we going to do?" I asked with straight attitude. I believe in reacting.

Choking and sobbing, Kayla struggled to find her voice. When she could not, she reached for Danielle and cradled her face against the crook of her neck and cried some more.

"Hey, girl, it's gonna be all right," Danielle replied soothingly. "Just tell us what you want to do."

"I-I don't want t-to do anything," she stuttered.

I tossed my hands in the air and headed for the door. "You know what? I'm too through! It's obvious I'm gonna have to handle this myself."

"Nae-Nae, shut the hell up." Danny gave me a look of warning. "Kayla, how do you want to handle this? If you love that bastard and you plan to get back with him tomorrow, then there is no point in us getting involved." She looked over at me as she spoke. What the hell is she looking at? I rolled my eyes.

Kayla sniffed and slowly eased out of Danielle's arms. For the longest time she sat there with her hands folded in her lap, looking pitiful as shit. Finally, in a tearful voice, she spoke. "You can do whatever you want. Right now I just want to go to sleep."

"Do you have a headache? Want some ibuprofen?"

She nodded and Danielle raced up to the bathroom to raid her medicine cabinet.

"Don't worry, Kayla. We're gonna take care of this for you," I said softly.

She sniffled and I handed her another Kleenex.

"Renee, you can do whatever you want," she began and paused long enough to blow her nose. "For real this time—it's over between us." She lifted her chin. "I will never forgive him for what he did to me."

"That's whassup!" I cheered, then reached for my cell phone and dialed. "You ain't said nothin' but the word."

"Who you calling?" Danielle asked suspiciously as she came back into the room carrying a cup of water and a bottle of pills that she handed to Kayla.

I put the phone to my ear and headed toward the door. "Don't worry about it."

Just as I heard someone say "Hello," that trick snatched the phone from my ear. "Damn, Danny! Quit playing!" I tried to get my phone back but she held it out of my reach.

"Renee, what's going through your head?"

Danny knows me like the back of her hand. "Don't worry about it," I retorted. "Just help your girl get herself together so we can go and get somethin' to eat. I'm starved."

"Who were you calling?"

"Tommy," I confessed reluctantly.

"Tommy? For what?" She dropped her arm and I snatched my phone back.

"Why you think?"

Danny popped me upside my head.

"Ow!" I rolled my eyes at her. "What the hell you do that for?"

Her frown hardened into stone. "Don't get yourself in some shit you can't get yourself out of."

"Danny, I know what I'm doing. I promise no one will be hurt."

She looked at me for the longest time like she didn't believe me before she finally dropped her hand from her hip and returned to Kayla's aid.

I moved outside and hit TALK again. Tommy answered on the second ring.

"Damn, Nae-Nae, whaddaya doin' hangin up on a nucca?"

I couldn't help but smile. "My bad. How you been?"

"Shit, I can't complain. Pockets fat. I got pussy comin' at me left and right. Shit, a brotha is livin' large."

"That's whassup." Enough of the small talk—it was time to get down to business. "Listen, you seen Peaches?"

"Nah, not for a minute."

"Well, I need him, so find him and get back with me quick."

"Why, whassup?"

I quickly told him about Leroy beating my girl down.

"Sounds like Reverend Brown needs a reality check."

"That's my plan." I told him I was heading to Mama B's to eat and to find Peaches and have him meet us there. I had just returned my phone to my waist when Danielle came out of the house alone.

"Kayla said she don't feel like eating."

"Whatever. I ain't got time to be waiting on her ass."

Danielle gave me a long, hard look. "Nae-Nae, there is no point in us getting involved. You know her as well as I do, and she's gon' take that fake-ass preacher back tomorrow."

"It doesn't matter. Regardless of how stupid she is, he shouldn't have put his hands on her. If we don't do anything, then he's gonna think he can keep getting away with that shit."

She nodded. "Yeah, you sho' right. Let me try talkin' to her again. I'll meet you there in a few minutes."

I hopped in my rental car and took off to the little hole-in-the-wall restaurant that had some of the best pancakes in town. The only bright spot in my morning was that I was going to see Tommy.

The two of us go way back. He's a hustler that will slit a nigga's throat in a heartbeat. We've been friends for years. I'll admit we used to fuck at one time, but after that fizzled and we both moved on to the next, we stayed close friends. One thing for sure—he's got my back.

Fifteen minutes later, I was sipping my coffee thinking about how some men just don't have any respect for women. That was one positive thing I could say about my husband. John would never put his hands on me regardless of how much I pissed him off. And believe me, I've given him more than enough reasons.

Shortly after the waitress took my order, Danielle came strolling into the building. As soon as she spotted me she came over to my table and lowered into the seat.

"How's Kayla?" I asked between sips.

"How do you think she is? Depressed, blaming herself for what happened."

I just shook my head. There wasn't really anything to say at this point. I had already decided to handle it myself.

"So what are you planning to do?"

"Get back at his ass. He's been treating her like shit for years."

"True, but she lets him." She reached for her water and took a sip. "You gon' let Tommy and his boys whoop his ass?"

"Nah. That ain't good enough. Those bruises will heal. I need to hurt him where it hurts."

A slick smile curled her lips. "You know I'm down for whateva."

"Good." I knew Danielle would have my back. As soon as our waitress came and took her order, Tommy arrived with Peaches.

I smiled when I saw him—I mean her—sashaying her hips as she moved toward our table. I don't understand all that gay shit, but if Peaches says he's a she, then so be it. He was wearing tight jeans and a loud orange ruffled blouse. I must admit, he has fooled so many people. Shit, he looks better than me on a bad day and that ain't easy to do. Part Mexican, Peaches has long, raven-black curls and a smooth nutmeg complexion. He doesn't need makeup, although most of the time he wears it and usually it's so much he looks like a damn clown with rosy red cheeks and all that doggone eye shadow. Today he was wearing dark shades with a polka-dotted orange-and-black scarf tied around the neck like he was somebody important.

"What's up, chicas?" "she" said as she dropped her butt into a seat beside Danielle.

Tommy dropped a kiss to my cheek and took the seat next to me. We all exchanged greetings as our waitress arrived with our food.

Peaches pressed a hand to her chest and gasped. "Uh-uh! No, you didn't order food and forget 'bout me," she said in that high-pitched, flamboyant way.

"Would you like to order?" the waitress asked.

"Of course. Don't you hear my stomach growling?" Peaches smacked her lips and gave an exaggerated pout.

Tommy shook his head and butted in. "Just give us the same thing they're having." He rolled his eyes at me. His cousin got on his last nerve. She'd been embarrassing him for years; her behavior was the main reason why.

"So what's up?"

"Reverend Brown beat my girl up."

"Oh my goodness!" Peaches gasped. "He's a trip."

Danielle sucked her teeth, then asked, "You still messing with him?"

Peaches rolled her neck with straight attitude. "Why you all in my business?"

"Ho, don't try and act all innocent. I know you were fucking him."

Peaches smiled. She loves it when you call her a ho. "How you know that?"

"'Cause I do."

Tommy started laughing. "Peaches, you really fuckin' that old cat?"

"Cuz, puhleeze. He ain't the only leader of that church I'm fucking. Them freaks like it down and dirty."

Danielle held up an open palm. "Peaches, the last thing I

want to do is hear about you and yo' men. Now, you gonna help or what?"

"I'd love to. Leroy's been into some sick BDSM shit lately and had the nerve to try and choke me," Peaches said as she snaked her neck.

Danielle didn't have a clue what that meant. "What's BDSM?"

"Bondage, domination, sodomy. Crazy shit, but he's paying, so I'm willing to do whatever it is he wants to do."

I shook my head. He'll pay a fag but he won't give Kayla shit. I don't understand it.

"So, chicas. What do I get out of this? Leroy is my money-maker."

"How about two tickets to Chris Brown's concert?" It had been on the radio all week. He was going to be in St. Louis next month.

"Oh my goodness! I love him."

"Bet. I'll have them to you by Friday."

Peaches' eyes danced with excitement. I knew she would be easy to please.

"Everybody in on this?" I glanced around the table as they all nodded their heads. "Good." I leaned forward. "This is how it's gonna go down." Reverend Brown was going to regret ever putting his hands on my girl.

Chapter 15

Kayla

She lowered her body into the hot bubble bath and closed her eyes.

Leroy beating her up was definitely an eye-opener. She had wasted four years of her life loving that man and trying to be everything she could possibly be for him. She brushed a tear from her eye and thought of all the times she had put her kids second to cater to his needs and it made her sick. All she had ever wanted was to be loved. She never got it as a child.

Kayla had been raised by Delores Sparks, an overweight woman with low self-esteem who was a dummy when it came to men. For years, her three girls watched her jump into one relationship after another that lowered her feelings of self-worth even more. After years of repeating the cycle, her kids never understood why she just didn't have a clue.

Delores had a knack for attracting losers. Convicts, drug dealers, men without jobs, all of them wanted the same thing—her money and a chance to lay between her jiggly thighs. As a registered nurse, one would have thought she had some kind of common sense. Instead, she allowed one after the other to move in. She'd even come home to find her television missing, and still didn't have a clue. It was no wonder her daughters had no idea how they should be treated by men. The countless men she had seen in and out of her mother's life were no better

than her alcoholic father. He showed up at their house whenever he needed money, banged their mother, then robbed her
wallet. To this day Kayla didn't even think he knew her real
name because all he had ever called her was Ms. Piggy.

She met Anthony, Kenya's father, at nineteen, and their relationship moved no further than the bedroom. He never took
her anywhere and refused to be seen with her "big ass" in public. When she found out she was pregnant with Kenya, he questioned if he was the father, even though she had been a virgin
when they met. Asia's father was no better. Eric was a law student she had supported thinking he would marry her as soon
as he passed the bar exam. Instead, a month after passing the
exam, he joined a law firm in San Francisco and left Kayla behind because she wouldn't look good on his arm. After that
there were countless others who treated her like crap, and she
had come to believe that love just wasn't meant for her. Then
Reverend Leroy Brown came to lead their church and she fell
in love. She tried to fight her feelings. Even got down on her
knees and prayed to God, but it was no use—she loved him regardless of how wrong she knew it was. And then he admitted
his feelings to her and they tried to deny the attraction but
eventually lost the battle. They started meeting at hotels outside of town for a few stolen moments together. She knew it was
wrong and that she would probably burn in hell, but Leroy told
her he wasn't happy and that he was leaving his wife and she believed him. No matter how many years passed, and even when
his wife "accidentally" got pregnant, she believed in her man
and took his word. She still didn't understand why. Her friends
told her she was stupid and even a little voice in her head
agreed, but she just couldn't bring herself to accept that she
had wasted all those years for nothing, because as far as she was
concerned, what difference did it make that she was waiting? It
wasn't like she had any other prospects. But now things were
different. After seeing Leroy with Tracy, she knew it was over
between them, that their relationship had run its course, and it
was time for her to move on. And that was what she thought she

had done with Jermaine. She was ready to make a new beginning that didn't include Leroy, or his siddity wife. She had even
thought that being the Christian he claimed to be, Leroy would
just accept that she was through waiting around for him. But
that was before he had come to her house and acted a fool.

Kayla took a deep breath. Maybe she should have gone to the
police and reported the incident. She had never been a fighter.
That was one thing she admired about her friends. They stood
up for what they believed in and didn't let anything or anyone
stand in their way. But not her. She had always been afraid of
confrontation or of bringing unwanted attention to herself. And
an incident like this would definitely bring a lot of attention.
What she worried about most were her girls.

Another tear rolled down her cheek as she remembered that
shortly after Leroy had left, Kenya had come down the stairs.
Kayla was balled up beside the coffee table, too weak and humiliated to move. The last thing she had wanted was for her
daughter to see her that way. The room had been destroyed.
The table overturned. Her shirt ripped. Her panties gone. At
the sight of her mother's bruised face, Kenya screamed. All
Kayla could do was hold out her arms to her daughter. She'd
sat on the floor holding her for almost an hour before she had
finally found the strength to pull herself together long enough
to get her girls away from that madness. Kayla drove up to her
mother's house and didn't even bother to get out. As soon as
she answered the door, Kayla peeled off. She was certain Kenya
had already revealed all the horrid details. As soon as her cell
phone started ringing, Kayla answered long enough to assure
her mother she was okay. The minute she got home, she had
called a locksmith to come and change all the locks, adding two
additional ones, and paid the ridiculous weekend rate.

The phone rang, startling Kayla from her thoughts. She took
a deep breath, leaned out of the tub, and reached down for the
cordless phone on the rug. She glanced down at the Caller ID
and paused. PRIVATE. *Should I answer it?* She pressed TALK, then
put the phone to her ear.

"Hello?"

"Kayla? Kayla, honey . . . I'm so sorry." Her stomach churned. It was Leroy. He was crying loudly into the receiver. "I'm so sorry. The devil made me do it. The devil made me. Please forgive me, for I have sinned." Her lip quivered and she couldn't bear to hear any more and ended the call. Immediately, the phone started ringing again. She turned the volume down, then sank lower into the water. Somehow she had to find a way to make Leroy understand it was over.

Chapter 16

Renee

"Damn, I shouldn't have eaten those tacos," Danielle said with a groan.

I gave her a sympathetic look. "Me neither, but they sho' were good," I added as I made a right at the next corner.

"Maybe we need to swing by my house for a few minutes so I can use the bathroom."

"Uh-uh. We don't have time for that. Reverend Brown is picking up Peaches in less than an hour. We've got to get to his house before they do."

"If you say so." She went quiet for a minute. I could feel her brain working and gave her the time she needed to think. "You sure you want to go through with this?"

"Damn straight." It was time someone taught Reverend Brown a lesson. He had fucked-over a lot of women through the years, but this time he had messed with the wrong one. Kayla was one of the most committed people I knew, even to dogs that didn't deserve it. She ended friendships over that fool when all Leroy had to do was love her. Instead, he wanted to put his hands on her. I just didn't get it. Several years back, I had warned his ass to leave her alone—otherwise, I was going to expose his infidelities. We were in Jamaica, and Nadine had spilled the beans that Leroy's wife was pregnant with another baby. Kayla was upset. Me, Nadine, and my sister Lisa were all trying to convince her to kick up her heels and get over that fool. Anyway, I was in our hotel room alone when the phone rang.

"May I please speak to Kayla?"

My brow rose with curiosity. "May I ask who's calling?"

"Yes, a good friend."

I sucked my teeth. "Uh-huh. This must be Reverend Leroy Brown."

"Uh, no. You've got me confused with someone else. My name is Clarence."

"Clarence, my ass," I spat as I lowered onto the bed. "Reverend Brown, I know this is yo' trifling ass. You need to be ashamed of yourself."

"Who is this?" he inquired.

"Don't worry about who this is," I barked in the telephone. "What you need to be worrying about is me telling your pregnant wife about your latest escapade."

"You wouldn't do that," he said, trying to sound all bold and shit.

"The hell I won't. I love Kayla and don't want to see her hurt. So I'll tell you what. You stay the fuck away from her and I won't let the church know where you spend your Wednesday afternoons."

"Now, sister, you don't—"

"I ain't your sistah. Now, I know all about you sleeping with them Campbell twins and about you going to the motel with Bonnie, only to find out she was a he, so if I was you, I wouldn't fuck with me, 'cause I play for keeps."

He hesitated for a long moment. "So what is it that you want?"

"For you to stay the fuck away from Kayla and I mean it. Let her have a chance to find someone who truly loves her, not the games you be playing."

He started laughing. "You can't stop me from seeing her."

"Oh, yes I can. Personally, I don't know what she sees in you. Now, what I should be asking is what the hell she wants with you and your little-ass dick. Oh yes, I've seen the pictures."

"Pictures?"

I giggled inwardly before continuing. "Didn't you know? See, you used to mess with Shanika Martin, who is really John-John from over on Eighth Street. One afternoon when he—oops, I mean she—had your arms tied to the bedpost, she had her older sister, Ursula, in the closet taking pictures. You should be ashamed of yourself. Does your wife know you're on the DL?"

"I'm n-not on the d-down low," he stuttered nervously.

"That's what they all say."

I laughed in his face and finally I heard him sigh and say, *"I do love Kayla."*

"Then if you truly love her, you'll leave her alone."

"What will I tell her?"

"The truth. You never had any intention of leaving your wife."

"That's not true. I did. It's just hard when you have so many people looking up to you and then Darlene got pregnant and everything changed."

"Yeah, yeah—save that sappy-ass story for someone who cares." I heard the knob turn, so I spoke quickly. *"Don't call her again or else."* I hung up the phone.

Of course, Kayla found out and went off on me for butting my nose in her love life. Whatever. She needs me to fight her battles for her, and I'm more than happy to, especially since Leroy didn't take my threat seriously. Now he was going to have to pay the piper. Kayla wasn't strong enough to stand up to him but I was.

In a way I guess I can say I owed Kayla one. I'm gonna quit faking the funk and tell you the truth. While in Jamaica, I did sort of fuck her man. He wasn't actually her man—he was someone she was dating, but when she dropped him like a hot skillet, I was there to scoop him up. I didn't even know she really cared about the man until she walked in while we were in midstroke. I've never seen her so hurt before. Well, I guess it's time to pay my dues.

I pulled onto Rock Quarry Road and started searching for the house. "All right, help me find it. Kayla says it's at the end of the picket fence with red shutters." I slowed the car to a crawl while we scanned both sides of the street. The dozen or so houses on the road were definitely off the beaten path.

"There it is." Danielle pointed to a small ranch house on the left. The yard was in serious need of work. Weeds had taken over the flower beds. The screen door was swinging back and forth in the wind. "No wonder this place isn't rented."

"I think that's just an excuse so he can justify keeping it for his own nasty pleasures." I turned my nose up just thinking how stupid his wife was to put up with his mess. If it was John, I would have put a stop to this kind of shit a long time ago. The part that gets me is that everybody knows what's going on at this house—and I do mean everybody. So why does Darlene just sit back and allow that mess to happen? I guess that's the million-dollar question.

"I'm gonna park over here." I pulled up in front of a house at the end of the street that was in the midst of construction and climbed out. The house looked to be recently framed— lumber was scattered everywhere. I would have to watch where I stepped because the last thing I needed was mud on the bot- toms of my new canvas sandals. "Okay, we need to hurry and go set up." Danielle got out and we put our purses in the trunk, then I reached for a small camcorder.

"All right, let's get into position." I handed Danielle a digital camera and shut my trunk. As we moved down the street I glanced around to see if anyone was watching. Luckily, the street was relatively quiet.

Danielle's eyes were sparkling with amusement. "I can't be- lieve we're doing this."

"Well, believe it," I mumbled. I looked left to right, then zipped up the driveway. I ain't gonna lie—my heart was beating hard. "Where's the key?"

Danielle reached into the back pocket of her jeans and re- moved the key to his front door that we had to pry from Kayla's hands. Can you believe she didn't even want to give us access to Leroy's house? I told you her ass is stuck on stupid.

Hands shaking, Danielle struggled with the door. While she fumbled with the lock, I glanced around and made sure no one was watching. "Hurry, girl."

"I'm hurrying," she replied in a shaky voice.

The last thing we needed was for Leroy to pull up while we

were breaking into his house. Finally, the door opened and we quickly slipped inside and turned the lock behind us. We took a deep breath and tried to get our hearts to stop racing. Breaking into someone's home was some crazy shit. Thank goodness the crime rate in the area was low and folks in this neighborhood didn't feel the need to install security systems.

I clicked on the light, then glanced around the living room. Nothing special, but definitely nicer looking than the outside. Worn brown leather furniture. Beige carpeting. Big-screen television and an entertainment center, which included a complete stereo system. Pornographic magazines were spread out on the coffee table. "Look at this shit," I said with a hint of disgust.

"What do you expect from a sleazeball?"

"I guess." I clicked off the light and followed Danielle down the hall. The only room with a bed was the last room on the end. Queen-size bed. Dresser with television on top. A private bathroom to the right, directly across from a closet with two folding doors. I pulled back the doors and stepped inside, then pointed the camcorder toward the bed. Filming would require keeping the door slightly ajar, but other than that, we had a clear shot. Danielle and I took a seat on the bed while we got our equipment ready.

"Girl, he's gonna die when he finds out what we've done," Danielle said as she put film inside the camera.

"Well, let's hope he doesn't find out."

The plan was to video Reverend Brown fucking Peaches, then pass the tape around to all the church members. He humiliated Kayla, and in turn, we planned to destroy his entire world. That would teach him to fuck with me and mine.

Danielle turned to me and paused before saying. "You know I'm down for whateva you want to do, but you sure you want to take it to the extreme? The church ain't gon' take lightly to him being on the DL."

I scowled. "Then he should have thought about that."

I have never been considered a Christian woman—goodness, no, not with my nasty mouth and track record. But I believe there is a God in heaven watching over us. Truth be told, He needs to do something about all these hypocrite pastors, preaching in the pulpit on Sunday and fornicating all the other days.

I took the camera from her. "You should have made Kayla come with us."

Danielle pursed her lips. "You know as well as I do, she doesn't like confrontation. That's why she stood there and let that man beat her ass."

I removed the cap from the camera and handed it back to her. "Make sure you use this button here to zoom real close to his face. I don't want there to be any question as to who is in that bed with Peaches."

"All right," she replied. "Ooops! Excuse me."

"Excuse you for what?" And then the smell hit me. "Damn, Danny! Ugh!" I moved over toward the bathroom and tried to gulp as much fresh air as I could.

"Sorry." She fell onto the bed, laughing her ass off.

"Damn, girl, you can't be doing that shit!" I yelled even though I had laughter in my voice.

"I told you I shouldn't have had those tacos."

"No, you shouldn't have. Stanky ass." I was still laughing and holding my nose while I moved over to the closet. "Come on. Let's get in position before they get here." Other than a few clothes hanging in the closet, it was relatively empty. Danielle rose and slid in on the right side of the closet and I was on the left. "Don't even think about farting up in here," I warned.

"I'm good now."

I lowered onto the floor, then turned on the camcorder and decided I'd better practice recording before they got here. While gazing down at the screen, I pressed the red button, then said, "We are here in the closet of Reverend Leroy Brown's house on Rock Quarry Road where he meets all his freaks. In a few minutes he will be arriving with his Monday night flavor." I pressed PAUSE and Danielle and I died laughing.

"You're crazy!"

I had tears in my eyes. "I was trying to keep from laughing.

Can you just imagine them church folks' faces when they get this tape?"

"I wish I could be a fly on that wall."

"So do I." I lowered the camcorder to the floor and pulled my knees to my chest. Danielle crossed her legs Indian-style and slid farther in the corner. There was a long silence while we waited and listened. My phone was on vibrate, awaiting Peaches' call. "So tell me, what's up with you and Calvin?"

"Like what?"

I could tell she was trying not to laugh. "You know what I'm talking about. Did you give him some?"

Danielle slid her sandaled foot over to my side of the closet and nudged me playfully in the leg. "You nosey."

"Damn right. I want to know what's going on. So, did you give him some or what?" I wasn't ashamed about asking because like she and I always say, "Inquiring minds want to know."

Danielle clicked her tongue. "Ain't you nothing. I would have gotten me some if you didn't come bangin' on the door Saturday night like a damn fool."

"My bad." I shrugged and tried to appear nonchalant about the whole thing. "Hey, I can't help but feel some type of way about the whole thing. I mean, come on, I think you should have been woman enough to have at least told me first," I said with a little hurt in my voice. I wasn't really hurt, just wanted to make Danielle feel bad about fucking around with one of my exes.

"True. And if I had told you, would that have made it okay?"

"No," I said after a long moment. "But at least I wouldn't have been surprised."

She nodded, understanding where I was coming from. "Actually, I don't know how I hooked up with Calvin in the first place 'cause even though he's fine, you know he isn't my type. But after that shit went down at the club with Ron, he followed me home to make sure everything was okay. Then while he was there, Ron started bangin' on the door and actin' a damn fool, and I thought to myself, why do I need this drama in my life when I've got this nice man sitting in my living room? One thing led to another and Nae-Nae girl, the next thing I knew we were up in my bed."

I couldn't resist a grin. "Did you get a chance to see what he was working with?"

Her eyes sparkled, the way they do when you've got a secret you're dying to tell. "Shit, yeah. He's got a nice dick, but Ron's got him beat."

My eyes grew large. "What?" She was nodding and grinning at the same time. All I could do was shake my head. "Damn—I guess so, since you put the negro's name on your car. Is he on your house, too?"

She stuck her middle finger up at me. "Forget you. I ain't that stupid."

"I hope not."

"Nah, I ain't that crazy. Although Ron could patent that thang and make a lot of money."

"And my ass would be at the front of the line," I joked.

Laughing, Danielle reached over and gave me a high five. "I know that's right." She added, "Ron's been calling for the last two days, driving me crazy."

"He's fine, but that negro's psycho. What's he goin' to do about scratching up your car?"

"He said he'll have it painted if I take him back." Danielle rolled her eyes. "Girl, I'm not taking that fool back no matter how good he is in bed. All I want is my car."

"Is he going to give it back?"

"Nope."

I shook my head. "You sure know how to pick 'em."

"Yeah," she admitted around a frustrated breath. "I don't know why, but that type of man turns me on."

"Yeah, they turn me on, too. But you fuck 'em and send 'em back home to Mama."

She rested her chin on her knees. "I know. I just keep hoping that one of these days I'll be able to change one of them."

"When you're competing with the streets, you can't change them muthafuckas."

"You right."

My cell phone vibrated. "Ooh! That's Peaches letting us know they're here!" I hurried and shut off the light, then moved back into the closet and closed the folding door. "It's showtime." We waited for what felt like forever. Danielle was breathing so hard, I leaned over and tapped her arm. "Girl, quit breathing so hard or he'll hear us."

She cupped her mouth with one hand. I was starting to get nervous, so I had to make myself breathe deeply through my nose and out my mouth. As soon as I heard the key turn in the lock, my pulse jumped and I felt like something was lodged in my throat. *Relax*, I kept telling myself. I was doing this for Kayla and there was no way I could fuck this shit up. I slowly reached over for the camcorder and held it up, pointing it through the small space between the two folding doors. Danielle grabbed her camera and pointed it through a corner at the other end. We were both ready. Voices drew closer and I knew they were coming down the hall toward the room.

Reverend Brown stepped into the room and turned on the light. He then paused, sniffed, and said, "What's that smell?" I held my breath, certain we'd been caught. Dang, had Danielle's fart lingered that long?

Peaches stepped into the room, then dropped his hands to the waist of his low-riding jeans as he spat, "That's yo' bottom lip ya smelling. Now shut up and go get dressed."

I gasped and snickered at the same time. *That's my girl.*

Reverend Brown looked at Peaches for the longest time, eyes blinking. I was hoping he wasn't going to punch Peaches in the mouth because if he did, we would've jumped out and handled that muthafucka hood-style. Instead, he stared over at him with his hands cupped in front of him before he finally replied in a soft baby voice, "Yes, Mommy."

Yes, Mommy? Hold the fuck up. At the same time Danielle

and I turned to each other and even in the dim closet I could see her stunned expression. What's really going on?

Like a good little boy, Leroy moved to the bathroom and shut the door behind him. Peaches looked over at the closet and squinted his eyes like he was trying to see if we were inside. I quickly stuck out a couple of fingers so he would know the show was about to begin.

Peaches was doing the damn thing. Micro braids were hanging loose around his shoulders. I could see he was wearing his long Lola Falana eyelashes and had his lips painted red. His slender body was wearing the hell out of a pair of white Capri jeans and a halter top exposing a flat stomach and a pierced belly button. He looked like a pretty teenage girl.

I watched as he moved over to the radio and tuned the station to KISS 106.1. The Black-Eyed Peas' female singer was talking about her lady lumps, and Peaches, while waiting, was wiggling his little flat ass. By the end of the song, the bathroom door opened and Leroy came out. My mouth dropped to the floor. There he stood in the middle of the room, wearing a big-ass diaper with a pacifier in his mouth.

It was a good thing the music was on loud because Danny started laughing. I quickly clamped a hand over her mouth. "Be quiet or you're gonna ruin everything," I warned softly near her ear. Danny nodded and I slowly removed my hand. I pressed the red button on the camcorder and started filming. I ain't never seen no crazy shit like that before. Leroy was walking around the room like he was an eighteen-month-old baby.

"Good boy," Peaches replied. He was getting a kick out of playing the mama. He handed Leroy a rattle—he dropped his pacifier and started shaking the toy up and down and laughing.

"Goo goo, gaga."

I turned to Danielle and we started laughing and covering our own mouths at the same time. I almost dropped the camcorder. This shit was better than a movie. He reminded me of that cartoon character Baby Huey. My brain was already churning. I couldn't wait to see his wife's face when she got a copy of this tape. Leroy crawled around the floor, playing with his rattle, then tossed it across the room. Peaches retrieved it and as soon as he gave it back to Baby Leroy, he tossed it again, laughing and hitting Peaches upside his head.

"Bad baby. I'm going to spank you for that."

I wanted to laugh so bad I was ready to pee on myself. Peaches took a seat on the bed and had Baby Leroy lie across his lap with his head facing the closet. She spanked him across his butt and Leroy wailed like a baby although what I saw was smiles and grins while he howled in pleasure. It seemed that the sick bastard liked being spanked.

"Now, go play and be a good boy," Peaches said with a pat to the head.

Sniffling, Baby Leroy climbed off her lap and moved over to the floor to play with a small ball. He rolled onto his back and played with his toy while gurgling and slobbering like he was teething. After a while he stopped playing and stared over at the door. He was lying so still I just knew he could see us in that closet. My pulse raced. *Oh boy, now what?*

"What are you doing?" Peaches asked in a sweet-potato-pie voice. He walked over to where the baby was lying on the floor and sniffed. "Did you boo-boo on yourself?" he asked and Baby Leroy started sucking his bottom lip and began crying. I wanted to say, nah, that's Danny's stinky ass you smell. Peaches moved closer, then leaned over and put his nose down near his rear. "Ugh! You did boo-boo on yourself."

Baby Leroy started crying hard and sounded so pitiful, I almost felt sorry for him.

"There, there, don't cry. Mama's gonna change you then I'm going to give you a bottle and put you to sleep." Peaches took his hand and led him over to the bed where he made him lie down. While Baby Leroy lay there crying and slobbering all over the damn place, Peaches moved over to a small duffel bag and removed a clean diaper and a pack of baby wipes. I looked over at Danielle with my brow raised. I know he ain't about to do what I think he's about to do. I looked back in the camera as Peaches unpinned the diaper and, damn . . . Baby Leroy really had shit in his pants. Hell, nah! Peaches pulled off the funky diaper, then wiped his big, black ass with a baby wipe. I couldn't contain my laughter and neither could Danielle. We both tried to hold it in the best we could, but it was impossible, and by the look on his face, I could tell Leroy had heard us.

"Oh shit," Danielle mumbled.

Shit was right. She was laughing and groaning at the same time until the smell radiated over to my side of the closet. I thought I was going to pass out. Danielle's stanky ass had farted one of those quiet, hot farts that smells so bad you can't breathe or you'll throw up if you do. I tried to quiet her and hold my breath at the same time and couldn't. The smell from the closet and the room was just too much to bear.

"I've got to get home so I can go to the toilet."

We busted through the closet at the same time. Leroy was lying there like a good little boy while Peaches pinned on a clean diaper. As soon as the doors flew open, Peaches fell backwards onto the floor with a thump.

"What the . . ." Sitting up, Leroy's voice trailed off and his eyes grew large when he noticed me standing there. "What is going on?"

Still on the floor, Peaches sucked his gold teeth and faked ignorance. "That's what I wanna know, too."

Danielle pushed past me and dashed into the bathroom, leaving me to face Leroy alone. He looked like he was ready to beat my ass, so I swallowed and put on a tough front real fast. Maybe I'm crazy, but I ain't that damn crazy to think that muthafucka wouldn't hit me.

"What's goin' on? I should be asking *you* that, lying here in a big-ass diaper."

His demeanor changed as he suddenly remembered he was role-playing. "Why are you in my house?"

"I wanted to confront you in person about what you did to Kayla."

"I have no idea what you're talking about."

"Yes, you do and if you ever touch her again, I'll show this tape to everyone."

I could tell he hadn't noticed I was holding a camcorder because his expression changed to rage. He jumped off the bed and tried to lunge at me, but Peaches had pinned one side of his diaper to the mattress, so when he tried to jump forward he got yanked backwards and his head hit the headboard.

"Ow!" he cried, then struggled to free himself. Peaches looked from me to him, confused about what he should do before going to lend Leroy a hand.

By the look on his face, I knew it was time to get out of there. "Danny, let's go!" I heard the toilet flush and I went back to the closet to retrieve the Polaroid camera. As I came around the bed, Leroy rolled off and came at me. I panicked and did the only thing I could do with my hands full. I kicked him hard in the nuts.

He screamed and buckled over in pain. I pushed and he fell onto the bed, then I jumped around him quick just as Danielle came out of the bathroom.

"Let's go!" I grabbed Danielle's hand, then dropped it. "I hope yo' stanky ass washed your hands."

"Nae-Nae, shut up," she spat, then signaled for Peaches to come with us. "Leroy, don't try and follow us—otherwise we gon' tell everybody you're a freak."

Peaches fanned his hand. "Damn, Renee, what's that smell?"

"That's Danielle's stanky ass."

"I ate some bad beef. Let's go."

We dashed out the door before Leroy could put his pants on, and rushed into my rental car and pulled off. I couldn't believe that we had done it, but the evidence was right inside that camcorder.

"Ya'll bitches are crazy!" Peaches threw his hands in the air.

I smirked. "Yes, we are!" We all started laughing and talking at the same time. It was too hilarious. "Peaches, I can't believe you changed his diaper!"

"Yeah, right," Danielle chimed in. "What the hell were you thinking?"

He sucked his teeth and leaned forward on the backseat. "I'll do anything that fool wants as long as the price is right." He waved a stack of twenty-dollar bills at us.

I was driving and looking over my shoulder at the same time. "Hell, nah! He's pays you to be his damn mama. Shit, that's crazy!"

"His mother died when he was a little boy. I guess he misses having a mother figure in his life," Peaches replied around a snort.

I shook my head as I turned at the next corner. "And I thought I had seen and read it all. You know this shit is gonna end up in one of my books, right?"

"We know." Danielle advanced the film in the camera and I heard it rewind. "I'm taking this right to the one-hour photo tomorrow."

"Before I drop y'all off, I'm going to take this tape over to Tommy's so he can get it copied and distributed. Wait 'til the first lady sees this shit."

"Ooh, I will definitely be at church on Sunday." Peaches gave his usual throaty, goofy laugh and we joined right in. It was too hilarious for words. After a while, we grew quiet and listened to the Caribbean sounds of Sean Paul blaring from the radio.

"You think Reverend Brown is gonna mess with Kayla?" Danielle asked.

I pondered that thought for a minute. He wasn't supposed to know we were in the closet videoing him, but now that he knew, the first person he was going to contact was Kayla. There was no way I was getting her mixed up in this shit. "I'll ask Tommy to go and pay him a visit." I picked up my phone and while I drove I told my boy everything that went down. He agreed to grab two of his boys and go by and see if he could catch Leroy before he left the house. Relieved, I still thought it would be a good idea if I went and hung out with Kayla just to make sure. I turned my car at the next corner and noticed the white Impala waiting for the light to change. "Danny, isn't that your car?"

"Where?" She broke her neck trying to look through the windshield.

Peaches started laughing. "Yep, and that's Nita's sticky-finger ass behind the wheel."

"Hell, nah!" For the right price, Nita could steal anything out of the store, and I do mean anything.

"Nae-Nae, turn this car around now!" Danny was hot and seconds away from blowing a fuse. I drove to the corner, then after looking both ways made an illegal U-turn in the middle of the street and zoomed up to the corner. I watched the Impala make a left turn and I would have also made the light if it wasn't for some slow-ass Volvo driver in front of me who chose to stop instead of running the yellow light.

"Dammit! Move!" Danielle screamed. She was pissed and I don't blame her. Her man had stolen her car and now had his ghetto-fabulous-ass mama driving it.

As soon as the light changed, I started blowing my horn so the Volvo would hurry and get out of the way. Luckily, they pulled over and I zoomed past the car and down the road.

"Which way did she go?" I asked, looking in both directions. She was nowhere in sight.

Peaches pointed straight ahead. "There she is, in front of that Expedition!"

Following his directions, I spotted the car a couple feet ahead. I drove through a yellow light and followed the car as she made a right at the next corner.

"His mama wasn't allowed to drive my car while we were together so I don't know what makes him think she can drive it now with her non-driving ass. He's got life twisted!" Danielle

kept mumbling on and on about the rent-to-own company calling her house asking her to let Nita know her furniture payment was past due. Drama—like I said, she can't live without it.

Nita pulled into the housing project and parked outside a
beat-up-looking unit. Some girl with her butt on her back came
out and climbed in.

Peaches was starting to get excited in the backseat. "That's
Ron's sister, Carmen. She ain't nothing but a crackhead."

I pulled up alongside the Impala and Danny rolled down her
window.

"Uh, excuse me, Nita, but that's my car you're driving."

Nita's do-rag-wearing ass looked surprised, then pissed.
"Nah, it ain't. Dis Ronny's ride," she said angrily.

"How you gonna tell me whose car you're driving? You and
Carmen would want to get out of my car," Danny demanded,
her neck rolling.

"I ain't got time to be gettin' in the middle of y'all mess,"
Nita said with a look of disgust. "You gonna have to take dat up
wit' my son later. I just got my food stamps and we fin to go grocery shopping." She peeled off down the road and by the time
I reached the end of the corner, Nita was lost in the dust. We
were sitting there, engine idling. I'll have to admit, I was cracking up.

"Girl, you're always in the middle of some ghetto-ass shit!"

Danielle was shaking her head. "I don't know why I always
get the rejects." She reached for her phone. "He's got life twisted
if he thinks he's not comin' up off my car." I guarantee you
she's calling Ron.

Peaches clicked his tongue. "Nita and Carmen shop at
Moser's."

I glanced over at Danielle. "You want me to drive over and
see if she's there? While they're inside shopping you can hop in
your car and take off."

"Nah, as triflin' as his mother is, I can't do that and leave her
stranded."

"Why not? She can catch a cab."

Danielle shook her head. "Nah, don't worry 'bout it. I'll get it later."

"Whatever you say." I pulled off and listened as she and Ron argued on the phone. Danny didn't want her car back because as long as Ron had it, she still had a connection to him.

Chapter 17

Renee

After I dropped Danielle and Peaches off, I went over and hung out with Kayla until Tommy called and said that he had "put fear in that nigga's heart." Knowing Tommy, he made Leroy shit his pants again. I was cracking up and tried to give Kayla the details, but she put her hands over her ears and refused to hear anything else after I mentioned that big-ass diaper. I don't know how she can sit back and feel sorry for him after everything he has done to her, but Kayla has a forgiving soul just like Big Mama. Nevertheless, Kayla did agree to view part of the tape when the copies are made. I was relieved to hear that she'd had the locks changed. We played a couple of hands of Uno, then I headed over to drop the tape off. After shooting the bull with Tommy and his boy Pooky, I headed over to the hotel. The day had worn me out.

When I got back to my room, I glanced down at my cell phone and realized I had one missed call. I pressed VIEW and turned up my nose when I read the name displayed: Paul Perry.

I dropped my keys and phone on the dresser, then removed my shoes and lay back on the bed. I wasn't sleepy. Not yet. My mind was racing with too many thoughts. As much as I tried to clear my head, Paul was still on my mind. His call reminded me that staying with John wasn't the only thing Lisa had asked me to do.

I remember staring out the window of her room, hoping to hold it together while pleading with my sister not to ask that one thing of me.

"Renee, you've got to make peace with him so you can move on with your life."

Her words still echo in my mind. I remember telling her she was wrong. Paul no longer had a hold on me. But she didn't believe me. In a weak voice, Lisa told me only hours before surgery that I had to find a way to forgive our stepfather.

To me, forgiving him was like saying it was okay for the way he had treated me, as if it was no big deal. But that wasn't the case. It wasn't as simple as someone stepping on my feet or forgetting to send me a Christmas card and then saying I'm sorry. It just wasn't going to be that easy to forgive. What I had experienced, what I had felt—it took years to get there.

As a child, I was blamed for everything. That was pretty much the way it was, growing up with him. Lisa was his favorite and my brother, his only biological child, could do no wrong. I never knew my real father. He was murdered when I was very young. My mother was rarely home and when she was, she was always on the phone or too busy to care. She was mentally ill even then, but I was too young to understand. Besides, Mama was so pretty no one wanted to admit that something was wrong with her, including Big Mama. Then she started drinking and picked up the crack habit and there was nothing we could do for her then. I haven't seen her in years. I love her and think about her often, but I just don't have room for any more heartaches in my life.

It was bad enough that I grew up with a mother with a habit and a mental thing going on. Bernice had an excuse. She was sick and there was nothing she could do for me but go get help, which she had tried countless times and failed. But Paul, my stepfather—that's a different story. He didn't have an excuse for turning his back on me. It was as if the day he divorced my mother, me, his stepdaughter, was no longer his problem.

It's funny how I've suppressed so many things about my past

and still can't remember, but there are certain things you never forget. It's sad. It really is, and when I sit back, thinking about it, even now I want to cry. Those should have been the best years of my life. Instead, they're too painful to even think about. Growing up with not one but two dysfunctional parents is something no child should have to endure.

I remember when my parents were still married. Mom was working at the hospital—I can't remember doing what. So after Paul got home from his accounting job, he was stuck watching the three of us. Bedtime was at eight o'clock. Even if the sun was still out, we had to bathe and get in the bed. Lisa and I shared a room, so we'd slide into our matching twin-size beds and talk until we both drifted off to a better world in our dreams. On one particular night, I remember Paul was working late—it was tax season and everybody was trying to make that paper. Mama had to leave for work early, so she had put us to bed and left around seven. Paul was due to get home before eight. I remember being asleep, dead to the world, when I felt someone yank me out of the bed. I startled to bright lights and Paul standing all up in my face, screaming and yelling. My heart was hammering in my chest. I was about nine at the time, half-asleep and scared out of my wits because I had no idea why he was yelling at me. All I did was lie there and think, *What did I do this time?*

It took a while but I finally realized Paul was yelling at me because he had forgotten his house key, and I didn't hear him knocking at the door. Can you believe that shit? It was my fault. It was the dead of winter in Chicago. Realizing he didn't have his keys, he started banging on the door, but no one came. After a while, he went to one of the neighbors to use their phone. A long time had passed before Lisa heard the phone, got up, and answered it. She then went down and let him in. Next thing I know, he's screaming and hollering at me. Not my brother, who was still sleeping peacefully in the other room. Just me. Come on. I was a little girl. And what I couldn't understand was how the hell it was my fault that he locked himself out and I didn't hear him banging at the door. To this day I haven't forgotten that night or the way he treated me, and I never will because I've never slept that hard again. I'm too afraid to.

The last time I saw Paul was at Lisa's funeral. Afterwards, we had a big dinner at the church we attended with Big Mama while she was alive. I was joking with John about Deacon Davis falling asleep during the funeral and how loud he was snoring before his wife shrugged him with her elbow. I mentioned that he sounded a lot like my husband. Then my stepfather had the nerve to get all in my Kool-Aid.

"I know my daughter ain't talking about the way someone snores."

I rolled my eyes and John laughed. "The way Renee says it, she doesn't snore."

"That girl could keep Snow White awake." Paul chuckled, rumbling his big belly. "I remember one time I was locked out." He turned to me, eyes dancing with amusement. "You remember that time I worked late and couldn't get in?"

How could I forget, I wanted to tell him. It was one of the most traumatic times of my childhood, I wanted to scream. Instead I sat back and listened as he told John the story. I wanted so badly to yell at him about how he had made me feel. But I didn't because it was Lisa's funeral and it would have broken her heart. She wanted so badly for me and Paul to make peace and get along. But it isn't that simple. I just can't forgive him for turning his back on me. He chose to be my father, not the other way around. I didn't ask him to put his name on my birth certificate. But he wasn't there when I needed him.

A tear slid from my eye down to the pillow as I remembered Bernice walking out on us and coming home to find that disconnection notice on the door. Paul drove down from Chicago to pick up Lisa and my brother but not me. I wasn't welcome in his house. I was barely seventeen, but it didn't matter. He took them and left me behind. I had no choice but to move in with Mario's crazy, young ass. Here I was, going to high school and working two part-time jobs. No more running track. No more hanging out with friends and being a teenager. Instead I was cooking, cleaning, and washing his dirty drawers. My senior year was a nightmare. Mario used to knock me up the right and left sides of my head because I wanted to still be a child and hang out with friends and make my own decisions, but he was so possessive and crazy, all I could do was obey his rules. But what could I have done? I had nowhere else to go, and was too ashamed to complain. In the meantime, I tried to maintain my relationship with Lisa and Andre, but Paul refused to let me call his house. I rarely got to see them, yet Lisa wants me to make peace with Paul because now that he's going to church, he's a changed man. Well, if he'd changed that much, then he would have picked up the phone by now and apologized to me for not being a father when I needed him most.

I rolled over on the pillow and stared up at the ceiling. I don't know why I let him still get to me. All I know is I'll never treat my kids that way. I try to give Tamara and Quinton everything I never had growing up—adequate clothing, family time together, and love. Lots of unconditional love.

I think about Andre and the way he blames our mother for ruining his life. He thinks Paul is pitiful, but my brother doesn't hold anything against him. Andre and I have never been close. He calls every once in a while and I remember to send him a Christmas card, but other than that neither of us have made much of an effort to be closer. Now that Lisa's gone, you would think we'd cling to one another, but that's not the case. The only people I have in my life are John, the kids, and my friends. For someone who everyone thinks has it all, my life is pretty pathetic.

Chapter 18

Danielle

Danielle pulled into her driveway. For once, all of the lights were off and everything was quiet. With Ron out of her life and Portia gone for two weeks, her house would be exactly the same way she left it. This morning, she'd put Portia on a plane to Memphis to visit her oldest sister, Constance. She'd been visiting her aunt every summer since she was five, and even though she was pregnant, she still insisted on going. On the ride to the airport, they had discussed the baby and her decision to keep it. Although the last thing she wanted to be doing was raising another baby, Danielle was strongly against abortions. Nope. She might as well get ready to take on the role of grandmother while Portia finished high school. While driving, she had wanted to call her sister and give her a heads-up, but Portia objected, insisting on telling her auntie herself.

Danielle climbed out of her car, feeling like she had the weight of the world on her shoulders. She knew that the very second Portia told her aunt she was pregnant, Constance would blow her top and was going to be calling her just so she could chew her out. Constance believed that since she successfully raised three girls without a man, her younger sister could at least manage to do the same with just one child.

Her stomach grumbled and Danielle placed a palm across it. No more tacos for her. She still couldn't believe she'd come barging out of the closet, rushing to use the toilet while Reverend Brown was getting his poopy diaper changed. She smiled despite the pain in her stomach. She had seen some wild, kinky stuff in her life, but that one took the cake. She and her girls would be laughing about that for a long time.

After entering the house, she went to the kitchen and removed a bottle of milk of magnesia from the refrigerator and took a swallow. While leaning against the counter, she remembered the look on Reverend Brown's face when they stumbled out of that closet. Laughing, she took another swallow. The moment was priceless. She knew it was wrong but she actually felt good about what they had done to Leroy. He deserved it. Tommy was certain to have that tape circulated around the church in no time.

Her doorbell rang. She put the bottle back in the refrigerator and went to the door. It was Calvin. "Hey."

"Hey, yourself. I was in the neighborhood and saw your car so I thought I'd stop and see how you were doing."

Stepping aside, Danielle gestured for him to come in. "I was just getting ready to curl up on the couch. So come on in and make yourself at home while I go and change into something a little more comfortable." The jeans she was wearing were too tight for comfort around her belly. Danielle went to her room, her heart beating a mile a minute. Despite the fact he used to date Renee, she wanted him and she wanted him bad, and maybe part of that was because she knew her relationship with Ron was now over.

After taking a quick shower, she slipped into a pair of cotton low-ride shorts and a wifebeater. She generously spread scented mango lotion on her legs and arms, then walked back into the living room, where Calvin was laughing at something on television. Whatever the program was, it was quickly forgotten when he spotted her coming down the hall.

"You smell good," he commented as she flopped down on the couch beside him.

"Thanks." Danielle curled her legs beneath her and pretended to be watching television, all the time aware that he was staring at her.

"If I'm not mistaken, I think I saw someone driving your car this afternoon. A woman?"

She groaned. "Yep. That's Ron's mama. I saw her, too."

His brow rose curiously. "And you're okay with that?"

"No," she began around a heavy sigh, "but I just don't feel like dealing with them right now. I've got too many other things on my mind."

"Anything I can help you with?" Calvin patted his thighs and signaled for her to drape her legs over them. She did and he reached for her feet and began to massage them.

"Portia's pregnant," she announced with an exaggerated sigh.

"What?" he stalled from massaging before starting again. "I'm sorry."

"Yeah, so am I."

"Who's the father?"

She shrugged. "I don't think she knows, which is sad. She's wants to keep the baby."

"How do you feel about that?"

"I don't believe in abortions, so I'm okay with that."

"Good. Neither do I."

"Between my mother and me, we can help her take care of the baby so she can graduate from high school."

"That's going to mean a lot to her. She might not realize it now, but she will eventually."

Danielle nodded and pushed a strand of hair out of her face. "I want her to have a chance out here. You can't do much of nothin' without a high-school diploma, even working at McDonald's."

"Tell me about it."

"I really want her to go to college, but that's only if she still wants to go."

"What's her father saying about this?"

Danielle looked him straight in the eyes. "He's pissed off and blamin' everything on me, like I can watch her every hour of the day. When I told him she decided to keep the baby, he wasn't too happy about the idea. The thought of teen pregnancy is embarrassing to him. Anyway, after he got done screaming, he has agreed to help."

"I can't blame him," he commented while stroking his chin. "If she was my daughter, I'd be upset and looking for the muther-fucka responsible."

"That's exactly what he said."

"Can you blame the man?"

Danielle thought about it a moment. "No," she finally admitted. "I don't blame him at all."

"So now that I'm here, what can I do to make you feel better?"

"Just keep doing what ya doing."

He kneaded the balls of her feet. Danielle leaned back against the cushions of the couch and got comfortable. "Mmm, you've got skills."

"That's not all I have."

She chuckled softly and closed her eyes.

"You know I like you, right?"

She nodded. "Yes, I know."

"How do you feel about me?"

She opened her eyes and looked over at him. His Adam's apple was moving up and down while he waited for her answer. "I like you even though you used to mess with my girl."

"That's was over ten years ago. Renee wasn't thinking about me then and she definitely ain't thinking about me now."

True. She couldn't resist a smile. Renee had probably screwed three dozen men since her relationship with Calvin. "Actually, she could care less."

She didn't miss the hint of excitement that lit his eyes as he said, "Good, then that means we don't have anything to worry about. I ain't gonna lie—I like you, Danielle. I want this to be more than a sexual thing between us."

"So do I, but I'm just getting out of a bad relationship and need a little time to get my head on right."

"Okay. But don't keep me waiting too long."

Danielle settled back on the couch again. "I won't," she said with a smile.

"Good. In the meantime, let me give you something to think about." He slid from beneath her legs, then lowered on top of her and crushed his mouth to hers. With a moan, Danielle wrapped her arms around him and gave in to the moment, enjoying the kiss. Finally, Calvin came up for air and stared down at her. "Mmm, I can definitely get used to this."

So can I.

Chapter 19

Kayla

Hearing a knock at the door, she looked out the window and spotted Jermaine's car in her driveway. *Dang!* She knew it was just a matter of time before he showed up.

Slowly, she stepped back, hoping he hadn't seen her. The reason she had parked her car in the garage was so no one would know she was home.

"Kayla, I see the curtain moving so I know you're in there."

Dang! That was a stupid move. There was no way she could let him see her. The swelling had gone down, but her lip was still cracked and there was a dark bruise underneath her eye.

"Kayla, please let me in. I'm worried about you. Tina told me you were in a car accident. I just want to make sure you're okay."

Kayla lowered her eyelids and felt guilty for lying. It had been a week since her rape and she hadn't been to work since. Instead, she had called her boss and lied that she had been in a car accident and was too beaten up to come in. *Lord, forgive me.* At least she hadn't lied about being beaten up, although instead of hitting the steering wheel, she had been hit with Leroy's fist.

Her pulse quivered. Leroy had been calling her every day begging for her forgiveness, and said that if the Lord could forgive him, then why couldn't she? She was so tired of him using the Bible for his own twisted purposes. Thank goodness she'd had a locksmith out to her house, because the night after Renee had videoed him while hiding in the closet, Kayla had heard his unsuccessful attempt at trying to use his key before he started banging on the door and acting like a fool. Why couldn't he just leave her alone and let her be happy?

Another knock at the door startled her. "Kayla, baby, please talk to me. I've been calling your house and you've been ignoring my calls."

It was true. She had been. Taking a deep breath, she turned the lock on the door and peeped out around the chain.

"I'm fine, Jermaine. Just not up for company right now."

He gave her a sad smile. "How are you feeling?"

"A little sore."

There was a long pause before he said, "Can I come in just for a few minutes?"

Hearing the pleading in his voice, she hesitated for a moment. "I don't want you seeing me this way."

"Kayla, you are beautiful to me no matter what has happened to your face."

Tears pushed to the surface. He was so kind. What had she done to deserve someone like him in her life?

Sensing her reluctance, he quickly added, "I just want to make sure you're okay, then I'll leave. I promise."

She closed the door long enough to remove the chain, then stepped aside so he could come in. After shutting the door, she turned around and met the look of compassion on his face.

"Oh, baby. I'm so sorry," he mumbled before holding out his arms to her. Without hesitation, she moved to him and buried her face against his chest. Jermaine held her close to him.

He pulled back slightly, stared down at her battered face, then pressed his lips firmly to hers. Kayla wished she could freeze this moment forever.

"Come sit down." He took her hand and moved over to the couch and took a seat, pulling her down beside him. "Now, tell me what happened."

She swallowed. Here she goes, lying again. "I was riding in the car with uh . . . Renee, and she tried to make a left turn and someone was trying to make a right and they slammed into her rental car." *Lord, please forgive me, but Renee owes me.*

"Thank God you're okay."

"I told you I was okay. Just need a couple of days for the bruising to go down."

"Did you hurt anything?"

Yes, my pride. "My side is sore. I think I have a couple of bruised ribs but I'll be fine."

"I know you're fine, but how are you doing?"

She couldn't resist a grin. It was her first in days. Somehow she felt like a load had been lifted from her heart. Jermaine was definitely good for the soul.

The phone rang, startling her. She ignored it. Her daughters had gone down to the lake with her mother and she had just talked to them. The only person who had been blowing up her phone was Leroy, and he was the last person in the world she wanted to talk to.

"You want me to get that?" Jermaine asked after the third ring.

She quickly shook her head. "No. I don't feel like talking to anyone right now."

Jermaine reached up and stroked her chin. "Tell me, what can I do to make you feel better?"

"Just seeing you has made all the difference."

"Good. I'm here for you whenever you need me—all you have to do is call."

"Thanks."

He shook his head. "You just don't know how much you mean to me, do you? Kayla, I'm crazy about you. I have been since the first day I met you, only you've never seemed to notice a brotha. I've never asked you this before, but are you involved with someone?" At her silence, he continued. "I assumed that you were and figured if you wanted me to know, you would have told me. Well, now, I'm going to be up front with you, I'm tired of waiting and I need to know if I even have a chance before I start putting my feelings out there."

She closed her eyes and willed away the tears. If he had asked her that a week ago she would have politely told him she was involved, but her life had changed so much in such a short period of time. "No, I'm no longer involved with anyone." There—she said it. And to her surprise, it felt good to know that she was finally going to put the past behind her.

"I'm glad to hear that." Leaning forward, he pressed his lips to hers in a single kiss, then pulled back and gazed at her surprised face. "How about a comedy? I got one in the car I had picked up from the video store last night that I haven't had a chance to watch. Watching it with you would be a lot more fun. I could sit here and hold you in my arms."

She nodded. "I would like that very much." Pleased with her answer, he went out to his car.

Kayla glanced down at her black slacks and simple white blouse. Renee was right. She was definitely going to have to do something about her attire. Quickly, she went over to the small bathroom behind the kitchen and checked her appearance. Every time she looked at her face in the mirror she wanted to cry. She stared at the stranger whose face was bruised black and blue all over. Surprisingly, Jermaine had not been turned off by her appearance. A smile creased her lips, just knowing that for once a man saw her for who she was on the inside.

The telephone rang. Kayla went over to the phone in the kitchen and read the Caller ID. It was coming from the church, so it couldn't be anyone but Leroy. Reaching up, she turned off the ringer. She hated to do that, but for one day she just wanted to have peace and quiet and a chance to think about something other than Leroy and what he had done to her.

Jermaine returned and she walked into the living room just as he turned on the television. "My boy said this is supposed to be extra funny."

She met the look of amusement on his face and got a warm

feeling inside at his attempt to cheer her up. "Good, I could use a good laugh."

He slid the movie into the DVD player but before he could turn it on, the local anchorwoman, Katherine Smith, popped onto the screen with a newsflash. Kayla peered at the television and gasped when she realized the tall blonde was standing outside of Mt. Carmel Baptist Church.

"*. . . Reverend Leroy Brown was brought in for questioning regarding a videotape police received of him and what appears to be a teenage girl. The police refuse to comment any further at this time except to stress that as of right now, Reverend Brown isn't being charged with anything. He's just being questioned about the identity of this young girl. Right before we were getting ready to air this segment, a copy of the tape was anonymously handed to the station. Now we are about to show you a clip from that tape, but I want to warn you that it isn't suitable for children.*"

Kayla cringed as the video she'd refused to see popped onto the screen. She'd know Leroy's room anywhere. There he was, wearing . . . *oh, my, God* . . . Renee wasn't lying, a diaper. He was walking around the room pretending to be a baby with a pacifier in its mouth.

"What the hell?" Jermaine mumbled as he sat down on the couch beside her.

"*If anyone knows the identity of this young girl, please call the police. This is Katherine Smith with Channel 8 News.*"

Kayla hurried from the room and made it to the bathroom just in time to throw up.

Chapter 20

Danielle

"Danielle, you have a call on line two!"

"Okay." She set the IV bag down on the counter, then walked around the triage window to the phone. It had been nonstop since she arrived this morning, one delivery after another, and she was glad for a few seconds to stop and rest her feet. She moved over to a chair behind the desk and lowered herself, reaching for the receiver and pressing the flashing red button. "This is Danielle."

"Danny?"

"Mama?"

"Chile, where have you been? I've been calling you on your cell phone all morning."

Danielle groaned inwardly, then lowered her head. Leave it to her mother to track her down. "I've been busy. What's so important that it couldn't wait?"

"It's all over the news. Reverend Brown was arrested this morning. Chile, he's a pedophile."

"What?"

"Yes, there's some video floating around with him forcing some sweet teenage girl to change his diaper!"

Oh, no. Danielle swung around in the chair. "Mama, where did you see this video?"

"Sister Stevenson came over and showed me a copy she got

from Sister Jefferson, who got it from Brother Jamison. Chile, it's sad, so sad. There are also snippets of it on the news. I'm sure it's going to make the front page of this evening's paper."

"Danielle, Mrs. Rogers in room three needs to go to the bathroom," the receptionist announced.

"I'll be right there," she replied, then removed her hand from the mouthpiece. "Mama, I got to go."

"Okay, but on your way home, pick me up a *Tribune*," she cried just before she hung up the phone.

She couldn't believe it. The video that wasn't supposed to go any further than the church had circulated through the community. To top it off, they thought Peaches was an underage child. Danielle tossed her head back and laughed—then, after several seconds, she stopped. As much as she wanted to laugh at the entirely ridiculous situation, she couldn't. Leroy was in serious trouble. *That damn Renee.*

Chapter 21

Renee

I stepped off the plane and walked through the Baltimore-Washington International Airport, not at all happy to be home. I've got a book due at the end of the summer that wasn't close to being done, so I had plenty to do. But now that the kids were gone, being home meant John was gonna want some cootie-cat on the regular and I truly was not in the mood. What bothered me the most was that I went to Columbia with the intention of getting me some and didn't get a damn thing. It's crazy. David turned out to be a joke. I even thought Vince, my St. Louis connection, would have been able to break me off a piece before I had to catch my plane, but as timing would have it, he was in Memphis visiting his mother.

I turned my phone on and immediately my voice mail went off. I put the phone to my ear and quickly went through the messages.

"Nae-Nae, girl, I got some more drama for you. You will never guess what's going on! Call me the second you get this message."

I deleted Danielle's call. I just wasn't in the mood for any more drama. The last couple of days had taken a toll on me. Danielle dating Calvin. Ron stealing her car. Leroy beating up Kayla. And Danielle and I videoing his sexual fantasy. The last couple of days I've been having this bad feeling about what we did. I don't know why, since I didn't even like Leroy's no-dick

ass, but at the same time I was second-guessing my hasty decision to ruin his ministry. We all have skeletons in our closet, but
there are some that are better off never coming to light. His in-
discretions were going to destroy the lives of so many, including
his children. That's the part that bothered me the most. I could
care less about him and his anorexic wife, but it's the kids I didn't
want to hurt. We should have just let Tommy and his boys beat
Leroy's ass instead. I'll have to give Tommy a call when I get home,
but I'm pretty sure it's already too late. I had already given him
the tape and Danielle had given him the pictures two days ago.

Pushing the thoughts aside, I called John to let him know I
had landed, then went to the carousel to retrieve my bag. As
usual, by the time I moved outside, I spotted the Escalade waiting. The second John spotted me, he climbed out of the SUV
and came around to retrieve my bag.

"Hey baby," he said, then leaned down and pressed his dry,
cracked lips against mine. I quickly returned his kiss, then climbed
into the car.

Soon we were on our way. I leaned my head back against the
headrest and closed my eyes. Again, I wished that Vince had
been in town so that I could have got me a taste of what he had
to offer, because it was a lot better than what I was going to get
when I got home.

"You hungry?" John asked.

I shook my head and squeezed my eyelids tight. He was so
nice that I felt bad about not wanting to be bothered by him.

"You okay?" I heard him say.

I had to bite my tongue to keep from snapping at him. "I'm
fine. Just tired."

"I figured as much. I've got a surprise for you."

My eyes snapped open. "What?"

He reached over and squeezed my hand. "Wait and see."

I forced myself to do just that, although I hate surprises and
he knows that. It wasn't long before I found out his surprise.
He pulled into the parking lot of the Ramada Inn and killed
the motor. "What are we doing here?"

"I thought we'd spend the night together."

Oh, hell nah! "Don't you have to work tonight?"

Dragging his eyes from the road, he smiled over at me and said, "I took the evening off to spend it with my lovely wife."

It was obvious he had gone to a lot of trouble to arrange a romantic evening alone with his wife. I just wished that woman was someone other than my black ass, because I felt sick to my stomach.

John climbed out and while he retrieved our bags from the back, I made myself get out of the vehicle and follow him through the lobby. When we moved past the registration desk to the bank of elevators, I knew then he had already been in our room, waiting for my arrival.

"I wish you had told me you were planning this. I would have taken a nap on the plane," I scolded as we rode up to the fourth floor. I was trying to come up with every excuse that I could.

"Once we get in the room, if you want to take a nap, that's fine."

He always says that shit, then the second I climb under the covers and close my eyes, he's on my ass like flies on shit. I followed him off the elevator and down the hall to a room on the left. John unlocked the door and signaled for me to enter first. Reluctantly, I stepped inside, and there, sprawled across the bed, was a dark chocolate brotha holding his dick.

My eyes widened with surprise. He was hung like a horse. "Oh shit! Sorry, we're in the wrong room," I said, although I couldn't take my eyes off him.

I started to back up, but John moved up behind me and whispered close to my ear, "No, we're not. This is my surprise for you."

I forced my eyes off the brotha long enough to look at John like he had lost his damn mind. "What?"

He lowered the bags to the floor, then took my hand and led me over toward the bed. "Renee, meet Shemar."

Sexual chocolate smiled, then licked his lips. "The pleasure is all mine."

I looked from him to John and back again. "Okay, what's going on here?"

John wrapped his arms around me. "I thought we'd add a little spice to our marriage." He kissed my lips, then released me and turned to that sexy muthafucka on the bed. "Shemar, she's all yours."

"What the hell you mean, 'she's all yours'?" He had to make himself clear 'cause as horny as I was, *me ready to love 'em long time* and the last thing I needed was a big misunderstanding.

John moved to a chair in the corner and took a seat before responding. Humor shimmered in the depths of his eyes. I could tell he was getting a big kick out of this whole thing. "It means that Shemar is going to make love to you while I watch. Do you have a problem with that?"

I stared at him, surprised by the dominant tone of his voice. Where was my husband, and who the fuck was this man that the Martians sent back on Earth to replace him? Meanwhile, Shemar rose from the bed and stood in front of me. I gazed up at him and swallowed the large lump in my throat. Did he just say this fine brotha was going to fuck me while he watched?

I'd be lying if I said I didn't like what I saw, because I did. He was tall with chiseled abs. Dark hair covered his chest in an inverted V that traveled down to a long, extra-thick dick that was hard enough to knock a muthafucka out cold. Shemar was looking at me and I knew that before I left that room, I'd be getting some of that. I couldn't move and just stood there while he slowly unbuttoned my blouse. He then removed my bra. My nipples were hard as rocks and screaming, "Suck me."

"Play with her nipples," John commanded.

Oh, yes, please do! Obediently, Shemar reached up and rolled my nipples between his fingertips. His sudden warm touch took me so off guard, I gasped. John never played with my breasts this way and I was loving it. Speaking of John, I was starting to feel guilty, so I glanced over at him. Hell, nah! I couldn't believe it! John was watching hungrily while slumped in the chair, stroking his crotch. He smiled and licked his lips and I mouthed, "thank you" and blew him a kiss.

Shemar unzipped my shorts and I wiggled out of them before he motioned for me to lie across the bed. I followed his orders and lay on my back, my body vibrating with anticipation. He removed my red thong and within seconds was snacking on my honey-pot. I wrapped my legs around his head and rocked into his tongue as he dipped in and out. I was so turned on by the whole thing I was moaning and shit. For years I had fucked around on my husband, only feeling slightly guilty when I returned home. But here I was, messing around with a brotha right under my husband's watchful eyes, and he didn't give a shit. This was like a dream. That shit had me so turned on.

Rolling my head to the side, I watched John unbuckle his pants and reach inside for his dick. He stroked his erection with his eyes glued to the two of us. I wondered what he thought about me lying across the bed with my legs spread, and another man's tongue and hands arousing me in ways he'd never been capable of. But by the way he was beating off, John seemed to be just as turned on.

"Fuck her, dammit!"

Oh. My. God. Now John, that's what I'm talking about! Shemar quickly slipped on a condom.

"Mrs. Moore, I want you doggy-style."

He said nothing but the word. It was my favorite position, one that my husband had never been able to perform properly. Hopefully, John was taking notes. I got up on all fours. Shemar climbed up on the bed, then positioned himself between my legs. My heart was beating hard against my ribs as I felt him searching for the entrance into Kittyland. Without much time to prepare, he plunged hard, driving deep inside me.

"Yeah!" I cried out.

"Yeah, that's it," John hissed at the same time.

Oh, shit, he felt huge inside me. Had it been that long? He was spreading me, forcing me to take him deeply. I felt every thick inch of him. "Ooh, yes," I panted.

"There you go, baby," John crooned while he continued to watch and stroke his meat.

Shemar moved his hands to my ass, where he held me at just the right angle for his thrusts. I enjoyed every deep, deliberate stroke. I squeezed my muscles and gripped him tightly and it wasn't long before he began plunging harder and faster. It felt so good I wanted it to last but I had been deprived for too long.

"Ah, baby," I cried. "Oooh!"

"Yeah, baby," John moaned. "Take all that dick!"

Oh, I was doing exactly that. I was mindless with intense pleasure. The bed rocked. The headboard banged. I was screaming and Shemar and John were cussing. It was then that I noticed the camcorder on a tripod in the corner. I found myself staring into the camera, licking my lips. I looked over at John, who was working his meat like he was churning butter.

"Come here," I breathed. He definitely had earned a little TLC.

He rose from the chair and moved over and stood in front of me and I took his dick in my mouth. I'd be damned if I was going to be the only one in this home movie.

Chapter 22

Danielle

The past couple of days have been unbelievable.

Danielle leaned back on her couch, gazing across the room at the bouquet of flowers Calvin had delivered to her job at lunchtime. Never in her thirty-seven years had a man ever done anything that nice for her. She had always been the giver and rarely ever received, and if she did get something, it was because she had given the muthafucker the money to buy it for her.

Curling her legs beneath her, she took a moment to reminisce about dinner the night before. Calvin had taken her to CC Broiler's, fabulous dining at its best. She had driven by the restaurant numerous times before, but had never eaten there. The restaurant didn't even open until dinner, so she should have known it was going to be just that good. Calvin ordered appetizers, then suggested they have lobster and prime rib. Both at the same time! She couldn't believe it. He had even ordered a bottle of Moët. While eating, they had such a good time talking and laughing. She told him about her career as a nurse and her dreams to go back to school and become a registered nurse. He shared his life as a university police officer. When the meal finally ended with dessert, their waiter arrived with the bill. Instinctively, she had reached for her purse like she had always done after dinner with some wannabe. Only this time her date stopped her and shook his head.

"Baby, I got this," Calvin had said.

It made her feel good inside 'cause a man had never been that good to her before. Never. Ever. Ever.

Afterwards she invited him back to her house to show him just how much she had appreciated his generosity. They shared a bottle of wine while she talked about her failed marriage and the future plans to raise her grandbaby. He listened without interrupting and she appreciated every minute of his company. When she reached down inside his pants and told him they could go up to her room, Calvin had declined, saying he wanted to take things slow and get to know her better first before they moved to that level.

Instead he made her lie back on the couch and remove her panties. She did as he requested. Already she was wet. Calvin slowly lowered onto his knees on the rug in front of the couch. A lopsided grin was on his face. Using his hands, he spread her legs and pushed her thighs apart. Goodness, she couldn't bear for him to tease her. He let his lips rub across her skin. Her coochie quivered. Her nipples hardened.

"Oh!" she cried and swayed slightly when he brushed lightly against her sensitive clit. Calvin clamped two hands on her hips and pulled her forward.

"Relax, baby. All I want to do is make you feel good," he said huskily. "Just let me taste it."

He moved his mouth between her legs and dipped his tongue between the soft folds. Back out. Then in again. Her body trembled. Her clit pulsed. Cum ran down her inner thigh. He spread her folds apart and opened them, then explored her thoroughly with his mouth. She moaned and lost herself in the excitement of it all. For several minutes all she did was lie there, keeping her gaze fixed on his face while he delved deeply into her. He draped her thighs across his shoulders and slid her lower on the couch. He then resumed eating her out. Lightly his tongue raked across her pink flesh and she jerked and wiggled in his hands, but he held her still for his mouth. Using his hand, his thumb found her clit and circled it. She sucked in a breath at the erotic gesture.

"Oh, yeah," she purred. She brought her hand to his head, then slid her palm down over to his earlobe and across to his forehead. He licked and sucked until her body was rocking with sensation. Suddenly, she gave a sharp cry and her hands clasped his head. She trembled violently and erupted in a sharp orgasm. "Yesssssssss," she cried, then collapsed on the cushions.

Calvin rose and lifted her into his arms and settled her comfortably in his embrace. Her eyes were still closed. He waited patiently until she opened her eyes again.

He kissed her forehead. "How do you feel?"

"Wonderful," she said and laughed bashfully as she buried her face against his chest. He continued to hold her while they finished their wine, then went home. This morning at work, flowers had arrived with a note saying that he looked forward to seeing her tomorrow. Tonight he was working second shift.

So this is what it's like to have a good man.

Yeah, she was going to love every minute of it.

She was trying to think of something she could do to show Calvin how much she appreciated him being there for her when she needed someone to talk to, when her thoughts were interrupted by a knock at the door. She swung it open and was surprised to find Ron standing on the other side. You would think after throwing a brick through her window and stealing her car, he wouldn't be stupid enough to show his face around her house. She figured wrong. Not only was he here, but he'd brought the Impala with him.

"What do you want?" she asked with her hand on her hip.

Ron didn't appear the slightest bit fazed by her nasty attitude. He stood there grinning and licked his thick lips. "Yo, sexy, can we talk?"

"We ain't got nothin' to talk about," she said with a roll of her neck. But even as she said that, she stepped back so he could step in. Ron brushed passed her, leaving a trail of Sean John cologne.

Danielle closed the door and struck a pose. "Okay, what do you want to talk about?" she demanded.

"I came to bring yo' car back. I felt bad about everythang."

She rolled her eyes. "You should."

"I'm sorry, boo. But when I saw you with ole' dude, I lost it."

"You were with that hoochie, but did I trip? Nah," she replied, rolling her neck with each word.

"That's 'cause you don't love a nigga anymore."

She simply folded her arms and looked him up and down, and despite everything he had done to her, she liked everything she saw. Ron was fine as hell. He reminded her of Allen Iverson. Same complexion. Six feet. A buck-eighty soaking weight. Cornrows. Tattoos starting at his neck and working their way down to his wrist. His good looks was the reason why she always looked the other way when he forgot to pay a bill or slipped money out of her purse when she wasn't looking. Well, not anymore. She glanced over at the bouquet of roses for strength. There was no way she was going to let him know that she was turned on just by looking at him.

"Well, thanks for bringin' me my car back. Now you can leave."

He licked his lips again. "Can I holla at you a minute? I mean, are you really ready to call it quits?"

"You did that yo'self. I'm tired of the games, Ron. I want to be appreciated."

"I do 'preciate you." He pouted and actually looked hurt.

She folded her arms across her chest, determined to stand her ground. "I want a man to take me out sometimes."

"You saying I ain't never taken you out?"

"McDonald's don't count."

"Ai'ight. Well, I can do that. I got a job today at Square D. I start on Monday."

"Good for you. Now you can leave."

"Damn, Danielle. Why you always gotta have an attitude wit' me?"

"Why? I don't know. It may have somethin' to do with the fact you haven't done anything but use me since we've been together."

"And I'm tryin' to make up for that. Come on, boo. I'ma treat you right this time. Tell me you don't miss me." He reached out and tried to touch her face but she slapped his hand away.

"I don't miss you," she lied.

He looked so good in his jeans hanging off his sexy ass, showing the waistband of his Sean John boxers, and that damn wifebeater emphasized his muscled arms. She took a deep breath and prayed for strength.

Ron took a step closer. Danielle took a step back.

"It's over between us. The sooner you realize that, the better off we'll both be."

"I'm not ready for it to be over." He was so damn sure of himself. She wasn't even about to go there with him. Watching him lick his lips again was not helping matters.

"Well, it's too late. You've had your chance."

"Boo, how about givin' yo' man another chance at keeping that pussy happy?"

She swallowed. "Sorry, but somebody took over that job." She hoped by telling him somebody else was hitting it, he would just leave. *Yeah, right.*

"I betcha he ain't puttin' it down like I do."

He sounded confident. Danielle rolled her eyes. "I'm not even fin to go there wit' you."

"'Cause you know it's true. Don't you?"

She wasn't even about to justify that question with an answer. The truth of the matter was nobody knew how to lay the pipe like Ron did. He even ate pussy like a champ. She didn't know what Calvin was going to be like because she hadn't had him yet. But at least he could eat some pussy.

"Come on, boo. Tell the truth. You miss this dick, don't you?"

"Would you just shut up!" she cried, then took a step back. He was driving her crazy. Her coochie was purring, "Yes, yes!" while her mind was saying, "Hell no!" If she didn't get him out of here quick she was going to do something stupid.

His expression told her he wasn't happy with her attitude. "I can't believe this shit. I try to come over here and show you how sorry I am, and all you want to do is throw shit in my face about you bein' with anotha nucca. I'm not gonna stand around here and listen to this shit."

"Good, then there's the door. Oh, and give me back my car key."

"You right. You right." He made a show of pulling his keys out of his pocket and removing the large black one and holding it out to her. "Here. Take it."

Danielle reached for the key and as soon as she grabbed it, Ron pulled her against him.

She tried to push him away. "What are you doin'?"

He held on tightly to her waist. "Just one last kiss and then I'm out."

She hesitated. His eyes looked sincere enough. He lowered his head and pressed his thick, juicy lips to hers and it was all she wrote. *Damn*, she ain't had none since she had put him out.

He reached down and unbuckled his pants and they fell to his ankles and his dick sprang straight out at her, and before Danielle knew it, she was holding it in her hand. They just don't make them like that anymore, she thought as she stroked the head with her thumb. By the time he took her hand and led her up the stairs, she was more than ready.

They stepped into the room and he moved over to the night-stand.

"Why you turning on the light?" she asked.

"'Cause tonight we gonna fuck with the lights on."

His cocky manner made her coochie wet. She loved when he talked dirty. Danielle took her clothes off and watched as he did the same. Uh-uh-uh. *Damn, that nigga is fine.* It was why she put up with so much shit, because good dick was hard to find.

He gripped his hammer in his hands. "You wanna give all dis up?"

The back of her throat went dry. All Danielle could do was stare as he stood there stroking his meat.

"Come here, boo." The endearment always made her feel funny inside.

She moved over to stand in front of him and he turned her around so that she was facing the full-length mirror behind her door.

"I want you to see what I'ma 'bout to do to you."

She watched as his large, chocolate hand skimmed to the swell of her breast, cupping it so softly. She cried out.

"Keep looking."

She sucked in a breath and returned her gaze to the mirror. Ron gave her a look of satisfaction that he had power over her body. He squeezed her nipple between his thumb and forefinger and she fought a mix of pain and pleasure that caused liquid to flow down her inner thighs. His fingers slipped down her stomach to her clit where he teased and played. She moaned and her head fell to one side but she refused to close her eyes and miss a single thing. Nothing felt as good as when Ron touched her. Heat built as he stroked her nipples.

"You belong to me. Can't no otha mofo make you feel like I do."

His fingers slid down past her clit and slipped inside. Starting with two fingers, he quickly moved up to four and she watched with fascination as she stretched to accommodate him. She cried out. Against her behind, she felt his dick jerk.

"Lean over."

She leaned over the foot of the bed and stuck her ass out. From where she was, she could see every thrust inside her wet coochie. She was able to watch him move in and out. Watch his fingers as they caressed her clit. She watched him watch her. Seeing the look on his face in the mirror pushed her on.

With each thrust, he slapped her ass until she was crying from a combination of pain and pleasure. Oh, it was so good.

For two years his dick was the only thing her pussy knew. The only one it loved. She tightened her muscles around him, drawing him further in. He slammed into her and she could hear his balls slapping against her ass. She came hard, exploding around him. He came with a long, hard moan and she quivered one more time, then squeezed her muscles and milked him dry.

Ron pulled out, then carried her over to the bed. "I told you this pussy belongs to me."

Danielle curled into him and sighed. What he said was so true.

Chapter 23

Kayla

"This is nice."

"Yes, it is."

Candles. Soft music. Wine. Kayla had never experienced anything like this before.

Jermaine had invited her to his home for dinner. She had raced home, quickly ordered the girls a pizza, and had showered and changed, then hurried south of town. Dinner was fabulous. His house was beautiful. Two-story. Five bedrooms. Thirty-five-hundred square feet. The forty-five-foot-long living room was separated from the formal dining room by a two-sided fireplace. After dinner, he had given her a tour of his house and they were now both sitting on a basil-colored sectional sofa, listening to John Legend's mesmerizing CD. She had kicked off her patent leather flats and had sunk her toes into his plush, barley-colored carpet. Yep. Jermaine's upscale home was not only beautiful, but peaceful, making the evening perfect.

Well, almost.

Her cell phone vibrated for the third time since her arrival. She reached for her phone and glanced down. It was Leroy. He'd been calling her every thirty minutes, and the only reason why she hadn't turned her phone off was because the girls might need her.

"Is everything okay?" Jermaine asked curiously. Once again, he had noticed her staring down at her phone.

"Yeah, I'm fine," she replied, forcing a cool, relaxed smile.

"You don't look fine. Are the girls okay?"

"Yes, everything's fine." He was so nice. She didn't know how in the world he could be interested in her. Jermaine deserved far better, because right now the only thing she seemed to be able to think about was Leroy. He was the last person she wanted on her mind, but because she was so overcome with guilt, she couldn't think about anything else.

As president of the local chapter of the NAACP, minister of the largest church in the city, and a prominent member of the community, the videotape circulating around the city with Leroy and that fag was slowly destroying his career. She felt sorry for him. Kayla knew she shouldn't—not after the way he had beaten her like she was stupid. But she did, nevertheless. How can we pray to the Lord for forgiveness if we can't do the same?

Kayla was certain there was something they could do to help him. For the last couple of days, she had been unsuccessful at reaching Renee by phone. Danielle said she didn't want to have anything else to do with that mess. However, she did mention, to her surprise, that the underage woman in the photo was Parnell Carver, a.k.a. Peaches. Kayla had to pause the tape just to make sure it really was little Parnell from around the way, and almost fell out when she discovered it was. It was one big fiasco. She had gotten a copy of the tape from her mother, who had gotten a copy from her sister, who'd gotten a copy from—

She shook her head. It was just too crazy for words. The Mt. Carmel Baptist Church was having an emergency business meeting tonight to discuss the matter.

Kayla took a deep breath and willed her heart to cooperate. Despite everything, she still loved him, and it hurt knowing that Leroy really was on the down low. It was one thing for her friends to tell her, but seeing it was an altogether different matter. What was even worse was the embarrassing video with him wearing a diaper while playing with a freakin' rattle! Her heart actually went out to Darlene. Surprisingly, she didn't feel vindicated at all. Instead, she felt sick to her stomach because she, as well as her two friends, were to blame for this whole fiasco.

Her phone vibrated, bringing her mind back to the present. She glanced down at it. Discovering it was Leroy, she finally decided to just turn off the ringer.

Jermaine reached over and cupped her chin with his hand, then tilted her head so that she was looking directly at him. "Hey, it's okay. You can tell me whatever is bothering you."

"It's nothing, really."

"Sure there isn't some other man you'd rather be with?" He said it like a joke, but the expression on his face said he was serious.

Kayla leaned forward and pressed her lips to his, then met his intense gaze. "The only place I want to be is right here with you." She hugged him, then gazed over his shoulder and out the window. Her body was here with Jermaine, but her heart and mind were a million miles away.

Chapter 24

Renee

Sex was off the hook. I'd always wanted dick and was now getting it left and right. John had taken the week off and we were meeting different brothas on the regular. It was like swinging, only John wasn't participating. His goal was to find the right dick for me.

"Did he make you feel good? Did he fuck my wife right?" He jacked off his dick with each question.

We were home in our bedroom after spending the evening with Dante. Dante's thing was so big it was like two dicks in one. I don't think I've ever seen a head that fat before. But it turned out to be another satisfying evening that ended with me sucking off my husband.

"How good was he? Baby, tell me all about it."

I slipped off my clothes and lay on the bed beside John. As I explained how it made me feel being fucked by another man, my husband listened and continued to jack off. Talking about it, I was growing horny again. I reached down, offering to stroke his dick for him, but he pushed my hand away.

"Keep talking. Tell me how he made you come."

Closing my eyes, I thought about Dante fucking me the way my husband never had and described it in detail. By the time I had finished, John's balls were so tight, he flipped me over onto my back and rammed his little dick inside of me.

"Does he make you feel like Daddy?" he asked while trying to mimic the move.

"No," I denied. "Nobody makes me feel like you." I lay there moaning as he plunged in and out until he finally came.

Afterwards, I lay there, expecting to feel lucky to have a man who allowed me the privilege of being satisfied by another man with his blessing. Instead, it bothered me. I don't know what exactly was bothering me, but it was something. I guess I could consider this new twist in our sex life research for my next erotic novel, but damn, how much material does one woman need?

Long after he was asleep, I moved quietly across our cherry-wood floors to my large office on the first floor. I had a lot on my mind and the best thing for me to do when I needed to clear my head was write. I moved over to my desk and lowered myself into my chair and pulled up a blank screen and quickly started typing everything that had happened this week. The sex. My husband's excitement. Remember what I said about the Martians? For real, that's not my husband sleeping upstairs. Listening to the sound coming from the room above me, I shook my head. I think I'll take back the part about that not being my husband. Don't nobody else sound like a chainsaw while they sleep but him.

After I got done writing, I paused and took a moment to read over the three pages of notes. Here I was, getting everything I wanted, and yet I still wasn't happy. What's wrong with me? I reached for a Kleenex. I've been crying a lot more lately. Is my life that twisted up? Well, let's see. I have a mother with issues, a stepfather who hates me, a sister who's dead, and a husband who gets off on watching other men fuck his wife.

Overhead I could hear the ring tone on my cell phone. I didn't feel like running up to see who it was and John was sleeping too hard to notice. Thirty seconds later, my office phone rang. I glanced down at the Caller ID then answered it.

"Hey, Danny."

"I figured you were in your office."

I cleared the frog in my throat. "I felt inspired," I said, trying to pump laughter into my voice when I wanted so badly to cry.

"I just wanted to let you know that Peaches came forward today."

"Oh good," I said with a sigh of relief. Danielle had called me after Leroy had gotten arrested to tell me they thought Peaches was some teenaged girl. After I had got done laughing because the situation, although serious, was pretty funny, I called Tommy and asked him to handle it.

"You should have seen Peaches. He was on television sucking that shit up. You would have thought he was auditioning for a commercial or something. Batting them fake lashes, puckering his lips. Girl, it was a straight comedy show."

I twirled the phone cord around my finger and laughed. "Dang, I wish I could have seen it."

"Nae-Nae, now you know my mama recorded that shit. I'ma have to send you a copy."

"You do that." I reached for a peppermint in my candy dish on the end of my desk. "I still can't figure out how that tape got all over town."

"Easy. This is Columbia. A town this small where everybody knows everybody, it's bound to happen. This has been the talk of the town. Everybody stoppin' and asking, 'Have you seen the videotape?' and now that everyone knows Peaches is a man, not a woman, Nae-Nae girl, it's 'bout to go bananas up in here!"

I tossed my head back with laughter. "Oh, shit. I ain't thought about that. Hell, nah! Girl, that is crazy." Shit was about to hit the fan for real, for real. I sobered as a thought hit me. "Did Peaches say anything about who recorded the video?" The last thing I needed was my name in the paper.

"Shit, no! I said he gave an Academy Award performance. He acted like he had no idea anyone was taping them and he was so hurt and disappointed that someone would be putting Leroy's business out in the street. He pursed his lips and stared at the camera at the exact moment they zoomed in on his face, and said in that high-pitched voice of his, 'There's a lil' freak in all of us.' Girl, I fell out!"

"You are lyin'!" I screeched.

"Nope. He sure did. Ask my mama."

I chuckled softly and leaned back in the chair. This was some funny shit and you betta believe it's going in one of my books. "Okay. We need to come up with a plan. What are we going to say when it comes out that we made that tape?"

"Humph! Why can't we just tell them the truth? Nah, I guess if we do that, then they can get us for breakin' and entering."

"We didn't break shit. Remember, we had a key."

"Yeah, but then we'll have to admit where the key came from."

I pondered that thought for a moment. "Okay, how about we let Tommy handle it? All he's got to do is tell Leroy we have pictures with him and John-John that's gonna leak out if he runs his mouth."

"What? You got pictures of him with John-John?"

John-John is another fag we know from the old neighborhood. "Nope, but he doesn't know that. A while back, John-John and his sister Ursula were blackmailing him for money. She had taken pictures of him from the closet and milked him for some money before handing over the originals. So I know he doesn't want that story to get out."

"Damn! You never told me about that. You would think after that happened he would have been smarter about who he's dealing with."

"Or at least checked the closet first." We both exploded with laughter. "I'm glad that everything is going okay down there. Have you talked to Kayla?"

"Yeah, and she and Jermaine are still kicking it."

"All right!" I was so glad she had finally moved on.

"Anyway, I got my fingers crossed that we've seen the last of Reverend Brown in her life."

"So do I." I don't know why, but long after we got off the phone, I kept thinking about that saying, "it ain't over until the fat lady sings." While sucking on that peppermint, I had this strange feeling that no matter how much we tried to protect Kayla, it wouldn't be enough.

Chapter 25

Danielle

Danielle woke up to light kisses along her arm. She opened her eyes and found Ron smiling down at her.

"I didn't think you'd ever wake up." He brushed his lips across her forehead.

"What do you expect when you're trying to wear a sistah out?"

He rolled on top of her and pushed her thighs apart. "You betta believe I'm branding this pussy so all them otha mofo will know this's mine." He pushed up into her again and she held on for the ride. Danielle gasped as he plunged deeper. It didn't get any better than this. For the last three days, she had been dodging Calvin's calls. She tried not to take Ron back but with all that he had swinging between his legs and the way he worked it, he made it almost impossible to resist. He was a damn good lover and he knew it. It was that cocky attitude that made the dick feel even better. This time he promised to treat her right.

"Whose pussy is it?" He pulled all the way out.

"Your pussy."

"And don't you forget it." He slid in hard and fast.

The rhythm increased and she spread her legs wider apart. Danielle wanted to make sure she felt everything he had to offer. It wasn't long before she was screaming.

"Ron!"

"I'm right here, gurl. Givin' you all this dick." He draped her legs over his shoulders and plunged hard. Within seconds, she came, then he started moaning hard and came shortly after. Ron collapsed on top of her. She lay there for the longest time, running her hand along the muscles of his back. She loved this man. She didn't want to, but she did. Even after all the shit he had put her through. She must have lain there for the longest time, because the next thing she knew, Ron was snoring.

She pushed him off of her. "Ron, get up!"

"What?" he answered in a sleepy voice.

"Get up. I got errands to run."

"Handle yo' business." He rolled over onto his stomach.

"You got to go."

"What?" He sat up in the bed so quickly, she jumped.

"You heard me. I got to run to the store and do a few other things before I go back to work tomorrow and you've got to go."

"I can't believe this shit. I thought we were getting back together."

Her brow rose. "Who told you that lie?"

"You mean to tell me I've been fucking like a champ for nothing?" He huffed and looked clearly insulted. "I can't believe this shit! I thought since you let me lay all up in that pussy, we were tryin' to work shit out."

"That doesn't mean you can stay here." He was getting on her nerves. "I'm not gonna lie. I would love to work things out if that's possible. But we can do that with you stayin' at yo' mama's house."

"I don't want to be with Mama. I want to be here wit' my boo."

He climbed out of bed and her eyes strayed down to his dick. She licked her lips. Ron was hard again. He noticed her looking, then started moving toward her with that sexy-ass smirk on his face.

"Come on, boo. We'll be here waiting when you get home." He had his dick in his hand, waving it at her so she'd know who *we* were.

Her pussy pulsed and she felt herself weakening. Just as he reached her, she stepped out of his reach and into the adjoining bathroom. "Don't even try it. This time, things are gonna be my way or not at all." She met his eyes and didn't dare look down, because if she did there was no way she could stay strong and resist some more good loving.

"I love you, boo. I ain't tryin to run no game. All I'm tryin' to do is show you things are gonna be different. It took seein' you wit' another mofo for me to get my head right. From now on, I'm gonna treat my girl the way she 'posed to be treated."

She would be lying if she said that what he said wasn't music to her ears. Not to mention, it turned her on. Ron stood there looking sexy as hell. He had a body that put Tyrese to shame and a dick long and hard enough to slay a dragon.

"Let's talk about this tonight."

With a smile, he rushed forward and scooped her into his arms. "Whateva it takes, boo. Now give yo' man some." He carried her back over to the bed and she got up on all fours. He positioned himself but before sliding in, she heard him ask, "Can I keep the Impala so I can come over later?" He then slid in just the head and waited for her response.

She was dying to feel him again and would have agreed to just about anything. "Yeah," she replied as he slid all the way in and out, and in. They found their rhythm and she was seconds away from coming when she heard a car pull into the driveway. She peered out the window, not knowing who it was until the car opened and her sister climbed out. Her daughter hopped out on the other side.

"What in the world?" she mumbled with her brow drawn. Portia was supposed to fly back tomorrow. Why in the world did Constance have to come back with her?

"Ron, stop. Portia and my sister are here." And she looks mad as hell.

"Baby, how you gon' ask me to stop?"

"Easily." She pushed him away, then rolled over and quickly slipped on a pair of shorts and a t-shirt. She slid her feet into a pair of flip-flops and finger-combed her hair. Portia opened the door just as she was coming down the stairs.

"Hey Portia, how was your trip?"

She shrugged. "It was okay."

"Okay?" Danielle began as she lowered onto the couch. "You usually have a ball. Hey, sis. I didn't know you were coming up."

Constance turned to her with dark, piercing eyes. "I wasn't, but when Portia told me she was pregnant, I wanted to talk to you in person."

She curled her feet beneath her. *Oh boy, here we go.* "Yeah, whassup?" She followed the direction of her eyes to Portia, who was fidgeting nervously in the corner.

"Portia, have a seat and tell your mama," Constance said as she lowered onto the couch.

Danielle looked from one to the other. "What?"

Before her daughter could answer, Ron came down the stairs. "Hey, Portia. Whassup?"

Constance looked from Portia to Ron. "Don't tell me this is Ron?"

Danielle rolled her eyes. Her sister never understood her insatiable taste for younger men. "Yeah, and he was just leaving."

Constance jumped from the couch and blocked Ron's path. "Oh hell, naw! He's not going anywhere."

"Yo, Danielle, you betta get this bitch out my face."

"Bitch?" Constance swung at him, but Ron managed to duck just in time. "I got yo' bitch!" She balled her fist and was ready to throw down, but Danielle jumped in between the two of them. "Portia, tell your mama what you told me."

Portia played with her hands.

"Tell her!" Constance demanded.

"Tell me what?"

Constance looked at Ron, shooting him evil dart eyes. "That she's pregnant by this young muthafucker standing in your living room!"

What? Stunned, Danielle looked from Ron to Portia, who refused to look at her. This couldn't be happening. "Ron, is this true?" she asked in a panicked voice.

Ron started laughing. "Yo, I don't know what she told you, but that girl is lyin'."

"You're the liar!" Constance screamed. She was still struggling to break free of Danielle's grasp, swinging and kicking, but she wouldn't let her go. "Sweetie, tell ya mama the truth!" she demanded.

Portia just sat there, crying and squirming on her seat.

Ron was frantic. "Boo, please . . . I ain't touched that girl."

Danielle looked from one to the other. "Portia, is what Constance said true?"

There was a long pause before she finally choked out, "Yes."

Ron punched the air. "Why you lying!" He looked at Danielle and pleaded for her to believe him. "Baby, why would I touch some little girl when I got you?"

Portia sprung from the chair and propped a hand at her waist. "You did touch me. You told me you loved me and that we were going to be together." Tears were trailing down her face.

"Man, quit lying!"

Danielle couldn't believe this was happening. Not Portia and Ron. Constance broke free and swung her fist at Ron's head, hitting him on the side of the face. They started shouting obscenities at each other and as soon as her sister lunged at Ron a second time, she jumped in. "Stop it!" Danielle screamed.

Portia rolled her eyes. "Mama, I know you're not gonna believe that thug over me!"

Danielle closed the gap between them and when she was close enough, reared her hand back and slapped the shit out of her. Portia fell to her knees, holding her face. "I'm tired of the lies. Get your hot ass out of my house!" Tears welled the bottoms of her daughter's eyes.

"I know that's right!" Ron shouted triumphantly. He then moved beside Danielle and put his arm around her waist. She jumped away.

"Don't touch me because I don't have anything to say to you, either." Backing up, her eyes traveled from one stunned face to the next. "By the time I get home, all three of you had better be out of my house." Danielle retrieved her purse from the table and rushed out the door.

Chapter 26

Kayla

This has to be heaven.

Kayla couldn't believe how much her life had changed. Jermaine definitely had to be a gift from God. On Sunday she went with him to his church in Jefferson City. She couldn't begin to explain how proud she felt walking in on his arm. She saw the looks of surprise and the whispering, and she knew they were wondering how someone who looked like her could be with someone like him. Well, believe it. She walked with her head up and her man on her arm as she and her girls took a seat near the front of the church. In a few short weeks, she had realized that she didn't need a minister to be happy. She could be content with having a spiritual man in her life who simply loved her and her daughters.

On Monday, they both took the day off from work and went to Six Flags with the girls. Kayla had never been big on riding anything other than the Ferris wheel; just being there was more than enough excitement for her. They dropped by Applebee's on the way home and had a wonderful dinner. Jermaine laughed and joked with Kenya and Asia and she could tell they really liked him.

That evening after the girls were too tired to do anything but hang out in their rooms and watch television, she and Jermaine sat on the couch holding hands and kissing.

"Thank you for a wonderful day."

"The pleasure was all mine." He brushed his lips against hers again and she felt her toes curl. They kissed and kissed some more. He tasted so good and made her feel even better. There was no question about it; this was the happiest time of her life.

"What are we going to do when we get to work tomorrow?"

He squeezed her hand. "Act as natural as possible. I'm not ashamed to be with you nor do I feel like I have to hide how I feel. At the same time we don't need to broadcast our business out in the street."

Kayla smiled and tears itched at her eyes. She'd never had an open relationship with a man before. They'd always slipped in the back and left the same way, pretending not to know her until they wanted some more. It had been the same with Leroy. Lies and more lies about a life together that was never going to happen, when all she had ever hoped and prayed for was a good man who loved her back. She believed that she had finally met that man.

They watched a movie together with him lightly caressing her arm. Around midnight, she checked to see if her girls were asleep. They were. She returned to the living room and took Jermaine's hand.

"Follow me." She led him upstairs to her bedroom. After weeks of putting him off, she was finally ready to take their relationship to the next level.

Chapter 27

Danielle

At the end of her shift, Danielle clocked out, then moved through the hospital toward the parking lot at the far west of the building.

She hadn't spoken to Portia or Ron in days. Portia was staying with her mother, and Ron? She didn't care where he was. She didn't know who was telling the truth, and right now she was too hurt to care about either of them. The only thing she did know for sure was that Portia had a tendency to cry wolf, which made the situation that much more difficult. As she walked across the parking lot, she remembered the look on Portia's face after she'd slapped her. She didn't mean to hit her, but after everything her daughter had been putting her through for the last several weeks, Danielle felt the slap was well deserved.

Moving toward her Durango, she noticed Calvin was leaning against it, waiting for her. *Oh, no.* She had been avoiding his calls for days. He obviously wants an explanation, she thought with a heavy breath. Her life definitely couldn't get any more complicated. As she neared, Danielle observed his attire and couldn't help comparing Calvin to Ron. He was dressed in simple blue jean shorts that showed off massive thighs and calves and a red button-down shirt that was neatly tucked in and secured with a black belt. On his feet were sneakers, a brand she didn't recognize. The two men were so different. Ron wouldn't be caught dead in anything but white Ts, a new pair of Air Force Ones, and a pair of sagging jeans. He always managed to look sexy as hell.

"Hey," Calvin said as she came within several feet of him.

"Hey yourself." Danielle removed the heavy purse from her shoulder and rested her hips against the car. She then looked up into his piercing brown eyes and for the longest time, neither of them said anything.

"What've you been up to?" he finally asked.

She shrugged. "Nothing."

"Nothing?" Calvin chuckled with disbelief. "Nah, it must be something, because I haven't heard from you."

Danielle reached for her keys and opened the driver's side door, then stuck her key in the ignition and lowered her windows to allow some of the heat to escape. "I've been busy."

"Busy with the janky-ass nigga who stole your car." It wasn't a question.

Looking over at him, she shrugged and replied, "So what if I have?"

"Is it like that?"

"Listen," Danielle began, then paused and took a deep breath. The last thing she wanted was to get into it with him. "I'm tired and I really don't have time for this right now. I'll talk to you later."

"Hey, wait a minute," Calvin said and caught her by the arm before she climbed onto the seat. Reluctantly, she turned around and looked up at him while he spoke. "I think I deserve at least an explanation. Come on, Danny. I thought we were trying to do something here."

He was right. It wasn't fair to leave him hanging. "I like you, Calvin. I really do, but I've got a lot on my plate right now and this isn't a good time for me to be starting a new relationship."

There was another long pause before he released his hold. "Thank you. Now, was that hard? All you had to do was just tell me the truth. I'm a lot more understanding than I look."

Danielle gave him her first smile all day. "Thanks, Calvin. Lately, I don't know if I'm comin' or going."

Reaching up, he caressed the side of her face. "How about you get rid of some of that stress and go out to dinner with me tomorrow night?"

She gave him a skeptical look. "I don't know."

"They're having a lobster fest at Red Lobster."

His words made her smile.

"Girl, you know you want to say yes," he said, and nudged her lightly in the arm.

He was right; she did want to say yes. With all of the drama in her life, having someone treat her to a night out was a breath of fresh air. She knew it was unfair to be using him for a free meal, but what the hell. "All right. It's a deal."

Calvin looked pleased by her answer. "I'll pick you up tomorrow around seven."

As soon as Danielle got home, she went straight upstairs and took a shower. By the time she came out, Ron was sitting on her bed. "What the hell are you doing in my house?"

"Yo, we need to talk."

Rolling her eyes, she moved over to her underwear drawer. "We don't have anything to talk about."

He grabbed her arm and pulled her around so she was facing him. "Yes, we do."

Danielle stared up at his pleading face. "Okay, then talk."

"Yo, I didn't touch Portia. I swear."

She watched his eyes, hoping to see something that would make her think that this time things were really different. Instead the expression resembled the same one she had seen many times before when he promised to have his baby mamas stop calling her house. "I don't know, Ron. I just need some time to think this over. Why would Portia say something like that if it wasn't true?"

His arms snaked around her and she found herself flush against his solid body. The only things keeping them apart were a bath towel and his clothes. "I don't know why, boo. I think she's just jealous of what we got. Her baby's daddy must not want nothin' to do wit' her." He lowered his head and pressed his forehead against hers. Danielle continued to stare up at him, hoping what he was telling her was true.

"I just need some more time," she said softly. Taking a deep breath, she tried to ignore the yearning rushing through her veins.

"I swear to you, I'm tellin' you the truth. I ain't messed with that girl. Why, when I've got you." Tilting his head, he pressed his lips to hers and unconsciously her arms moved around his waist while he deepened the kiss. She loved this man, and despite Portia's many flaws, she loved her as well.

Ron's hands skimmed the tops of her breasts and it took everything she had to pull away from him. Breathing heavily, she glared at him and said, "Get out. When I make a decision, I'll let you know."

He gave her a long, hard look, then wiped his nose with the back of his hand. "Yeah, ai'ight," he replied, then turned on his heels.

Chapter 28

Renee

We pulled up in front of the hotel, and John eagerly climbed out and handed the valet the keys to his Escalade. Quickly, I checked my lipstick, and by the time he walked around to my side and opened the door, I was ready.

I stepped out of the car and moved up the circle driveway, dressed to impress in a form-fitting white spandex dress and matching stiletto heels. My hair hung loosely around my face. I looked good and smelled even better. I've got to give my girl Kimora Simmons her props—her Goddess perfume is the bomb.

"This is going to be great," John said, eyes gleaming with excitement. If anyone should be excited, it was me. I was going to sample some new dick. Any woman who chose him was going to get the short end of the stick, no pun intended. However, I'll have to admit he looked good. Tonight's event is an all-white affair, and he was dressed in a white linen outfit offset by a thick gold chain.

As we took the elevator up to the seventh floor, I tried to hide my excitement. It had been three weeks since that afternoon in the hotel with Shemar. Since then, I'd seen him six times. Each and every time he'd satisfied my insatiable need for dick. John's always sitting there watching, but if he doesn't care that another man is banging his wife better than he could, then neither do I. Tonight we're attending a swingers' party. Invitation only, compliments of Shemar. I couldn't wait to see what Philadelphia had to offer. It's strange, but a few weeks ago, I was unsure of this new lifestyle that John had introduced me to, but after a while I had warmed up to the idea. It is what it is. My marriage has gotten a whole lot better.

We got off the elevator and followed the sound of music coming from the end of the hall. A long table was set up outside the revolving nightclub on top where the party was being held.

"Names, please."

"Sasha and Donovan Hall." What? You thought we'd use our real names? Hell, no. I'm a published author and my husband is head of a major government project. We've got too much to lose if word got out that we're swinging. She handed us our badges and together we stepped into the room.

I walked in, expecting to see folks butt-naked and fucking in every corner of the room. Instead, everyone was standing around, dressed in white and looking damn good. No hoochie mama gear in the house. Shemar had explained that everyone in attendance was well off. No scrubs or lowlife muthafuckas were allowed to be here. If couples weren't pulling in at least six figures, then you weren't getting through the door. Last week, John and I had to complete a long application that had to be approved for membership. It was funny to see how many siddity muthafuckas were trying to get their freak on.

We walked around the room and I was disappointed not to see Shemar. Either he hadn't arrived or was already down the hall fucking someone else. John must have noticed the stares I was getting from some of the other couples, because he put his arm around me and pulled me proudly to his side. We stopped periodically to shake hands and introduce ourselves. There were quite a few bugaboos, but also several men that looked good enough to eat. I caught one particular brotha staring at me. There was a petite woman on his arm but I wasn't looking at her. My eyes were on him. Tall, in white pleated slacks and a spandex shirt that strained against the muscles in his arms. He was every bit of six-three and fine as hell. Damn, he looked tasty. I made certain to steer John in their direction.

"Hello," he said as we drew closer.

I held out my hand. "Hi, I'm Sasha and this is my husband, Donovan."

He shook both our hands. "Pleasure meeting both of you. I'm Tyler and this is my wife, Daphne."

I looked at the woman on his arm. Short, dark-skinned. With a pair of big-ass titties. She wasn't much to look at. I never understood how fine muthafuckas like him always ended up with the mud ducks when they could have anyone they wanted. Shit, I can't talk. Hell, I'm with John's homely ass.

John quickly shook her hand. "Hello. Nice meeting you both." Daphne licked her lips and gazed up at my husband as if she liked what she saw. Good. John could spend the next hour tweaking *her* damn titties for a change. That would give me a chance to be with Tyler alone without my freaky-ass husband watching. I looked up at Tyler in time to see him wink at me. I don't know how I knew, but just looking at him I knew his ass could fuck.

"We've never done this before," John admitted.

"Neither have we, but my wife and I have been curious for a while."

We found a booth in the corner and the four of us took a seat, ordered a round of drinks, and made small talk, discovering we had a lot in common. John was sitting beside Daphne and Tyler was next to me. An hour later, he was caressing my leg, his hand creeping higher by the second.

John rose. "We're going to go dance." He took Daphne's hand and escorted her out onto the floor, where he pulled her into his arms and the two started slow dancing. I felt a hand stroke my clit. I jumped and gazed up at Tyler.

"I see you're not wearing any panties."

His deep, robust voice excited me. "Should I have?"

"Not at all. Open your legs."

I spread my legs wider and he rubbed some more, dipping

two fingers deep inside my coochie while he stroked my clit. Shit, I ain't gonna even lie to you. The shit felt soooo good.

"You like me playing with your pussy?"

"Oh, yeah," I purred as I rocked my hips and met each of his strokes. I reached over and unbuckled his pants and removed his dick. Hell, yes! The brotha had a dick. It wasn't the longest thing in the world but it had depth and just enough length to reach my g-spot.

I spotted my husband and Daphne returning, so I released him and slid across the bench. Only minutes after they returned to their seats, Tyler suggested that we go on down the hall to their room. I was dripping wet and more than ready to get my freak on. John took my hand and we followed them. He was smiling and I could tell he was excited. My body shuddered with anticipation. We stepped into the room and took a seat on one of the beds while they sat on the other. There was a long, awkward silence before Daphne spoke.

"Why don't I come over there and you move over here with Tyler?"

She ain't say nothing but the word. I nodded, then eagerly moved over to the other bed and onto Tyler's lap. My husband and Daphne were the furthest things from my mind. Tyler was kissing me, and with his thick, juicy lips I must say the brotha had skills. I deepened the kiss and allowed his tongue to invade my mouth, then I met him stroke for stroke. Eventually, he pulled my dress up over my head, then his mouth closed around my nipple and my gasp quickly turned to a whimper as his teeth gently raked the little peak. Damn, he's good. No tweaking, no irritating, just plain old sucking. I leaned back and enjoyed his tongue swirling around one hard peak.

"Oh yeah," I moaned as he sucked the other nipple into his mouth.

He slipped his hand beneath my dress and skimmed his thumb between my thighs. I eased my thighs apart and one of his long fingers traced the creamy opening between.

"You feel that?"

"Do I? Oh hell, yeah." He stroked his thumb over my clit and my breath caught. "Oh, yeah!" He licked my nipples like a man trying to make a dessert last as long as possible. As if he wasn't already driving me crazy, one thick finger parted my lips, then drove deep. I closed my eyes and moaned.

"You're so wet."

Hell, he ain't seen nothing yet.

"I can't wait to sink my dick inside you."

For a long moment there was no sound but breathing as he twisted his fingers, then pushed inside me up to the knuckle. Pleasure raced down my spine with each magical stroke.

"Now I want to feel you come on my fingers," he said, then thrust deep inside me while simultaneously circling his thumb over my clit. I rocked my hips against his fingers. Desire radiated everywhere as he drove deeper with one, two, three fingers. I cried out. Hallelujah! His breath caught, then released a growl. "That's it. Let me feel you clamp down on my hand."

Within seconds, I came. The climax was explosive. I was rocking my hips back and forth, trying to take everything he had to offer.

Dazed and panting, I watched as he rose to his feet. Sweat rolled down between my breasts and my thighs were quivering with anticipation. I was still sitting on the corner of the bed. Towering over me, he took hold of the back of my head then looked down at me with a fierce expression on his face. "Open your mouth."

I looked at his dick, inches from my mouth, then leaned over and took the round head between my lips.

"Hell, yeah!" he groaned as I took as much of his dick as I could in my mouth. Hearing his reaction urged me on. I pulled back, swirled my tongue over the head, and he shuddered. I loved the power I had. I licked each and every vein snaking his dick, then swooped in again and sucked him in and out. I increased my speed and watched as his thighs rocked on either side of my face. Oh, yeah. This was going to be easy. I sucked harder as he pumped deeper inside my mouth. I put my hands at the base of his dick because I'll be damned if he was going to gag me with that thing. His body began to shudder when I heard moaning coming from the other bed. I released him and cum started spraying all over my face at the exact moment I glanced over to see Daphne down on all fours and John slamming his dick in her. She was howling like a damn dog. *What the hell?* I couldn't believe he was doing it doggy-style because he had never been successful with me. What was even worse was the fact that Daphne seemed to be enjoying it. I don't know why, but suddenly I was no longer aroused and was suddenly turned off by the whole thing. John enjoyed fucking a total stranger better than he enjoyed screwing his own wife. He couldn't do me dogging, but he didn't have any problem fucking that way with another bitch. The script had been flipped on my ass and I didn't like it one bit.

Chapter 29

Kayla

"Kayla, I'm getting ready to make love to you."

His words were like a breath of fresh air. *Make love.* She had dreamed and hoped for this moment when a man said those words and truly meant them. The day had finally come. If this was a dream, then she never wanted to wake up.

His lips traveled down across her breasts, where he stopped long enough to lavish each nipple thoroughly before moving to the other. Traveling down past her belly, she felt his hands as he tugged down her panties. Lifting up slightly, he eased them over her hips and down past her ankles, then tossed them aside.

"Spread your legs so I can see how badly you want me."

His directness made her clit clench. Oh me. Oh my. She opened her legs and could feel liquid sliding from her vagina. With a smile on his face, he leaned forward and tortured her clitoris with the tip of his tongue.

"Please!" she cried, begging for more. "Don't stop!" She wanted this moment to go on forever. He moved his tongue to the center of her, dipping and diving into her warm, wet center. She bucked against him. Breathing shallow, Kayla tried to fight the intensity. But it felt *sooo* good, she was powerless. She tried to maintain control but it was sweet torture.

Jermaine withdrew his finger, then inserted two. Withdrew

again and inserted a third deep inside her and stilled as her walls clenched around him.

"I want you in my life. I want you to be my woman."

At the impact of his words, her hips jerked. "Yes!" she cried.

He then leaned forward, replacing his hand with his tongue, and licked her up and down, spending a little extra time at her clit. No one, not ever in her thirty-eight years, had ever gone down on her and made her feel this good. Tears pushed to the surface.

"I'm crazy about you."

She rocked her hips against his tongue, wanting, needing. It was difficult to think and listen to what he was saying when all she wanted was for him to be inside of her. "Oh, yes, Jermaine. I'm crazy about you, too."

He moved between her legs, trembling with anticipation. His eyes darkened as he stared deep into her eyes. Moments later, he slid inside of her ever so slowly and she wanted to cry.

"Look at me," he asked sweetly.

Kayla opened her eyes and gazed up at his handsome face.

"I want the world to know how special you are to me," he whispered as he began to move. With each slow stroke, he kissed her nose. Her lips. Her forehead. She had barely had a chance to catch her breath when he rocked his hips back, then reentered her. Intensity began to build inside her and his thrusts became deeper. She exploded, rocking back and forth, and cried out his name. Jermaine plunged faster, then came inside her with a groan until finally his body collapsed.

"I love you," he whispered against her lips.

Kayla gasped, then searched his eyes, disbelieving what she had heard. "Did you . . ."

"I said I love you." He dropped a kiss to her lips. "Baby, I've been in love with you for a long time. You just never bothered to notice."

She started crying, bawling.

Jermaine rolled onto his side and pulled her against him. "Baby, what's wrong?"

"You're the first person who has said that who I honestly believe is not just telling me what he thinks I want to hear. I actually believe someone truly loves me."

He held her close, running his hand down her back, comforting her. "When I love, I love with everything I have. I don't believe in doing anything halfway. Who couldn't love you? You're beautiful with a good heart and you're a woman raised in the church. My mama always said you can't go wrong with a churchwoman."

She chuckled softly against his chest. It felt so good to laugh.

"Seriously, if you give me your heart, I promise I'll never do anything to hurt you."

Hours later, she woke with a smile on her lips. She curled into a ball and squeezed the pillow to her chest. *So this is what love is?* Jermaine had stayed long enough to make love to her a second time, kissing her from head to toe, paying close attention to the middle. He held her in his arms until she drifted off to sleep before heading home. *This is what it is like to be loved and appreciated by a man.* For the past couple of weeks, he'd been doing everything in his power to make her feel important, putting her needs first. God had blessed her with a good man. She had been praying for a long time and her prayers had finally been answered.

She inhaled, drawing in Jermaine's masculine scent. It was like a bad dream that she had finally managed to pull herself out of. Jermaine was loving, passionate, and truly wanted to be a part of her life. All the things Leroy never had been, at least not to her. She still found it hard to believe that Leroy was into kinky, weird sex. Diapers and spankings—who would have ever guessed that? Even though Peaches had come forward, everyone was still gossiping about him. The rumor mills were milking it for everything it was worth. Leroy was forced to resign his seat on several local organizations. It was bad enough they had thought Peaches was a teenager, but it was even worse now that the community knew he was having sex with another man.

Kayla closed her eyes and willed herself to go back to sleep.

Church was in a couple of hours and there was no way she was missing an opportunity to step into her heavenly father's house with a fine man on her arm. She had a lot to be thankful for. And she planned to sing praises to the son, the father, and the Holy Ghost for helping her to finally see the light. And for bringing a good man like Jermaine into her life.

Her body relaxed and she had just drifted off to sleep again when the phone on her bedside table rang. Kayla reached over and grabbed it by the third ring.

"Hello."

"Kayla."

Her eyelids flew open. "Leroy. What do you want?"

"I-I just called to say good-bye." His voice cracked. Her stomach clenched. Leroy was crying.

"Good-bye?" Surprise had suddenly changed to fear. "What do you mean, good-bye?"

"It means . . . it's over. I've been asked to leave the church. My wife left me. My friends have turned on me and almost all of my clients have canceled their insurance policies with me." His voice was thick with sorrow and she felt a pang to her chest. *What have we done?*

"I'm sorry, I—"

"No, you don't have anything to be sorry about. I brought all this on myself. As the Bible says, you reap what you sow."

Kayla sat up in the bed, stunned by Leroy's words. Never in all the years they were sleeping together had he ever taken the blame for anything wrong he'd done. In fact, everything had always been her fault.

"I just wanted to say good-bye." She heard the defeat in his voice.

Even though they were no longer together, she was still concerned for his welfare. "Where are you going?"

He hesitated. "I'm going home."

Something in his voice made her ask, "To Macon?"

"No. To my heavenly father."

Panic seared through her blood. "Leroy, what are you talking about? You know suicide is a sin. The consequence is eternal damnation."

"I can't continue like this. My life is over."

There was no way she could let him kill himself. His blood would be on her hands. It was her fault his life was ruined, not Danielle's, or Renee's. They had only been trying to help her.

"I think you need to pray about this. Tomorrow, things will be better," she reassured him, wanting him to believe that.

"Tomorrow, I'll be going home to face what the Lord has in store for me." There was a pause. "Good-bye." The phone went dead and Kayla sat there for the longest time, her mind racing with possibilities. Leroy wouldn't really take his life, would he? As a minister, he knew that would mean going straight to hell. She groaned. If she was in his shoes, she would probably do the same. She'd been shamed and humiliated all her life. Ms. Piggy. Fat Albert's sister. A father who didn't love her. Men used her. But for Leroy it was different. He had been admired and highly respected in the community. Baptized hundreds of folks' kids. Provided services to people he'd known all his life. Big house. Fancy car. Platinum credit cards. With all that gone, he had nothing left to live for except his faith, and it appeared that had been taken away as well.

In a panic, Kayla jumped off the bed and reached for her jeans. She then pulled her gown over her head and replaced it with a red t-shirt. She barely had her tennis shoes on by the time she grabbed her keys and dashed out the door. It was all her fault. If she had not gone out with the girls that night, she wouldn't have run into Jermaine and none of this would have happened.

That doggone Renee, and her need to feel vindicated. She should have insisted that she butt out. A few minutes ago, Kayla was willing to take all of the blame, but if Leroy died, his blood was going to be on all their hands. Kayla put her foot on the gas and headed south of town. "Please Lord, let him be all right."

She squirmed nervously in the seat as she drew closer to the secluded neighborhood. At the top of the hill, she pulled into his driveway, then used her keys to get in.

"Leroy!" she called as she moved through the house. "Leroy!" She panicked when she didn't find him in the bedroom or bathroom. Heading back down the hall, she had just stepped into the living room when a hand snaked out from behind the closet door, grabbed her hair, yanking her head back so hard, she thought her neck would pop.

"I knew you would come." Leroy snarled, then slapped her with his open hand. Kayla struggled to get free, but he had her head pulled back in an agonizing position. All she could do was brace herself when he slapped her the second time with the back of his hand.

"Why are you d—"

Before she could get it out, he released her head and threw a punch that busted her lip again and sent her flying across the coffee table. "You are so predictable," he said with a sickening grin as he spoke in a voice that was so calm it was scary. He raised his arm, prepared to back-hand her again, but this time Kayla managed to dodge the blow. Swallowing blood, she saw the crazed look in his eyes and panicked. She rolled off the table and landed on her feet, then quickly moved behind a burgundy recliner. From where she was standing, Leroy looked like a bull ready to charge at any second. Holding onto the back of the chair, she tried to keep her fears under control long enough to get away. Standing between her and the front door, was Leroy.

Leroy began to bob and weave. When he moved left, she went right. When he went right, she moved left.

"Why are you doing this?" she cried.

He chased her around the chair. "Because it's your fault. Everything that happened was because of you. You try to act like you're a God-fearing woman, but you're a whore!"

Her breath came out in short gasps. "I didn't mean for—"

Leroy grabbed her and she watched as his big hand came crashing down toward her face, sending her sprawling onto the floor. "I lost everything because of you!" he exploded. "My wife and my kids hate me!"

She screamed and rolled away and cradled the immense pain to her face. Her cheeks throbbed, her nose was swollen. She tried to get to her feet, but Leroy rolled her onto her back and climbed on top of her. He was cussing and quoting scripture at the same time. She fought him with all she had, but he had the upper hand.

The next blow hit her in the eyes and she swore she felt her eyeball pop. It hurt so bad she screamed and started crying. The second blow got her in the nose. Nothing could begin to prepare her for that pain. The third caught the side of her head. After that, he balled his fist up and the blows just kept coming, and coming, and coming. She kicked and screamed but no one was coming to help her. As he made hamburger out of her face, all she could think about was this was not the way she intended to die. What would Kenya and Asia do without her? A cry lodged in her throat. All these years, she had put Leroy first in her life—at times, even above her Lord and Savior, Jesus Christ. Kayla lay there, eyes closed, arms by her side, trying to make peace with God. When had she stopped fighting? She wasn't sure.

Leroy rose and towered over her. The look on his face reminded her of her grandfather, Reverend Sparks, only seconds before he was getting ready to beat her behind for acting up in church.

"See what you made me do to you?" Leroy accused as he reached for his belt buckle and unfastened his pants. "This is all your fault," he howled. She swallowed, preparing to take whatever punishment he had yet to dish out. Leroy kicked her in the leg, then the arm, and shoulder. She managed to curl up in a fetal position, trying to protect her head and disfigured face.

He reached down, trying to yank her jeans over her hips, and something told her to fight. She wasn't sure where the idea came from. She fought against the dizzy feeling in her head and the pain in her arms and legs, then took a deep breath. Counting to three, she kicked her foot out and got him right smack between his legs. With a howl, Leroy released her and buckled over.

Somehow Kayla found the strength to pull her body off the floor and moved as fast as she could through the house into the kitchen. She reached for the door, then struggled as quickly as she could to unlock it and get it open. Just as she turned the knob, Leroy grabbed her by the neck, pressing firmly against her windpipe.

"The devil made me do it." He wore a crazed look while tears streamed heavily down his face. Kayla struggled to get his hands from around her neck, kicking and moving until he had her bent over the sink.

She reached around frantically and felt metal, cool and sharp, against her fingertips. A butcher knife. She reached as far over as she could and grabbed the handle and swung the blade toward Leroy.

"Owww!" he yelled. Releasing her, he struggled with the knife that was sticking out of his shoulder. "I'm going to get you for this!"

Kayla didn't stand around. While he frantically tried to remove the blade from his body, she hastily moved over to the door, turned the knob, and fled. Peeling out of the parking lot, she almost crashed into another car coming up the street. The driver blew his horn with annoyance, but she ignored it and rushed down the street, breathing hard and crying at the same time.

"This is so unreal," she chanted as she headed toward home. She mopped the tears from her eyes and tried to maintain control, crying and staring out her rearview mirror. She couldn't believe Leroy had tried to kill her. She was shaking so hard her teeth chattered. All she wanted to do was go to sleep and start a new day that Leroy was no longer a part of.

Within minutes she was home. As soon as she got to her room, she pulled the bloody shirt over her head, then pulled her jeans off and went into the bathroom. Once under the spray of water, her body shook and she started crying again and the tears wouldn't stop.

"Lord, please forgive me, for I have sinned." She prayed until the water ran cold, then turned off the faucet and climbed out. She didn't dare look into the mirror, afraid of what she might see. Instead, she dried off, shuffled into her room, and slipped on a fresh pair of cotton shorts and a t-shirt. She then went down to the kitchen and retrieved a long knife and carried it up to her room and placed it under her pillow. In the back of her mind, she feared that Leroy might come to finish what he had started, and if so, she wanted to be prepared. She crawled under the covers and after tossing and turning, she finally drifted off to sleep.

Kayla felt like she had just gone to bed when she heard the doorbell ringing. She rolled over onto her side and ignored it, hoping whoever it was would take the hint and go away. However, the ringing changed to pounding on the door. "All right, all right," she grumbled as she slowly got up from the bed. Pain exploded through her body and she groaned. Leroy had definitely done a number on her. Kayla descended the stairs and moved to the door and looked through the peephole. As soon as she saw the two police officers standing on her porch, she was instantly wide awake. Reluctantly, she opened the door.

"Kayla Sparks?"

Puzzled, she looked from one to the other before answering, "Yes?"

"I'm Detective Garrison and this here is Officer Tatum," he said, referring to the female uniformed officer standing beside him. "Ma'am, can we ask you a few questions?"

She looked past them to the officer in her driveway as he pressed his palm against the hood of her car. Her stomach clenched. "Uh . . . yeah . . . sure." She stepped aside so they could come in. Immediately, she saw their eyes traveling quickly around her living room. "What can I do for you?"

The detective removed a notepad from his breast pocket. "Do you know a Leroy Brown?"

Shaking nervously, she backed toward the couch and took a seat. "Yes, I know him."

"When was the last time you've seen him?"

"It's been a while. U-uh, quite a while. He's the minister of the church I used to attend."

The female officer stepped forward, wearing a puzzled look. "What happened to your face?"

Kayla startled. She had forgotten all about her face. Big black-and-blue bruises were also on her legs and arms. "I um . . . had an accident."

Detective Garrison cleared his throat. "Ms. Sparks, we need you to come down to the station to talk."

"Talk?" She looked from one to the other. "Talk about what?"

"We need to talk in reference to an incident that occurred at 425 Rock Quarry Road last night."

Oh, no, she thought. Leroy had gone down to the police station and pressed charges against her. *Just be honest.* "Does this have anything to do with me stabbing him?"

The detective's brow rose. "Yes."

She nodded and gave a defeated sigh. "I figured that." She rose and the female officer stepped forward.

"Kayla Sparks, you are under arrest for assault with intent."

"What?" she gasped. "But it was self-defense."

"Please turn around."

"Wait a minute. Look at my face. All I did was stab—"

"Ma'am," Detective Garrison interrupted as the officer cuffed her. "You have the right to remain silent . . ."

Kayla was in a state of shock as they escorted her out to the patrol car.

Chapter 30

Renee

I got up early that morning, hoping to spend a few hours in my office working on my latest erotica, *Expose*. It was due in to my editor the first of September and I was running a little behind schedule. I wasn't worried—I work well under pressure. It fact, sometimes that's when I produce my best work. Moving into the kitchen, I found my schnauzer, Nikki, already waiting by the door.

"Ready to go outside?" She started frantically wagging her tail. "Okay, sweetheart." I opened the sliding door and she scurried out into the backyard. Smiling, I watched her go take care of business. Nikki had been in our family for years, and as far as I was concerned, she was one of my kids. I glanced out at the clear sky. The pond behind my house was calm and the breeze was cool. It was going to be a good day.

After making a cup of coffee, I went into my office and logged onto my e-mail account. There were over thirty, but none of them was something I had to attend to immediately. While sipping my coffee, I read over the last scene I had written and began to outline details for the next two. I'm not big on outlining, but for someone with adult A.D.D., I've got to have an agenda. Otherwise, I never manage to get anything done.

John had already left for a ten o'clock meeting, so I had the house to myself for a change.

Last night, he and I went to dinner at Daphne's house. Afterwards, we all went into the family room and got busy. While Tyler banged me doggy-style, John screwed Daphne in a recliner. I watched in envy as he dicked her until they both came. Once we got home, John wanted to go over every detail about how turned on he got watching another man fuck his wife. We then made love and I must say it was the best sex we'd had in years. But as I was lying there, I started feeling so cheap, like a ho. It was one thing for me to mess around on my husband, but now that the roles had been reversed, it didn't feel good at all. I couldn't help wondering if this was the Lord's way of telling me something. I had fucked around for so many years without thinking twice about it, and now it was my turn to see what it felt like.

What in the world was I doing with my life?

That was a good question, and I didn't know how to answer it. All I knew was that something was going to have to change because this new life was not at all what I wanted.

The doorbell rang. I was still wearing my pajamas, so I peeked out my office window and saw three women standing on my front porch toting Bibles. Damn! Jehovah's Witnesses! I reared back from the window and crept onto the mauve chaise in the corner of my room and waited. They rang the doorbell again.

I shook my head. I don't understand why it is so hard for them to get the hint.

"Hello?" one of them called through the door.

Oh, no, she didn't. Then they started knocking. And you think that's bad? I spotted one who had come over to my office window and was peeking through the glass. She looked straight at me and waved.

Now, see, I was trying to be nice, but these Bible-carrying heffas have gone too far. I rose and moved out to the door where they were waiting.

"Can I help you?"

They each smiled, and the one in the middle, wearing a big straw hat, held a pamphlet out to me. "Good morning. We would like to share our magazine."

I shook my head. "Listen, I'm really busy right now."

She gave me a solemn nod. "Okay, then we can come back tomorrow."

"No, don't come back tomorrow. I work from home and don't have the time or the interest."

The one on the left with big, beady eyes pointed her finger at me and said, "Did you know that the Lord will be coming to take us home soon?"

"Yes, ma'am." I may be a bitch, but I do try to respect my elders. "I'm Baptist."

The one on the right had been sizing me up since the moment I opened the door, wearing a red silk robe. "What kind of work do you do at home?"

"I write erotica."

She placed a hand to her chest and looked appalled. One of the others started fanning herself with her publication.

Smacking my lips, I continued, "Yes, I write those sex books. And my heroine was just getting ready to give a blow job when you rudely knocked on my window."

Those women jumped off my porch and hurried away like they had just realized they'd stepped through the gates of hell.

I shut the door and chuckled. I knew I was wrong for doing that, but at least I didn't have to worry about them knocking on my door again. My office phone rang and I reached over and grabbed it by the third ring.

"Hello?"

"Renee, this is Danny."

"Hey, girl," I greeted as I sank onto my chair.

"You need to get yo' ass on the next plane back down here."

Something in her voice caused a moment of alarm. "Why, whassup?"

"Kayla's been arrested for murder."

Chapter 31

Renee

I pulled off the Interstate and headed toward Nadine's house. As soon as I had gotten off the phone with Danielle, I caught an evening flight to St. Louis. Now it was almost midnight. I was tired and had never been much of a night driver, but it was Kayla we were talking about and it was going to take something stronger than a tornado to keep me from getting to Columbia. I still couldn't believe what had happened. Kayla accused of murder. No way. That girl wouldn't even kill a fly.

I was driving down the road, trying not to speed. My hands were shaking, my chest pounding. I was squirming on the seat, unable to stay still. I don't think I've ever been so scared in my life. Danielle didn't have any more information at the time, but Nadine, who's a divorce attorney, was trying to get as much as she could.

I pulled in front of her large, brown stucco house. Danielle's car was already in the driveway. I knocked on the door and Jordan answered it. "Hey, come on in."

I stepped into the foyer and walked across the oak hardwood floors to the dining room, where Danielle and Nadine were already sitting. We hugged and then I asked for information.

Nadine gave me a grim look. "It doesn't look good. Kayla went to Leroy's house last night. She said he tried to kill her so she grabbed a knife, stabbed him in the shoulder, and ran out the door. Then the police received a call this morning and found Leroy lying in his kitchen, dead. He had been stabbed seventeen times in the chest."

I was livid. "Seventeen times! What the hell happened?"

"She has no idea."

"Did you get to see Kayla?"

Nadine nodded. "She looks a mess. He definitely did a number on her. I wouldn't have blamed her if she *had* killed his ass."

Even though I already knew the answer, I had to ask. "Did she?"

Nadine shook her head. "I spoke to Kayla and she said that she only stabbed him once."

"So someone must have come to the house after she left."

"That's what I was thinking, but there's no proof. Kayla's fingerprints are the only ones on the murder weapon. She was seen fleeing from the scene of the crime."

Damn, what was Kayla thinking?

"I told her not to say another word—I hired a criminal attorney to represent her."

I was pleased to hear that Nadine was handling things, because I wouldn't have had the slightest idea where to begin. "Can we at least get her out on bail?"

"Her bail hearing is in the morning."

I slumped back in the chair. There was nothing else we could do at this point but wait. Danielle was sitting there, staring at me, saying nothing at all. A flicker of annoyance darkened her features.

I gave her a curious look. "What's goin' through your head?"

She suddenly jumped out of the chair like a crazy lunatic, screaming, "It's all yo' fault!"

Nadine caught her just before she lunged across the table. "Hold up," she said softly.

I was stunned beyond words. Slowly I rose from the chair. "How is this my fault?"

Danielle pulled away from Nadine and came and stood all in my face. "If you hadn't been so quick to get back at him, none of this shit would have happened! That videotape is yo' fault."

"Don't act like you didn't have anything to do with it," I said to Danielle.

Through her sobs, Danielle responded. "I can admit that I was wrong. I should have respected Kayla's wishes and left that whole thing with him whooping her ass alone. But I didn't. Instead I helped you video that triflin' negro in a diaper, then you insisted on giving that video to Tommy so he could circulate it through the church. Only that tape made it to the television stations and the doggone police station. We ruined his life, his kids' lives, and Kayla's." Her fists were balled and tears were streaming down her face. I know she wanted to kick my ass and I couldn't blame her.

I sat back in the chair, quiet as a church mouse. Danielle was right. All this shit *was* my fault. My attempt at rectifying the situation had only made the situation worse.

Nadine was staring down at me. Leave it to the lawyer to break the silence. "Renee, is that true?"

I raked a hand across my face before finally saying, "Yeah, it true. It's all my fault."

For once, Nadine didn't bother to comment and I was glad for that because it's hard as hell for me to admit when I am wrong. As she went over to the couch, her disappointment was obvious. Danielle shuffled over to the window. Her arms were crossed and she was holding her stomach. She has this ulcer thing that always emerges whenever she's upset.

"Everybody, I'm sorry."

Danielle tsked under her breath. I was tempted to tell her to go ahead and try and kick my ass and get it over with because maybe a good fight was what we needed to get past this. But leave it to attorney Nadine Hill to intervene.

"Look," she began, her eyes swimming with tears. "There's no point in dwelling on what happened. What's done is done. What we need to be doing now is finding a way to get Kayla out of this mess."

I nodded. She was right. "Do you know how much her bail's gonna be?"

"For murder, probably close to a million."

Danny swung away from the window. "What? How the heck we gonna afford to get her out?"

I glanced at Nadine, wondering the same thing. "We need to come up with ten percent, right?" She nodded. That was a hundred thousand. Hell, even John didn't have that much money lying around to spare.

She sat up straighter on the chair. "Don't worry. It's already covered."

My brow rose. "Really? Who's got that kinda change lying around?"

"Jermaine," Nadine reported gleefully.

Danielle and I locked eyes, both surprised.

"Jermaine? Damn!" I sprang from the chair and tossed a fist in the air. "Kayla finally found her someone with some money."

Chapter 32

Kayla

Kayla clung to Jermaine's arm as they left the police station the next morning. The media was everywhere. The news had spread through Columbia like wildfire. The moment they left the building, microphones were pointed in her direction.

"Kayla, did you kill Reverend Leroy Brown?"

"Ms. Sparks, were the two of you having an affair?"

"No comment," Jermaine said and pushed through the crowd, steering her to his car. Kayla shielded her face from the camera.

"The public has the right to know!" a reporter shouted just as she closed the door. She was going to lose her mind before this was all over.

Kayla leaned back on the seat and closed her eyes. It was unreal. She had been accused of murder. A tear ran down her cheek that she didn't even bother trying to brush away. The ordeal gave her the right to cry, especially after everything she had gone through for the last several hours. Leroy was dead. He had been stabbed repeatedly in the chest and neck. A shudder raced through her body as she recalled the horrible crime-scene photographs the detective had spread across the table. The sight was more than she could handle, and she ended up standing in front of a trash can throwing up. How could someone have done something so hideous? No one, not even Leroy, deserved to die like that.

"Hey, you doing okay over there?"

With her eyes still closed, she nodded. Jermaine reached over and clasped her hand. By the way he squeezed it, she knew he didn't believe she was okay but was trying the best he could to comfort her, and she appreciated that.

What have I done to deserve someone like him?

She had been committing adultery for four years. Intentionally, she had disobeyed God's laws, although after each and every time they had made love, Leroy had insisted that they both got down on their knees and ask the Lord for forgiveness. She raised her eyelids. What a fool she had been.

Looking out the window, she noticed that Jermaine was going south instead of north. "Where are we going?"

He briefly tore his eyes away from the road. "I'm taking you to my house. The media is bound to be camped out at your place the rest of the day."

"I hadn't thought about that."

He laced his fingers with hers. "Don't worry. You'll be safe with me."

She nodded and relaxed on the seat. Before leaving the jail, she called her mother from a pay phone. After listening to her scream and call her every name in the book, she got her to agree to take Kenya and Asia to Birmingham to visit her folks until everything blew over. The last thing she wanted was for her daughters to be affected by this madness.

Jermaine pulled onto the circular driveway. The garage opened and he slowly entered and lowered the door behind them. Once out of the car, he took her hand and escorted her inside. It was impossible not to feel the serenity radiating around the room. Jermaine turned around and wrapped her in his arms.

"Thank you so much for bailing me out. I don't know how I could ever—"

"Shhh," he said, and when he had her attention he lowered

his head and pressed his lips to hers. After a while he pulled back and gave her a long, serious look. "Kayla, I love you and I know you don't have an evil bone in your body. But I've got to know what's going on. Is it true? Were you involved with this minister?"

Kayla closed her eyes briefly. She had known it was just a matter of time before she was going to have to tell him the truth. She just wished she had done it long before now.

She took his hand and led him into the living room. Once they were seated across from each other, she nodded and said, "Yes, Leroy and I were involved for over four years."

He gazed at her long and hard before asking her, "Did you know he was married?"

She swallowed and somehow found her voice as she nodded. "Yes. I was once a member of Mt. Carmel Baptist Church." Just as she feared, she saw the look of disappointment in his eyes. "I know what I did was wrong, but you have to understand, I was so alone back then. All I've ever wanted was for someone to love me. Kenya's father used me and refused to claim his daughter. I supported Asia's father for three years while he finished law school and as soon as he joined a law firm he dumped me. The only name my father knows me by is Ms. Piggy. Men look and laugh at me and call me fat." She was crying so hard now she could barely get the words out. Jermaine tried to hold her but she held up her hand. "Wait—please let me finish. I was so lonely and Leroy started paying me attention. For the first time, someone actually listened to what I had to say. Then he told me his marriage was in trouble and I believed him. He told me that he loved me and was going to divorce her so that we could finally be together, and even though I had doubts, I needed to believe in him." Pausing, she gazed down at her hands for the longest time. "Leroy was my whole world and I had invested so much time in him and our relationship that there was no way I could allow myself to believe that it was just one big lie."

"I can understand that."

Kayla shook her head, then lowered her eyelids. "But I can't. Not anymore. It makes me sick every time I think about all the times Renee, Danielle . . . and Lisa," a sob caught in her throat as she remembered, "tried to tell me the truth about him but I refused to believe them."

He took her hand. "Baby, you're not the first woman to become a victim of a man's false promises."

"But for four years! Dear Lord, what's wrong with me? It took finding him in the bed with another woman for me to finally see him for who he truly was. Even when he put his hands on me, I still felt sorry for him."

"You're a loving person who sees the good in everyone. There is nothing wrong with that," he added in a soothing voice.

Kayla wiped her cheeks.

"What happened that night?"

Nodding, she reached for a tissue and wiped her eyes. "Umm . . ." She took a moment to catch her breath. "Leroy had called shortly after midnight, saying he wanted to apologize for the way he treated me and that he was going home to the Lord that night. I knew he was talking about killing himself. He was crying and I never heard him that way before. I know it was stupid, but I rushed over there to stop him. I couldn't help it, but I blame myself for what happened to his life. If I had never said anything to my friends, they wouldn't have taped him with Peaches and none of this would have happened."

"Wait a minute. Your friends made that video?"

"Yes, after he beat me up."

He squeezed her hand. "So you weren't in a car accident."

Her heart sank as she remembered the lie she had told. "No—I'm so sorry."

He nodded knowingly, kissed her forehead, then encouraged her to continue.

"Anyway, when I got there I couldn't find him, so I was running through the house, and then out of nowhere he came and knocked me across the room. He yelled that I was so predictable and that he knew I'd come over. He kept hitting me until I finally stopped fighting. Then he tried to pull my pants down to rape me. Something told me to keep fighting for once—not to give in."

Jermaine squeezed her hand and she glanced up beneath the tears and gave him a smile. "I kicked him in the nuts, then got up and tried to get away, but he caught me around the neck. I reached over and felt the knife in my hand and grabbed it and stabbed him in the shoulder. Then I ran out that door." She looked up at Jermaine, needing so badly for him to believe her. "I swear to you, when I left he was cussing and going off, but he was not dead."

"I believe you."

The look in his eyes told her he honestly did believe her. She threw herself into his arms and held on for dear life. She hated that she needed him so badly but she did. Her body shook as the tears came and she cried silently against his shoulder.

"I'm not going anywhere. When I told you I loved you, I meant it. No games. No conditions. Love to me is being there when someone needs you most. Sharing in their pain, and trying to find ways to bring them joy and comfort. Lean on your man, baby, because that's what I'm here for."

She pulled back slightly and gazed up at him. Had it not been for the murder charges hanging over her head, life would be nothing short of perfect. "Thank you, Jermaine. I don't know what I would do without you. This has been hard enough as it is. And it is only the beginning."

His eyes sparkled with compassion. "Just hold on. Everything is going to work out. You'll see." He brought her hand to his mouth and kissed her knuckles.

Fat teardrops leaked from her eyes. "I hope so. Someone came into that house after I left and killed him. I'm certain of that."

He was quiet for a long moment and she could see the wheels in his head turning. "Do you have any idea who would have wanted him dead?"

"Probably quite a few people. The more I'm learning about him, the more I think that. My first choice would be his wife. Lord, please forgive me, but if I was Darlene, I'd want him dead. He has given her every reason. His secret life destroyed her. I heard she has the house up for sale and is planning to leave town. As small as Columbia is, I don't blame her. Life around here will never be the same again."

"Do you know if he was messing with other men besides the one on the video?"

"I've been hearing rumors for years but never wanted to believe them." She nibbled her bottom lip nervously. "I wonder how many other women, or men, he used to invite to his house? I was his Thursday girl, Tracy had Wednesday." She scowled and snuggled closer into his comforting embrace. "There's no telling how many others there were."

He clasped his fingers with hers then planted a kiss to her cheek. "Don't worry, baby. Put it in God's hands and he'll make everything all right."

"I can only wish." Kayla had a strong feeling she had already used up all her wishes. Getting her out of this was going to take nothing short of a miracle.

Chapter 33

Renee

It was all over the news and on the front page of every newspaper. I stared down at a recent photograph of Leroy and wanted to scratch his eyes out. Even dead, he still managed to have a hold on Kayla's life. Well, not for too much longer. Not if I could help it. After she got off work, Danielle scooped me up and we rushed over to Jermaine's house. There was still tension between Danielle and me, and this wasn't the first time we'd gotten into it. There was one time we didn't speak for almost a year over something as trivial as money. She's my girl and even though she does stupid shit and pisses me off, we've been friends for too long to let anything get in the way. Besides, if she still wanted to kick my ass, she'd be more than welcome to try after we found a way to get Kayla out of this mess.

Danielle pulled up in front of a bad-ass house. Dayum! Jermaine really did have it going on. We moved up the stairs and Kayla greeted us at the door. I hugged her close.

"Girl, everything is going to be all right. I swear to you," I whispered for her ears only.

She released me, then nodded. "God will find a way. I'm certain of it."

I wish I had her faith. Although I am a strong believer that the Lord helps those who help themselves, and that is exactly what I planned to do—help her. Kayla signaled for us to follow her through the gorgeous, custom-built home to a large family room.

I wagged my eyebrows. "Gurrrl, this is nice."

"Thank you." I jumped at the sound of Jermaine's voice. I had no idea he had come up behind us. "Sorry about that," he said.

"No problem. How are you doing?"

"A lot better now that I've gotten my baby out of jail." He moved over to Kayla and pressed his lips to hers. "I'll let you spend some time alone with your friends. I'm upstairs if you need me." She nodded and he kissed her once more before waving at us and turning on his heels.

Danielle and I looked at each other, and the minute he left the room we raced over to Kayla, giggling like two starstruck teenagers.

"Hot damn, girl! Where did you get him?" Danielle screamed.

"I know. Does he by any chance have a brother?" I chimed in. She giggled with us and it felt like we were back in high school, freaking out over the star basketball player. I was glad that we were able to take her mind away from her problems, even if it was just for a few seconds.

Kayla sat on the couch. I moved to a matching chaise lounge while Danielle flopped down in the chair.

"How are you holding up?" I asked.

"I'm okay," is what she tried to say, but instead a sob blocked her windpipe. "Really I am. Jermaine has been real supportive."

"We see," Danielle and I said at the same time. The three of us laughed, then quickly sobered.

Kayla wiped a tear from the corner of her eye. "Mom has the girls and the attorney Nadine hired has agreed to take the case."

"Oh, good," Danielle said with a sigh of relief. "Do you feel like telling us what happened?"

She swallowed, then shifted uncomfortably on the couch. "I was so stupid. I don't know what I was thinking. Leroy called, threatening suicide. Like a nut I ran over there, trying to stop him. Only I don't think he really planned on killing himself. I think it was just an excuse to get me over there. The moment I walked in the door, he attacked me." My stomach churned as she tried to get herself together. "He lost his mind. He tried to rape me . . . again. At first I was going to just lie there and let him have his way, but I prayed about it and the Lord gave me the strength I needed. I kicked him in the crotch and got away long enough to grab that knife, then I stabbed him in the shoulder and ran out the door." She shook her head. The tears were flowing. "He was still alive. When I left him, he was trying to pull the knife out. You both have to believe me."

I gave a dismissive wave. "Girl, puhleeze. I believe anything you say. I know you don't have it in you to kill someone. Now, if it was me, I would have stabbed his ass a long time ago, for real, for real."

Danielle rolled her eyes. "Nae-Nae, shut the hell up. The last thing we need to hear is you talking about stabbing someone."

I pursed my lips and bit my tongue. I would have cussed her ass out, but it wasn't about me. I was here for Kayla. "Why did he go off?"

She hesitated before saying, "He blamed me for ruining his life." She tried to control her voice but couldn't. Danielle moved over to her and cradled her face against her chest as she wept.

"It's not your fault," Danielle cooed while stroking her back.

She and I looked at each other at the same time. Feelings of guilt assailed me again. Damn! Both of them had every right to be mad at me. All this was my fault. Of course, Kayla would never say that because she was such a loving and forgiving person. I wish I was that way, because if I was, I wouldn't have plotted to pay Leroy back and none of this mess would have happened. Torn between cussing and bawling like a baby, I just closed my eyes and wished I could take it all back.

Kayla released a heavy breath. "His funeral is scheduled for Friday. I think the whole city is planning to attend." I know Kayla well enough to know she was wishing she could attend as well. If she thought for a moment that either one of us would go on her behalf, she was crazier than I thought.

We stayed for over an hour before Jermaine came down to see if everything was okay and if we needed anything. Danielle and I decided it was time for us to leave. We shared a group hug, then just stood close to Kayla, who stared at our faces through a waterfall of tears. After one final hug, we promised to come back tomorrow.

We climbed back into Danielle's car and headed to her house. "Girl, this is bullshit. You and I both know that Kayla didn't kill anyone."

She looked at me out of the corners of her eyes. "It doesn't matter what we think. The police and the Boone County prosecuting attorney both think she did."

I nibbled on my lower lip, trying to think. There was no way I could let my girl go down for some shit that I started. I was going to have to find a way to help clear her name.

I swung around. "Have you seen Peaches?"

Danielle shook her head. "I haven't seen that fag since he was on the news."

"We need to find him. He has to know something—otherwise he wouldn't have just disappeared."

"Maybe I can talk to Tracy."

I couldn't stand Tracy. I was once messing around with this fine muthafucka that Tracy called herself liking as well. I was at his house, and he had run to pick up his mama from work. I stayed there, watching television. The phone rang and my nosy ass moved over and read the Caller ID. As soon as I saw her name pop off, before I realized what I was doing, I had picked up the phone and answered it.

"Hello," I purred.

"Hello? Hello? Who's this?"

"Who's this?"

"This's Tracy. I need to speak to my man," she demanded with attitude.

"Well, your man's licking my cootie-cat, and . . . ooooh, it feels so

good." I had hung up, laughing. Ever since then she couldn't stand my ass. But she knew better than to step to me, 'cause I would have kicked her narrow ass.

"That's a good idea. Y'all cool, right?"

Danielle shrugged and frowned at the same time. "Yeah, we speak, but that's about it."

"That's all we need." Damn, I needed a drink. "Okay, this is what we're going to do. I'm going to try and find out where Peaches is, while you locate Tracy's ass. Somebody knows something, and if the police aren't going to do their job, then I guess we'll have to do it for them."

Chapter 34

Danielle

Danielle pulled into her driveway. With everything going on with Kayla, she was glad Portia was still staying with her mother. Danielle was ashamed to admit that she didn't know how to handle the situation. Her daughter had been screwing *her* man. If Portia had been some ho on the street, she would have whooped her ass. But she couldn't do that. Portia was her daughter.

She moved into the kitchen and without bothering to check her messages, she looked down at her Caller ID and noticed Calvin had called. She didn't know what she was going to do with him. After he had taken her to Red Lobster, she had been honest with him when she told him she wasn't looking for a relationship right now, but she wanted to at least be friends. He had agreed, for now. Calvin was a very nice guy but there was no point in leading him on when she was still sprung over Ron's ass.

The phone rang, startling her. She groaned when she realized it was her mother. But if she didn't answer it, she would keep calling until she did.

She grabbed the phone and reached into the refrigerator for a bottle of water.

"When are you coming over here?" her mother asked.

"For what?"

"So the three of us can sit down and work this out."

"Mom, there is nothing to work out. My daughter is supposedly pregnant by my ex-boyfriend. What am I supposed to do, give her a medal?"

"No, but you can't turn your back on your daughter, either. She needs you."

"Then her fast tail should have thought about that before she slept with him."

"I told you before that Portia don't keep no clothes on," she huffed. "Always walking around with butt cheeks hanging out. He was too young for you, anyway. He was more her age. You shouldna had him in your house in the first place."

"Mama, please."

"Please nothing," Victoria cut in. "Those sonabitches ain't looking for nothing but a place to lay their heads."

"Shoot," Danielle pouted. "I got it from you, messing with those young negros." Her father was nine years younger than her mother.

Victoria stuttered. "You got to pay to be the boss. Besides, your dad and I never shacked up. We went straight to the judge and got married."

"Whatever," Danielle mumbled to herself. If she argued, her mother would never let her get off the phone.

"You can't be mad at your daughter. You need to be mad at him because he knew better."

"I'm not ready yet."

"Then you need to get ready because whether you like it or not, you're about to be a grandmother."

Danielle hung up and walked down to her room. *Hot ass.* She'd raised her daughter better than that. True, she knew she liked them young herself, but that wasn't the point. She just couldn't talk to her daughter. Not yet.

Danielle went into the bathroom. A hot bath was in order. Something, anything to relax her mind, because right now she was mad at the world. Portia. Ron. Renee. Though she didn't know why she was wasting her time being mad at Renee. Nae-

Nae was always going to be impulsive and vindictive. That just was the way she was, which was why it was her job to keep her best friend in line.

She put the stopper in the drain and reached for the faucet to pour a hot bath. *I'm just as responsible for this mess as Renee is,* she thought as she walked into her room and started taking off her clothes. She had been taught a long time ago that God don't like ugly, yet she had gotten a big kick out of making Leroy feel like a fool.

Danielle unsnapped her jean shorts and they dropped to the floor along with her panties. Naked, she reached for her night-gown and went back into the adjoining bathroom. Even though the tub was only half full she climbed in. The house was so quiet, all she could hear was running water, the thoughts racing through her head, and her older sister Constance screaming at her. She lay back against the inflated pillow and squeezed her eyelids tightly together, hoping to block the scene from her mind. But there was no way she could run from her problems. The situation was not going away—instead it was going to linger in the corners of her mind until she decided to do something about it.

Danielle reached up and turned off the water, then pulled one of her knees to her chest while she thought over the situation. She had two problems: a daughter who had a bad habit of "crying wolf" all the time, and a man she loved. Now, if Portia wasn't always trying to find ways to get attention, she wouldn't have given her confession a minute's thought. All it would have taken was one phone call to her brother and the muthafucker would be on the next train out, with a couple of black eyes to take along for the ride. Only that wasn't the case. Instead, Portia accused Ron of having sex with her, and she had allowed it because she thought he loved her. It was a sick and twisted— a grown-ass man sleeping with an underage girl, but she knew that it happened all the time. Hell, she'd had men trying to hook up with her when she was the same age. She also remembered lying on several occasions just so she could see what it was like to date an older man.

Danielle scowled because this time, that was not the case. Ron knew how old Portia was. She allowed her mind to travel back, hoping to remember anything that might make her think her daughter just might be telling the truth. She remembered working late and coming home to find the two on the couch playing a competitive game on Ron's Playstation. Ron had even picked Portia up from school a couple of times when she had been unable to do it. Danielle pressed a hand to her forehead. She was going to go crazy thinking about this. They had been together for over two years and not once could she remember an incident that made her think something was going on between her daughter and Ron.

She released a heavy breath because her mother was right. Portia did have a tendency to walk around with her shorts up her ass. With her overweight body, it was nothing nice to look at. On numerous occasions she had to check her on it, and quickly reminded her a man was in the house.

But like Ron had told her, what in the world would he need with a little girl when he already had a grown-ass woman? That's true, she thought while lathering her washcloth and smoothing it across her body. Day or night, she'd always been willing to satisfy her man's needs, so he never needed to think about any other woman. Especially not Portia. She settled back against the pillow and closed her eyes again. "Lord, please help me figure it out." Somehow she had to find a way to fix everything that had gone wrong in her life.

Chapter 35

Renee

"How was the movie?"

Kayla grinned, then nodded. "Funny as all get-out. Thanks for bringing me."

I looped my arm with hers. "That's just the beginning. We're going to go and she what bargains we can find at JCPenney's, then go have dinner. I heard there is a new seafood place not too far from here."

She nodded in agreement and I could tell she was starting to relax, which made me feel good. It had been over a week and the media was still having a field day at my girl's expense. Kayla had been forced to take a leave of absence from work and was hiding out at Jermaine's. I was so tired of watching her feel sorry for herself that I had invited her to drive up to Jefferson City for a girls' day out. It was a Wednesday. Everyone was at work, so the mall was relatively quiet. I treated us to pedicures and then we had our faces done at the cosmetic counter.

"Have you talked to Danielle?" Kayla asked as we were strolling through the mall.

"No. I know she had to work today, but I've been trying to reach her for the last two days and she hasn't returned any of my calls. She's probably trying to decide what to do about Portia and the baby."

Kayla stopped dead in her tracks. "Baby? Portia's pregnant?"

"Yep, but you didn't hear that shit from me." I signaled for her to come over and look at a gorgeous sapphire necklace I spotted in the jewelry store window. I wasn't big on wearing much more than gold loops and a ring or two, but every now and then I saw something that I thought I should have.

"Oooh, Renee, that's beautiful!"

"Yes, it is. I reached inside my purse to see if I had bothered to bring my platinum Visa, and was pleased to find it in my wallet. "Come on. I think I'm going to buy it."

We went around to the door and practically ran into a woman with her hands full of bags. "Oops, my bad." I reached down for the Victoria's Secret bag that had fallen onto the floor and handed it to her.

"Thank you. I—" Her words startled both of us when we realized it was Darlene. Wife to the dearly departed Reverend Leroy Brown. As soon as she realized who we were, she gazed up toward the ceiling and shook her head. "Lord, please give me strength."

Kayla stepped forward. "Darlene, please believe me," she pleaded. "I had nothing to do with Leroy's murder."

"I can't believe you have the nerve to stand here and tell me you're not responsible for my husband's brutal death! How dare you!" She bored evil eyes into Kayla.

I could tell Kayla was frustrated. "Mrs. Brown, please . . ." She allowed her voice to trail off as defeat slumped her shoulders.

While giving her shoulder a comforting squeeze, I suggested softly, "Kayla, why don't you go over to that bench and have a seat." She shook her head. Damn, why now, of all times, does she decide to be stubborn? "Do it, please."

Reluctantly, she turned and walked over to a bench at the center of the mall.

"Well, if you'll excuse me, I need to get home and get down on my knees. If I wasn't a Christian woman, I would have scratched her eyes out." Darlene turned and started walking away, but I moved into step beside her.

"Mrs. Brown, can you please give me just a few moments of your time? I'm tryin' to help clear my friend."

She stopped dead in her tracks and started spitting her venom. "Clear her? She killed my Leroy. The two of them have been messing around for years and finally they both got what they deserved." Her tone was cool and detached.

"I'm quite aware of that. I'm also told that you've known about it for years and didn't seem to care."

"How do you think it makes me feel to know that my husband was messing around with someone who looks like that, when he had all this at home?" Her skinny ass struck a pose so I could see what *all this* meant. Truth be told, Darlene was one ugly bitch. Dark-skinned with that ashy look that no amount of Vaseline could cure. She had a serious overbite, a thin, sunken face, and bulging frog eyes. I was tempted to tell her Kayla was more woman than she could ever be, but I know when I need to shut the hell up.

"It's one thing to mess around, but it's another to disrespect me. Now, I know a man is going to be a man. And it ain't anything but that devil that was tempting my Leroy with those women."

And let's not forget about his craving for men, but I wasn't about to go there. "I can tell you that Kayla stopped seeing Leroy weeks ago."

"Weeks? Is that supposed to make me feel better? I was quite aware of my husband slipping out a couple of hours here and there. But all those weekends he pretended to be going out of town to be a guest speaker and insisted that I stay at home, now that's another thing." She paused and shook her head. "All those fishing trips that he and Deacon Williams were supposedly taking, I knew something wasn't right. It wasn't until three weeks ago I went into the garage and discovered he'd forgotten his tackle box."

"He wasn't with Kayla. He must have been with another one of his women."

"There weren't any others," she bellowed. "Only her."

I laughed in her face. "Mrs. Brown, I know you don't believe that. He was sleeping with that slut Tracy Branch, and I know you've seen the videotape—he was also screwing a fag."

"Miss, don't disrespect my husband or me!" she cried, drawing the attention of several bystanders. "Hasn't your friend already done enough? My family is in shambles and I'm a nervous wreck. I don't know how I'm going to manage to live another day without him."

I glanced down at her bags. "It looks to me like you're doing a pretty good job of getting on with your life."

Darlene tilted her chin defiantly. "Shopping makes me feel better. Besides, Leroy always said not to mourn death but to celebrate life and that's what I'm trying to do." Her sour face then twisted into a devilish smirk. "I guess I shouldn't be too mad at Kayla. After all, she did make me an extremely rich woman. While she's rotting in jail, I'll be living in Florida and riding around town in my new Mercedes." She winked. "Excuse me, but I've got some more shopping to do." I watched her swish her little narrow ass around the corner before I joined Kayla, who was waiting eagerly to hear what I had to say. "That crazy bitch thinks Leroy walks on water."

"What did she say?"

I scowled. "Nothing worth repeating. Although she is under the impression Leroy used to pretend to go fishing and instead was spending the weekend with you."

"I wish. All he ever gave me was a quick, cheap screw," she returned with a dejected look.

I could tell she was about to get depressed again. I rose and pulled her up to her feet. "Come on. Let's not let her ruin our day."

We still went to dinner, but I could tell her heart was no longer in it. I wanted to go find Darlene myself and give her a piece of my mind for messing everything up.

After I dropped Kayla off at home, I decided to go by Danielle's house unannounced and see why her ass ain't been answering the phone. I made a left onto her street and before I even reached her house, I spotted the Impala in her driveway. *Ain't this a bitch.* Don't tell me she let Ron's freeloading ass back into her house. I climbed out and walked up the driveway. The door was open and as soon as I stepped onto the porch, I could see straight through the storm door into the living room and neither of them were in sight. Knowing Danielle, they were probably in her bedroom getting busy. It takes a ho to know one, and I know my girl will drop her draws for a thug in a heartbeat.

I rang the doorbell repeatedly, knowing good and well it was going to piss her behind off. I didn't care, because it was the only way I knew she would hurry to the door. I heard footsteps and thought it was her, but instead Ron came around the corner.

"Hey, Renee, come on in." Ron's honey-coated voice oozed into my head and I couldn't help smiling as he unlocked the door and I stepped in.

"Where's Danny?"

"She'll be right down."

I tried not to stare, but damn, the brotha looked good. He had come to the door with no shirt on and had a body that very few muthafuckas could hold a torch to. In fact, in a pair of jean shorts, he showed off the sexiest set of calves I have seen in years. Shit, maybe I need to find me a thug. Not to date, just to fuck.

Ron reached for a white tee on the couch, lowered it over his head, then grabbed a set of keys off the coffee table and headed toward the door. "Tell Danny to hit me on my cell later."

"Uh-huh," I mumbled. My eyes followed him out the door and down the driveway. He hopped into the Impala and started the car. Music blared, bass thumping as he peeled around the corner.

"Hey, girl." Danielle came bouncing down the stairs, taking them two at a time in a slamming two-piece Rocawear shorts outfit.

"What you all smiles for? You must have gotten you some."

Blushing, she moved over to the couch and took a seat.

"Girl, I don't blame you. As fine as he is, I don't think I could stay mad at him, either." I gave her a high five and we started laughing.

"You seen Kayla?" she asked.

I nodded, then sat in the chair across from her and told her about our shopping adventure, including running into Mrs. Brown.

"She's crazy."

"Yep. I wouldn't be surprised if that anorexic bitch didn't kill him herself," I said.

Danielle's eyes grew large. "Dayum! Me, either."

"Crazy as she is, she at least gave me a clue." I told her about the fishing trips. "I don't think they were fishing. I bet you Deacon Williams was covering for Reverend Brown so he could be with another one of his skanks."

"I agree."

"Now I just have to find out who she is."

"Or he," Danielle corrected.

"Right."

I leaned back in the chair, trying to make some sense out of everything that was happening. "Deacon Williams and my grandfather go way back. I'm going to drop by and see if maybe, now that his boy Leroy is gone, he'll tell me what really happened. He's a Christian man so I'm sure he's ready to cleanse his soul."

Nodding, Danielle added, "While you do that, I'll keep trying to reach Tracy. I left her two messages at her mama's house and she ain't bothered to call me back yet."

"Then drop in on her ass. She don't work and got four kids. How far can she be?"

Danielle cackled. "I know that's right." She laughed, then asked, "Have you seen Peaches yet?"

I gave her a grim look. "I've been asking around. Even Tommy is trying to find him."

"He'll pop up eventually," Danielle replied confidently.

But personally, I wasn't so sure. "I don't know, Danny. I'm

starting to think that maybe Leroy might have done something to him as well."

She gave me a worried look that I was amazed to see, considering she and Peaches never cared much about each other. "Do you really think so?"

"Right now, anything is possible." I glanced up the stairs curiously. "It's quiet. Where's Portia?"

Danielle quickly looked down at her acrylic nails, "I put her hot ass out."

I drew in a deep breath. "Why'd you do that?"

Her voice was cool and detached. "Because she lied and said she was pregnant by Ron."

"What!" I sprang from the chair like a jack-in-the-box. "Hold up! Wait a minute. My goddaughter told you she was pregnant by Ron, and you put her out?"

She straightened her shoulders. "Yep, sure did. She's staying over there with my mama."

"What is Ron saying about all this?"

She drew in a deep breath. "He said she's lying."

Is this bitch stuck on stupid or what? "Of course he's gonna say that. Do you think he's gonna admit fuckin' around with your daughter?" I shook my head in disbelief. I'd met some dumb women in my lifetime, but Danielle takes the cake. "How the hell you gonna take some negro's word over your daughter's?"

Danielle gave me a dismissive wave. "'Cause she lies too damn much."

"How you know she isn't telling you the truth for once?"

"Because I know."

"No . . . because you don't *want* to know. Whatever. There is no way in hell I would believe dick over blood."

She looked over at me with those slanted eyes of hers and tried to get me to understand. "You don't know how Portia is, but I do. She lies all the time to get attention, and I know she's lying. She just doesn't want to see me happy."

"First off, how the hell can Ron make you happy? That muthafucka may be fine, but he ain't got a pot to piss in."

"He may not have much, but at least he's trying. He got a job and is planning to start paying bills around here."

"Ain't you heard this sad love song before? Come on, Danielle. How can you turn your back on your daughter?" I rolled my eyes. "See, if it had been Tamara, all she'd have to do is tell me once that some nigga was trying to touch her and I'm gonna do a Lorena Bobbitt on his ass."

Danielle shook her head. "You don't understand. Yo' daughter doesn't act like mine. Portia is off the chain and driving me crazier by the day. All this sneaking out and meeting men on the Internet, and pretending someone raped her. Now she's pregnant and claiming that my man is the father."

"Wait a minute. Yo' man . . . What happened to Calvin?"

She pursed her lips with attitude. "I thought you didn't want me being with Calvin."

"I told you I didn't care if you were with him. I just wished you had given me a heads-up. But, I'd rather you be with him than with Ron's ass. Come on, Danny, he might be screwing your daughter."

There was a long moment of silence. "How do I find out for sure?"

I can't believe this ho. She is more afraid of losing a man than her own child. What is wrong with this world? "What does Portia say?"

She gave me a disbelieving look. "She says she loves him and that he promised her they would be together after the baby is born."

I can honestly say I can't blame Portia for falling for his fine ass. Ron is a chocolate bar definitely worth sampling. I can see any teenage girl falling for him. "Well . . . what's something that only a person who's fucking him would know?"

Danielle gave me a long, thoughtful look before finally saying, "He's not circumcised."

My jaw dropped. "Ewww! You've been messing with a dirty dick." I started waving my hands in the air like they were on fire.

"He's not dirty," she replied defensively. "Ron's the cleanest man I know."

"But he ain't circumcised. Yuck!"

She rolled her eyes. "Girl, whatever."

I could tell that I pissed her off by talking about her man, but so what. "Okay, so then all you have to do is have Portia describe his dick."

"Yeah, I guess," she said, unconvinced.

"What do you mean, you guess?"

"I mean, I guess you're right."

"Damn straight I'm right. Is his thing long, fat, does it have a curve?"

Her jaw twitched with amusement. "Ain't *you* being nosy."

"No, but you need to have her describe it. We already know she knows what the rest of his body looks like. Hell, I saw that when he came to the door." And damn, did that shit look good. "But no one should have seen his dick but you."

"Okay, I'll ask her."

"When?"

"Tonight."

"Why not now?"

"Because I need a moment to prepare," she informed me.

"Prepare for what? Putting the muthafucka out? Girl, please."

"Renee, just let me do this my way."

"Whatever. " I rose from the chair, pissed off and ready to go get my cousin Murphy and have him whoop Ron's ass. "You need to handle your business—otherwise, I'm gonna ask my goddaughter myself." I turned on my heels and headed back out to my car. This shit gets crazier by the second.

Lisa, girl, shit is crazy down here. Kayla's been charged with murder. Danielle's man is fucking her daughter, and me, well, I don't know what to say about my fucked-up situation except to say that this shit has got to come to an end—soon.

Chapter 36

Danielle

She slept late the next morning, not at all ready to face what she was about to do. Renee had made a good point. Some way, somehow, she had to know for sure if her daughter was lying.

"Boo, you up?" Ron mumbled as he stirred in the bed beside her. Turning on his side, he swung an arm around her waist.

"Yeah, I'm up."

"Good, can yo' man get some attention this morning?"

Her hand traveled down between his legs to find him hard as a rock. She rolled over and straddled him, then took every inch with one push. "Ooh!" she moaned. Every time he was inside of her, he made her feel so complete. A perfect fit. Danielle rocked her hips slowly at first, then sped things up.

"Yeah, boo, that's what I'm talking about. Ride this dick," Ron managed between groans.

She rocked hard while he joined in and moved beneath her.

"Tell me you don't like this."

Like it? That was a stupid question. She loved it. Danielle made a sound in her throat but didn't answer. How could she give all this up? It had taken her years to find the perfect dick and now she might have to let it go. She rose up and down and plunged hard, wanting it like a hungry woman trying to get a meal. There was a chance that she might not ever have this again and she wanted to get all she could.

Ron tapped her lightly on the butt. "Roll yo' ass over."

Obediently, she got down on all fours and Ron positioned himself behind her and plunged inside. She sucked air between her teeth at the contact. He pushed in and out until he had her screaming and speaking in tongues. Danielle came, then came again. While he stroked, he slapped her ass and gave her a thorough spanking. Oh, was it good, and she couldn't get enough.

"Yes, baby, fuck me!" she cried.

Ron smacked her ass again. "Whose pussy is it?"

"It's yours. Only yours."

"You promise not to give my shit to some other nucca?"

He didn't have to worry about that. "I promise. This pussy belongs to you." And she meant it.

Ron then reached for her hair and pulled it while his body tensed. Trembling violently, he came long and hard, and she right along with him, then they collapsed on the bed together. After a while he reached across her to the nightstand.

"Boo, here's two hundred."

Danielle sat up straight on the bed and glanced from him to the money and back. "For what?"

"What you think? To help wit' the bills. I told you I'm gonna start doing right by you," he announced proudly.

Danielle lowered her head to his chest again. She loved him so much, she didn't know what she was going to do. "Can I ask a question?"

"Yo, you can ask me any thang."

She wrung her hands nervously before saying, "Has Portia ever seen you with . . . with yo' clothes off?"

Ron pushed her head off his chest and sat up so he could look down at her face. "What kind of question is that?"

"One that requires an answer," she replied with a roll of her neck. "I want to know if my daughter has seen you naked."

His eyes shifted nervously before he finally shook his head.

"Nah, boo. That girl ain't seen my shit. Damn! I thought we squashed this thang."

She hugged him close. The last thing she wanted was to mess things up between them. "I know, I know. But she *is* my daughter."

"Yeah, and your daughter has a serious problem. What the hell do I need with a kid when I got a fine-ass woman lying right here?" He winked, then tickled her underarm and she squirmed and screamed.

"Okay, stop it!" Danielle tried to push his hand away, but he pinned her hands at her side and straddled her.

"Damn, Danny. I know I've fucked up in the past, but I'm tryin' to do right by you, boo. Give yo' man a chance." He kissed her and she moaned. "Man, you got my dick hard again."

"Oh, really?" she cooed. "So what we goin' do 'bout it?"

"Watch and see." He pushed her thighs apart and slid all eleven back in, banging and pumping until she thought she would explode because it was so good. She wrapped her legs around his neck and Ron stroked her long and deep. She clung to him, her breath jagged. Finally, when she didn't think she could take another second, he exploded inside her.

He lay there holding her for the longest time. Something in her heart told her that her man was telling her the truth. Ron had been serious about trying to change. But the maternal part of her said she needed to talk to her daughter and give her a chance to explain before passing judgment. Danielle breathed a deep sigh. Before the day was over, she was going to have to choose between her man and her daughter.

The phone rang and she pushed Ron's snoring body off of her so she could grab the phone. "Hello?"

"Hey, this is Veronica."

It took a second for her to recognize her cousin's voice. "Why you whispering?"

"'Cause I don't want no one to hear me. You still looking for Tracy?"

Danielle instantly sat up straight. "Yeah, you seen her?"

"She's here right now, waiting to get her toes done."

"Okay, I'll be there in a flash."

"Ai'ight."

Danielle hung up the phone and dashed to take a shower.

Dressed in white Apple Bottoms capris and a red midriff blouse exposing her flat, pierced belly button and wearing white strappy sandals with rings on all her toes, Danielle strolled into the nail salon. Glancing around, she was pleased to see Veronica sitting in front of the foot tub, scrubbing Tracy's feet.

"What's up, girl?" Veronica said when she glanced toward the door.

"Nothin'," Danielle replied, then made eye contact with Tracy and acted surprised. "Girl, I didn't even recognize you. What's goin' on?"

"Nothing. Just treatin' myself. What's been up wit' you? I haven't seen you in . . . a long-ass time."

Her grin widened. "Same here."

"Cuz, you can go ahead and take that seat there and I can get started on your feet in a minute."

Danielle gave Veronica a puzzled look, then noticed she wanted her to play along. "Oh, yeah. Okay." She slipped off her shoes and took the seat beside Tracy and waited while Veronica poured her water.

After a while Danielle said out of the blue, "It's first Sunday, so I am going to try and go to church this weekend."

"Aunt Bea will be happy to hear that," Veronica chimed in.

While she scrubbed the bottoms of Tracy's feet, Danielle watched her expression as she asked, "Tracy, you still attend Mt. Carmel?"

She nodded. "Yeah, girl, but we've got drama at our house."

"Yeah, I heard Reverend Brown was murdered."

"Uh-huh," she said, all loud.

"I was reading in the paper they now have a possible sus-

pect," Danielle paused, then snapped her finger and faked ignorance. "What's that girl's name?"

"Kayla Sparks," she spat, loud and ghettolike. "I know that
bitch did it, too."

Danielle gaped. "What?" She tried to act like she loved to
gossip. "Why you say that?"

"Because she was mad when she found out I was getting
some of that, too."

Danielle had to try and hold it together. "Isn't he married?"

"And?" she rolled her eyes and watched as Veronica painted
her toes red. "Darlene knew I was screwin' her man. Came up
to me and made sure I knew she knew. She had the nerve to
laugh and said she could care less who was getting that, because
wasn't nobody getting his check but her."

"Shit, no! Gurrl, she sounds crazy."

"*Crazy* ain't the word. All that wench cared about was the sta-
tus she received bein' married to Leroy's ass."

"She's better than me because after I saw that video I would
have stabbed his ass."

Veronica's eyes grew large and round. "Girl, wasn't that some
jacked-up shit!" She clapped her hands and laughed louder
than was called for. "I think I watched that video three times.
Tracy, girl, what you doing messing with that fool?"

She sucked her two front teeth. "I didn't know he was
messing with Peaches. I seen them talkin' a couple times, but
I never put two and two together 'til I saw that tape. I remember dropping by his little home away from home—that's
what he called it—and saw all these cars out front. Girl, he
was having this party. It was on a weekend he told me he was
going fishing. I thought a couple of those cars looked familiar, but before I could get inside, Leroy met me on the porch
and told me he and his wife were entertaining and I had to
leave. It wasn't until after the video that I realized that
raggedy Ford Escort parked out on the curb had belonged to
Peaches."

So that explained the fishing trips. He was entertaining a bunch of fags.

Veronica shook her head as she applied polish to her toes. "Tracy, you're a better woman than me 'cause there ain't nothing a fag can do for me."

Danielle splashed her feet in the warm water. "I heard he wasn't workin' with much."

"Shoot, that man might not be working with much, but he could lay it on you. And he could eat some good pussy."

Danielle laughed along with her, then gave her a high five. "I know that's right. I'm surprised his wife didn't have the po-po knocking down your door."

Her eyes grew round and wide like she thought she knew something she didn't. "Girl, they came, and I told them all about my relationship with Leroy, then I gave them my alibi. I was in St. Louis kickin' it wit' my girls. There's this new club called The Loft that is off the hook."

The bell over the door rang and Danielle's cousin Nina came through the door. As soon as she spotted her, she went over to where she was sitting.

"Whassup, cuz? I heard about your girl being arrested. Y'all get her out on bail yet?"

Danielle swallowed and tried to give her cousin the signal to shut the hell up. "Yeah, she's out."

Curious, Tracy looked from Danielle to Nina. "What friend?"

Before she could respond, Nina answered for her. "Kayla—you know, the one they think killed that minister."

Quickly, Danielle rose and removed her feet from the soaking water. It was time to go.

"Oh hell, nah! You been sittin' here all this time shooting the shit wit' me so you could go back and tell yo' friend?"

"Yep," Danielle replied without hesitation. "I'm tryin' to clear my girl's name."

"Your *girl* killed my man."

"She didn't kill him, but someone did. I was tryin' to find out what else you knew 'bout him."

"All I know is that my man is dead and yo' girl's big, fat ass killed him. I hope she rots in that jail." Her neck rocked as she spoke.

Tired of listening to her talk bad about Kayla, Danielle reached out and snatched the wig from her head, then headed toward the door. Tracy started cussing and screaming, but Danielle ignored her fake ass and kept right on going.

Chapter 37

Renee

I went over to catch Deacon Williams at work—he owns a small copy shop near campus. I knew him from back in the day. He and my grandfather had been really good friends, and Big Mama used to be a very active member of their congregation. I parked my rental in the lot next to a blue VW Bug with a sticker on the back window that read, HE IS THE ANSWER. I strolled inside the air-conditioned building and glanced around at the rows of copy machines. By the summer traffic in the lobby, I could tell business was definitely good. I walked to the desk, asked if Deacon Williams was in, and was escorted to his office in the back.

The second he saw me, his beady brown eyes sparkled with laughter. "Well, if it isn't little Nae-Nae. I haven't seen you in years." He came from behind the desk and hugged me.

"It's good seeing you, too. How are the twins?" I asked, referring to his albino-looking daughters.

"Fine, fine. Please, have a seat." He sat behind his desk and pointed to a group photograph on the end. "We took this last year. That's Norita's two children and those are Cappy's."

Good Lord, three generations of ugliness. They definitely took after their mother because for an ol' head, Deacon Williams wasn't half bad. Salt-and-pepper curls, paper-bag-brown skin. and a tall, medium build.

"What can I do for you?" he asked, getting right to the point.

I cleared my throat and tried to put on my most pitiful expression. "I'm sorry about Reverend Brown. I was told the two of you were very close."

"Thank you," he replied with a solemn nod. "His death was a shock to all of us. But he's in a better place now."

"The reason why I'm here is that Kayla Sparks is my best friend." I watched his face change. "Please, hear me out."

He took a deep breath, then nodded grimly.

"I've known Kayla for years and so have you. She was a member of your church for over a decade before your boy preyed on her vulnerability. Now she's being accused of murdering him and I'm trying to do everything I can to help clear her name," I explained.

Deacon Williams fingered his mustache as he spoke. "I believe everyone is innocent until proven guilty, but in this case, I prefer not to take sides. Instead, I'm leaving it in the hands of the Lord."

"Sorry if I can't do that. I know Reverend Brown was messing around with both women and men." He squirmed at that bit of information.

"Listen, I wish you all the best in helping your friend, but I prefer not to discuss Reverend Brown's extramarital affairs because they are all lies."

"Lies?" I gave a quick short laugh. "Didn't you see the videotape?"

"Yep, and it was a fake, just like the one that framed R. Kelly."

Oh, he was definitely touched in the head.

"Listen, all I want to know is who else was he messing with?"

"How would I know?"

"Because you were 'posed to be with him on those alleged fishing trips."

"Young lady, you're on a goose hunt," he replied impatiently.

"I don't think so. I was curious about those fishing trips the two of you took."

He glanced down at his watch. "What about them?"

"Was he really going fishing with you, or were you just covering for him and his fag parties?"

He looked vaguely amused. "He and I were fishing."

I frowned. "Then how was it that three weeks ago he forgot his tackle box?"

Deacon Williams hesitated for a moment and refused to meet my gaze as he wiped beads of sweat from his forehead. "We shared mine," he retorted defensively. "Now, if you'll excuse me, I've got a lot of work to do." He sprang to his feet and so did I.

"I don't believe you. I think he was meeting some woman or man and you covered for him—unless, of course, the two of you were involved."

He was practically foaming at the mouth. "I bet your grandmother is turning in her grave. What Leroy chose to do when he wasn't in the pulpit was his business and he'll have to answer to God for that. Now, if you'd excuse me."

I walked back to my rental car. His ass was lying and I was going to find out why.

Chapter 38

Danielle

Danielle pulled into her parents' driveway. Closing her eyes, she took a deep breath and prayed for the strength to go through with what she was about to do, then climbed out and went inside.

"Hey, Mama."

Victoria turned around, a hand on her hip, and glared. "About time you got your narrow behind over here. I don't know what's gotten into you."

She groaned. This was the reason why she had suggested to her mother that Portia come over to the house to talk, but no, her mother refused to let her grandbaby out of her sight until she was sure everything had been squared away between the two of them.

"Mama, that's why I'm here now," Danielle whined as she sank into a seat at the table.

"But it shouldn't have taken you this long. That's your daughter in the other room. Your flesh and blood. You never turn your back on your child for a piece of meat, because thugs come a dime a dozen."

"He's changed," she replied defensively. "Ron has a job now and even gave me money to help pay the bills."

"Whoopty-do." She pointed a fork at Danielle. "That's because he's trying to get back in your good graces. Once he starts getting comfortable again, then everything is gonna change, mark my word."

"Mom, I didn't come over here for this."

"Just answer one question for me. How could you take the word of some lowlife over the words of your own daughter? Uh?"

"Mom, you and I both know that Portia lies all the time to get attention. I can't separate fact from fiction with that girl. Just last month she was accusing a college student of raping her."

"And as her mother, it was your job to stand by her. Now, hear me out. That's what mothers are for. We fight our children's battles. We try to protect them from harm." She paused long enough to take a seat across from her. "Do you remember that yellow man your Aunt Donna used to date?"

Danielle nodded.

"The minute you told me that sleezy bum put his hand under your skirt, I went upside his head with a skillet. I didn't go asking questions, because there wasn't a damn thing to think about."

Danielle never forgot "Uncle David." He was a fabulous piano player. Every time she visited Aunt Donna, Danielle would sit on the bench beside him and watch his fingers glide across the keys. One afternoon he decided to teach her how to play "Chopsticks." Danielle skipped over to the bench in her new pleated skirt and patent leather shoes and sat beside him. He showed her the first two bars and it wasn't long before she had it down pat. Next thing she knew, he was telling her how beautiful she was and sliding his hand up her knee. Her mother had taught her as a child that if a man, no matter if he was even her "damn daddy," touched her in a way that made her feel uncomfortable, to come and tell her. The second his hand slid across her crotch, she sprang from the bench and into the kitchen, where her mother was sitting picking collard greens.

Blinking, Danielle returned to the present and gazed over at her mother's determined face. "Mama, I know what you're saying, but if I was to jump every time Portia cried wolf, I'd be in jail."

"I'm not saying come out swinging, but side with your daughter until you discover the truth. Men come and go, but your children are forever."

"Mom, I just don't know."

"Then you'd better figure it out quick, because the longer it takes you, the harder it's going to be to mend the mess between y'all." She shook her head. "Your daughter's been over here crying her eyes out while you've been over there entertaining. I thought I raised you better than that. How would you have felt if I had turned my back on you the first time you got pregnant?"

"I wasn't . . ." She stopped short when her mother glared at her, then suddenly remembered a time in her life she had tried to block from her mind. *How quickly we forget.* She had just turned sixteen when she had discovered she was pregnant by her boyfriend of three months. Ryan Jackman was her first. Danielle thought he would stand by her, but instead he dumped her, claiming the baby wasn't his. She had waited six weeks before she finally broke down and told her mother she was pregnant. Instead of screaming and hollering, her mother had pulled her into her arms and said, "We all make mistakes." Her mother told her whatever she decided about the baby, she would stand by her. She didn't want it but couldn't see depositing the embryo at the nearest Planned Parenthood, either. After weeks of praying to the Lord for guidance, she started spotting and eventually miscarried.

"You have allowed yourself to stray too far from the church. Have you even bothered getting down on your knees and asking the Lord for help?"

"No," she mumbled.

Clearly disappointed, Victoria shook her head. "See, that's the problem. Any Christian woman wouldn't have dreamed of choosing a man over her only child. Now march your butt right down that hall and make things right!"

Danielle went down the hall to her daughter's room. Growing up, the room had belonged to her. Portia was curled up on the bed with her headphones on, sound asleep. As she watched her, Danielle's heart softened. She remembered all of the nights she had strolled into her daughter's room to tuck her into bed long after she was asleep. Danielle watched her for what felt like forever before she took a seat on the end of the bed, then tapped Portia lightly on the arm. "Portia, wake up."

Disoriented, Portia mumbled something Danielle didn't understand before she shot up straight against the headboard. Her eyes were wide with surprise that quickly changed to fear. "Hey," she finally said.

Danielle briefly closed her eyes. *Lord, please forgive me for striking my child.* She believed in discipline, but the last thing she had ever wanted was for Portia to be afraid of her.

"How have you been feeling?" When she reached up to brush a strand of hair away from her face, Portia flinched before she relaxed.

"I've been okay," she replied weakly.

She nodded. "Don't forget you have an appointment next week with the gynecologist. We'll get to see how far along you are." Danielle lowered her hand and sighed. "I guess I need to be getting the spare room ready for my grandbaby."

Portia's eyes grew round with surprise at the smile on her mother's lips, and a single tear rolled down her cheek.

Danielle's own eyes swam. She pulled her daughter into her arms and held her while they both cried. "I'm sorry," she whispered near her ear. "I'll never put my hands on you again."

Sniffling, Portia eased out of her arms. "No, Mama. I'm not mad at you. I've been giving you a hard time lately. If it was my daughter, I would have knocked her out a long time ago." Shrugging, she continued. "I don't know why I do the things I do."

Danielle patted her back lovingly, then slowly dropped her hand. "I just wished that you would try to work with me. I love you, Portia, and I want you to know that if there is something or someone bothering you, you can come to me."

"Okay, Mama."

Reaching over, she grasped her daughter's hand, then took a deep breath. "Right now I need you to tell me the truth. No matter how you answer, I won't get mad."

Portia nodded. "Okay."

Danielle swallowed hard and asked the most difficult question of her life. "Is Ron the father of yo' baby?" she asked, although deep down, she already knew the answer.

Her bottom lip quivered, then heavy tears flooded her cheeks. After a moment, Portia nodded. "Yes." She started crying hard. "Mama, I'm so sorry. I know it was wrong, but he was so nice to me and made me feel so pretty. It only happened once. I swear!"

The pain of the truth was like a knife to her heart. She pursed her lips to keep from crying again, and held out her arms. Portia threw herself against her and held on tightly. Danielle's heart started to pound fast. She couldn't believe this was happening. But this was her baby and if she didn't stand by her, who would? "I believe you. But if I'm going to put him out, I have to have something to make him stop lying to me."

Portia looked at her with sad, confused eyes. "Something like what?"

Danielle swallowed. She still couldn't believe what she was about to ask, but she didn't have much choice. "What's his *thing* look like? If you can tell me that, I can catch him in a lie." Deep down, Danielle knew she needed something else to back up her daughter's story.

Portia sat there for the longest time, wringing her hands together, and Danielle could tell she was uncomfortable with the question, but she had to know.

"Well . . . he has that skin on his thing." Her words were barely above a whisper but loud enough for her mother to hear nevertheless. Danielle sat there for the longest time, stunned as the truth had finally sunk in.

"Pack yo' things. I'll be by to pick you up in the morning. Right now, I've got some business to take care of."

Portia looked scared. "Please, Mama. I don't want to get Ron in trouble. I-I let him touch me."

"It doesn't matter," she said reassuringly. "You are a kid and Ron's a grown-ass man. You can't consent to shit." Pissed as hell, Danielle rose. "I'll see you later." From this point on, the only part Ron would ever play in her life would be through the blood of her grandbaby.

Chapter 39

Kayla

Kayla swallowed thickly, but the frog in her throat refused to budge. "I love you, Kenya."

"I love you, too, Mommy."

She was choking with tears when she lowered the phone to the cradle. Kayla slowly crossed the living room, her arms folded across her chest for comfort. Things weren't looking too good. She didn't have an alibi for the time after Jermaine left her house till Leroy's body was found. She was so scared that she was going to spend the rest of her life in jail, she had called her mom in Birmingham and asked her to bring the girls back so she could spend as much time with them as she possibly could.

Kayla glanced around with a look of despair. She had met with her lawyer this morning, then dropped by her house to pick up her mail and spend a few moments in her own home alone. Jermaine was against the idea and would have a fit when he found out, but it was something she felt she needed to do. Afraid there were still reporters lurking in the corners, she had parked around the corner and snuck in through the back. The first thing she did was check her voice mail, and she wished that she hadn't. *Murderer, home-wrecker,* and *fat slut* were just a few of the obscenities. Appalled, angry, and wounded, she didn't even bother listening to the next twenty-seven messages. The mail was just as bad. Letters with no return addresses, threatening her life and the welfare of her children. Sinking to the couch, Kayla cried softly. What in the world was she going to do? She was touched that Nadine and Renee were taking care of her legal expenses. And extremely grateful they had retained one of the sharpest lawyers in the city, especially when her own life and freedom were at stake. But her legal representation was the least of her worries. If only she could say the same about the rest of her life.

She hadn't killed anyone, and the whole situation and all of the accusations only added to her frustration. Someone came into that house shortly after she had left and killed Leroy and in the process had framed her for his murder.

"Why, Lord!" she shouted, then slammed her hand down onto the coffee table. She paid her tithes every month. Every night she was down on her knees in prayer. She even tried to live her life according to the Good Book. Almost.

Thou shall not commit adultery.

Swallowing, she was unsuccessful at removing the lump from her throat. She was wrong for getting involved with Leroy and now she was paying for it. But the only one who had the right to determine her fate was God, not a courtroom with a jury of thirteen.

Falling to her knees, Kayla bowed her head and closed her eyes. "Lord, I come to you as your humble child because what I did was a foolish act. Please cleanse and make me whole again." For the next twenty minutes, she prayed for forgiveness.

Kayla rose and paced around the room, feeling slightly better but worried just the same. With each passing hour, her day in court drew nearer. This morning she and her lawyer tried to come up with names of folks who might be able to shed some light on Leroy's recent behavior and help clear her name. So far they hadn't been able to come up with any evidence to prove that she wasn't responsible for killing him. All they had was a list of references who could vouch for her character, although their testimonies would carry very little weight against the evidence the prosecuting attorney's office had already collected. DNA, Leroy's blood on her shirt, the witness she almost ran her car into, her admitting she stabbed him, and—oh yeah, let's not forget her fingerprints on the murder weapon. The rest of their evidence was circumstantial but damaging just the same.

Tears flooded her eyes. She hadn't even been able to come up with any other possible suspects because everyone she thought of had an alibi. *Everyone has an alibi but me.* She had one, all right. She was at home in her bed asleep. Unfortunately, she had no way to prove it, or her innocence, thus far. Kayla knew that if they didn't come up with something soon, she was in very hot water.

The phone rang, startling her. She listened to it ring, too afraid to answer it. No one knew she was there, anyway. Moving over to the window, she stared at the neighborhood children out in the playground behind her house. She had spent years, right in this house, watching her own girls out back while she prepared dinner. Tears raced down her cheeks and fear pounded her heart at the thought of never being able to see them again. She couldn't bear losing her children, and her mother having to raise them for her. She wanted to see them grow up, go off to college, and someday fall in love and start families of their own.

Think, Kayla, think.

She *had* been thinking. For the last several weeks, that's all she had been doing, and she couldn't come up with a single possibility. According to her lawyer, two hours after she had stabbed Leroy in the shoulder, Deacon Williams had arrived at the house and found the body, lying on the kitchen floor. For the longest time she sat there wondering what the deacon was doing at the pastor's house at one o'clock in the morning. Maybe if she found out the answer to that question, she might be able to find out who really killed him.

Chapter 40

Danielle

By the time Ron put his key in the lock, Danielle had all his shit in garbage bags right inside the door. He stepped in, looked down at the bags, then over to Danielle, who was sitting on the couch with her legs crossed and arms folded, waiting. "Danny, whassup, boo?"

"You're moving out, that's what!"

Eyebrows knitted close together, he stepped forward. "Yo, you always trippin'! What I do now?"

"Portia described your dick," she stated firmly. "How would my daughter know you're not circumcised?"

Ron's face fell. Obviously, he never expected to hear those words coming from her mouth. "Okay, I-I can explain that," he stuttered nervously. "She walked in on me one time I was in the shower. I never mentioned it 'cause I didn't wanna start nothin'."

Danielle rolled her eyes. She wanted so badly to believe him, but Ron had had every opportunity to come clean. Maybe then she might have believed him. Now it was too late. "I don't believe you."

"Come on. What I gotta lie fo?"

"'Cause you're a man and that's what men do—*lie.*"

"Yo, this is crazy. Boo, I thought everything was cool wit' us?"

"That was before you decided to take advantage of my daughter!"

"I ain't touched that girl." He raked a frustrated hand across his face. "Okay, I'm fin to be totally honest." At her continued silence, he relaxed his stance, then continued. "Me and Portia were cool as shit, then one day she came running out her room half-naked and tried to kiss me."

Her eyes grew large and round. "And you slept with her?"

"Hell, naw! I ain't never touched that girl. I swear. I told her that shit wasn't cool and if she tried it again, I was tellin' you."

"You're lying!" Danielle screamed and hurled a paperweight at his head. He ducked and it hit the wall.

"Why you buggin'? All I'm tryin' to—"

She cut him off. "Get out! Otherwise I'm callin' the police, and if you ever bother me again, I'm goin' to charge you with rape."

He stood there for the longest time with an expression of disbelief before finally saying, "You're gonna regret this."

"And don't take my car!"

He tsked. "You got life twisted if you think I'm walkin' wit' all these bags."

"Then you better go call Tyrone, because you ain't takin' my car!"

Ron grabbed the two bags and headed out the door. Danielle came out behind him. "You heard what I said!" she repeated. Completely ignoring her, he pulled his keys out of his pocket and opened the trunk. "You heard what the fuck I said?"

He glared over at her, then gave her a bitter laugh. "What you gon' do, call the cops? You forget. My name's on this car, too." While she stood there, he loaded the trunk and slammed it shut. Danielle dashed over and blocked the door so he couldn't get in. "Move the fuck outta the way!"

Folding her arms, she refused to budge. "Make me."

"Listen—I'm not fin to put my hands on you."

"You are a sick bastard—you know that!" she screamed, pointing her fingers in his face.

Shaking his head, he laughed. "Yeah, all right. Whateva you say. Now move, 'cause I'm outta here."

"You ain't going nowhere because I'm callin' the cops and pressing rape charges against you!"

He gave her a smug look, then held up his hands in surrender. "Yo, lock my black ass up! And I'll have my lawyer bring in a dozen nuccas who'll testify they slept wit' Portia's slutty ass."

Danielle swung and got him right under the jaw, then threw another punch that he caught. "Get off me!" she screamed as he pressed her arms to her side. "Get off me!"

"You need to calm the fuck down," he mumbled close to her ear. "Look at you, actin' like a damn fool. Got the neighbors watchin' and shit."

For the first time she noticed the couple across the street standing in the door staring. "Let me go!" She jerked away from him and dropped her hands to her knees while she tried to catch her breath. "I can't stand you. You make me sick!"

Ron just stood there looking down at her, shaking his head with this amused look on his face. "You know what? You and yo' daughter are two crazy-ass mofo." Turning, he opened the door and she watched as he climbed in and flipped her off.

This time she did nothing to stop him.

Chapter 41

Renee

"Hurry up with the drinks!" I yelled.

"Just hold your horses."

Nadine was in Danielle's kitchen making our third round of margaritas. She was slow as hell. I could have hopped in my car, driven five blocks to a little hole-in-the-wall, ordered a drink, and been back, at the rate she was going. Tonight was girls' night out, and the mood wasn't right without a drink in our hands. At least that was the case for me. Our job tonight was to cheer Kayla up.

We were all laid out in the living room. Me on the couch, Kayla in the chair, and Danielle on the love seat. Everyone, including Kayla's nondrinking ass, was tipsy as hell. And we couldn't have a girls' night out without Lisa. My eyes traveled over to the five-by-seven photo Danielle had placed on her coffee table. *See, sis, we haven't forgotten about you.* Lisa had always been the levelheaded one of the bunch. We definitely need her wisdom to vibrate through the room tonight.

The CD in the five-disk player changed. "Ooh! That's my song!" Danielle cried.

"Ho, every song is your song." Danny's been saying that same shit for the last half hour, although I'll have to admit that was my song as well. Oh, yeah! The room filled with the sultry sounds of Luther Vandross. I hummed along with him, and Danny and Kayla both started singing off key. By the end of the song, Nadine finally moved into the living room carrying a blender filled with heaven.

"About damn time," I said without malice as I held out my glass. She went around and filled each of our glasses before returning to her seat at the other end of the couch.

Danielle rose and held up her glass. "Okay, let's make a toast."

"A toast to what?" Kayla asked.

"A toast to our fucked-up lives!" she cried, then fell back onto the love seat, cracking up.

"I second that," Kayla replied, waving her glass in the air.

"Hell, I've got to toast to that as well."

I snorted rudely. "Nadine, puhleeze. What's fucked-up with *your* life?"

"Jordan wants to have a baby," she admitted between sips.

Danielle gave a hard laugh. "That ain't nothing. My man was screwing my daughter."

"What?" Nadine cried.

Kayla gasped. "Say it ain't so."

"It's so," she answered with a gloomy look. "And I really thought Ron and I had a chance."

So it was true after all. Damn, I wouldn't put that shit on anyone. "Did you do what I told you to do?"

She took a sip, then nodded. "Yep, and she described it in full detail, foreskin and all."

"Foreskin!" Nadine cried. "Eeew! You were messing with some brotha who wasn't circumcised?"

"Like you never have?" Danielle challenged.

Nadine calmed down. "Okay, once, but that was by accident."

Kayla wasn't letting it go that easily. "What do you mean, by accident?"

"That football player I met while we were in Jamaica," she confessed.

I started laughing loud. "RD? What? So I guess that means you really did screw him?"

Nadine shrugged, faking nonchalance. I could see through her ass. I always could. "If you want to call it that. I was just trying to figure out my sexuality."

"What she means is, she was trying to fight the fact she was digging pussy by trying one more dick."

She gave me a disapproving look. "Why you always got to make things sound so damn nasty?"

I spread my legs and rubbed my crotch suggestively. "'Cause I am nasty."

Kayla reached for the photograph. "Lisa, you hear this mess? Your sister ain't changed a lick."

"Oh, I've changed quite a bit. Y'all just haven't noticed. This is my second trip down here in a month, and I still ain't had no Columbia dick."

Nadine's jaw dropped. "Now I know you're lying."

"Since when do I lie?"

"She's right," Danielle chimed in. "If she got some, we would be the first to know."

Kayla wagged a finger in the air. "Uh-uh, that ain't even true. Not no more. To this day, Renee refuses to admit she slept with Everton."

Danielle's brow rose. "Who's Everton?"

"The front-desk clerk at that hotel we stayed at in Jamaica."

I gave Kayla a serious look. "I admitted that I slept with that crazy muthafucka."

Nadine was quick to agree. "Yeah, he was definitely psycho."

Danielle pouted. "I hate that I didn't get to go."

"There'll be other trips."

"So tell me, what are you planning to do about Ron?" I asked between sips.

"Last night Kee and his crew beat his ass."

I tossed my head with laughter. "I ain't mad."

"Yep, he's lucky he didn't kill his ass for fuckin' with his niece.

Kee's pretty certain Ron's arm is broke. He made him sign over my title and got my car back."

"Lucky you."

Kayla rose. "Okay, so are we going to toast to our messed-up lives, or what?"

"No, we're going to toast to our fucked-up lives," I amended while trying to scramble to my feet. Nadine and Danielle also stood and held their glasses high. "Here's to making our lives better."

"Hear, hear," we each said, then took a sip from our glasses and lowered back into our seats.

"So, Jordan wants to have a baby?" Danielle asked.

While nodding, Nadine pressed her lips together. "Yeah, she says her biological clock is ticking."

"So what y'all going to do?"

Her shoulders deflated. "I guess we'll find a sperm donor."

"Hey," I interrupted. "That reminds me of the Spike Lee joint, *She Hate Me.* Anybody seen that?"

"Yes," Nadine replied, "and no, she's not planning on sleeping with a man. Jordan wants to be artificially inseminated."

"Girl, that shit's expensive. You're better off letting some negro bang her for a six-pack and a bucket of chicken." Nadine tossed her shoe at me and got me square in the chest. I guess I deserved that one.

Nadine's wounded look was quickly replaced with a smirk. "Okay, smart-ass. Your turn to tell us what's so fucked-up about *your* life."

I took another sip from my straw before dropping the bomb. "Hell, y'all think you're lives are bad—well, guess what? My husband and I have been swinging."

"What!" Nadine fell off the couch.

Kayla's eye shifted from one of us to the other. "Swinging? What's swinging?"

Danielle decided to explain. "It's when couples have sex with other couples."

She gasped, then shook her head. "Why am I not the least bit surprised?"

I nodded and took another sip. "Oh, yeah. I've had quite a few mandingos."

"So what's the problem?" Nadine asked as she returned to her seat at the other end of the couch. "You've been complaining about John in bed for years."

"But now it's too much." I sat up straighter on the couch. "This may sound crazy, but now I'm actually fucking around on my husband with my husband. And it's no longer any fun. I like spontaneous sex, not that kinky shit my husband schedules for me. It takes the fun out of it."

Kayla shook her head. "You are too much."

"Does he get his groove on, too?" Nadine asked.

"Yeah. And he seems to be getting off on that shit. He ain't never been able to fuck me doggy-style, but he managed to fuck some big-titty bitch that way with no problem. Oops—sorry, Nadine." As sensitive as she is about her breasts, I knew she would kick my leg.

"Forget you. That's why John's pimping your ass."

"And that's why you're a dyke," I retorted.

"Don't knock it 'til you try it."

I snorted rudely. "Whatever. I am strictly dickly—ain't that right, Danielle? Oh shit, I forgot. I guess you can't say the same."

"Yousa damn liar!" she cried defensively.

I rolled off the couch, cracking up. "Girl, you know you were rubbing pussies with Trish!"

Kayla gasped. "What? Tell me it ain't so."

Danielle rolled her eyes. "It ain't so."

Nadine gave her a skeptical look. "I don't know. Y'all were pretty close."

"Close?" I gasped. "I walked in just as she was strapping on."

Kayla held up her hand. "Wait a minute. You need to start at the beginning because neither of you bothered to tell me this story."

Danielle looked over at me and rolled her eyes. "That's because I swore them to secrecy."

"Well, the secret's out now." Kayla's eyes sparkled with anticipation as she reclined the chair. "All right. I'm listening."

I shifted on the couch. "Okay, Da—"

"Uh-uh, heffa," Danielle interrupted. "The only one telling this story, is me."

"Okay . . . we're all ears." I jumped up and grabbed the pitcher. "But first let me whip up another round." I dashed into the kitchen, tossed in a whole lot of tequila and triple sec, then grabbed the ice and margarita mix. I was having a ball hanging with my girls. Tonight was long overdue. I added a couple more cubes of ice to the blender and listened to Kayla in the living room talking about Jermaine. I was so happy he had come into her life. Now the only thing standing in the way of her future was Leroy's murder, and I wasn't leaving Columbia until her name had been cleared.

I skipped into the living room. "Okay, I'm back!" Everyone held out their glasses at the same time. I quickly filled them to the rim, and even spilled a little on the floor that Danielle will have to shampoo later. Right now everyone was dying to hear Danny's story. "All right." I ran over, picked up Lisa's picture, kissed it, then plopped down onto the couch. "Tell us the story."

Nodding, Danielle took a sip. "Okay. I met Trish while attending that nine-month LPN program. She was cool as shit and we became study partners."

"Uh-huh. Y'all were studying, all right," I mumbled under my breath.

"Shut up." Danielle tossed a pillow at me before continuing. "She would come over and we would lie across my bed and study, and sometimes we fell asleep. I didn't think nothing of it—then one evening I woke up and found her standing over me wearing a strap-on. Rubber dick flapping in the air!"

All four of us drunk bitches were laughing so hard we were crying.

"What a minute!" Kayla cried while still laughing. "She was actually naked, wearing a strap-on?"

Nodding, Danny wiped tears from her eyes.

"What did you do?" Nadine asked between chuckles.

She looked over at me as she continued. "I didn't get a chance to do anything because Nae-Nae used her key and walked in."

"'Cause I knew something wasn't right with that girl. Her hair was too damn short and she always wore these oversized shirts so you couldn't tell how big her titties were."

Nadine intervened. "I thought she was cute."

"You would!" Danielle and I screamed in unison.

Blushing, Nadine tried to explain. "Well she had the longest lashes and the sexiest lips."

"Shut up! I'm about to be sick," Danny groaned.

I reached for the pitcher and topped off my glass again. "She walked like a man," I sang. "Talked liked a man. Hell, she even dressed like a damn man."

"She did not," Danielle defended. "She wore jeans like everyone else."

"Yeah, but we ain't wearing a rubber strap-on underneath."

Nadine spit her drink across the couch and the laughter was nonstop.

My eyes traveled from one to the other. "That girl was getting ready to work Danny with that big chocolate thunder. She was standing there, stroking it up and down like that shit was real. I cupped my hand and demonstrated what I meant. "I told her to get the hell up out of there. She put on her pants with that thing hangin' on the side of her leg, then bounced. As soon as she was gone, me and Danny burned her sheets."

"Did she ever talk to you again?" Kayla asked, clearly intrigued.

After taking a sip, Danielle shook her head. "Nope, she played my ass. Found herself some other bitch she was hugging and lip-locking with."

"So tell us, Nadine. Do either you or Jordan use a strap-on?"

The question caught her off guard. "Hell, no. That's a butch.

Jordan and I are both females. We find other ways to make each other feel good."

"What? Licking pussies?" I asked, and grinned at her mortified expression.

Kayla frowned. "You are so damn nosy."

Nadine stirred her drink with her straw before saying, "I saw Trish a couple of weeks ago at The Red Hot Chili Pepper."

"What's that?"

"It's this new alternative club."

I was intrigued. "Men dancing with men and women be dancing together?"

Nadine nodded.

I couldn't resist saying out loud what had come to mind. "Let's go."

"You're kidding." Nadine looked surprised.

"Nope," I replied, then rose to my feet. "I'm serious. Let's go." I was tipsy and down for anything.

We all hopped into the Durango. System thumping. I hung out the window and flashed my boobs at a blue Caprice Classic filled with some young thunder cats trying to get our attention. They followed us, but as soon as they saw us stop in front of the gay club, they shouted, "Dykes!" and peeled around the corner. We were laughing so hard, it was ridiculous.

Danielle parked on the corner and the four of us staggered to the door, holding on to each other. I paid everyone's cover charge, then we moved inside the dark, smoky interior and started leaning and rocking with the crowd. The floor was packed, the music hot. I was amazed to see that gays knew how to party, too. I was also surprised at how many fine-ass gay men there were in Columbia. No wonder a good black woman couldn't find a man, because they were all in this muthafucka. While the three of them moved out onto the dance floor, my lush ass pushed through the crush of bodies toward the bar.

"Let me get a tequila and pineapple," I said to a sweetie pie behind the counter. He was a handsome specimen, wearing a wifebeater, with muscles bulging.

"Coming right up." He reached beneath the bar and removed a glass. I couldn't stop staring and shaking my head. It was a doggone shame for anyone to look that good. Shiny bald head. Goatee. Milk chocolate. He definitely looked like he would melt in my mouth.

"Here you go, sexy." He slid the drink in my direction.

I licked my lips. "Please tell me you like women."

A lopsided grin curled his thick lips. "I like women."

"Shit! Then how—"

He pressed two fingers to my lips. "I also like men."

Damn! I pushed his hand away 'cause ain't no telling where them fingers been. "That's a damn shame," I muttered as I tossed a five on the counter. He moved to the other end of the counter and I took one final look, groaned, then turned around and rested my hip against the bar. Every seat was taken, even around the bar. I stared off onto the dance floor, watching people bumping and grinding. Women were rubbing on other women. Men were groping other men. I'll have to admit, seeing it up close and personal wasn't as bad as I thought it would be. Hell, the shit was funny. Especially Kayla, Nadine, and Danielle, who were all to the far right, making a sandwich with Nadine in the middle. Bodies rubbing, palms tightly holding to each other's hips. Hell, nah! I started laughing, then quickly downed my drink. There was no way I wasn't capturing this moment. I removed my cell phone from my hip and pushed through the crowd toward the three of them. As soon as I was in close range, I aimed and clicked my camera phone.

"What are you doing?" Danielle screamed.

"Taking a picture of y'all nasty asses!" I yelled back over the bass blaring from a nearby speaker.

"Give me that phone!" Danielle came at me. Laughing, I pushed through the crowd, while trying to upload the photo to my online photo album. The transfer was at eighty-five percent by the time she grabbed my arm. "Hey!"

"Delete that photo. Now!"

I put the phone behind my back, out of her reach. "Oh, hell no. I'm going to make a copy for everyone, even Trish."

We were wrestling and laughing at the same time when Danielle stopped abruptly and said, "Isn't that Peaches over there?"

I followed the direction of her gaze and sure enough, Peaches' skinny ass was a few feet away, grinding with some little white dude on the dance floor. The song ended and I turned and moved in their direction just as Peaches stuck his tongue in the dude's ear and pivoted on his heels. Pushing through sweaty bodies, my speed was hindered when a tall dude stepped in my line of vision. By the time I made it to a clearing, Peaches was nowhere to be found.

"Where'd he go?" Danielle asked as she joined me.

My eyes traveled quickly to my right and left. "I don't know, but he's in here somewhere. Let's see if we can find him." We spent the next few minutes trying to cover every corner of the club, but it was hard to do with so many folks in the way. As little as Peaches was, his gay ass could have been anywhere. "Damn!" My head was throbbing, a combination of too much to drink and the loud bass.

"He must have left already." Danielle looked equally pissed off.

"Let's not mention to Kayla that we saw Peaches. She's having a good time and I don't want to ruin it for her."

"I agree. But now what?"

I shrugged. "I don't know, but right now I need to pee."

"I'll come with you."

We followed the neon sign at the back of the club to the bathrooms. Men on the right. Women on the left. We were just getting ready to step through the door when Peaches came out of the men's room, wiping his mouth with the back of his hand.

"Peaches! Where the hell you been hiding?" I demanded to know as I walked up to him.

He looked stunned, then relaxed and rolled his eyes at me. "I shouldn't be speaking with y'all heffas after getting me mixed up in that shit. Leroy's bitch ass tried to beat me like a stepchild."

I ignored his dramatics. "So you had reason to kill him?"

Appalled, he pressed a palm to his chest. "Uh-uh, Ms. Peaches ain't killed nobody. I was on vacation."

"Vacation where?" Danielle asked.

"Not that it's any of your business," he began while rolling his neck. "I was so upset after seeing my name all over the news that one of my sugar daddies bought me a trip to Jamaica. Shit, they got some mandingos over there."

Been there, done that. "Have you heard about Kayla being arrested for Leroy's murder?"

He nodded. "And I don't blame her for killing him."

Danielle intervened. "Kayla ain't killed his trifling ass, but we're trying to find out who else might have wanted that man dead."

"Shit, maybe someone who doesn't want the whole town to know his ass liked a good licking every now and again," Peaches said with a dramatic pose.

My brow rose. "Someone like who?"

Peaches' thick lips curled in a slow, sinister smile. He signaled for us to move in closer, then glanced over his shoulder before he whispered, "Didn't I tell you . . . Leroy ain't the only member of that church I'm messing with." He wiped his mouth, winked, then pointed to the men's room. "Catch y'all chicas later." After tossing his purse over his shoulder, he sashayed back toward the dance floor.

I glanced at Danielle, nodded, then moved to the men's bathroom and pushed the door open. We stepped in just in time to see Deacon Williams coming out of the far stall, zipping his pants. Shocked, we all gasped, then froze.

He was the first to relax. Then he moved over to the sink and turned on the faucet. "What are you ladies doing in the men's room?" he asked while he calmly washed his hands.

"We should be asking you that, especially since every man in here is gay," Danielle replied as she stood by my side, her arms folded across her chest.

I started laughing. "You gay muthafucka. When you were

supposed to be fishing, y'all were doing that *Brokeback Mountain* shit."

His face snapped to me. "I ain't gay! Reverend Brown was gay," he barked. A muscle flexed nervously at his jaw.

Talk about calling the kettle black. "You just finished letting Peaches suck your dingdong. What do you call that?"

He simply shrugged. "A mouth is a mouth."

"And a dick is a dick, right?" I countered coolly.

"That doesn't make me gay," he retorted defensively.

"All y'all down-low brothas are in denial." I shook my head and propped a hand to my hip. "Now I know why you killed your boy Leroy. You were afraid if he went down, it was just a matter of time before you did, too."

He gave a nervous laugh and the skin around his mouth grew tight. "You can't prove I had anything to do with his death. The only suspect the police have is Sister Sparks. Now, if you ladies will excuse me, I need to get home." He moved toward the door.

"How would Lula feel if she found out her husband was getting his balls lickity-licked?" I yelled, halting his departure.

He swung around so fast, me and Danielle both jumped back and fell against the stall door. With his fist balled, he looked like he was about to hit me before his stance relaxed and he started laughing again. "Like I said before, you can't prove it. You ladies have a good night." He huffed past us, then pushed through the door.

"I knew something was up with him!" I shouted the moment the door shut.

"Yeah, but we can't prove it?" Danielle asked wearily.

I scrubbed my hand over my face, then shifted restlessly around the bathroom. "There has to be something."

"We already know he was there because he was the one who found Leroy's body and called the police."

I took a few seconds to ponder a possibility. "I bet you he's also the same sugar daddy who bought Peaches a ticket to

Jamaica. Deacon Williams didn't want him around while every-thing went down."

Danielle's hazel eyes regarded me for a moment before she nodded and signaled for me to follow her. We moved through the club, looking for Peaches to confirm what we already knew, and couldn't find him anywhere. I then sent David Lovell a text message to call me so I could tell him there was another suspect in Leroy Brown's murder.

Chapter 42

Renee

Okay, David Lovell is going to make me put my foot up his ass. He had finally called me back at two in the morning as I was crawling into bed. And he had the nerve to think he was about to make a booty call. Muthafucka, I don't think so. He'd had his chance and blown it—although I did tell him that if he helped us solve Kayla's case, I just might consider letting him rub my cootie-cat again. I then told him everything that happened last night, and all he could say was, "I'll look into it."

I checked with him again at eight and he still hadn't brought Deacon Williams in for questioning. I don't understand it. Do I have to do all the damn work?

Around nine, I sat up in my comfortable hotel bed and reached for my laptop. Like I said before, I've got a deadline that I have to meet. I spent two hours writing a sex scene that made my ass horny as hell, then put my laptop down and went to take a shower. While under the spray of water, I tried to think of a plan of action. Hell, I'm not a detective. That's David's job. But there was no way I was letting my girl go to jail without knowing I'd done everything in my power to help her.

Stepping out of the shower, I reached for a towel and wrapped it around my body, then went back into the room. I looked over at the box of chocolates that I had bought earlier from Nadine for her church's fund-raiser. I wasn't planning to eat it all, but I love to support a good cause. As I stared at the box, an idea came to mind. I could go door-to-door through Leroy's neighborhood, selling candy and asking questions at the same time. I know the police had already canvassed the area, but what could it hurt to try again? Everybody isn't always willing to talk to the police.

I got dressed, told Danielle what I was planning to do, then hopped in my car and headed out toward Leroy's whorehouse. I was halfway there when Tommy called. "Whassup?"

"Peaches got arrested."

"What?" I almost ran into another car and had to pull my ass over. "What happened?"

"The ticket to Jamaica had been bought over the Internet with one of Leroy's stolen credit cards."

"Oh no!"

Tommy sucked his gold tooth. "The police think that maybe Peaches killed him, stole his wallet, then hopped a plane."

"That's crazy." I wasn't about to tell Tommy that it was partly my fault Peaches had gotten arrested. David had come through after all. My lips curled upward. He must really want to play with my cootie-cat.

"I got my attorney trying to get him out on bail."

"Please keep me posted."

"I will."

I hung up the phone and squeezed the steering wheel tightly. Someone had killed Leroy, then stolen his wallet, setting it up to make it look like Peaches could be a suspect. My gut still told me it was Deacon Williams. Now I just needed to find a way to prove it.

I pulled onto Rock Quarry Road and parked at the very end of the street, then went door-to-door asking questions while trying to sell candy. Some people were helpful and even bought one or two bars of chocolate. Others slammed the door in my face. I was working the other side of the street, a few doors down from Leroy's house, when I recognized the elderly woman that answered it. "Hello, Ms. Ruby."

She peered at me before her eyes sparkled with recognition. "Well, if it isn't little Nae-Nae. Chile, come on in." She held open the door and I stepped into a living room that smelled like Ben-Gay. She signaled for me to have a seat and I watched her slowly move over to the couch. She reminded me of Big Mama. Silver-gray hair. Small, wire-rimmed glasses. A face covered with moles. Ms. Ruby had grown thin, and moved like her old bones were ready to give out.

"How's your mother doing?" she asked. Growing up, she had lived next door to us.

I stared across the couch at her for a long, intense moment before glancing away. "I haven't seen my mother in years."

She nodded knowingly. "She still hasn't kicked that habit yet?"

I shook my head.

She placed a small, wrinkled hand over mine and said, "Pray and have faith that in time she will find the strength to overcome her weakness. You know it ain't nothing but that devil."

"I know." We grew quiet and then I decided that instead of trying to pawn candy off on such a sweet old lady, I would just cut to the chase. "Ms. Ruby, are you familiar with Reverend Brown's murder?"

Her face sobered. "Yes, it was so sad."

"My best friend Kayla is being accused of his murder."

Slowly, she shook her head. "I saw it on the news. Such a sweet child. Always has a smile. Waved at me. I remember one time I needed help getting groceries out the car. I didn't even have to ask. She came across the street and gave me a hand."

"Kayla didn't kill him."

"I believe you," she replied, squeezing my hand. "Please tell her I'm praying for her."

"I will," I said, then shifted on the cushion. "Ms. Ruby, I'm trying to find out what really happened that night after Kayla left." I quickly told her what I knew about the night of the murder.

She gave me a long, thoughtful look, then folded her hands

onto her lap. "I remember waking up at midnight. I had fallen asleep on the couch as usual watching *The X-Files.* I just love that show. Ms. Tabby was meowing, wanting to go outside. When I opened the door, I saw this VW Bug pulling out from the new development next door to me. I remember wondering why someone would risk parking their car over there and getting stuck in all that mud. But as it pulled away, I remembered seeing that same car in front of Reverend Brown's house several times before."

My heart was pounding rapidly in my chest. "What color was it?"

She frowned thoughtfully. "It was either black or dark blue."

"Would you be willing to tell this to the police?"

Nodding, she replied, "If it will help that sweet friend of yours, I will."

I stayed long enough to have lunch, then said good-bye and went out to my car to call the girls. Kayla said she left Leroy's house shortly after eleven and Deacon Williams reported he didn't find Leroy's body until after one. So if that was the case, what was his car doing pulling away from the neighborhood around midnight? Ms. Ruby seemed confident about the time.

While dialing Danielle's number, I couldn't help grinning. I had finally found something to connect Deacon Williams to the murder.

Chapter 43

Danielle

She picked up a pair of booties and her heart fluttered. She was going to be a grandmother. A smile curled her lips. Teenage pregnancy was nothing to be proud of, but there was nothing she could do about it now except support her daughter's decision and get ready to spoil her grandbaby.

Danielle put the booties in her cart, then moved to the next aisle. She had come to Wal-Mart to buy food, not shop for baby clothes, but as she was moving down the aisle, she couldn't resist. As she gazed down at a pink ruffled dress, she couldn't help but hope that Portia had a little girl. However, after having only one child herself and the drama that came with girls, maybe she needed to pray for a grandson. Nadine had a boy and so did Renee, and both claimed that little boys were so much easier to raise.

"Excuse me, can you suggest a gift for a baby shower?" she heard someone ask.

"Sure, the easiest . . ." She swung around and her voice trailed off as she gazed up to find Calvin standing over her. Danielle's heart started to pound rapidly. He had a fresh new haircut and was casually dressed in jean shorts that showed off fabulous legs and a shirt that strained across his massive chest. "Calvin." She said his name like she was almost afraid to believe it. "Hi."

"Hey, yourself. I'm surprised to see you here."

She shrugged, then swallowed as she finally managed to pull herself together. "I'm supposed to be grocery shopping, but I couldn't resist."

His smile widened. "That means you've accepted your daughter's pregnancy and it's sunk in that you're going to be a grandmother?"

"Yeah, you know what they say—if you can't beat 'em, join 'em. Besides, I think this whole experience is going to have a positive effect on my daughter. She's been reading baby books and asking a lot of questions about her future, especially college, a subject I couldn't even get her to consider before," Danielle said while nervously fingering her hair.

"Good, I'm happy for both of you." He touched her arm and they shared a smile before Danielle dropped her eyes back into the basket. "Think you can spare a few minutes and help me pick out a gift?"

She nodded and looked up again. "I would love to."

"It's for my niece," he explained. "She and her husband are expecting their first child in four weeks. The doctor told her it was a girl."

"Okay, girls are easy to shop for. But I learned a long time ago that the easiest thing to do is to buy a gift card. They'll know what they need more than you will. It also prevents buying the same gift as someone else."

Calvin removed a gift card from the display. "Then a gift card it is."

"Good choice. Just go up to the register and you can put as much money on the card as you want."

"Thanks, Danielle."

"No problem."

There was a long silence before Calvin cleared his throat. "Well, I better get out of here. Good seeing you again."

He then turned on his heels and was several feet away before she finally found the courage to shout, "Wait! Calvin! Can I ask you a question?"

He slowly turned around and eyed her with measured curiosity. "Sure."

Her expression grew serious as she took a step forward. "Do you miss me?"

"Yes," he said without hesitation.

"Good, because I miss you, too." Without ceremony, Danielle dashed over to where he was standing, tossed her arms around his neck, and kissed him passionately on the lips. She was relieved when she felt him relax against her. Danielle didn't care who was watching. All she cared about was how good it felt to be held by him again. What a fool she had been to let him go. Her thug days were finally over. After her experience with Ron, she had learned to appreciate someone like Calvin. Good, single men were few and far between. Now that she had a second chance, she wasn't going to blow it.

"You must really miss me," he replied when she finally released him.

"I do." She kissed him again. "You think maybe you can sneak away with me next weekend? I would love to spend some time in St. Louis, getting to really know each other in more ways than one."

He nodded. "I think that can be arranged."

"Good. I'll call you later."

He kissed her once more, then went to the register up front. Danielle stood there for the longest time, grinning like a damn fool.

Chapter 44

Renee

Later that afternoon, I rushed over to Danielle's and we spent the next hour discussing the case. "Okay, according to Ms. Ruby, she saw Deacon Williams's car around midnight, but he said he didn't arrive at the house until after one o'clock. And even then, David said he was driving his Lincoln."

Danielle's face collapsed. "So what did he do, kill him then run home and change clothes and switch cars?"

"Hell, yeah," I replied and shifted uncomfortably in the chair.

"Is David going to question him?"

"He's going to look into it," I said sarcastically. "I guess we're going to do his job for him."

"So what are we going to do?" Danielle asked, biting her bottom lip.

"I rode by the church on my way over here and the bulletin out front said they are having a concert this evening, which means Deacon Williams is going to be at the church."

"What are we going to do, rob his house?"

I chuckled. "Nope. I'm crazy, but not that crazy. But we are going to find that raggedy-ass VW Bug of his and break into it."

"Oh, good. For a minute there I thought you wanted me to do something illegal," Danielle replied sarcastically.

"It's only illegal if we get caught." At her skeptical face, I dropped my feet to the floor and sat up straighter. "Come on,

Danny. Who else can I do my dirt with but you? Nadine can't risk being disbarred. Kayla is out on bail. That leaves you."

"You remember what happened with your last crazy scheme." At my silence, she released a heavy breath, then said, "All right, I'm game."

"I knew you'd have my back."

Portia stepped into the room. "Mama, would you like me to cook dinner tonight?"

Danielle looked over her shoulder and smiled. "Yeah, that would be great. Nae-Nae, you eating?"

"As long as it ain't Hamburger Helper."

"It's not," Danielle reassured me.

I flashed a wry grin. "Sure, then I'll stay for dinner."

As soon as Portia left the room, I turned to her and asked. "What's she cooking?"

"Tuna Helper," she said and laughed. Before she could duck, I tossed a pillow at her.

As soon as we finished eating, which I have to admit tasted mighty good, we hopped in Danielle's SUV and drove over to Deacon Williams's house. He lived on the side of town not many black folks could afford. Big, two-story, stone-front houses with large backyards and immaculate lawns. I turned off the main road, then climbed a wooded hillside, passing miles of farmland. At a fork, the road circled to a secluded neighborhood surrounded by mature woods. Deacon Williams's house was on the corner.

"You think anyone's home?"

I slowed the car down almost to a crawl. "I hadn't thought about that. I assumed everyone had gone to church." I looked up at the house. In the driveway were three cars—one had a plastic cover over it. "Let me park around the corner so we can get out." I made a left and pulled up the street, then parked. I got out and glanced around to see if anyone was looking. We started walking up the street and passed his house while gazing up at it surreptitiously.

"You think anyone's home?" Danielle asked again as we turned around to pass his house a second time.

"There's only one way to find out." I made a quick detour across his front lawn to the front door.

"Wait a minute!" Danielle called after me. "What are you planning to do?"

"I'm not planning to do anything. You are. Lula knows my face, but she doesn't know you. Just go up to the door and pretend you're at the wrong house." I moved over to the side of the house and waited as Danielle reluctantly climbed the stairs and rang the doorbell. After she rang a second time and no one came, she moved away.

"I don't think anyone's home," she said with a sigh of relief.

"Cool." I signaled for her to follow me. "Let's check these cars and see if we see that same red clay from that new construction site."

While she looked at a Cougar, I walked over and looked under the plastic cover and frowned when I found a red Cooper instead. "Damn!"

"What?" she cried, clearly startled by my voice.

I shook my head. "Nothing." I walked over to the Tahoe and checked each of the tires and was disappointed not to find any red mud.

"Okay, now what?"

I nibbled on my lips. I wasn't sure what to do at that point. "We need to find that Bug."

"Maybe one of his kids drove it to church," Danielle suggested.

I snapped my fingers. "That's a good idea. I knew I kept you around for some reason." Danielle nudged me in the arm. "Okay, let's get to the church and see if we can find it. The Lincoln is missing, and I know they had to have traveled in more than one car."

We hopped back into her car and drove out to the copy shop to make sure it wasn't there. It wasn't. Then we made the ten-minute drive to Mt. Carmel Baptist Church. Slowly I drove through the large, unpaved parking lot on the side of the church, searching for the Bug. I spotted the Lincoln parked in front.

"There it is!"

Sure enough, at the back of the church was another group of cars, and there in the far corner was the Bug. I parked at the end of the dirt road and we climbed out and ran over to it. It was the same one with the sticker on the window I had seen parked outside the copy shop.

"Okay, this is it and it has red mud on the treads of the tire. Now what do we do?"

I frowned. There was red mud at the church as well. That was not going to be good enough unless they were going to take some soil samples, and who knows how long that mess would take or if they would even take my claim seriously. "We need to come up with something else." I checked all of the doors and found them locked. Damn! Peering in, I didn't see anything that looked incriminating. "You got a crowbar or a hammer and screwdriver in your car?"

"As a matter of fact, I've got my daddy's toolbox still in my trunk."

While she ran back to her car, I leaned back and waited. The church was rocking with the song, "The Presence of the Lord Is Here." There was so much sin going on behind those walls it was ridiculous. And Christians wondered why so many people stray from their faith.

"Okay, here," Danny replied, all out of breath.

I positioned the screwdriver directly over the lock and hit it with the hammer several times before finally knocking it through. After lowering the tools to the ground, I raised the trunk and we both looked inside. Danielle and I glanced over at each other at the same time, stunned.

Inside the trunk was a bloody shirt, a Bible engraved with Reverend Brown's name, a white, bloodstained towel, and a pair of white gloves. It was too good to be true.

Danielle shook her head. "He couldn't possibly be that stupid."

"No. He thinks he's untouchable and smarter than everyone else, and because of that, he didn't feel he needed to hide the evidence." I reached for my phone and called David. My fingers were shaking so hard I could barely punch the numbers.

When he finally answered, he sounded sleepy. "Hello?"

"David. I got it!" I cried excitedly. "I got the evidence we need to prove that Deacon Williams is responsible."

"What? Okay, slow down." He suddenly sounded wide awake.

"I said," pausing to take a deep breath, "I found the evidence we need to clear Kayla." Tears were running down my face and as soon as Danielle noticed, she started crying as well. Somehow, I managed to tell David what we had done.

"I'll get an officer over there as soon as possible. Don't touch anything! We can't do a thing until we get a search warrant."

"How long is that going to take?"

"Probably at least an hour. We—"

"An hour! I can't sit here that long. Church will be over by then!"

"Renee, just calm down. That's why I'm going to send over an officer. Now sit tight and try and stall."

I hung up the phone.

Danielle nudged me in the side. "What did he say?"

I wiped my face, then leaned back against the car and looked over at her. "He said he'll send an officer over right now. We need to guard this evidence until he gets here. When does church get out?"

"Now."

Oh, shit! She was right. People were slowly coming out of the church and moving toward the parking lot.

Danielle looked nervous as hell. "What're we gonna do?"

"I don't know!" My heart was pounding so hard I thought it was going to come straight through my chest. Now that I had broken the lock, the trunk refused to stay closed. Quickly, I leaned back against it and crossed my ankles like it was the most natural thing to do. Danielle leaned against the side of the car and we tried to pretend we didn't notice folks staring and pointing at us. It wasn't long before two men headed our way. My heart started pounding even faster until I recognized one of them. "Cary! Whassup, cuz?" He was my Uncle Larry's son.

"Whassup with you, cuz?" He gave me a hug. "I didn't know you were back in town."

"I just got back," I said as my eyes traveled to the man standing beside him.

"Yo, this here is James Groves."

I smiled. "Whassup? This's my girl Danielle."

She rolled her eyes. "We already know each other." The look she gave meant there was a story to be told and I couldn't wait to hear it, but right now I needed my cousin's help.

"Hey, Cary. I need you to stand here with me until the police come."

His brow arched. "Why? Whassup?"

I didn't have time to be explaining. "Trust me. Something big is about to go down."

Sure enough, I spotted Deacon Williams coming out the church with some woman who pointed in our direction. The damn busybody had gone running to tell on us.

"Oh, shit—oops, I mean shoot." *Lord, please forgive me for cussing at your house.* "Here comes Deacon."

He ran over to where we were standing, eyes narrowed dangerously. "What are you doing?"

"Waiting for the police." I grabbed onto my cousin's arm and pulled him closer for protection.

"Get away from my car," Deacon Williams demanded.

I shook my head. "Sorry, but this car contains evidence to a murder."

Standing there, he raked a frustrated hand across his face. "I told you I didn't have anything to do with that—now leave!"

"No."

He reached for me and tried to yank me from the car, but

Cary grabbed his arm and pushed him away. "You back up. That's my cousin you messin' wit'."

Deacon Williams gave him a nervous look. "Then talk some sense into this girl and send her away."

"The police are on their way," Danielle chimed in.

It grew quiet and I noticed several church members standing around, trying to figure out what was going on. I was more than happy to fill them all in. Glancing over at Deacon Williams, I pursed my lips, then said, "I finally figured it out. I think you were afraid that Reverend Brown was going to bring you down with him, and because of it you killed him. You were afraid the whole city was going to find out you were a fag as well."

"I'm not a fag! Leroy was the fag. He was the one that insisted on meeting those faggots every month. Not me!"

"Yeah, but you went with him and was gettin' a little booty as well. If that don't make you a fag, I don't know what does." By now, more church members had started to gather around a large oak tree nearby.

Deacon Williams glanced around frantically, almost pleading for us to hear him out. "You don't understand. He called me talking about ending his life. He said that he was confessing everything, including the role that I played. Don't you see? We couldn't let him destroy us as well."

My brow was drawn. "*We?*"

Danielle caught on as well. "Who's *us?*"

Tossing his head back, he gave a short, sinister laugh that ended with tears streaming down his face. "You're obviously not as smart as you think. What you don't understand, young lady, is that if Leroy wanted to take his own life, then fine, but he didn't have to take me down with him! Then Sister Sparks stabbed him in the shoulder and by the time I got there, he was going on and on about how he had to make it right. We got into an argument and the next thing I knew, he was dead! You see, we had to." He repeated it over and over as he looked around at the congregation standing and listening. At that exact moment, Darlene's anorexic-looking ass walked across the parking lot in a wide-brimmed hat and an expensive pink suit, wearing white gloves. Her eyes traveled from Deacon Williams's teary-eyed face to the congregation.

"What's going on out here?" she asked. I noticed her jaw twitching nervously.

Danielle stamped her foot triumphantly. "I knew she killed her husband!"

I had to give her her props on that. "Yeah, you did say that. Deacon, I guess she's the *W* in *we.*"

Darlene's eyes snapped to her left. "Deacon, what have you been telling these people?"

His shoulders drooped with defeat. "It's over, Darlene."

She looked around uncomfortably. "I have no idea what you're talking about," she stammered.

Her skinny ass was going to lie 'til the end. Using the end of the screwdriver, I lifted one of the bloody gloves out of the trunk. "Save it. Couldn't nobody else wear these itty-bitty gloves but you. They're just like the pair you got on now."

Anger seared her face as she glanced around at the crowd with her hand planted firmly at her hip. "Who are y'all to judge me? The only person I have to answer to is my father in heaven. That man tried to ruin me. Now, I could deal with the women but the men? Oh no, that was a totally different story."

Deacon Williams grabbed her by the shoulder. "Darlene, you don't have to do this. I already confessed."

She shrugged his hand away and held her head up with pride. "No, I can't let you take the blame for what I did." Her lower lip quivered. "When Deacon told me Leroy was planning to confess all his sins in front of God and the church, I went with him to see him that night. I pleaded with him to just leave well enough alone. But no, he wanted to come clean about his lifestyle, and I wasn't having that. I've worked too hard to get where I am for him to just take it all away. I saw that bloody knife lying on the counter and I stabbed him. And even after he fell, I kept on stabbing him until Deacon Williams walked through the door and pulled me off him. It wasn't until then that I realized he had stopped moving."

Members started whispering under their breath and shaking their heads. Darlene searched through the crowd, looking for one person who understood why she had done what she did, but there was none. Well, at least no one would admit it.

"Why are you all looking at me that way?" she demanded as she spun around and faced the crowd. "He ruined me and his family with his sick, twisted behavior." Deacon Williams tried to cover her mouth, but she violently threw an elbow back into his chest. "Leave me alone! I killed him, okay? Is that what you wanted to hear? I stabbed him, and by the time Deacon pulled me off, he was dead. He then tried to cover it up for me." Her eyes zeroed in on him. "Isn't that right, Deacon? Only he was too stupid to get rid of the evidence!"

From a distance, sirens could be heard. Darlene dropped to her knees and sobbed openly. Deacon Williams took off, running across the field, and a couple of male members tackled him in the grass and held him down until the police cars arrived. My shoulders relaxed. I gazed over at Danielle, who grinned while tears were running down her face. Hell, everyone was crying. But for me, they were tears of joy because finally, everything was going to be all right.

Chapter 45

Kayla

God is good. Yes, he is. Kayla sank into a chair with a smile. Finally, everything really was going to be all right. A week had passed since Deacon Williams and Darlene's confession, and she was free, cleared of all charges, and she was the happiest she had been in a long time. All that her friends had done to help her warmed her heart. There was no telling what would have happened if they had not come to her aid. She owed them her life. Renee, with her wild self, had instigated the mess with Leroy, but she had been willing to admit her mistakes and show her how sorry she truly was. She knew better than to expect her to say it out loud, but she'd shown her how much their friendship meant. Actions definitely speak louder than words. Renee had confronted a killer and hadn't backed down no matter what. Earlier this morning, Nadine, Danielle, Renee, and Kayla had breakfast before Renee had to leave for the airport. She hated good-byes and this time was even harder.

Kayla shifted on the seat and smiled. She was going to miss Renee, but she was relieved that life was back to normal. Next week, she would finally be returning to her job that her boss said would be waiting for her whenever she was ready to return.

Hearing a horn blowing outside, she reached for her purse and went to the door. Jermaine was taking her to her mother's house. Kenya and Asia were finally coming home. A tear rolled down her cheek as she realized just how much she missed them. Things were going to be different this time. She had a lot to be thankful for. Two beautiful girls and a man who loved her. Kayla had not known it was possible to feel so comfortable and fulfilled in a relationship. Finally, she had everything she could possible need and want. And she had her Lord and Savior to thank.

Chapter 46

Danielle

While stirring a pot of spaghetti sauce, a smile curled Danielle's lips. Everything was going to be all right with all of them. Kayla had Jermaine, she had Calvin, and Renee was on her way home to her big house, her husband, and their new swinger lifestyle. Shaking her head, Danielle was still stunned by that confession. What was surprising was that as much as Renee messed around on her husband, you would think that she would be down for the idea. Instead, all of it made Renee a little uncomfortable. She wanted to have her cake and eat it, too. Hell, she even wanted ice cream and caramel topping. So it probably had pissed her off to discover she couldn't always have what she wanted, and even when she got it, she took the risk of someone else wanting the same kind of things—that someone being her husband. At breakfast, Danielle didn't have a chance to ask Renee what she was planning to do about her husband's newly discovered fetish. Personally, she believed it was finally time for Renee to make some decisions about her future.

Danielle carried a boiling pot of spaghetti over to the sink and poured it in the strainer. Life couldn't be better. She was even starting to get excited about her grandbaby, even if Ron was the father. But that was neither here nor there. At least the baby would have good hair. She chuckled at the crazy thought.

Somehow she had to focus on the positive things and forget the others. Ever since her return home, she and Portia had been getting along beautifully, and they were both making an effort to work together as a team. Portia had been doing her chores without waiting to be asked, and was even preparing dinner on occasion. Yep, life was good. She even had a loving and attentive man who knew how to treat a woman. Calvin was a blessing from God and she would definitely be a fool to let a good man like him go. They were leaving for St. Louis on Friday and she could hardly contain her excitement.

As she poured cool water over the pasta, her lips curled upward as she reminisced about the previous evening. They had finally made love again and it was definitely worth telling her girlfriends about it over breakfast. Calvin could hold his own.

Danielle turned the burner down low, then went up to Portia's room to tell her it was time for dinner. After knocking on her door and not getting an answer, she turned the knob and stepped in and found the room empty. Hearing water running in the bathroom at the end of the hall, she realized Portia was taking a shower.

Seeing dirty towels on the floor, she instinctively walked over and picked them up. No wonder she couldn't find half her towels, she thought wearily. They were here, buried in Portia's room. Danielle frowned. Portia had been doing a fabulous job of keeping the house clean, but her room was another story altogether.

Picking up a gold bath towel, she heard something drop. Looking down, Danielle spotted a small, leather-bound book. She reached for it, flipped it over, and realized it was Portia's journal. Staring at it, she was tempted to open it, but she tried to respect her daughter's privacy. Danielle stood there, listened for the water, and after several seconds convinced herself that she was the mother and she had a right to know what her teenaged daughter was up to.

"I'll look at just one entry, then I'll put it down," she murmured to herself, then flipped to the center of the book.

I saw Ron's dick today. He wasn't too happy that I walked in on him so I played it off and stepped out of the bathroom. I've never seen a thing with the skin still on it. But dang, it was big! I promise you, I'm going to get some of that before the school year's over.

Stunned, Danielle flipped forward several more pages.

Tomorrow my mother is working evenings and I plan to finally make my move on Ron. The plan is to come running out my room butt-naked, pretending I saw a spider.

Fingers shaking, she turned the page.

I can't believe Ron rejected me. Even after I told him I loved him, he tossed it back in my face and said he loved my mama, not me, and that I needed to find a boy my own age. I hate him! I hate him. Just wait, I'm going to get him back.

Danielle flipped until she found an entry dated the day after she had put Ron out.

Well, my plan worked. Mom believed me over Ron and put his butt out. Heehee! You should have seen his face. That's what he gets for treating me that way. Now Mama thinks I'm pregnant by him when I'm really carrying Andre's baby. Yuck! That was the worst sex I've ever had. Too bad the rape story didn't work. I sure hope my baby comes out looking like me.

Danielle dropped the journal to the floor and stood there for the longest time, stunned.

Chapter 47

Renee

I pulled into Northern Hills, an upscale subdivision that showcased half-million-dollar homes. As I rode past block after block of immaculate, two-story houses with professional landscaping, I sighed. Could I really give up all of this? Rubbing my forehead, I told myself I was just tired, and now was not the time to be thinking about my future. It had been a long couple of weeks but all was well.

Kayla finally had a wonderful, devoted man in her life who loved and accepted her. In time I hope she will learn to love herself as well. My girl Danielle had found happiness with Calvin. I'm still feeling some type of way behind that, even though I am trying to be open-minded. After all, that was in the past and I didn't want Calvin when I had him. Seriously, I'm glad it was someone like Danielle who got him, because if I see her with another young buck, I'm gonna have to stick my foot up her ass. I'm envious of her man, but that drama with Portia, I will definitely pass on. Fucking the same man as your daughter? Now that is definitely something to write about. Hopefully, Danielle has learned a very valuable lesson.

Lessons. I guess we all need some of those. On the flight home from St. Louis, I thought long and hard and I realized something. I'm scared of being alone. My life was always hard. I struggled to make it on the streets by myself, trying to figure out

what to do and who was out there for me to turn to. I didn't
have a mother I could run to or a father, either. I was scared
and it ain't nothing worse than being scared of what tomorrow
will bring. I struggled for years trying to make it. Then the kids
came and I struggled even more, counting pennies and trying
to make quarters work like dollar bills. It was hard and I don't
want to ever go through that again. That's why John means so
much to me; with him, I don't want or need for anything.
Working outside the home is optional, not a necessity. I like
that.

I know I have two degrees, but I don't know if I'm ready to
get out there and take care of myself. It's not that I can't—it's
that I don't want to. And that's my problem. I have grown ac-
customed to a certain lifestyle, and selfishly, I'm not ready to
give that up. But what I've decided to do is start saving money,
and I mean real money. Open up another account that I can't
touch and start tucking money away. Money from my books
and money I plan to be making while teaching this fall. Yes, I
got a call from the director of the English department at
Delaware State University. He was so impressed with my back-
ground that he offered me an adjunct position, working with
their creative writing program. So, there you have it. I have a
plan to get my life back and I'm going to stick to it this time.
Although I am planning to stay a little longer, that shit John
wants me to do is over. No more swinging. I just can't take it
anymore. I want one man who can satisfy me mentally, physically, sexually. I don't need two or three.

By the time I pulled up in front of our two-story colonial, I
was feeling pretty good about my decisions. I turned into the
driveway, then parked and climbed out and took it all in. Four
thousand square feet and it had everything in it a woman could
ask for, and more. I swung my purse onto my shoulder. I didn't
bother putting the car in the garage, since I planned to run to
Wal-Mart a little later. While turning the key in the lock, I
found I was looking forward to taking a long bubble bath and

was thankful that John worked second shift. Believe me, by the time he gets home tonight, I will be snoring. But tomorrow, we are definitely going to talk about us.

As I stepped into the house, I heard my office phone ring. I started to ignore it, but it was a workday and business is business. I caught it by the fourth ring and put the receiver to my ear.

"Hello?"

"Hey, baby?" I knew that voice anywhere.

Slowly I lowered into the chair. "Daddy?"

"Hey, how are you doing?"

"I-I'm doing fine," I replied and noticed my voice was shaking.

"I don't want to keep you, but I was wondering if you and your family would like to come and spend Thanksgiving with us this year. Carol and I would love to have you."

Carol was his second wife of fifteen years. "I don't know. L-let me talk it over with John and get back to you." His invitation had caught me completely off guard.

"Okay. That's fine. Andre's planning to come, too, with his family." There was a long pause and I just didn't know what else there was to say. "Renee?"

"Yeah?"

Paul cleared his throat. "I really want to try and work on our relationship. I've done a lot of things that I'm not proud of, but I . . . I just would like a chance to make things right."

I immediately wanted to sob, but I refused to let him hear me cry. "I'll get back with you." Before he could respond, I hung up the phone, then sat there for the longest time in a daze. Did Paul really just call and say he wanted to make it right between us? Part of me yearned for my daddy, while the other part was still bitter and hated him for everything he had done.

Head pounding, I rose from my chair and climbed the stairs toward my room. I needed to get some sleep and then I could think about Paul and his request to be a part of my life. Right now, I was anxious for a long, hot bath. I went down the hall to my room and turned the knob. I had barely stepped into the room when I froze in my tracks.

For a second my brain refused to acknowledge what my eyes already knew. There, on my bed on my expensive sateen sheets, were John and Shemar doing it doggy-style. John was on top and Shemar was on the bottom with his ass in the air. He was crying out with pleasure as John plunged in and out of his back door. The two were going at it like they were running a marathon. Shocked, my hand flew to my mouth, then I slowly retraced my steps right back out of the bedroom door.

TROUBLE LOVES COMPANY

ANGIE DANIELS

ABOUT THIS GUIDE

The suggested questions are intended to
enhance your group's reading of
Angie Daniels's novel.

Discussion Questions

1. After Danny and Calvin tried to make Ron jealous and the two men got into a fight on the dance floor, was Renee wrong for not coming to her friend's aid?

2. Do you feel Danny was wrong for getting involved with Calvin, especially since he used to date Renee?

3. Why do you think Kayla put up with Reverend Brown for so long?

4. Do you believe Renee is responsible for Reverend Brown's death? Should Kayla blame her?

5. You've heard the saying, "You reap what you sow." Do you feel this is appropriate where Renee is concerned? What about Kayla? Danielle?

6. Would you have handled Portia's situation differently? If Portia was your daughter, would you have chosen your man over her?

7. Would you have forgiven Portia and accepted her pregnancy?

8. Now that Danielle's found the diary, what do you think is going to happen?

9. If you were Calvin, would you have given Danielle a second chance?

10. Do you think Renee will finally leave her husband?

GREAT BOOKS, GREAT SAVINGS!

When You Visit Our Website:
www.kensingtonbooks.com

You Can Save Money Off The Retail Price
Of Any Book You Purchase!

- **All Your Favorite Kensington Authors**
- **New Releases & Timeless Classics**
- **Overnight Shipping Available**
- **eBooks Available For Many Titles**
- **All Major Credit Cards Accepted**

Visit Us Today To Start Saving!
www.kensingtonbooks.com

All Orders Are Subject To Availability.
Shipping and Handling Charges Apply.
Offers and Prices Subject To Change Without Notice.